RANDOM
HOUSE
LARGE
PRINT

RULES OF VENGEANCE

Also by Christopher Reich
Available from Random House Large Print

The Devil's Banker
The Patriots Club
Rules of Deception
The Runner

Also by Christopher Reich
Available from Random House Large Print

The Devil's Banker
The Patriots Club
Rules of Deception
The Runner

RULES OF VENGEANCE

RULES OF VENGEANCE

Christopher Reich

RANDOM HOUSE
LARGE PRINT

This is a work of fiction. Names, characters, places, and incidents either are the product of the author's imagination or are used fictitiously. Any resemblance to actual persons, living or dead, events, or locales is entirely coincidental.

Published in the United States of America by Random House Large Print in association with Doubleday, New York.
Distributed by Random House, Inc., New York.

Cover Design by Will Staehle and John Fontana
Cover Illustrations by Peter Crowther Associates / www.debutart.com

The Library of Congress has established a Cataloging-in-Publication record for this title.

ISBN: 978-0-7393-2843-9

www.randomhouse.com/largeprint

FIRST LARGE PRINT EDITION

10 9 8 7 6 5 4 3 2 1

This Large Print edition published in accord with the standards of the N.A.V.H.

To James F. Sloan
Deputy Assistant Director,
United States Secret Service
Director, Financial Crimes Enforcement Network
Assistant Commandant for Intelligence,
United States Coast Guard

With respect and admiration for a life lived
in service of the United States of America

RULES OF VENGEANCE

<REUTERS> NEWSFLASH LONDON 11:38 GMT

A POWERFUL CAR BOMB EXPLODED THIS MORNING AT 11:16 GMT IN THE LONDON BOROUGH OF WESTMINSTER. IMMEDIATE CASUALTIES ARE SAID TO NUMBER FOUR DEAD AND MORE THAN THIRTY WOUNDED. THE TARGET IS THOUGHT TO HAVE BEEN RUSSIAN INTERIOR MINISTER IGOR IVANOV WHO WAS TRAVELING IN A MOTORCADE FOLLOWING AN UNPUBLICIZED MEETING WITH BRITISH BUSINESS EXECUTIVES. THERE IS NO WORD YET AS TO WHETHER IVANOV WAS AMONG THE INJURED.

DEVELOPING . . .

London
Storey's Gate, Westminster
11:18 GMT

The world was on fire.

Flames licked at the ruined cars littering the roadway. Coils of black smoke choked the air. Everywhere there were bodies sprawled on the sidewalk and in the street. Debris rained down.

Jonathan Ransom lay on the hood of an automobile, half in, half out of the windshield. Lifting his head, he caused a torrent of fractured glass to scatter across his face. He put a hand to his cheek and it came away wet with blood. He could hear nothing but a shrill, painful ringing.

Emma, he thought. **Are you all right?**

Recklessly, he pulled himself clear of the windshield and slid off the hood. He staggered, one hand on the car, getting his bearings. As he took a breath and cleared his head, he remembered everything. The convoy of black cars, the tricolored flag waving from the antenna, and then the brilliant light, the sudden, unexpected wave of heat, and the liberating sensation of being tossed through the air.

Slowly he picked his way through the bodies and the wreckage toward the intersection where he'd seen her last. He was looking for a woman with auburn hair and hazel eyes. "Emma," he called out, searching the bewildered and panicked faces.

There was a crater where the BMW she'd driven across the city and parked so precisely had detonated. The vehicle itself sat five meters away, blazing fiercely, essentially unrecognizable. Across from it was one of the Mercedes, or what was left of it. No survivors there. The blast had shattered the windows of every building up and down the street. Through the smoke, he could see curtains billowing forth like flags of surrender.

Up the street, a thin blond woman emerged from the smoke, walking purposefully in his direction. In one hand she held a phone or a radio. In the other she gripped a pistol, and it was pointed at him. Seeing him, she shouted. He could not hear what she said. There was too much smoke, too much confusion to tell whether she was alone or not. It didn't matter. She was police and she was coming for him.

Jonathan turned and ran.

It was then that he heard the scream.

Immediately he stopped.

In the center of the road, a man tumbled from the wreckage of a black sedan and crawled away from the burning car. It was one of the Mercedes from the motorcade. Flames had seared the clothing off his back and much of the flesh, too. His hair was on fire, enveloping his head in a curious orange halo.

Jonathan ran to the suffering man, tearing off his

own blazer and throwing it over the man's head to extinguish the flames. "Lie down," he said firmly. "Don't move. I'll get an ambulance."

"Please help me," said the man as he stretched out on the pavement.

"You're going to be all right," said Jonathan. "But you need to stay still." He rose, searching for help. Farther down the road he saw a police strobe, and he waved his arms and began to shout. "Over here! I need some medical attention!"

Just then someone knocked him to the ground. Strong hands yanked his arms behind his back and handcuffed him. "Police," a man barked into his ear. "Make a move and I'll kill you."

"Don't touch him," said Jonathan, struggling against the cuffs. "He has third-degree burns all over his body. Get a poncho and cover him up. There's too much debris in the air. You have to protect the burns or he'll die of infection."

"Shut it!" yelled the policeman, slamming his cheek to the ground.

"What's your name?" asked the blond woman, kneeling beside him.

"Ransom. Jonathan Ransom. I'm a doctor."

"Why did you do this?" she demanded.

"Do what?"

"This. The bomb," said the woman. "I saw you shouting at someone back there. Who was it?"

"I don't—" Jonathan bit back his words.

"You don't what?"

Jonathan didn't answer. Far up the block, he'd spotted a woman with ungoverned auburn hair maneuvering through the crowd. He saw her for only an instant—less, even—because there were police all around, and besides, it was so smoky. All the same, he knew.

It was Emma.

His wife was alive.

One Day Earlier . . .

1

The most expensive real estate in the world is located in the district of Mayfair in central London. Barely two square miles, Mayfair is bordered by Hyde Park to the west and Green Park to the south. Claridge's Hotel, the world headquarters of Royal Dutch Shell, and the summer residence of the sultan of Brunei are within walking distance of one another. In between can be found many of the world's best-known luxury boutiques, London's only three-star restaurant (as awarded by the Guide Michelin), and a handful of art galleries catering to those with unlimited bank accounts. Yet even within this enclave of wealth and privilege, one address stands above the rest.

1 Park Lane, or "One Park" as it's commonly known, is a luxury residential high-rise located at the southeast corner of Hyde Park. It began life one hundred years ago as a modest ten-story hotel and over time has served as a bank, a car dealership, and, it is rumored, a high-class brothel for visiting Middle Eastern dignitaries. As real estate values began to spiral upward, so did the building's aspirations.

Today, One Park stands some twenty stories tall and is home to nineteen private residences. Each occupies an entire floor, not counting the penthouse, which is a duplex. Prices start at five thousand pounds, or a breath under eight thousand dollars, per square foot. The cheapest residence goes for 15 million pounds; the penthouse, four times that, 60 million pounds, or nearly 90 million dollars. Owners include a former British prime minister, an American hedge-fund manager, and the purported leader of the Bulgarian underworld. The joke around the building is who among them is the biggest thief.

With so much wealth gathered beneath one roof, security is a twenty-four-hour concern. At all times, two liveried doormen cover the lobby, a team of three plainclothes officers roams the premises, and two more occupy the control room, where they keep a constant eye on the multiplex of video monitors broadcasting live feeds from the building's forty-four closed-circuit television cameras.

One Park's imposing front doors are made from double-paned bulletproof glass, protected by a steel grate and secured by magnetic lock. The doors' German manufacturer, Siegfried & Stein, guaranteed the lock against a direct hit from a rocket-propelled grenade. The front doors might be blown clear off their hinges and across the spacious marble lobby, but by God and Bismarck,

they will remain locked. Visitors are granted entry only after their faces have been scrutinized via closed-circuit television and their identity confirmed by a resident.

For all intents and purposes, One Park is impregnable.

Getting in was the easy part.

The trespasser, operational designation "Alpha," stood inside the master bedroom closet of residence 5A of 1 Park Lane. Alpha was familiar with the apartment's security system. Prior reconnaissance had revealed the presence of pressure pads beneath the carpet alongside the windows in every room and at the front entry, but none in the closet. There were other, more sophisticated measures, but they, too, could be defeated.

The intruder crossed to the door and flipped the light switch. The closet was palatial. A shoe rack stood against the far wall, and next to it a rolled-up flag of St. George and two Holland & Holland shotguns. The owner's clothing hung along one wall. There was no women's clothing to be seen. The residence belonged to a bachelor.

To the left were stacks of yellowing periodicals, bound newspapers, and manila files, the meticulously accumulated bric-a-brac of a dedicated scholar. To the right stood a mahogany dresser with several photographs in sterling frames. One showed a fit, sandy-haired man in hunting attire, shotgun under one arm, in conversation with a similarly sporty Queen Elizabeth II. The trespasser recognized the owner of the apartment. He was Lord Robert Russell, only son of the duke of Suffolk, England's richest peer, with a fortune estimated at five billion pounds.

Alpha had not come to steal Russell's money, but for something infinitely more valuable.

Kneeling, the intruder removed a slim packet from a work bag. A thumbnail punctured its plastic wrapping. Alpha deftly unfolded a foil-colored jumpsuit and stepped into it. Care was taken to ensure that the suit covered every square inch of exposed skin. A hood descended low over the brow and rose over the jaw to mask the nose and mouth. The jumpsuit was made from Mylar, a material often used for survival blankets. The suit had been designed for one purpose and one purpose only: to prevent the escape of the body's ambient heat.

Satisfied that the Mylar suit was in place, the intruder removed a pair of telescopic night-vision goggles and affixed them comfortably, again working to cover as much skin as possible. A pair of gloves came last.

Alpha cracked open the closet door. The master bedroom was cloaked in darkness. A scan of the area revealed a motion detector attached to the ceiling near the door. The size of a pack of cigarettes, the motion detector emitted passive infrared beams capable of detecting minute oscillations in room temperature caused by the passage of human bodies through a protected space. The alarm's sensitivity could be calibrated to allow a cat or a small dog free rein of the premises without triggering the alarm, but Robert Russell did not own a house pet. Moreover, he was cautious by nature and paranoid by dint of his profession. He knew full well that his recent work had made him unpopular in certain circles. He also knew that if the past were to be taken as an indication, his life was in danger. The sensors would be set to detect the faintest sign of an intruder.

Even with the thermal suit, it was not yet safe to enter the room. Robert Russell had equipped his flat with a double-redundant security system. The motion detector constituted one measure. The other was a microwave transmitter that relied on the concept of Doppler radar to bounce sound waves off the walls. Any disturbance in the sound waves' pattern would activate the alarm.

A survey of the bedroom failed to locate the transmitter.

Just then a voice sounded in Alpha's earpiece. "He's leaving the target. You have eight minutes."

"Check."

Stepping out of the closet, Alpha moved swiftly to the bedroom door. No alarm sounded. No air horn. No bell. There was no microwave transmitter in the room. The bedroom door stood ajar, granting a clear view down a hallway and into the living area. Gloved fingers increased the night-vision goggles' magnification fourfold. It required fifteen seconds to locate the ruby-red diode high on the foyer wall that signaled the location of the transmitter. There was no way to disable the diode. The solution lay in tricking it into thinking it was operating normally.

Drawing a miniature target pistol from the jumpsuit, Alpha took careful aim at the diode and fired. The pistol did not shoot a bullet—at least, not in the conventional sense of the word. Instead it launched a subsonic projectile containing a crystalline epoxy compound. Designed to flatten on impact, the epoxy would effectively block the sound waves and reflect them back to the transmitter. Still, for less than a second, the sound waves would be disturbed. The alarm would be triggered.

But there it would end.

The beauty and the arrogance of the double-blind alarm lay in the necessity to trigger both mechanisms at the same time in order to activate the alarm. If the thermal sensor detected a rise in temperature, it would cross-check with the motion detector for a corresponding disruption in the Doppler waves. Similarly, if the Doppler-based motion sensor was disturbed, it would verify with the thermal sensor that there had been an increase in room temperature. If in either case the response was negative, the alarm would not be activated. The redundancy was not installed to make the room safer, but to guard against the possibility of a false alarm. No one had ever considered it possible to defeat both systems at the same time.

The projectile hit its target dead on. The ruby-red diode vanished. The room was clear.

Alpha checked the time. Six minutes, thirty seconds.

Inside the living room, it was necessary to fold back the carpet from the walls. The pressure pads were located as noted on the schematics. One was placed in front of each of the floor-to-ceiling windows looking over Hyde Park, and the third in front of the sliding glass door that led to the balcony. Each required one minute to disable. There was another near the front door, but Alpha didn't bother with it. The entry and escape routes were the same.

Four minutes.

Free to roam the apartment, the intruder made a beeline for Russell's study. Alpha had been inside the apartment before and had made a point of memorizing its layout. A sleek stainless steel desk occupied the center of the room. On it were three LCD monitors arrayed side by side. A far larger screen, some ninety-six inches across, hung from the wall directly opposite him.

Alpha directed a halogen beam beneath the desk. The computer's central processing unit sat on the floor at the rear of the foot well. There was no time to copy its contents, only to destroy it. Alpha slipped a handheld electronic device from the work bag and swiped it several times over Russell's CPU. The device delivered an immensely powerful electromagnetic pulse, obliterating all data.

Unfortunately, the information was also stored in a more permanent location: Robert Russell's estimable brain.

"He's pulling into the garage," announced the voice in the earpiece.

The time was 2:18 a.m. "Everything's a go," said Alpha. "Get lost."

"See you back at the fort."

On the desk was a web tablet, an all-in-one touch screen that controlled the apartment's automatic functions. With a touch Russell could turn on the television, open or close the curtains, or adjust the temperature. There was another, more interesting feature. If one hit the security button, the screen divided itself into quarters, each showing the view from one of the building's closed-circuit cameras. The top left quadrant showed Robert Russell leaving his car, an Aston Martin DB12. Russell appeared entering the basement foyer a moment later. A few seconds passed and he entered the bottom left quadrant, this time inside the elevator. At thirty, he was tall and lean, with a full head of tousled white-blond hair that drew looks wherever he went. He wore jeans, an open shirt, and a blazer. Somewhere in the past, he'd earned a black belt in Brazilian jujitsu. He was a dangerous man in every respect.

He stepped out of the elevator, and a moment later appeared in the final screen, standing inside his private alcove and pressing his pass key and thumb to the biometric lock.

Alpha walked into the kitchen and opened t freezer. On the top shelf were two bottles of vodk sheathed in ice rings. "Żubrówka," read the labels. Polish vodka made from bison grass. The vodka tasted like warm velvet.

The tumblers to the front door slid back. Robert Russell's heels clicked on the marble floor. The trespasser took off the balaclava, unzipped the jumpsuit, and waited. The disguise was no longer needed. It was essential that Russell not be frightened. His keychain held a panic button that activated the alarm.

Russell walked into the kitchen. "Jesus, you scared the hell out of me," he exclaimed.

"Hello, Robbie. Care for a drink?"

Russell's smile faded rapidly as the facts arranged themselves in his razor-sharp mind. "Actually, just how the hell did you get in here?"

He had barely finished the words when the trespasser, operational designation Alpha, brought the bottle of vodka and its ice sheath down on his skull. Russell collapsed to all fours, the keychain skittering across the floor. The blow left him stunned but not unconscious. Before he could call out, Alpha straddled him, grasped his jaw in one hand, his hair in the other, and wrenched his head violently to the left.

Russell's neck snapped like a rotted branch. He fell limp to the floor.

It took all of Alpha's strength to drag the body across the living room and onto the balcony. Alpha ung his arms over the railing, then grasped Russell's legs, hefted the dead weight, and rolled the body over.

She did not wait to see Lord Robert Henley Russell strike the granite stairs 35 meters below.

2

Kenya Airways Flight 99 inbound from Nairobi touched down at London Heathrow Airport at 0611 British Summer Time. The manifest listed 280 passengers and 16 crew aboard the Airbus A340. In fact, the number was well over 300, with a dozen infants piled on their mothers' laps and a handful of standbys clambering into the fold-down seats meant for flight attendants.

Seated in row 43, Jonathan Ransom checked his watch and shifted uneasily. Flight time had clocked in at exactly nine hours—thirty minutes faster than scheduled. Most passengers were delighted by the early arrival. It meant beating morning rush hour into the city or gaining a head start on the day's sightseeing. Jonathan was not among them. All week departures out of Jomo Kenyatta International Airport had suffered lengthy delays because of an ongoing strike by local air traffic controllers. The previous day's flight had arrived in London six hours late. The day before that, it had been canceled altogether. Yet his flight had arrived not only on time, but ahead of schedule. He wasn't sure whether it was luck or something else. Something he didn't want to put a name to.

I shouldn't have come, he told himself. **I was safe where I was. I should have played it smart and stayed out of sight.**

But Jonathan had never ducked a responsibility and he wasn't about to start now. Besides, deep down he knew that if they wanted to find him, there was no place too far away, no spot on the globe too remote where he might hide.

Jonathan Ransom stood a few inches over six feet. Dressed in jeans, chambray shirt, and desert boots, he looked lean and fit. His face was deeply tanned from months of working beneath the equatorial sun. The same sun had chapped his lips and left his nose freckled with pink. His hair was shorn to a soldier's stubble and cut through with gray. His nose was strong and well shaped, and served to focus attention on his dark eyes. With his two-day beard, he could be Italian or Greek. A bolder guess might place him as a South American of European descent. He was none of these. He was American, born in Annapolis, Maryland, thirty-eight years earlier to a distinguished southern family. Even in the narrow seat, he appeared to control his space instead of allowing it to control him.

To channel his nerves, Jonathan gathered up the varied journals, articles, and reviews he'd brought to prepare for the medical congress and tucked them into his satchel. Most had names like "Diagnosis and Prevention of Tropical Infection" or "Hepatitis C in Sub-Saharan Africa: A Clinical Study" and had been

written by distinguished physicians at distinguishe
universities. The last was printed on simple copier
paper and carried his own name beneath the title.
"Treatment of Parasitic Diseases in Pediatric Patients," by Dr. Jonathan Ransom, MD. FACS. Doctors Without Borders. Instead of a hospital, he listed his current place of work: United Nations Refugee Camp 18, Lake Turkana, Kenya.

For eight years Jonathan had worked for Doctors Without Borders, the humanitarian relief organization dedicated to bringing medical care to areas of acute crisis. He'd taken his skills to Liberia and Darfur, to Kosovo and Iraq, and to a dozen places in between. And for these last six months he'd served as principal physician at the Turkana camp, on the border of Ethiopia and Kenya. The camp's current population numbered upward of one hundred thousand persons. Most had come from the horn of Africa, displaced families fleeing war-ravaged regions in Somalia and Ethiopia. As one of only six physicians at the camp, and the only board-certified surgeon, he spent his time caring for everything from broken ankles to bullet wounds. But this year his crowning glory lay in another department. He'd delivered a hundred babies in 140 days without losing a single one.

At some point along the way, he'd become an expert on parasitic diseases. With the world community paying increasing attention to the problems of disease and poverty in developing nations, doctors with experience "on the front lines" were suddenly in gue. Early in the spring, he'd received the invita-ion from the International Association of Internists (IAI) to deliver a paper on the subject at its annual congress. Jonathan did not enjoy public speaking, but he'd accepted all the same. The subject merited wider recognition, and the opportunity to address such an influential body didn't come along often. It was an obligation he couldn't shun. The IAI had paid his fare, booked the flight, and arranged his accommodation. For a few days he'd have a real bed to sleep on, with clean sheets and a firm mattress. He smiled. At the moment, the prospect sounded inviting.

It was then that Jonathan saw the police escorts and his heart did whatever it did when you couldn't catch a breath and you felt paralyzed from the neck down.

Two blue-and-white Rovers belonging to the British Airport Authority drove alongside the aircraft, their strobes lit and spinning. In short order, two more vehicles joined their rank. Jonathan pressed his back against the seat. He'd seen enough.

Emma, he called silently, his heart roaring to life. **They've come for me.**

"They'll be watching you. You won't see them. If they're good, you'll never even be aware of it. But make no mistake, they're there. Don't let your guard down. Ever."

Emma Ransom looked at Jonathan across the table. Her tousled auburn hair fell about her

shoulders, the flames from the hearth flaring i
her hazel eyes. She wore a cream-colored cardigan
sweater. A sling held her left arm to her chest in
order to immobilize her shoulder and allow the
gunshot wound to heal.

It was late February—five months before Jonathan's trip to London—and for three days they'd been holed up in a climbing hut high on the mountainside above the village of Grimentz in the Swiss canton of Wallis. The hut was Emma's rabbit hole, her escape hatch for the times when things got too hairy.

"Who are 'they'?" Jonathan asked.

"Division. They have people everywhere. It might be a doctor you've worked with for some time, or someone just passing through. An inspector from the UN or a raja from the World Health Organization. You know. People like me."

Division was a secret agency run out of the United States Department of Defense, and was Emma's former employer. Division ran the blackest of black ops. Clandestine. Deniable. And, best of all, without congressional oversight. It was not an intelligence-gathering agency per se. Its members weren't spies, but operatives inserted into foreign countries to effect objectives deemed essential to U.S. security or the protection of its interests around the globe. That objective might involve the manipulation of a political process through extortion, blackmail, or ballot rigging, the destruction of a geopolitically sensitive installation, or, more simply, the assassination of a powerful figure.

All Division operatives worked under deep cover. All assumed false identities. All carried foreign passports. Shorter operations ran to six months. More complex ones could last two years or more. Prior to posting abroad, every effort was made to construct a meticulously documented legend. In the event that an operative was caught or exposed, the United States would deny any association with the individual and would make no effort to secure his or her release.

"And what am I supposed to do?" Jonathan asked. "Stay here in the mountains for the next twenty years?"

"Go on with your life. Pretend I'm dead. Forget about me."

Jonathan set down his cup of tea. "I can't do that," he said.

"You don't have a choice."

He took her hand in his. "You're wrong. I do have a choice and so do you. We can leave here together. We can go back to Africa or to Indonesia or . . . oh, hell, I don't know . . . but we can go somewhere. Somewhere far away where they won't think of looking."

"No such place exists," whispered Emma. "The world's grown much too small. There aren't any far-flung corners anymore where one can just draw the curtains and disappear. They've all been discovered and have webcams and someone waiting to build a five-star resort. Don't you see, Jonathan? If there were any way that we could stay together, I'd jump at it. I don't want to leave you either. Last week, when I disappeared down that crevasse, you didn't just lose me. I lost you, too. I wasn't sure whether I'd ever see you again. You've got to believe me. We haven't any other option but to split up. Not if we want to stay alive."

"But—"

"No buts. That's just the way it has to be."

Jonathan began to protest and Emma put a finger to his lips. "Listen to me. Whatever happens, you mustn't contact me until I say it's all right. No matter how much you miss me, no matter how certain you are that no one's been watching you and that everything is safe, you mustn't think of it. I know it will be hard, but you have to trust me."

"And if I do?"

"They'll know. They'll get to me first."

Ten days earlier, Jonathan and Emma had come to Switzerland for a long overdue vacation. Experienced mountaineers, they had decided to climb the Furka, a peak situated midway between the villages of Arosa and Davos. The climb ended in disaster when a violent storm caught them on the mountain and Emma fell while descending a steep incline. Jonathan had come off the mountain believing his wife dead. The next day he received a letter addressed to her. Its contents unlocked a door to her secret past. He might have ignored it, but that wouldn't have been his way. On general principle, he avoided the easier path. Instead he delved into Emma's hidden world, anxious to discover the truth she'd kept hidden since the day they had met.

His search had ended on a hilltop outside of Zurich, with four men dead and Emma wounded.

That was three days ago.

Jonathan squeezed her hand and she squeezed back. He couldn't deny the affection in her touch. But was it love? Or was it rote?

Suddenly she was up, making a circuit of the hut. "You've got enough provisions for a week. Stay put. Nobody knows about this place. When you leave, act as if I'm dead and gone. That's just the way it is. Get that through your head. Use your American passport. Go back to work. Take whatever assignment they give you."

"And Division? You don't think they'll mind?"

"Like I said, they'll be watching. But you needn't worry. You're an amateur. They won't bother you."

"And if they do?"

Emma stopped, her shoulders tensing. The answer was evident. "It's me they want."

"So when will I see you again?"

"Hard to say. I've got to see if I can make things safe."

"And if you can't?"

Emma stared at him, a sad smile turning her lips downward. It was her code for "Don't ask any more questions."

"You've got to give me more than that," he said.

"I wish I could, Jonathan. I really do."

With a sigh, she threw her rucksack onto the cot and began stuffing her belongings into it. The sight panicked him. Jonathan stood and walked toward her. "You can't leave yet," he said, trying to talk in his professional voice. The doctor advising his patient, instead of the husband ruing the loss of his wife. "You shouldn't even be exercising your shoulder. You could reopen the wound."

"You didn't care so much about that an hour ago."

"That was . . ." Jonathan cut his words short. His wife was smiling, but it was an act. For once he could see through it. "Emma," he said. "It's only been three days."

"Yes," she said. "Foolish of me to wait so long."

He watched as she packed. Outside, it was dark. Snow had begun to fall. In the nickled moonlight, the snowflakes looked as fragile as glass.

Emma placed the rucksack on her good shoulder and walked to the door. There would be no kiss, no labored goodbye. She grasped the door

handle and spoke without looking back. "I want you to remember something," she said.

"What?"

"Remember that I came back for you."

The plane taxied to the arrival gate. The cabin lights blinked as the aircraft switched to auxiliary power. Passengers stood and opened the overhead luggage bins. In seconds the main cabin was a maelstrom of activity. Jonathan remained seated, his eyes on the police cars that had parked at right angles to the plane. No one was going anywhere yet, he said to himself. Unbuckling his safety belt, he shoved his satchel under the seat in front of him and positioned his feet so that he could stand up quickly. His eyes darted up and down the aisles, looking in vain for an avenue of escape.

"Ladies and gentlemen, this is the captain speaking. Please retake your seats. Police officers are coming aboard to conduct some business on behalf of Her Majesty's government. It is imperative that you clear the aisles."

With a collective moan, the passengers found their seats.

In his seat in row 43, Jonathan leaned forward, his muscles tensed. He spotted the first of the policemen a moment later. He was dressed in plain clothes and followed by three uniformed officers with Kevlar vests strapped to their chests, pistols worn high on their hip and in full view. They bullied their way down the aisle, making a beeline for him. There were no smiles, no apologies. Jonathan wondered what they had in mind for him. Whether he would be interrogated by English authorities or the Americans had made a deal to have him turned over to their care. Either way, the outcome was foreordained. He would be "disappeared."

He decided to protest, if only to be noticed. He had to leave some evidence of his resistance.

As the plainclothes officer approached, Jonathan stood.

"You," barked the policeman, pointing at Jonathan with his walkie-talkie. "Sit! Now!"

Jonathan started to push toward the aisle. He wouldn't sit. He would fight. He knew he would lose, but that was beside the point.

"I said sit," the policeman repeated. "Please, sir," he added in a polite voice. "We'll be off the aircraft in a minute. You'll be able to leave then."

Jonathan sank back into his seat as the column of policemen swept past. Turning his head, he watched as they confronted a clean-shaven African male seated in the last row of the economy cabin. The suspect protested, shaking his head, gesticulating wildly with his hands. There was a shout, a scuffle, a woman's piercing scream, and then it was over. The man was out of his seat, hands raised above his head in a gesture of surrender.

Jonathan saw that he was a small man, bent as driftwood, wearing a heavy woolen sweater that was much too warm for the English summer. The suspect was speaking Swahili, or a dialect of Kikuyu. Jonathan didn't need to understand the language to know that he was saying it was a mistake. He wasn't the man they were looking for. Suddenly the accused reached for his bags in the overhead compartment. A uniformed police officer shouted and tackled him to the floor.

Moments later, the African was cuffed and led from the plane.

"I'll bet he's a terrorist," said the elderly woman seated next to Jonathan. "Just look at him. It's plain as day."

"I wouldn't know."

"You can't be too careful these days," the woman added forcefully, lecturing her naive seatmate. "We've all got to keep a sharp eye. You never know who you'll be sitting next to."

Jonathan nodded in agreement.

3

It was called the Black Room, and it was one of five special operations centers manned by Her Majesty's Immigration Service at London Heathrow Airport. BR4—Black Room Terminal 4—was located in a stuffy, low-ceilinged office directly above the Terminal 4 arrivals hall. Immigration officers sat at a control board running the length of the room. A multiplex of video monitors was arrayed on the wall in front of them. Closed-circuit cameras positioned on the ceiling and hidden behind two-way mirrors focused on the travelers queuing for passport control. A wireless communications link connected BR4 with the passport inspectors on the floor.

As the world's busiest airport, London Heathrow saw 68 million travelers pass through its gates each year, arriving from or en route to 180 destinations in Great Britain and abroad. Ten million of them counted as international arrivals, an average of 27,000 persons entering the country every day. It was the Immigration Service's job to process these arrivals with an eye toward ferreting out those with a criminal bent and denying them entry into the United Kingdom.

Manipulating the closed-circuit cameras, the men and women seated at the control board proceeded systematically down their assigned queue, snapping photographs of each arriving passenger. The photograph was fed into Immigration Service's proprietary facial recognition software and checked against a database of known offenders. In the event of a positive response, the suspect would be approached by one of the dozen or so undercover immigration officers scattered throughout the hall and guided to a private room, where he or she would be interrogated and a decision taken regarding his or her status.

The same cameras were equipped with a package of invasive scanners that measured a subject's body temperature, heart rate, and respiration, as well as a still-classified imager capable of detecting facial tics for unconscious tell signs invisible to the naked eye. All the data was fed into a software program named MALINTENT that assessed with a 94 percent degree of accuracy whether the subject was harboring criminal intent.

"I've got a hot one," said the officer manning post three.

A supervisor approached. "Who is it?"

The officer brought up an image of a Caucasian male with dark skin and close-cropped hair standing at the inspection booth. "Jonathan Ransom. American. Came in on Kenya Airways out of Nairobi."

"How hot?"

"Temp's running at ninety-nine comma five. Respiration elevated, with a heart rate of eighty-four. Facial indicators read plus six out of ten. Borderline malicious."

"Is he on our books?"

A swipe of Ransom's passport had sent the information contained on the travel document's biometric security strip to the UK's domestic law enforcement database of wanted criminals or "persons of interest," as well as similar databases maintained by Interpol, European Union member countries, the United States, Australia, Canada, and a dozen other countries friendly to the cause. "Nothing outstanding against in the UK."

"And the States?"

"Still waiting." Ransom's name and passport number were then sent to the FBI's national criminal database, where they were matched against a watch list containing the names of suspected terrorists, individuals with warrants outstanding, and anyone with a felony conviction.

"Looks like a decent bloke," commented the supervisor as he studied Ransom's image on the monitor. "Probably worked up because of that arrest on board. Who'd the CT boys take down, anyhow?"

CT stood for counterterrorism, of late the largest component of the London Metropolitan Police force, numbering some five thousand officers and support staff.

"Supposedly some Al-Qaeda supremo. A regional commander or something like that." The officer did a double-take as the requested information began to stream in. "We've got something from Interpol. Ransom had a warrant issued for his capture six months back by the Swiss Federal Police."

"What for?"

"Murder of two police officers. A bit strange, though. It says that the warrant was rescinded after six days."

"That it?"

" 'No further information indicated,' " read the officer, swiveling in his chair and looking at his superior for further instructions.

"Patch me in," said the supervisor, putting on a pair of headphones. "Let's have a listen."

The officer activated a microphone on the passport inspector's jacket and an audio feed was delivered to the supervisor's headphones.

"Dr. Ransom, is it, sir?" said the passport inspector with seeming disinterest. "Are you visiting the United Kingdom on business or pleasure?"

"I'm attending a medical conference at the Dorchester Hotel. I don't know if that's business or pleasure."

"I'd say it qualifies as business. Will you be staying long?"

"Three days."

"Not making any time for sightseeing?"

"Maybe on my next visit."

"And you'll remain in London for the duration?"

"At the Dorchester, yes."

"What's your next destination?"

"I'll be returning to Kenya."

"That your home, then?"

"For now."

The inspector thumbed through the passport. "Sierra Leone, Lebanon, Sudan, Bosnia, Switzerland." He looked Jonathan in the eye. "Been a few places, haven't you?"

"Wherever my work takes me."

"What did you say you do?"

"I'm a physician."

"The last one who makes house calls, by the look of it. Just a few more questions, sir, and then you'll be free to go. Have you been feeling ill lately?"

Inside Black Room 4, the supervisor put down his headphones. "Anything from the Yanks?"

"Ransom's on some kind of diplomatic list. If he boards a flight to the States, we're to notify an agency in D.C. Gives a number here."

"What about the Swiss arrest warrant?"

"Nothing. What do you think? He some kind of spook?"

"Don't know, but I think it's time we find out for ourselves. Let's pull him in for a 'how do you do.' Is room seven free?"

"Leave him be."

It was a new voice. A confident mid-Atlantic baritone that brooked no exception. All heads turned toward the rear of the room.

"Let him walk," said the American. His name was Paul Gordon, and he had come to the United Kingdom as part of the immigration assistance program run out of the United States Department of Homeland Security's Customs and Border Protection agency.

"Let him walk?" asked the supervisor. "Why? Do you know the man?"

"Just do it." Gordon offered a pained smile. "Please."

"You're sure?"

"Yeah, I'm sure."

"All right, then." The supervisor radioed down to the passport inspector. "No interest on our end. Let him go."

Paul Gordon watched on the monitor as Ransom gathered up his satchel and passed into the baggage claim hall. He waited a decent interval, then left the room, descended a flight of stairs, and opened an unmarked door that led outdoors. He checked that his phone had a signal, then activated speed dial and pressed the number 1. A groggy male voice answered. "Yeah?"

"Sorry to wake you, but an old friend of yours just flew into London," said Paul Gordon.

"Who?"

"Dr. Jonathan Ransom."

"Jesus."

"Yeah, I thought you'd want to know."

4

"Murder squad."

Detective Chief Inspector Kate Ford of the London Metropolitan Police flashed her badge at the uniformed constable standing guard at the entrance to 1 Park Lane. "I'm looking for Detective Laxton."

"Morning, governor," replied the constable. "He's inside speaking to the building concierge. I'll ring him for you."

"Do that." As Kate pulled into the circular driveway, she made a quick visual of the crime scene. A half-dozen uniforms manned the perimeter, keeping pedestrians and joggers moving along smartly. Blue-and-white security tape cordoned off the north end of the driveway and the stairs leading into the building. A sheet covered the corpse, but nothing had been done to clean up the blood. That was as it should be, she thought, as she brought her car to a halt and killed the engine. Everything appeared to be under control.

It was 5:45 a.m. by the dashboard clock. Kate angled the rearview mirror toward her face and ran a five-second diagnostic. Makeup all right, hair fine, eyes clear. **First day back,** she told herself. **Make it count.**

She opened the door and stepped outside. An ambulance was parked a few meters away. Its crew lounged against the bodywork, smoking, chuckling. "This is a crime scene, not a pub on a Friday night," she said. "A man died here. Show some respect." She yanked a cigarette out of the fat one's mouth and flicked it to the ground. "Get in the cab and wait till we call you."

The driver tucked his chin into his neck. "Yes, boss."

Katherine Elizabeth Ford was thirty-seven years old, tall and blond and rail thin. She was dressed in a navy blazer, white T, and razor-creased slacks, and as she crossed the drive she appeared to gain not only speed but purpose. **Like a shark coming in for the kill,** someone had once said in the squad room. **Yeah, but a shark's got a sense of humor,** came the response. Her face was all right angles, her nose sharp as a ruler, jaw set against the rigors of the coming day, blue eyes narrow as gun slits. She knew that she stood too straight, walked too fast, and didn't laugh loudly enough at the boys' jokes. But that was her way, and damn the lot if they didn't understand.

"Hello, there, Katie!"

A trim silver-haired man emerged from the building. In a natty gray suit and pearl tie, he was dressed too nicely for a detective pulling night duty. As he jogged down the stairs, he held a hand on his head to guard his hair against the swirling morning breeze. **God help me,** thought Kate as she raised her hand in greeting. **It's too early for Pretty Kenny.** "Hello, Ken," she called, forcing a smile. "Bit of a mess, eh?"

Detective Ken Laxton of the Homicide Appraisal Team shook her hand and nodded at the body. "Bugger had to land on the stairs, didn't he? Missed a perfectly nice patch of grass three meters away." He laughed loudly at his joke.

"Where'd he fall from?" Kate asked, not sharing his humor.

Laxton pointed to a balcony halfway up the building. "Fifth floor. I'm seeing it as a jumper, plain and simple. Apartment was locked. The alarm was on. It's a biometric job. Needs a thumbprint plus a code. The place is the size of Buckingham Palace."

"What about family? Wife? Kids?"

"He was a bachelor. Looks like he'd decided he'd had enough of being alone and got on with it."

"So you're calling it a suicide," said Kate. "Fair enough. Did he leave a note?"

"Not that we've found." Laxton shrugged off the fact. "Like I said, he was a bachelor. No wife. No kids. Just his parents."

Kate mulled this over. The great majority of suicides left behind some kind of message. She'd learned that it didn't really matter who they wrote to, simply that they said goodbye. "You mentioned that his father was the duke of Suffolk? He the rich one?"

"To the tune of five billion quid. Owns half of

Covent Garden and the West End. Lord Russell here is the sole heir. Sorry to rouse you, but what with the title, I didn't want there to be any cock-ups."

As duty officer of the Homicide Assessment Team, Laxton was the first detective called to the scene of a suspicious death or suicide. It was his job to conduct a preliminary investigation and decide whether to call in the murder squad.

"No worries. You did the right thing."

Laxton began to say something, then bit back his words. "You all healed, then?" he asked after a moment.

"Better than new."

"You're looking wonderful," he said, sincerity thin as paint. "I'm sorry about what happened to Billy. We all are."

Billy was Lieutenant William Donovan, Kate's fiancé, as well as her superior in the Met. A month earlier, a high-profile arrest had gone bad when the suspect opened fire on the police without warning. Billy took a bullet in the chest and was dead before he hit the ground. Kate was shot twice in the lower abdomen. There was more to it than that, but she didn't want to think about it right now.

"At least it was fast," Laxton went on. "No suffering, I mean. Still, it must have been a surprise. One second you're knocking on the door, certain that you've got your man. Collar already pinned to the wall. The next, the bloke starts shooting like it's the O.K. Corral. Don't beat yourself up, Katie. Nobody else knew he had any priors. Why should you have?"

Kate met Laxton's eye. **You want me to cry, you preening little peacock,** she said to herself. **Well, I'm sorry to disappoint you.** "What's this one do, then?" she asked, pointing at the body lying at her feet.

Ken Laxton frowned. "No one around here knows. He came and went at all hours. By all accounts he was a serious chap. Not one of them carousers out burning through his millions."

"Run me through the protocol."

Laxton consulted his notepad. "Call came in at two forty-five. One of the residents heard the body hit. Lady on the second floor. One of them Saudi princesses. Said she thought it was a bomb. Al-Qaeda come to Hyde Park. Mayfair nick sent a radio car over. It arrived on scene at two fifty-five. They found him. The doorman identified the body."

"Anything else?"

"Doorman said Russell entered the building through the garage and went straight up to his apartment. No more than ten minutes passed before he fell from the building. He'd been out to the parents' for Sunday dinner."

"Was that a regular affair?"

"Like clockwork, according to the doorman. Left every Sunday at six-thirty."

"Anyone with him when he returned?"

"Doorman says no. He followed Russell on the

CCTV into the elevator and all the way to his flat. He's certain Russell was alone."

Kate made a mental note to interview the doorman herself. "Rather late to get in from the folks' house, isn't it?"

"Maybe the duke **likes** to eat at midnight."

"Maybe," said Kate. "Did the doorman notice if Russell was acting strangely? Drunk? Merry? Morose?"

"Doorman didn't speak with him, did he?"

"Yes, that's right. But you said another resident called it in. What about the doorman? Didn't he see anything? I mean, Russell practically landed right in front of his face."

"Too dark. You know how you can't see a thing out of a lit room. Same thing."

"What about the noise?"

"Listening to his iPod, wasn't he?" said Laxton. "Ask me, he's telling the truth, though I did catch a whiff of something on his breath."

"I take it it wasn't mouthwash?"

"More like a bit of Bushmills."

Kate stared at Laxton. "Wouldn't be the first time someone had a drink on duty."

Laxton colored, but said nothing. Two years earlier he'd been suspended for drinking on the job after the car he was driving mounted the sidewalk and nearly ran over a mother and daughter. The incident had cost Laxton a promotion to detective chief inspector and put a halt to any further advancement within the force. Kate knew all the details. The adjudicating officer had been Lieutenant William Donovan.

"So that's everything?" she asked.

"All yours," said Laxton. "Have a look around, but I'm sure it's just a formality. Russell's got some kind of security system up there. Motion detectors, pressure pads, thermal sensors. There's no way someone could have gotten into the place to harm him. Take my word, Katie. I know a jumper when I see one."

"Got it, Ken. Thanks."

"I'll stick around for a bit, if you need me," said Laxton, rocking on his heels.

"Aren't you set to go off shift at seven?"

"Doesn't matter. I'm happy to help."

It suddenly struck Kate why he was even more dressed up than usual. Russell's death was sure to stir up a hornet's nest of media attention, and Pretty Kenny wanted his share of the spotlight. He'd probably already worked out how appearing in the papers would return him to the Met's good graces and get him another crack at a promotion.

"That won't be necessary," said Kate.

"Really, I can stay. You might need an extra hand."

"I can handle it from here. I'll catch you back at the nick."

Laxton frowned, then stormed off.

"Oh, Ken," she called after him. "Who belongs

to the blue Rover over there?" She pointed to a navy four-door Rover parked next to the ambulance. No other private vehicle was parked inside the police tape.

"Don't know. It was there when we arrived."

Laxton stalked back to his car. The wind picked up, making a mess of his hair. For once Pretty Kenny left it alone.

Kate returned to her car and took a box of latex gloves from the backseat. "Sergeant Cleak," she called out as she slipped on the gloves. "The time is now six-oh-seven. Please note that as of this moment, we have officially taken charge of this investigation."

"Yes, boss." Reginald Cleak fell in behind her. Balding, stout, and possessed of untrammeled humor, Cleak was a thirty-five-year veteran of the Met and Kate's right hand. Over the years the two had done tours together in fraud, cybercrime, and most recently the Flying Squad, better known as "the Sweeney," the elite task force assigned to hunt down and capture armed robbers.

In one hand Cleak held a notepad, in the other a pen. The notepad was officially known as the "decision log." It was Sergeant Cleak's job to follow Kate around the crime scene and record every order, observation, and instruction she gave. The reasons were twofold: First, if Lord Russell had by some stretch of the imagination been murdered, and if one day his murderer was brought to the Old Bailey, the decision log would serve as a minute-by-minute record of every step taken during the investigation. Second, after the investigation and trial were completed, the log would be the subject of a thorough analysis conducted by the Murder Review Board.

"Victim is Robert Russell. Approximately thirty years of age. Cause of death, blunt force trauma resulting from a fall from the fifth floor of his residence at One Park Lane, London." Kate knelt. "Let's have a closer look, then," she said. "You may do the honors, Sergeant Cleak."

Cleak pulled off the sheet.

Russell lay facedown, his neck clearly broken, head bent grotesquely to one side. It appeared as if he'd landed head first. There was a lot of blood, but it didn't faze Kate. She'd seen worse.

The deceased was dressed in a blue blazer, jeans, and a collared shirt. The force of impact had scattered his shoes and personal effects to the far end of the driveway. Kate noted that his arms were splayed to either side of his torso and that the palms were turned up. She lifted his left wrist. The crystal of his Rolex wristwatch was shattered.

Odd, she thought.

No matter how committed jumpers were, they nearly always raised their hands to break their fall. The survival instinct was difficult to master. For Russell's watch to have struck the stairs in that fashion, his arms would have had to have been relaxed, possibly hanging at his side. It crossed her mind that Russell might have been sitting on the balcony railing and somehow fallen asleep. Instances of drunken students falling from their college windows after dozing off were common enough.

She ran the notion past Cleak. He shook his head, as if she were daft. "Look at the railing. Barely wide enough to set an elbow on."

"Yeah, you're probably right." Kate returned her attention to the body. It was then that she noted a prominent bump on the crown of Russell's head. She parted his thick blond hair. The scalp bulged as if a golf ball had been inserted beneath the skin. In a moment her eyes traveled from Russell's shattered Rolex to the balcony and back to the grotesque lump on the dead man's scalp. It was obvious that at some point, either during or prior to the fall, Robert Russell had been hit on the head.

"Interesting," she whispered, almost to herself.

"Excuse me, boss?" said Cleak.

"There's nothing below Russell's balcony. I mean no terrace, no window box, nothing."

"And so?"

"Gather up Lord Russell's belongings," said Kate, no longer whispering, but speaking clearly in the competent voice of a senior homicide investigator. "We'll need his wallet and his phone. And be sure to check all his pockets. Catalogue everything. I don't care if it's a used hankie. Next, find all CCTV cameras within fifty meters. I'm sure there's one somewhere along the street that was trained on the stairs.

Check the park, too. I know it was dark, but maybe the boys in the lab can find something. Put the doormen into separate rooms. I'll want a word. Oh, and get on to the alarm company. Find out what time Russell came home last night. And I mean to the minute."

"Yes, boss."

Kate stood and peeled off her gloves. "I'm officially declaring this a crime scene."

5

"Hands in your pockets, ladies and gentlemen."

Kate Ford opened the door to Lord Robert Russell's flat, followed by Reg Cleak and several members of the forensics squad. She took one look at the high ceilings and the expansive living room with its view of Hyde Park and whistled. "Not bad for a starter flat."

"Just a wee bit nicer than Lambeth Walk," said Cleak with sarcasm.

"Touch anything and that's where I'll send you." Kate examined the bolt locks embedded in the doorframe. One functioned vertically, the other horizontally. A biometric sensor was built into the wall, below an alphanumeric keypad and a video screen to show the faces of whoever was coming to visit. "Who was he trying to keep out?" she asked Cleak. "I'd have thought that three doormen on call day and night and that medieval portcullis downstairs would be sufficient."

Cleak pointed to the passive infrared sensor positioned high on one wall. "That's not all. He has himself a state-of-the-art system inside, too." Just then his phone rang and he stepped away to take the call.

"That was the security company," he said afterward. "Alarm was set at 1830. No activity reported until Russell returned from his parents'. He disarmed the system at 2:41:39 and turned it back on at 2:41:48."

"And he fell before 2:45," said Kate. "Whatever happened, it happened quickly."

They walked into the living room. Kate opened the sliding glass door and stepped onto the balcony. She observed that the railing was slim and metal, certainly too narrow for a man Russell's size to sit on. With a downward gaze, she confirmed that there was nothing protruding from the building that he might have struck as he plummeted to his death. From her vantage point, it appeared as if the body had actually veered toward the building as it fell.

She stepped back inside. Robert Russell had shared his parents' tastes as well as their money. The residence looked as if it had been furnished in 1909, not 2009. There was plenty of chintz and floral furniture, oriental rugs, and Louis XV chairs. There was a zebra-skin rug beneath the dining room table, a carved elephant tusk from the Raj, and even an oil of HMS **Victory** lying in wait for the French and Spanish fleet off Trafalgar. She'd stepped back in time. It was England at the height of the empire.

She walked into the kitchen, which was modern and up-to-date, with the Viking range she'd dreamed of and a Sub-Zero refrigerator big enough to hold a side of beef. A swinging door led into a formal dining room, which in turn gave onto a long hallway.

Halfway along the corridor, they found Russell's bedroom. It was more of the same: parquet wood floor, four-poster bed, curtains drawn, an oil of Russell as a teenager dressed in rugby kit, his cheeks rosy from exertion. The bed was neatly made, and a bouquet of fresh flowers stood in a vase on the side table. She opened the closet and peered in. A fleet of dark suits hung in perfect order, an inch separating each. A stack of pressed and laundered shirts sat on the dresser. Twenty-odd pairs of polished shoes were arrayed on custom-built shelves. "Look, Reg, he has a special place for his shoes. Got one of these at home, do you?"

Cleak stuck his head into the closet. "A regular Mrs. Marcos. Me? I've got my work shoes, a pair of tennis shoes, and my Sunday best. They all fit very nicely under the bed, thank you."

Kate picked up a pair. A label inside read "Made by John Lobb, Ltd. for R. T. Russell, Marquess of Henley." She whistled softly. "Our lord has a title."

Just then one of the forensics team rushed into the bedroom. "Come to the end of the hall," he said. "We've found Russell's command center."

"What do you mean, command center?" Kate asked.

"You'll see," came the reply.

It was a room from the future. If the rest of the apartment lived in the nineteenth century, Russell's office, or his "command center," as it had been aptly nicknamed, came from the twenty-first. The floor was of sleek travertine. The walls were paneled in some kind of glossy white wood. A long stainless steel desk occupied the center of the room, and on it were three slim monitors. More impressive was the massive video screen built into the facing wall. The screen measured at least 2 meters diagonally. Lighting came from halogens built into the ceiling. Like the rest of Russell's residence, the room was meticulously, even obsessively clean.

At either end of the desk stood neatly arranged trays piled high with papers. "Here's a timetable for Victoria Station," said Cleak, pointing to a brochure. "This one here's called 'Forecast of World Oil Production.' "

Kate leafed through several of the stacks. Some were Internet downloads from foreign news sites, others glossy company reports, and still others appeared to have been typed by Russell himself. The subjects ranged from weather patterns in Antarctica to something about a new military headquarters in Moscow to some mathematical sillyspeak about subatomic decay rates. She even found a copy of **Constabulary,** the monthly magazine "written by police for police." She wondered who had given him that.

"Anyone know what he did for a living?" Kate asked.

"Some kind of analyst or researcher, if you ask me," said Cleak.

"Yeah, but what kind?" She sat down at Russell's

desk and slid open the drawer. "Reg," she said, her voice gone hard as flint. "Better have a look."

Cleak gazed over her shoulder. "Very nice, indeed. And the latest model."

Inside the drawer lay a gray steel semiautomatic pistol and next to it a box of bullets. "Beretta?" asked Kate.

"Browning," said Cleak, who had served in the Queen's Guard years ago. "Standard army issue. Ten bullets in the clip, one in the chamber. Not a lot of range, mind you, but plenty of punch if you use it close in." He picked up the pistol by its nose and sniffed the barrel. "Hasn't been fired in a while."

"What do you suppose Russell needed one of those for?"

"Same thing he needed the bolts on the door and the **Star Wars** alarm system for. The man had enemies."

"I want to review the apartment's security videos for the past seventy-two hours. Both interior and exterior. Someone was in this apartment waiting for Russell when he arrived home last night. He didn't get that bump on the noggin hitting his head on the doorway. There has to be footage of the killer somewhere inside the building."

"Yes, boss."

"Have the body transferred to the coroner's office. Tell them I need a preliminary examination completed by lunch. I want to know just how seriously that blow to the head affected him."

Cleak nodded, listing each instruction on his notepad. As he did so, he made a not-so-quiet sucking sound. He stopped abruptly, aware that Kate was looking at him. "Two impacted wisdom teeth. Six-month wait to see an NHS dentist, or I can cough up a thousand quid to visit a private doc on Harley Street." He shook his head. "The wife has her heart set on Christmas in Bethlehem. I'll have to wait, won't I?"

"I can loan you the money. I'm flush. Got Billy's insurance. Have to spend it on something."

"Wouldn't hear of it," said Cleak, in a tone that said that was the end of that. He opened a package of chewing gum and folded two sticks into his mouth. "That'll cure it for a while."

Kate nodded, then turned back to Russell's desk and pulled the keyboard close to her. She hit the return key, thinking that the PC was in slumber mode. No one turned computers off anymore. The screen remained dark. She tried again, then rebooted the CPU. Finally the screen came to life. Dozens of icons indicating various files appeared, but the titles were all gobbledygook: letters, symbols, wingdings. "What's this, then?" she asked.

"The hard drive's been defragmented," said one of the forensics men. "Mind if I have a go?"

The tech took Kate's place and began to tap away at the keys. "Whole thing's shot. You'll have to take it to the lab, but even then I don't think you'll have much luck."

"What about the backup?" asked Kate.

"It's ruined, too. Someone did this deliberately. Two independent systems don't crash on their own. The hard drive's one thing, but not the backup. If you ask me, I'd say someone ran a very powerful magnet over both drives. It's like putting all your papers through a shredder at once, except worse. Not only is the stored data ruined, so is the hard drive holding it. Might as well have stuck a grenade inside the computer and set it off."

Just then the large flat-screen television built into the wall came to life. Kate looked at the keyboard, wondering if she'd somehow activated it with her typing. "I thought you said it was broken."

"Sshh!" said Cleak.

Activity in the room ground to a halt as all eyes focused on the screen, where a young woman sat in a dimly lit room staring into the camera. She was plain and disheveled, her brown, shoulder-length hair matted and uncombed, and she wore wire-rimmed specs and a black V-neck sweater.

"What the hell?" Kate looked over her shoulder.

"It's a live feed," said the computer technician. "Coming in off a DSL line. Must be independent of Russell's rig."

"Can she see us?"

"I don't know. The rest of Russell's computer is broken. I imagine that the camera is, too."

"Rob, you there?" she said. "It's seven. I know I'm early, but I had to reach you. Why aren't you answering your phone?" She looked to her side, then back into the camera. "Are you there? I can't see a thing. Don't you have your camera on?" She paused, expecting a response, and for a moment everyone in the room—Kate, Reg Cleak, the forensics men—held their breath, praying that she wouldn't terminate the connection.

"Tell me we have Russell's cell phone," whispered Kate.

Cleak shook his head, never taking his eyes from the screen. "Not yet. It wasn't on his body when he fell. No one's spotted it on the premises."

"Damn."

On-screen, the woman drew a breath and her manner hardened. "Mischa's in London," she said, leaning closer to the camera, as if vouchsafing a secret. "The entire team is coming. It's all very hush-hush. Some kind of under-the-radar visit to establish a new security protocol. Just the one seance, then it's back home. Scheduled for tomorrow at eleven-fifteen. Sorry, but I couldn't find out where. Whatever you said, it must have really scared them. God knows you've been right about this kind of thing before. Robbie, I'm frightened. The upgrades you talked about take months to implement. Seven days isn't long enough to even figure out where to start. Are you sure that it's going to happen so soon?"

From off-screen there came a bloodcurdling wail. The woman darted a look to her right.

"What the hell was that?" asked Cleak. "You think she's in some kind of danger?"

The wail grew louder. Kate stepped closer to the screen. "I've no idea."

The woman rose from her chair and disappeared out of the picture. She returned ten seconds later with a bawling infant in her arms.

"So much for your danger," said Kate.

On-screen, the woman continued. "Call me and tell me if you were able to figure out the stuff about Victoria Bear. I have no idea what your friend was talking about. Asked everyone I know and came up empty. Tell him it's about time he learned proper English. He's been here long enough. Victoria Bear. Probably got the whole thing cocked up. Anyway, I can't make heads or tails of it."

The infant continued to fuss and the woman rocked it gently. "Call me if you learn anything more," she said. "I mean, do I need to leave or anything? Just promise me you'll be careful. And call. Don't forget!"

The screen went black.

"What the hell was that?" said Cleak, folding his arms. "Did Mary Poppins just warn us about a pending attack?"

"I'm not certain," said Kate.

"Well, she sure as hell is. Seven days, she said, and she looked like she was scared out of her wits."

Kate turned to the computer technician. "Can you find her? I don't care what toes you have to step on. Just tell me, is it possible?"

"Possible," replied the technician. "But a long shot. First we need to learn which provider is giving Russell his cable hookup. From there, it's a question of following the transmission back to its source. Everything leaves a trail. Like Hansel and Gretel and their breadcrumbs. Problem is that if someone doesn't want you to follow it, there's plenty of ways to gobble 'em up."

Kate summoned Cleak. "Get on to Russell's parents and ask them a few questions about their son's profession, and if he happens to have a girlfriend, or if they happen to have a grandson, for that matter. But go easy. They've only just gotten the news. Oh, and Reg, ask them what time Russell left their place after dinner."

As she waited, Kate leafed through more of the papers on Russell's desk. There were titles like "Democracy in Estonia," "Open-Source Coding for the Military," and a whole pile dedicated to the Arsenal Football Club, which played out of North London. **He's a spy,** she thought rather crazily. **A spy with a football fix.** But what kind of spy communicated with mousy housewives with newborn babies?

Ten minutes later Reg Cleak came back into the room. "Russell left his parents' home in Windsor at eleven-thirty. Just after football highlights on BBC2."

"Eleven-thirty?" Kate ran a hand over the back of her neck. "That leaves nearly three hours unaccounted for. Maybe he hit the clubs, such as they are on a Sunday night, or maybe he visited a friend. Either way, I want to know. His car's downstairs. Send the plates to AVS. Ask them to run the number through their system and see if they get any hits."

AVS stood for Automobile Visual Surveillance, a division of the Metropolitan Police that monitored the thousands of closed-circuit television cameras positioned in and around London. Advanced software scanned the stream of images every three seconds, identifying each passing automobile's number plates and storing them in a temporary databank for five days. By searching for a given number plate in a given time period, it was possible to track a vehicle's movements from camera to camera as it drove across the city.

"I'll put some of the boys on it back at the nick," said Cleak.

"Anything about the woman?"

"Nothing. Russell's a bachelor. Parents don't know anything about his having a girlfriend."

"We've got to find her, Reg. She's our first priority."

Cleak nodded, all the while writing in his log.

"And what did the duke of Suffolk say about his son's job?" asked Kate.

"He teaches," said Cleak. "He's a don at Christ Church College, Oxford."

"A don with a Browning semiautomatic in his desk? What does he teach—marksmanship?"

"History. The duke wanted me to know that his son took a first when he was there."

"I'm sure we're all suitably impressed. Did the duke say what he studied?"

"Oh yes." Cleak picked up the pistol and admired it. "Russia."

6

"How the hell did he get to London without us knowing it?" asked Frank Connor, Division's newly appointed acting director, as he studied the photograph of Jonathan Ransom taken at the Terminal 4 arrivals hall of Heathrow Airport exactly three hours earlier. "The last you told me he was still at that godforsaken camp in Kenya."

"Turkana Refugee Camp. That's correct."

"Not looking very spry, is he? I don't know how anyone can survive in that hellhole. How long's he been there? Five months?"

"He arrived in Kenya at the end of February," said Peter Erskine, Connor's number two. "He hasn't left since. He suffered a bout of malaria two months back. Dropped twenty pounds."

"When was our last sighting?"

"A week ago. One of our contacts with Save the Children reported seeing him at the camp."

"Save the Children?" Connor flushed with anger. "Who will we be using next? The Make-a-Wish Foundation?"

He tossed the photo on top of Ransom's file, a binder stuffed four inches thick. The material inside dated back eight years, to Ransom's first assignment in Liberia. But Jonathan Ransom was not in any way affiliated with Division. He'd never received a U.S. government paycheck. In fact, until five months ago, he'd had no idea that he was working on its behalf. Ransom was what professionals in the trade call a pawn, a private individual manipulated to do the government's work without being made aware of its intent. Frank Connor had another name for them: schmucks.

Sighing, Connor removed his bifocals and rose from his desk. He would turn fifty-eight in a month, and at 4:38 Eastern Standard Time this fine summer morning, he was feeling every bit his age. Four months had passed since he was appointed acting director of Division, and those months counted as the hardest, most frustrating of his life.

Division had been created prior to 9/11 in the wake of the Central Intelligence Agency's failure to find and punish those responsible for the bombings of the Khobar Towers in Saudi Arabia and the United States embassies in Nairobi and Dar-es-Salaam and numerous other attacks against American interests abroad. The fire-eaters in the Pentagon were upset and eager for revenge. They argued that the CIA had grown soft, that it had become an organization of paper-pushers content to hide behind their desks. Instead of developing flesh-and-blood sources inside hostile territory, they were satisfied to wait for the next download of satellite imagery to study beneath their microscopes. The CIA didn't have a spy worth two cents on the ground in any of the world's hot spots and hadn't mounted a successful black op in ten years.

In short, the job of gathering intelligence could no longer be entrusted solely to the spooks in Langley.

It was the Pentagon's turn.

The United States military had the resources and the culture to put men into the field capable of taking the offensive in the global war on terror, referred to in directives and white papers as "GWOT," a name as ugly as the scourge it set out to defeat. "Proactive" was the watchword, and the former president liked the sound of it. One National Security Presidential Directive later, Division was created. A beast as secret as it was stealthy, to serve at his behest, and his behest only.

Division's first successes came quickly. The assassination of a Bosnian general wanted for genocide. The targeted killing of a Colombian drug lord and the pillaging of his networks. The kidnapping, interrogation, and, later, execution of several Al-Qaeda supremos in Iraq and Pakistan. All were important victories, and Division's reputation benefited accordingly. The operations it mounted grew in scope. More money. More operatives. More latitude to navigate the quicksilver currents of the gray world. Goals were no longer tactical but political. Removing a bad actor from the scene was not enough. Ideological factors were to be considered. Fostering democracy in

Lebanon and kick-starting the Orange Revolution in Ukraine were but two examples.

But success bred hubris. Not content to implement policy, Division began to make it. "Proactive" took on a new meaning. It was Acton's theorem all over again: power corrupts; absolute power corrupts absolutely. Inevitably, Division went a step too far.

In Switzerland six months earlier, a plan to foment war between Iran and Israel was foiled at the last moment by a Division agent gone rogue, and an international incident was narrowly averted. Behind closed doors, the president was forced to admit American involvement. Part of his penance involved the sharp curtailing of Division's mandate. Its operatives were recalled, its offices moved out of the Pentagon. Division's budget was halved and its staff sent packing. The coup de grâce came when it was decided that congressional permission was henceforth required to mount an operation.

In the eyes of the intelligence community, Division had been castrated. Word went out that it was only a matter of time until it was shuttered altogether. In the meantime, Division needed an interim director. And this time he would not come from the ranks of the military.

Frank Connor fit the bill perfectly. He was not a professional soldier. In fact, he had never worn his country's uniform. The closest he'd ever come to firing a weapon was blowing off an M-80 firecracker on the Fourth of July when he was a teenager. But, make no mistake, he was a fighter. Thirty years of toiling in the darkest corners of the Washington bureaucracy had honed survival skills a combat-hardened vet would envy. He'd worked at State, Treasury, and the Office of Management and Budget. He knew where the bodies were buried in every building in D.C. But for the past ten years he'd been a regular face inside the E-Ring of the Pentagon. He'd been at Division since the beginning.

Connor was the dumpy guy sitting in the corner with the wrinkled shirt and sweat rings under his arms who made sure all the **i**'s were dotted and the **t**'s were crossed. When Division needed a plane to ferry a team from friendly Kazakhstan into unfriendly Chechnya, Connor knew that only a Pilatus P-3 would do, and promptly made the arrangements. If an operative in Seoul required a dummy passport to cross into China, Connor could obtain one within twenty-four hours. (And you could be sure that it was clean, meaning that the number was duly registered in its home country and it would never raise a flag.) Need to bribe a corrupt dignitary? Connor would call an obliging banker at one of a dozen tax havens around the globe and the transaction would be taken care of. A shipment of Kalashnikovs to forces friendly to the cause in Colombia? Connor had the number of every arms dealer in both hemispheres memorized, and he probably knew their birthdays, too. The word was that Frank Connor made things happen. Quickly. Efficiently. And, best of all, secretly.

But equally important to his overseers at the Pentagon was what Connor didn't do. He didn't plan. He didn't intrigue. And he didn't dream. One look at his sagging cheeks, pouchy eyes, and lopsided gait, and you knew he was an inside man. Which was exactly what everyone wanted. An inside man to keep Division running until it could die a secret, clandestine death.

And Frank Connor wouldn't have disagreed. At least, not out loud. But Connor had his own ideas about the disgraced agency's future, and nowhere did they include a premature death. Despite the disaster in Switzerland, he was still a believer. And contrary to what his better-dressed, better-coifed, and better-informed bosses thought, Frank Connor **did** dream. He **did** intrigue. And he **did** plan. To his mind, Division was not dead. It was only resting. Gathering strength while waiting for a chance to reclaim its former glory.

Frank Connor's chance.

His days as an inside man were over.

"Did you get the information on the medical conference he's supposedly attending?" he asked.

"They've posted a website on the Net," said Erskine. "I downloaded the essentials. Take a look."

Connor studied the cover sheet. "International Association of Internists—21st Annual Congress. What's so important about a conference that it lures Ransom away from his beloved field hospital?"

"He's a keynote speaker. He's set to deliver a speech tomorrow morning."

Connor found the schedule of events. " 'Treatment of Parasitic Diseases in Pediatric Patients.' I think I'll take a pass. Where'd they say he's staying?"

"Dorchester Hotel."

"Not bad," said Connor, raising an eyebrow as he flipped through the pages. "How many men do we have over there?"

"In London? Four, but one of them is on leave."

"Four? You're kidding me." Connor shook his head. London was the intelligence capital of Europe. A year ago, Division had boasted posh offices alongside the U.S. embassy in Grosvenor Square, with a staff of twenty full-time professionals and another twenty contract men on call. "Get that sonofabitch on leave back, and I mean now. Set up a twelve-hour rotation at Ransom's hotel. Two men on, two men off. I want them on site and reporting back within the hour. And see what you can do about scaring up some more manpower. Get in touch with Berlin or Milan. They've got to have someone."

"Sure thing." Peter Erskine was thirty, pale, and runner lean, with black hair kept in place by a fistful of gel and shifty blue eyes that didn't miss a thing. He was third-generation spook. Deerfield, Yale, a Fulbright scholar, and a Bonesman to boot. His grandfather had worked with Allen Dulles in Switzerland during the Second World War and his father had been George H. W. Bush's deputy director of operations when "Forty-one" had occupied the director's chair at Langley in the mid-seventies. Erskine was the silk to Connor's sandpaper. The glimpse of ermine to reassure visiting dignitaries from the Hill that Division could be trusted.

Connor dropped the papers on the desk. "So he comes all the way from deepest, darkest Africa just to deliver a speech about tropical parasites to a bunch of wealthy doctors. I don't buy it. He must know that we're keeping an eye on him. She'd have warned him of that. Why would he compromise himself? He's there for another reason."

"I checked with the conference organizers," said Erskine. "Ransom was invited three months ago. They're paying his plane fare and his hotel expenses."

"No," said Connor, crossing his arms over his barrel chest and glaring at his deputy. "It's her."

There was no need to mention a name. "Her" was Emma Ransom.

Connor walked to the window. Division's offices had been moved to a nondescript office building in Tysons Corner, an "edge city" complex 15 miles southeast of Washington. It shared the building with the IRS and the Bureau of Weights and Measures. From his perch on the second floor, he looked across a forlorn stretch of Virginian asphalt and an auto repair shop. It wasn't exactly the Lincoln Memorial and the Reflecting Pool.

"She's there, Pete. It wasn't his idea to go to some highfalutin conference in London. He hates that kind of thing. It was Emma's doing."

"With all due respect, sir, I can understand her

wanting to see her husband, but why would she choose London? It's the most heavily watched city on earth. They have over fifty thousand closed-circuit television cameras set up around the city, and those are just the ones belonging to the government. The average Joe gets his picture taken fifty times just walking along Oxford Street. It'd be like going into a shark tank with a bloody nose."

"Sounds just like her," said Connor.

It was Emma Ransom who'd blown the operation in Switzerland and all but brought down Division. She figured number one on Connor's list of VIPs. There would be no going forward for Division or for Frank Connor until she was taken care of.

"What about Ransom's phone?" he asked.

"His cell? The number we have on file is registered to Vodafone."

Vodafone was the largest cellular phone carrier in Europe.

"We know anybody in their London office?"

"Not anymore."

Connor barely managed to suppress an expletive. He was Irish and Catholic and still went to mass twice a week. If he no longer quite believed, he still prayed with the fervor of a new convert. He was a man who believed in covering his bets. "When's Ransom's return flight?"

"Three days from now."

"Three days? So he's keeping a day free."

"Technically, yes, but . . ."

"But nothing. She's contacted him. She wants a meet."

"But why?" persisted Erskine. "She'd never risk a meet. Not there. Not now. Not after what happened in Italy in April. She knows we'll spot her husband coming into the country. She's better than that."

"Maybe. Maybe not." Connor placed his elbows on the table and cradled his meaty chin in his hands. His bloodshot brown eyes stared out the window, and when he spoke, it was as if he had forgotten that Erskine was in the room and was talking to himself. Rousing himself for the job to come. "We had a chance to take her out in Rome. We set the bait, we reeled her in, and then we muffed the job. Now, by the grace of God, we've been given another opportunity. She's in London. She's come to see her husband. I know it. And this time we're going to get her."

Connor placed two calls before going. The first went to an unsleeping suite of offices on the first floor of the Pentagon called the Defense Logistics Agency.

"I need a jet."

"Sorry, Frank. No can do. You're not on the list anymore."

"Forget about the list. This one's off the books." Connor tucked the phone under his chin while he rummaged through his desk for a passport. Canada. Australia. Belgium. He scooped up a Namibian passport under his work name of Standish and checked that the visas were intact. "So?"

"Is this about her?"

"One-way to London," Connor went on, as if he hadn't heard the question. "I believe you have a Lear on standby for the secretary. He won't be going anywhere today. The Saudis are going to press for an emergency meeting this morning. They want those F-22s bad."

"How the hell did you know—?"

"Fueled and ready in an hour."

"Frank, you're not making this easy."

Connor stopped what he was doing and stood up straight. "Don't make me bring it up," he said in the same easygoing voice. "Debts are so embarrassing."

Silence filled the line for ten seconds. "I can't give you the director's bird, but there's a Citation at Dulles that's fueled up with a crew on standby. Only thing is, it's on FlightAware, the FAA's tracking list. You'll be on the radar. That cause a problem?"

Connor considered this for a few moments. "No," he said, dropping the Namibian passport and picking up an American passport, the only one bearing his real name. "No problem there."

"Oh, and Frank . . ."

"Yeah?"

"I can throw in a flight attendant."

"That won't be necessary," said Connor, slipping on his jacket. "I'll be traveling alone."

The second call was placed on a secure line to a private number in England. Area code 207, for the center of London.

"It's me," he said when the party answered.

"Hello, Frank. Still handing out pink slips?"

"Finished for the moment. In fact, I'm calling to offer you a way back in . . . if you're interested."

"You know I am."

"Have any plans for tonight?"

"Nothing I can't break."

"Good. There's a cocktail reception I want you to go to. Dorchester Hotel. Six p.m. It's for a bunch of doctors, so you'll fit right in. Listen up."

7

It was late in the afternoon. In his suite at the Dorchester Hotel, Jonathan Ransom studied the schedule he'd received upon checking in. A cocktail reception was to begin at 6 p.m. **Business Attire Requested.** A handwritten note added: "Dr. Ransom, I'm looking forward to meeting you there to discuss your speech. Colin Blackburn." Blackburn was the president of the International Association of Internists, and it was on his invitation that Jonathan had come.

Jonathan showered and shaved. The bathroom was a vault of Carrera marble with towering mirrors and glamorous toiletries arrayed on the counters. He couldn't get out of there fast enough.

He dressed in a pair of gray flannels, a white button-down shirt, and a wrinkle-proof blue blazer. Reluctantly, he put on a tie as well, and even spent the extra few seconds getting the knot just so. The result wasn't half bad, he thought amusedly, looking at the stranger in the mirror. Someone might even mistake him for a doctor.

A sign in the lobby indicated that the cocktail reception was being held in the Athenaeum Ballroom. An arrow pointed the way. Opposite the ballroom entry, a woman was seated at a table handing out name tags. They were arranged alphabetically, but Jonathan wasn't able to locate his own. He mentioned his problem to the woman and gave his name.

"One of our speakers!" the woman boomed. "We have yours in a special place. I'll be right back."

A lanky man with wavy gray hair took up position at Jonathan's side. "You'd think that with so many advanced degrees floating around this place they could get things a bit more organized."

"Usually I find it's the opposite," said Jonathan. "Something about too many chefs."

"You're Ransom?" inquired the stranger.

"Do we know each other?" asked Jonathan guardedly.

"No, but I recognized you from the program." The man produced a brochure from his jacket and opened it to the inside page. Jonathan studied his photo. It had been taken in a passport studio in Amsterdam four years earlier. He wondered how they had gotten their hands on it. He didn't remember sending it in. "The name's Blackburn," said the older man.

"Dr. Blackburn. It's a pleasure."

They shook hands.

"Good flight?" Blackburn was near sixty, with dark, steadfast eyes and a no-nonsense manner. Jonathan liked him immediately.

"Early, if you can believe," said Jonathan. "These days that's more than you can ask for."

"Hotel taking care of you?"

"It's too much, really. You shouldn't have gone to the expense. The bathroom alone . . ."

"Like a Roman whorehouse. Between you and me, it suits my wife's taste to a T. I'm afraid you wouldn't last long at my house."

Just then the woman returned with Jonathan's name tag and pinned it to his blazer. While the other name tags were printed on three-by-five paper encased in translucent plastic, his looked half again as large and sported a blue ribbon.

"You're to wear it at all times," the woman instructed. "Some of our members aren't as good with names as one might like."

"Thanks." Jonathan shot a horrified look at his chest. He was pinned like a prize hog at the county fair. He turned to speak to Blackburn, but the older man had disappeared into the crowd.

The room was filling up. Jonathan observed that there were an equal number of male and female physicians present, most with their spouses in tow. All were dressed to the nines: the women in cocktail dresses, the men in dark suits. He headed to the bar and ordered a Stella. "No glass, thank you," he said. The beer was ice cold, just as he liked it, and he quickly drank half the bottle. A trickle escaped the corner of his mouth and he wiped at it with his sleeve.

"There is such a thing as a napkin," came a crusty British voice from over his shoulder.

"Excuse me, I—" Jonathan spun and looked into the face of a pleasantly chubby man with curly brown hair and merry blue eyes. "Jamie. What a surprise!"

"If you ever want to join me on Harley Street, you'll have to clean up your act," said Jamie Meadows. "My patients prefer their surgeon sharp. White jacket, polished shoes. Goodness, are those desert boots you're wearing?"

Jonathan clutched Meadows in a bear hug. The two had been at Oxford together, each the recipient of a fellowship in reconstructive surgery, and had shared a flat on the High for twelve months.

"What are you doing here?" Jonathan asked.

"Think I'd miss a chance to lob a few tomatoes at my old roommate?" said Meadows as he pulled his own copy of the conference brochure from his pocket and slapped it in his open palm. "Continuing education. Your speech is going to earn me two hours of credit. I'll give you fair warning. I've prepared several interesting questions guaranteed to raise a sweat when you're on the dais."

Jonathan smiled. It was the same old Jamie. "How have you been?"

"Not bad, all things considered," said Meadows. "Been in private practice for six years now. I'm doing the cosmetic thing. Boobs, bums, and brows. Not enough hours in the day. I've got a surgical suite in the office."

"What happened to the National Health Service? I thought you were headed off to the wilds of Wales to be an Accident and Emergency doctor."

"Not Wales, Cornwall," said Meadows in an injured tone. "Didn't last six months. The government's awful. Won't pay for a new kidney, let alone a new pair of knockers. What's a man with ambition to do?" He placed a hand on Jonathan's shoulder and pulled him close. "I wasn't kidding about the job. There's plenty of room in my shop if you decide to cross the street. Hours are long but the pay's handsome. Actually, it's more than that. Pru and I just bought a little shack in St. Tropez."

"I didn't know they had shacks in St. Tropez."

"They don't. They charge you a million quid and call them villas."

The two stood looking at each other, calculating the changes the years' passage had wrought. In his worn flannels and blazer, Jonathan felt scruffy, and for once perhaps even a shade insecure, standing next to Meadows, who was decked out in Savile Row's finest, his shoes polished to such a high gloss that Jonathan could practically see himself.

"Christ, we hated you," said Meadows. "Better than all the rest of us put together and a Yank at that. To top it off, you're actually still doing what we all promised. Tell me the truth: do you enjoy it?"

Jonathan nodded. "I do."

"I believe you." Meadows smiled, but it was a melancholy smile. "So, you still solo?" he asked, perking up. "Don't tell me you never married. You were such a monk at Oxford. Lived in hospital morning and night."

"No, I'm married," said Jonathan. "In fact, I met her just a few months after finishing up. Unfortunately, she couldn't make it."

"Is she back in Kenya?"

Jonathan answered quickly, and his duplicity surprised him. "No, she's visiting friends. I think she's the only one who hates these things more than I do." He added a larcenous smile to make the lie go down easier. "And you—kids?"

"Three girls. Eight, five, and one in diapers. Light of my life." Suddenly Meadows stood on his tiptoes and waved across the room. "There she is. Prudence. Didn't you know her up at Oxford? She was at St. Hilda's, took a first in chemistry, worked at Butlers on the High. Pru, over here!"

Jonathan spotted a slender, dark-maned woman waving back and making her way toward them.

"Pru, here's Jonathan," said Meadows, welcoming his wife with a kiss. "Tell him he looks as fat and out of shape as me. Go ahead. No need to spare his feelings. He's tougher than he looks."

"You look marvelous," said Prudence Meadows as she shook Jonathan's hand. "Jamie's been looking forward to seeing you."

"Actually, it's rather last-minute," said Meadows. "It was Pru who spotted your name on the brochure."

"Liar," said Prudence. "We signed up months ago. We've been looking forward to this for ages."

"Did we? Oh yes, that's right." Meadows dropped his shoulders, as if found out. "Caught me again.

Didn't want it to go to your head." He turned to his wife. "Listen, Pru, I'm trying to convince Jonathan to start selling his wares to the highest bidder, namely **moi.**"

"Do you work with Jamie?" Jonathan asked Prudence Meadows.

"Me? God, no. But close enough. I'm in pharmaceuticals, actually."

"Top sales rep in Britain," boasted Meadows. "Peddles enough Prozac to keep the entire nation stoned. Earns more than I do."

"Hardly," protested Prudence. "But really, Jonathan, you must come round to Jamie's place. There isn't a finer physician on all Harley Street."

"Go on," added Meadows.

"Oh shut up," said Prudence, gifting her husband with a jab to the ribs. She returned her attention to Jonathan. "It isn't all elective surgery. Jamie does plenty of reconstructive work as well. I understand that's your specialty."

"When I get a chance," said Jonathan. "Most of the time we're without the necessary equipment. I appreciate the invitation to visit your practice. I'm only here for three days, but if I have time I'd love to." Jonathan studied Prudence Meadows. She was pretty in an unassuming fashion, with narrow brown eyes and a vaguely sour cast to her lips. He jogged his memory for a sighting of her while he was up at Oxford all those years ago, but came up dry. He was certain they'd never met.

"Could you excuse me? I have to run," he said, gesturing in the opposite direction. "I need to go find the guy who invited me. Maybe we can get together tomorrow night?"

"Dinner. Our place," said Jamie Meadows. "I won't take no for an answer. Notting Hill. Number's in the book." Suddenly he lunged forward, and when he shook Jonathan's hand, his eyes were wet. "It's good to see you. All this time. I can't believe it."

"Likewise, Jamie," responded Jonathan, moved by the show of emotion.

"Anyway, till tomorrow," said Meadows, gathering himself. "Can't wait to hear the big speech. Give you the details about dinner then. Cheers!"

"Yes, good luck with your talk," said Prudence, smiling warmly.

Jonathan walked back to the bar and ordered another beer. The room was packed. Conversation had grown from bubbly to boisterous. No abstemious physicians here. He scanned the crowd for Dr. Blackburn, and when he didn't see him, he went down the corridor to the restroom. It was time to head out and get something to eat. No one could say he hadn't put in an appearance.

The door to the restroom opened. A moment later he spotted Blackburn in the mirror, plainly agitated. "Come on, then," said Blackburn. "Follow me."

"Excuse me?"

Blackburn nodded toward the door. "We need to hurry before they get here. Let's get a move on."

Jonathan stood his ground. "Who's 'they'?"

"You know." Blackburn walked out of the restroom. Puzzled, Jonathan followed. Blackburn led the way down the corridor, turned the corner, then threw open the door to a conference room. "What are you waiting for?"

Jonathan hurried inside. "What's this about?" he asked after Blackburn had closed the door behind them. "What do you mean, 'before they get here'?"

"There's no time for questions. Just do as I say. You can leave through the window. It's unlocked. Go to Green Park Underground station and take the tube to Marylebone. You'll have to change trains at Piccadilly. I was led to understand you knew your way around London."

"More or less."

"Right, then. Get out at Marylebone and head west on Edgware Road. Look for number sixty-one. It's a walk-up flat. Black door with golden numerals. You'll see some names and buzzers. Forget 'em. The door will be open. Go up to the second floor. Two C." Blackburn dug out a rabbit's foot with a single key dangling from it.

"What in the world are you talking about?" asked Jonathan as he took the key.

"Wait inside until you receive a phone call," instructed Blackburn, calmer now that Jonathan was paying attention. "You'll receive further instructions after we make sure you're clean."

"Clean?"

"Two of them have been keeping an eye on you at the cocktail party."

"Two of who? I didn't notice anyone."

Blackburn shot him a glance that said he was hardly surprised. "Get going. There's someone who wants to see you. And, I imagine, whom you wish to see as well."

Jonathan's heart caught in his throat. **She's here. She's in London.**

Blackburn moved to the door. "You must hurry," he said.

8

Fronted by the Meadow, a broad field of untamed grass and bordered by the meandering waters of the Isis River, Christ Church College, Oxford, was the picture of British higher learning. The college was founded in 1524 by Thomas Cardinal Wolsey, who had expropriated the grounds from a group of stubborn monks. Henry VIII stole it back from Wolsey and appointed the monastery church as the cathedral of the diocese of Oxford. As such, Christ Church was the only college at Oxford to be both church and institution of higher learning. But that kind of history belonged in guidebooks. All anyone knew about it today, including Kate Ford, was that its great hall served as the set for Hogwart's dining room in the Harry Potter movies. She was suitably impressed.

Kate ducked her head into the dusk of the porter's lodge and announced herself. "I'm looking for Anthony Dodd."

"Second floor. First door on the right."

She climbed the wooden stairwell. It was approaching six in the evening, and she was already bone tired. It was the videos that did it. All day she'd sat in One Park's security office reviewing tapes from the building's closed-circuit camera system in hopes of spotting Robert Russell's murderer. But no one—not she, nor Reg Cleak, nor any of the doormen who had worked the day before—had seen any unknown persons enter the building, or—**and this was the crucial point**—walk through the front door of Russell's residence on the fifth floor. Eight hours and not a single clue.

At four the coroner had phoned with news confirming that Russell's skull had been fractured before his fall. It was his opinion that the weapon was a blunt instrument, something akin to a ballpeen hammer. And though he couldn't say whether or not the blow had killed Russell, he was able to state with certainty that the blow had rendered him unconscious. The news confirmed her suspicion that Russell was already dead, or at the least incapacitated, when he'd fallen from his balcony, and had bolstered her belief that the assailant had been waiting for Russell upon his return. The question remained: how in God's name had he gotten in?

Reaching the second floor, Kate advanced down a gloomy hallway. The first door on the right stood ajar. Inside a cramped, sun-filled office, a burly young man in rugby kit was bent over a desk, shuffling through a stack of papers. Kate poked her head in. "Is this Professor Dodd's office?"

"It is," answered the student without looking up.

"Is he about?" Kate asked.

"He is indeed." The young man put down his papers and stood up. He was taller than she'd expected, at least six feet four inches, and handsome. His cheeks were flushed, his brow damp with sweat below a head of tousled brown hair. But it was his legs she couldn't help but notice. His thighs were as stout as tree trunks and striated with muscle.

"Where?"

"You're looking at him." Dodd nodded, stretching a hand to shake as he came closer. "Don't be embarrassed. I'm used to it. I'll be forty next week. I'm praying for my first gray hair."

"Lucky you," said Kate. "I've been plucking mine since I was thirty. Detective Chief Inspector Ford."

"I figured as much." Dodd moved his rugby ball off a chair and motioned for Kate to sit. "Can I get you something to drink? Water, beer, diet soda?"

"Water would be fine."

Dodd picked up a cell phone and called the scout with his order. "Sorry about the getup," he said afterward. "Coming from a practice. Season's almost here. I'm only a coach, but I like to stay in shape." He took up position, leaning against his desk. "Anyway, let's talk about Robert."

"You knew him well?"

"I was his tutor," said Dodd. "I supervised his doctoral work. We met twice a week for three years. We kept up contact since. I'd say I knew him well enough to know he'd never commit suicide. I take it you're not convinced either."

Just then Tom Tower stroked the hour of six.

Dodd's eyes shot to the window, and the two of them sat waiting for Great Tom to stop tolling. As the last bell died, he turned his gaze to her.

"No, Professor Dodd," said Kate. "We're not."

"Call me Tony. How can I help?"

"I'm interested in learning a bit about Lord Russell."

"What do you want to know?"

"Everything," said Kate. "Do you mind if I take notes?"

Dodd granted her permission with the wave of his hand. Kate pulled her notepad and pen out of her jacket. She did not carry a purse. Purses were for girly girls, and she'd never been one of those. Everything she needed—her badge and identification, her phone, her wallet, and her gun—she carried on her person.

"Robbie came up in '96," Dodd began. "He was an Old Etonian. But he was different. Humble, not arrogant. He was smart enough to know he didn't know everything. You don't see that often, not from that kind of family. The Russells go all the way back to the Domesday Book. They fought with William the Conqueror at Hastings. But Robbie didn't care about that. He was of the here and now. He put his nose to the grindstone from day one. He had a remarkable mind."

"How so?"

"He saw past the facts. Oh, he could memorize with the best of them." Dodd tapped his forehead. "He had an encyclopedia up there. But he went a step further. He saw patterns where mortals saw shadows. He identified trends long before they were anything but random events. He divined intentions. He even dared to predict. And he was right every damn time."

Kate nodded politely. **Patterns. Trends. Intentions.** This kind of talk was beyond her. Blather, she called it. She was an O-level girl who liked mayo with her chips and her Guinness lukewarm in a pint glass.

"What exactly did Russell study?"

"Twentieth-century Russian history. Postwar, primarily. His dissertation was titled 'The Case for a New Authoritarian State: Benevolent Despot or Totalitarian Czar?' He was not optimistic about the course that Russia is taking. He studied the language as well, though that was with another tutor. He spent some time in Moscow doing some work for a bank. He came back afterward and we took him on as a don."

"And is that what he taught? Russian history?"

"At first, yes."

"And now?"

Dodd rose abruptly and began pacing the office, cradling the rugby ball in his hands. "I'm not sure what he was up to lately, to be honest."

"But I thought you said you'd remained friends?"

"We are. I mean, we were. I can't bring myself to believe that he's gone."

"Did you see each other regularly?"

"Not for the past year."

"Do you recall the last time you saw him?"

"A month, maybe three weeks ago."

"Did he seem in any way distracted?"

"How should I know?" Dodd turned to her, his eyes wet and angry. He paused, and the rage left him. "We weren't close anymore. Robbie had his projects. I had mine. I'm in love with the past. He had his eyes on the future. We didn't talk shop."

"What about his students?"

"He didn't have any students. Not anymore. Robbie stopped tutoring a year ago."

"Then what exactly was his position at the university?"

Dodd stopped pacing and put the ball down. "You mean you don't know?" he asked, suddenly wary, off-balance. "Didn't they send you up here?"

"Who's 'they'?" asked Kate.

"I thought you'd been cleared for all this. I mean, don't all of you speak to one another?"

"I'm not sure I know what you're talking about."

Dodd stepped closer to Kate, and when he spoke, his voice had quieted and grown deadly serious. "Look, DCI Ford, it's like this. Robbie's work wasn't a matter fit for public inquiry. I thought you knew that."

"Was he doing something that might have jeopardized his life?"

"You're putting me in a hard spot."

"Am I?" asked Kate.

Dodd didn't answer. He stood looking at her, shaking his head. Up close, she could see the lines spreading from the corners of his eyes. She no longer found it hard to believe that he was forty.

"Would it surprise you if I told you that we have proof Lord Russell was murdered?" she asked.

Dodd turned away and moved toward the window. "Robbie knew what he was getting into."

"And what exactly was that?"

"The game."

"What game?"

"There's only one, isn't there?" Dodd glanced over his shoulder. "Now, would you go? I can't help you with this end of things."

"I can't find out who killed Robert Russell unless I know why someone wanted him dead. Please." Kate paused and guardedly met his eye. "He was your **. . . student,** after all. I think he'd want you to help us find who took his life."

Dodd considered this a moment, then looked away. "Five Alfred Street," he said. "That's where you'll find them. But don't expect them to talk to you. They're a secretive lot. It's the nature of the business."

"Who are they? What business are you talking about?"

"OA. Oxford Analytica."

Kate ran the name across her tongue until she was certain that she'd never heard of it. "What do they do?"

"What Robbie did best." Dodd's eyes drifted away from hers, to the open window and the looming form of Tom Tower. "They guess the future."

9

Emma is in London.

Jonathan pulled himself out of the window and hit the pavement at a jog. She was here. She had come to see him. He continued along Park Lane, then turned left onto Piccadilly. The sidewalk was teeming with pedestrians, tourists and locals mixed together, all appearing to be in every bit of a rush as he. **Slow down,** he told himself. **They're watching.** But who? Where?

According to Blackburn, two of them had been keeping an eye on him at the reception, but it was difficult to imagine anyone being able to follow him through this crowd. He trimmed his gait to a brisk walk, weaving through the oncoming legion. Every few steps he glanced over his shoulder. If they were there, he didn't see them.

Just ahead he saw the sign for Green Park Underground station. He descended the stairs recklessly and in the main concourse purchased an All-Day ticket, allowing him twenty-four hours of unrestricted travel on the tube. He was jogging again, and this time he didn't care who saw him. He didn't want to allow one more train to pass without his being on it. He followed the signs through the white-tiled tunnels until he reached the Bakerloo Line—northbound.

A breath of wind, a mounting roar, and the train bulleted toward the platform. He entered the last car and stood near the door, sweating despite the powerful air conditioning. He measured the journey in the beats of his heart. **Why don't I feel happy?** he wondered as the train lurched out of the station. Six months had passed since he'd seen Emma. By rights he should be thrilled. After all, Emma had told him she would contact him when the moment was right, and only then. But if anything, he was frightened. What was she doing in London at the same time as he? Why was she showing herself if she knew he was being followed? And he realized then that he wasn't frightened for himself but for her.

At Piccadilly he changed lines. The wait for the train was brief. As instructed, he got off at Marylebone and hurried through the long passageways. A line of commuters waited for the twin escalators that climbed to the surface. He dodged past them and took the stairs, attacking the steps two and three at a time. He reached the street a minute later, out of breath but calmer.

The Edgware Road was populated with block after block of cheap hotels with rent-by-the-hour rooms and run-down apartments. The area had always been popular with budget-minded tourists, newly arrived immigrants, and illicit couples. The tide of gentrification salvaging so many of London's scruffier neighborhoods had not yet reached this far north.

He found No. 61 on a leafy corner, across the street from a tobacconist and a Middle Eastern grocery. As promised, the door was open. The alcove smelled of roasted lamb and cigar smoke. Foreign voices fought behind cardboard walls. He climbed the stairs to the second floor. The key he'd been given slid into a well-oiled lock. Inside, the flat was dilapidated and mostly unfurnished. Damp rot ate at warped linoleum floors. Plywood took the place of the living room window. A naked bulb dangled from the ceiling. He turned it on, but it was dead.

In twenty seconds he'd ducked his head into every room and come back to the entry. The flat was empty except for a torn-up mattress, a few small tables, and an old black rotary dial telephone, circa 1960, sitting on the living room floor.

"Wait for our call," Blackburn had said. "We have to make sure you're clean."

Jonathan picked up the receiver and heard a dial tone. He hoped their surveillance methods were more modern than the phone. He ran a hand over his mouth. **Call,** he whispered to himself. **Tell me where I'm supposed to meet Emma.** He checked his watch. It was almost seven p.m. The sun's rays filtered through the soot-streaked windows, casting the flat in an antique light. He tried to open a window, only to find it had been nailed shut.

He waited five minutes, and another five. He looked down at the street. Evening traffic was a crawling, carbon-belching pageant. He paced until pacing grew unbearable, and then he sat, which was even worse. Back pressed to the wall, legs outstretched, he kept his eyes locked on the phone.

The room was hot and stuffy. The beer he'd drunk had kick-started his appetite, and now his stomach was moaning for something to eat. Suddenly he couldn't stand the waiting. He jumped to his feet and tried the window again. He was sweating now, his back wet, his forehead beaded.

Finally the phone rang.

Jonathan put the receiver to his ear. "Hello."

"And all these years I thought you liked it hot."

It was her.

But the clipped English voice hadn't come from the phone. It came from close behind him. He turned and saw Emma standing in the doorway, slipping her cell phone into her jeans.

"Hi," he said.

"Hi, yourself."

"What brings you to London?"

"A guy I know's visiting. I decided I might like to see him. Catch up on things. You know."

"Yeah, I think I do."

Emma tucked a strand of hair behind her ear, and he could see that her eyes were wet. He walked slowly toward her, wanting at first only to look at her. She was dressed as he always imagined her. Tight jeans, black T-shirt, sandals, her auburn hair falling in ungoverned ringlets to her shoulders. She wore an elephant hair bracelet on her left wrist and around her neck was the jade choker he'd given her for her twenty-fifth birthday.

He put a hand to her cheek, gazing into her green, steadfast eyes. "It's good to see—"

She kissed him before he could finish.

"I've missed you," she said, drawing back just enough to nuzzle his cheek.

"Me, too." Jonathan wrapped his arms around her, holding her close to him. "Been here long?"

"In London? A few days."

"You look good. I mean, better than the last time I saw you."

"The last time, you'd just yanked a bullet from my shoulder."

"I'd prefer to think I deftly removed it."

"Deftly or not, it hurt like hell."

"You have a good memory."

"Yeah, well, you know what they say—you never forget your first bullet."

"I thought it was your first kiss." Jonathan held her at arm's length, thrilled by the sight of her, by the feel of her. "How's the shoulder?"

Emma stepped back and demonstrated an admirable range of motion. "As good as new."

Jonathan nodded his approval. Suddenly he looked toward the door. "Does this mean no one followed me?"

"For the moment. In case you're interested, there's two of them."

"Two of who?"

"Two minders. One's in a blue tracksuit, posing as an OBG—that's an official bodyguard—for one of the poobahs staying at the hotel. The other was out front in his car. A tan Ford. Division always buys American. They had you until you reached the tube. I had to run some interference to get them off your tail."

"Well, thanks, then." He gazed around the beat-up flat, suddenly at a loss for something to say. "I hope you're not staying here."

"God, no," Emma said, but her eyes moved from his and she didn't elaborate.

"So what are you doing here, Em?"

"I told you I'd come when it was safe. I did some checking and found out you were traveling to London to attend this conference. It seemed like the right time."

"What about the guys at the hotel who were supposed to be keeping an eye on me?"

Emma shrugged. "Occupational hazard. I decided you were worth the risk."

Jonathan smiled. He suspected that there was something more, some reason that she was in London other than to see him. Emma gave her emotions short shrift. But he was too caught up in the moment to give it more than a passing thought. "I'm glad you came," he said. "I was beginning to wonder if I'd ever see you again."

"How are things at the camp?"

"Not bad, all things considered. We're short a few pair of hands, but we have adequate supplies for once. That's saying something."

"Enough antibiotics?"

"The Red Cross airlifts a pallet of meds to us once a month. We've got enough to keep malaria and dengue down. Something crazy happened last week. I've got to tell you about it. A girl was playing down at the river and a croc got hold of her arm. Took it off below the elbow. The father was watching. He got so upset, he wrestled the croc out of the water and killed it. It was a monster, twelve feet at least. Anyway, he cut open that croc, and there was his daughter's arm, intact, with barely a scratch. We were able to get the girl on the table less than an hour after the accident and reattach her arm. If we can stave off infection, I'm thinking she just might regain some use of her fingers."

"You and those hands," said Emma. "Magic."

"Excuse me?"

"Your hands. You're gifted. You're the best surgeon I've ever met."

"I wouldn't say that."

"I would. And I know from firsthand experience." Emma took his right hand and spread the fingers one by one, kissing each playfully, and then not so playfully. "And not just on the operating table," she whispered, stepping closer to him, so that their bodies pressed against each other and Jonathan could smell her scent. "As I recall, these hands are rather gifted in another department as well."

"I'm sorry, ma'am, but they're out of practice."

"Hmm? Are they? We'll have to see, now, won't we?"

She untucked his shirt and ran her own hands across his chest. Her hands changed direction, and Jonathan closed his eyes. "Doesn't take you long, does it, mister?" she said. "Christ, I'd almost forgotten."

Jonathan put his arms around her and lifted her up. "Forget the mattress."

Afterward, Jonathan lay back, feeling warm and sated, and maybe even happy. "We have to figure out a way for you to come back with me . . ."

"Stop right there."

He propped himself on an elbow, eager to explain. "No, no, not like that—I don't mean come back with me on the plane. I mean how you usually get around. Via Paris or Berlin or . . ."

"Jonathan—"

"Or Havana."

"Havana?" Emma burst out laughing. She pulled herself closer to him. "And from Havana, where to? Or should I even ask?"

Jonathan considered the question. There was something in her voice that led him to hope that maybe the question wasn't entirely academic. "Venezuela," he said.

"Venezuela? Caracas or Barranquila? They both have decent airports."

"I'll leave the choice to you. If neither's any good, you can hit São Paolo. Brazil doesn't have an extradition treaty with the U.S. Once you're in South America, it will be much easier to get to Kenya."

"By tramp steamer this time? Or do you have another idea?"

"I'm thinking more like by jet. I can't wait another six months to see you."

Emma nodded as he spoke, taking it all in. "And then I suppose we'll meet up at the Turkana camp?" she asked, in a less reasonable tone.

"Yeah. We'd be safe there."

"So I can just move in with you, or maybe you can build me a little thatched-roof hut in the forest where you can visit me every day after work or whenever you get bored, and we can get it on under the stars like we used to? Is that what you want, Jonathan? Keep your wife stashed away for some action on the side?"

He didn't reply. He'd picked up on the prickly timbre in her voice. At heart Emma was a realist, and she didn't tolerate forays into Never-Never Land.

"I just have one question," she went on. "What about the people who are watching you to see if I happen to turn up?"

"You said that they only picked me up when I came to London. There's no one watching me at the camp."

"You're sure about that?"

Jonathan nodded. "There's only nine of us permanently at the camp. And seven haven't left in over two years. I know them, Emma. They're not working for any government. Besides, I'm being careful. I don't ever mention your name. I only tried to contact you that once."

"What about Hal Bates?"

"Hal Bates? You mean lazy-eyed Hal from the UN Commission on Refugees? You think he's interested in me? Come on. The guy shows up once a month for a day or two, does a camp count, asks if we need any moldy K-rats, then scoots back to Nairobi. I don't even talk to him."

"Hal's a twenty-year man with the CIA. The UN thing is his day job. Every time he goes to the camp, he asks around about you. No strong-arming, mind you. Just the casual question here and there. 'By the way, old chap, happen to see Dr. Ransom with that overbearing wife of his? You know, the good-looking **mwanamke** with the decent pair of knockers?' That sound like Hal? He even takes a few pictures of you and sends them back to Langley, and they pass them down the line to Connor at Division. All in the name of intra-agency cooperation."

"That can't be," protested Jonathan. "I mean, someone would have told me. I know everyone who works there, the locals, too. They're friends. Even then, I keep an eye on them to see if they're watching me a little too closely. I am being careful, Em. I'd know if someone were watching."

"You don't know how to be careful," she said, with a sympathy that irked Jonathan. "You couldn't spot one of our networks if it were a snake crawling up your pants. We wouldn't let you."

"You're wrong!"

"And Betty?" Emma asked, not missing a beat.

"Betty the breakfast cook?" Jonathan was dumbstruck at the mention of her name. How could Emma know a thing about her? "She's fourteen years old. She's been in the camp for years. Are you saying she's an asset?"

"Not for a minute. But she doesn't need to be. All she has to do is keep a sharp eye and be ready to report if she ever sees you with a European woman who doesn't work in the camp. Last I heard, the going fee for a tip is a hundred U.S.—double that if the tip pans out. That's half a year's wage in that part of the world. What are you paying Betty the breakfast cook?"

"We don't," said Jonathan. "She gets her meals, a place to live that's relatively safe, medical care, and she attends camp school three days a week."

"Ah, I see. One of your friends. Someone whom you'd trust with your wife's life."

Case closed, thought Jonathan. He had no rebuttal. The verdict would be swift and damning. The defendant, Jonathan Ransom, is found guilty of recklessly endangering his wife. The sentence mandated for such a crime was death. But not his. Emma's.

She turned onto her side and he noticed a long

scar on her back, just above her kidney. He traced it with a finger. "This is serious," he said, sitting up, taking a closer look. "What happened?"

"Oh, that. It's nothing," said Emma. "I fell and cut myself, that's all."

The scar was five inches long, expertly stitched, and still puffy. "This was a deep incision," he said. "A surgeon did this work. What kind of fall was it, exactly?"

"It was nothing. Some broken glass, I think. Don't get yourself all worked up."

He knew she was lying. "Worked up?" he said. "I think about you every day. I wonder where you are and if you're safe, or if I'll even see you again. Then you show up out of the blue with a nasty scar on your side that you won't tell me about and act as if we're teenagers sneaking away from their mom and dad. How long do you expect this to continue? Am I supposed to live like a monk pining for you until one day some man or woman I don't know shows up and tells me you're dead?"

"No," said Emma, much too reasonably.

Jonathan fell back. "And you can't come with me?"

"No."

"And I can't go with you?"

"I don't think that would work."

"Then what, Emma? Tell me what will work."

"I can't."

"What do you mean?"

Emma looked at her watch and bolted upright. "Shoot! We've got to get you back to the hotel."

"Not yet. Not before you give me an answer."

But Emma was already standing. "We've been here much too long. There's a car downstairs. Get dressed."

"Okay, okay. Give me a second."

Grasping his hand, Emma led him to the first floor and out the rear of the building. On the pavement her actions grew crisp, disciplined. Her head turned to the left and right. She was in the open, which meant she was in danger.

They walked to a black Audi parked two blocks up the street. Using her remote key, she deactivated the alarm, then climbed into the driver's seat. Jonathan circled the car and slid into the passenger seat. Neither spoke during the drive to the hotel. She dropped him a hundred meters from the entry. He tucked his head into the open window. "When will I see you again?"

"Tomorrow," she said.

"For sure? How will I find you? Should I ask Blackburn?"

"Probably not a good idea," said Emma. "We'll find you. Now, go. And good luck with the speech. Don't be nervous. You'll do fine."

Just then a car honked. Emma threw the Audi into gear and accelerated into traffic.

Jonathan watched the car disappear, then walked to the hotel. He had barely stepped inside the lobby when a rotund, serious man hurried over to him. He wore a gray pinstriped suit with a carnation in his lapel. "There you are, Dr. Ransom. We've been waiting ages to speak with you. Where have you been?"

"Taking a walk in the park," said Jonathan. "I needed some air. Jet lag."

"Of course." The shorter man placed a hand on Jonathan's elbow and led him toward the reception. He was bald, with a ruddy complexion and dark, intelligent eyes. "Did you get my note?" he asked. "I scribbled a little something on your program. I thought it might be wise for us to coordinate plans before your speech tomorrow morning. The concierge assured me it had been sent up to your room."

"Your note?" Only then did Jonathan remember the elegant penmanship. **Looking forward to saying hello. Will require a few minutes to discuss your remarks.** "You sent the program?"

"Why, yes. Who did you think?" When Jonathan didn't answer, the man continued. "I do hope the accommodations are to your liking. Some of the members think it's a bit grand, but I believe we need to sequester ourselves in a discreet environment. We're physicians, not plumbers. Can't expect us to meet at Earls Court. But enough about that. How was your flight in? Everything go all right?"

But Jonathan didn't answer. He was no longer hearing the man's words. He'd finally gotten sight of his host's name tag.

It read "Dr. Colin Blackburn."

10

"I can't comment on Robert Russell's work for our firm," said the self-assured, arrogant man sitting across the desk from Kate Ford. "All of our contractors are employed on the basis of absolute confidentiality. It's not that we don't care to help with your investigation, it's that we can't. Rules are rules."

Sixty, with a crown of thinning hair, bifocals perched at the tip of a hawkish nose, Ian Cairncross, director of Oxford Analytica, fixed Kate with a bored gaze. The two were seated in his office at 5 Alfred Street. From next door at the Coach and Arms pub, the din of the evening crowd climbed the walls of the cobblestone alley and into the open windows. For ten minutes Kate had listened to a lengthy history of Oxford Analytica.

The firm had been founded thirty years earlier by an American lawyer who had worked as Henry Kissinger's assistant in the Nixon White House. While completing his doctoral work at Oxford, he'd stumbled on the idea. To his eye, the pool of dons and scholars at Oxford represented an incredible confluence of world-class experts on everything from economics to political science to geography. If he could harness this expertise, he could put it to work answering questions of utmost import to governments and multinational corporations around the world. He wanted the dons to analyze problems ranging from forecasting the future price of oil to guessing who would succeed the next Soviet premier. For all intents and purposes, Oxford Analytica was the world's first "overt intelligence agency." And that expertise was available to all comers, provided they agreed to OA's not insubstantial fees.

"The Met has rules, too," said Kate. "We're also forbidden to reveal details concerning cases we are presently investigating. For example, I'd be remiss in telling you that Lord Russell was keeping a loaded pistol in his desk at the time of his murder and that he was unable to make an effort to use it against his assailant. I'd also be remiss in telling you that Russell suffered a very nasty bump on his head before falling off the balcony, which might or might not have fractured his skull. And I have no right whatsoever to reveal that whoever was waiting for him when he returned home last night at two-forty in the morning not only managed to get past three doormen and a security guard monitoring cameras that covered every square inch of the building's public spaces, but also defeated a state-of-the-art alarm system tied in to the best private security firm in London. And the worst part is this: we have no bloody idea how the assailant got out, because Russell's alarm was still hot when we arrived. I can, however, freely offer my opinions," said Kate. "Would you care to hear them?"

Ian Cairncross nodded, his eyes a fraction too wide.

Kate went on. "Whoever did kill Mr. Russell was a professional. And I don't mean a thug from Brixton who'd done this a time or two before, but someone who'd been trained by the very best in the game. And I am not referring to an **overt** intelligence agency. I'd also posit that if for any reason that person believes that someone else—someone like you, for example—knew anything about what Russell was looking into, he wouldn't give a fiddler's fart before killing him, too."

Kate let her words sink in, noting the sudden funereal pallor of Cairncross's complexion.

"One more thing," she added. "In case you do decide to break any of your rules, I am authorized to offer you round-the-clock protection to make sure that you don't take a wee header off the balcony of your home—provided, that is, that you have one. A balcony, that is. I'm sure the address of your home is well known to everyone concerned." She cocked her head and smiled. "So if you don't mind, sir, I will ask one last and final time, what was Robert Russell working on?"

The answer was a whisper. "GSPM."

Kate sat back in her chair and took out her notebook. "Go ahead."

"Global Stress Points Matrix," said Cairncross, with a bit more force. "It's part of the early warning system we offer to our clients. GSPM is designed to forecast future risks. We've assembled a list of twenty core indicators that allow us to predict with a high degree of accuracy the course of events in the focus area."

"What kinds of things?"

"Who's going to be the next Japanese prime minister. The long-term rate of inflation in the U.S.A. The number of oil rigs coming online in Saudi Arabia and their effect on the price of oil."

"I don't think Lord Russell was killed over incorrectly guessing the price of a barrel of oil," said Kate.

"No," said Cairncross. "I dare say he wasn't. Robert took our GSPM program a step further. Are you familiar with open-source intelligence-gathering?"

Kate vaguely recalled seeing something with a similar title on Russell's desk, but she had no idea what it was all about. She said as much.

"It's where everyone's heading these days," said Cairncross.

"Who's everyone?"

Cairncross shot her a look from beneath his brow. "Suffice it to say that corporations aren't our only clients. There are some in this government, and others, who have shown an interest in our work. It used to be that for information to be deemed valuable, it had to be graded 'classified' or higher. If something was commonly known, then it was thought to be worth . . ." Cairncross paused to search for the right word. "As you so eloquently put it before, 'a fiddler's fart.' But that was all wrong. It turns out that all the information you need to ascertain what your friends and enemies are up to is already out there. The world is drowning in information. It's a question not of too little, but of too much. The problem is finding it. The Internet has brought us down from six degrees of separation to three at most. Look at the celebrity world. You may not know David Beckham personally, but you know who his best friends are, where he ate dinner last night, how much of a tip he left, and where he's going to travel the day after tomorrow. In another domain, that would be called actionable intelligence. Can you imagine if we'd known as much about Adolf Hitler or Joseph Stalin, or even Saddam Hussein? Who needs a Minox spy camera when your cell phone will do just fine? Everyone's a spy these days. People just don't know it. And the information is real time. It's happening **now.** That's what Robert was doing. He was setting up a trusted information network, a TIN, of individuals to gather that information."

"Are you saying that Lord Russell was a spy?"

"I'm saying no such thing. Oxford Analytica is not an intelligence shop per se. Robert was simply creating a methodology to collect accurate, timely information about a variety of subjects of interest to our clients. His forte was establishing these networks of highly placed sources who would speak to him off the record, as it were."

"TINs?"

"Exactly."

"And who were these sources?"

"Could be anyone. The deputy defense minister of Brazil. The chief financial officer of a gold-mining conglomerate in South Africa. A Russian general in charge of motor transport in Chechnya. Anyone who might possess real-time information of strategic importance. The point is that with technology the way it is, anyone with access to private information can report it anonymously and immediately."

"Sensitive subjects especially."

"Normally."

"Sold to the highest bidder."

"If you're insinuating any type of treasonous activities, you're off the mark," Cairncross shot back. "The world has changed. Borders are a thing of the past. Information doesn't carry a passport. It belongs to everyone."

"And yet Lord Russell kept a pistol in case there was someone with a less democratic view."

For once Cairncross had no response.

Kate went on. "I take it, then, that in the course of all this open-source intelligence-gathering he **wasn't** doing on behalf of the British, he found something he shouldn't have."

Cairncross plucked the bifocals off his nose and polished them with his handkerchief. "The events of this morning would seem to bear out your thesis," he said with equanimity, though he refused to meet her eyes.

"Didn't Russell give you any indication about what he was currently studying?"

"Only tangentially."

"Tangentially?"

"Yes . . . peripherally, so to speak."

Kate exhaled loudly. "Mr. Cairncross, I'm not interested in tangentially or peripherally or global space matrixes. I am interested in facts. Did Lord Russell share his discovery with you? Yes or no?"

Cairncross continued to polish his spectacles. "Robert did mention that he'd come across something that was keeping him up at night. He said that the problem was time-sensitive and that he was digging into matters where his interest wouldn't be appreciated. But that's all. I'm afraid it's not much to go on."

"Did he mention any kind of threat? An attack on British soil? Anything to do with the possibility of loss of life?"

"Good Lord, no," said Cairncross, and he appeared to be genuinely surprised. "Nothing like that. A few years back he put us on to the attempt on the Lebanese prime minister. I can assure you we passed that information on to the appropriate authorities in record time."

"If I recall, the Lebanese prime minister was blown sky high by a bomb in Beirut," said Kate.

"Alas, yes," admitted Cairncross. "We were too late to save the poor man. Otherwise, Robert's work has been strictly academic."

"Did he mention someone named Mischa? I'm

told that the name is a derivative of Mikhail. Both are Russian names."

"I don't know of any Mischa. I'm sorry."

"What about Victoria Bear?"

Cairncross shook his head. "May I ask where you obtained this information?"

Kate sat back in her chair and folded her hands. "I'm afraid I can't reveal that. I do have one last question: did Russell mention anything about a meeting tomorrow morning—something rather important?"

Cairncross pursed his lips, consulting some inner bank of information. "No, I can't say that he did. He was rather worried, though, about another matter. It was something he'd been studying for a while, really devoting all his resources to—"

Just then there came a firm knock and the door to the office opened a few inches. Kate caught a glimpse of a blond head, a square jaw, waiting in the hall. "Ian, a word . . ."

Cairncross looked at Kate, then away, but not before she caught the flash of panic in his eyes. "If you'll excuse me." He stood, and as he joined the man in the hall, Kate saw a hand fall on his shoulder and guide him out of sight.

Cairncross returned a few minutes later. "Sorry," he said. "Something's come up suddenly. I'm afraid our meeting must come to an end."

"You were saying that Russell was worried about something."

"Oil. A price shock. The only reason for that would be an attack on a major oil-producing facility somewhere, say Nigeria or Saudi Arabia. But I can promise you he never mentioned a Mischa. Perhaps Robert's death had nothing to do with his work. Who knows where his private tastes ran?"

"Perhaps," said Kate. If she wasn't mistaken, Cairncross had just tried to besmirch Russell's reputation. She slid her notebook into her jacket and stood. "The offer of protection stands."

"No, no," said Cairncross, stammering in his eagerness to escort her from the room. "That won't be necessary. I think we're all a bit unnerved by Robert's death. That's all."

Kate did not allow herself to be rushed. "Are you sure there's nothing else?" she asked, lingering in the doorway, wondering who it was that had interrupted their meeting and put a violent stop to the proceedings.

"Nothing at all."

She handed him her card. "If you think of anything else, tangential or otherwise, call me."

Kate stood outside the building, feeling deceived and cheated. She was sure that Cairncross had more to tell her, and her instinct told her it was something that might have proven helpful in finding Russell's killer. Moreover, the late-inning attempt to insinuate that Russell's sexual proclivities might have led to his murder angered her. Russell's death was no crime of passion. It was far too calculated for that. Swallowing her anger, she headed back to her car.

Her phone rang. It was Cleak's ringtone. "Yes, Reg."

"I'm at Russell's flat. You'll want to get down here as quickly as possible. We found it."

Kate stopped walking, putting a finger to her ear to hear better over the street noise. "Found what?"

"How the murderer got into Russell's flat."

"Tell me."

"You'll have to see it to believe it."

"On my way."

Kate hung up. And as she set off up the alley, she ventured a last look behind her. Her eyes rose to Cairncross's second-floor office. The window had been closed, and though the sun reflected off it, she was able to make out the outline of a blond head with a very square jaw watching her intently.

And who the hell are you? she asked the silent figure.

11

The components sat on the floor of the garage, stacked neatly against the rear wall.

Twenty sticks of plastic explosive, bundled into packets of four, each packet weighing five kilos and thermowrapped in orange plasticene.

Two 15-kilo bags of four-inch carpenter's nails.

Two 10-kilo bags of three-inch steel bolts.

Five 5-kilo bags of 00 buckshot.

Four 25-kilo sacks of Portland cement.

One reel of copper electrical wire.

One length of det cord manufactured by Bofors of Sweden measuring one meter.

One box of blasting caps. Ten count.

A can of stalignite gel, better known as napalm.

One cell phone (still in its factory packaging) and a SIM card carrying a stored value of twenty pounds.

Last but not least, the delivery device, recently detailed and sparkling beneath a raft of fluorescent lights, occupied the center of the garage.

A BMW had been chosen for the job. Expensive automobiles attracted less attention than cheap ones, and this one carried a sticker price of one hundred twenty thousand pounds, nearly two hundred thousand U.S. dollars when you included VAT. It was a brand-new 7-series, stratus gray with black leather interior, an elongated wheelbase, and conservative nineteen-inch rims. It was a car a diplomat might drive. A car that would look very much at home parked on the streets of Whitehall, the London district that was the site of many government offices.

One man stood in the garage, studying the automobile. He was wan and thin, dressed in a blue coverall. Except for his hands, he was unremarkable in every way. The left hand had only three fingers, the pinkie and ring finger lost to a faulty detonator. The right hand, though intact, was webbed with scar tissue and grotesque. When ignited, white phosphorus fuses with human flesh and cannot be extinguished with water. They were a bombmaker's hands.

He, too, had been smuggled into the country, though the route was less circuitous than that of the stolen BMW. He had come from Calais, France, spirited across the English Channel in a high-speed Cigarette motorboat and landed on a beach in Dover twenty-four hours earlier. After constructing the bomb, he would return to the same beach for the outward leg of his journey, but whether he would go back to Calais or elsewhere was unknown. Men like him did not publish their itineraries.

He had no name. He was known simply by his trade. **The Mechanic.**

The Mechanic circled the car, running a hand over the hood, the roof, and the trunk. Every explosive device was different and had to be constructed according to its specific purpose. To bring down a building required five hundred kilos or more of high explosives and the ability to gain close proximity to the target. For that, a truck or van was best, as was the willingness to sacrifice one's life. To maximize human casualties, fewer explosives were required, but more materiel, or shrapnel. Proximity was essential. Military-issue plastic explosives detonated at the rate of 8000 meters per second. The blast wave alone was capable of crushing a nearby automobile. At that velocity, a carpenter's nail would travel a long and deadly distance.

The job he was entrusted with this evening fell somewhere between the two. It took him six hours to complete.

When he was finished, he surveyed the BMW with a former policeman's eye. The vehicle appeared no different from before, which meant it neither listed to one side nor drooped on its suspension. The explosives were evenly distributed throughout the left-hand, or passenger, side of the automobile and concealed in the trunk, the rocker panels, the roof, and the engine.

The Mechanic designed his charges according to a three-tiered model. First he coated the chassis with napalm gel. Next he layered in the materiel (nails, bolts, buckshot). And last he shaped and affixed the plastic explosives.

The cement was used as a tamping agent. He

placed one bag of cement on the right-hand side of the trunk. The other bag he divided into smaller packages and spread throughout the engine cavity. The cement would thus deflect the force of the blast in the desired direction.

A standard cell phone attached to a blasting cap served to detonate the device. When the cell phone received a call, it passed along an electrical charge that ignited the blasting cap. The cap in turn ignited the det cord, instantaneously setting off the plastic explosives. The entire detonation sequence would last one one-hundredth of a second.

There was one last thing he needed to do. Crawling beneath the steering wheel, he installed an anti-jamming device. Targets had grown as sophisticated in protecting themselves as the assailants who wanted to kill them. It was not uncommon for vehicles to carry a wireless jamming device that blocked out all incoming phone signals as a defense against roadside bombs. The black box he wired to the car's internal battery would jam the jammer. It was a question of who was one step ahead of the other.

Finished, he hauled himself from beneath the automobile and stood up.

It was then that he saw her standing by the door.

"Is it ready?" she asked.

The Mechanic wiped his hands with a chamois cloth. The woman had bottle-green eyes and wavy auburn hair. Her beauty was as unexpected as her stealth. He knew better than to ask her name.

"Don't turn on the cell phone until you park it. They have scanners these days."

"What's its number?"

As he read it off, the woman programmed it into her own phone.

"Why the nails and bolts?" she asked.

The Mechanic darted a glance to a corner of the garage, but he did not answer.

"Why the nails?" she repeated. She had spent a week gathering the necessary materials, and the last-minute addition of nails, buckshot, and bolts bothered her. "The blast will be more than enough to do the job."

"To make sure the job is completed to my satisfaction," answered a gravelly baritone. A short, stocky man rose from the recesses of the garage and walked toward the car. A filterless cigarette dangled from the corner of his mouth. As always, he was dressed in a gray pinstripe suit of questionable quality. "Don't worry," he said. "It's a shaped charge. The blast will be confined to the target. Any collateral damage will be minimal."

"Hello, Papi," said the woman.

"Hello, child."

"Why are you here?"

"I came to wish you luck."

"Two thousand kilometers for a pat on the back? How nice of you."

"I thought my presence would impress upon you our commitment to the mission."

"I'm impressed."

Papi tossed his cigarette to the floor and ground it under his heel. "Nails, eh? They bother you? It doesn't surprise me. You always were more sensitive than you liked to admit."

"Cautious. There's a difference."

Papi frowned. He did not agree. "I took a risk in bringing you back."

"It was you who let me go."

"It was not a matter of choice. I could no longer pay you. The system was broken. It was a financial necessity."

"But we were family. Remind me, was I your daughter or something else?"

Papi raised a hand to her face and brushed his rough fingers over her lips. "I see your husband never taught you to shut your mouth. **Americans.** So weak."

The woman turned away brusquely.

"Many people are relying on you," Papi went on, fishing in his jacket for another cigarette.

"Especially you."

"Especially me. I admit it. I wanted to make sure you didn't have any last-minute misgivings."

"Why should I?"

Papi picked a fleck of tobacco from his tongue. "You tell me," he said offhandedly, firing his lighter, a dented Zippo that he had owned as long as she'd known him.

"Are you forgetting Rome?" Emma Ransom untucked her T-shirt and showed off her scar. "Going back isn't an option."

"Just so we both know that." The stocky man kissed Emma on both cheeks, then pressed the car keys into her hand. "Good hunting."

12

More than twelve hours after Lord Robert Russell's residence at 1 Park Lane had been declared a crime scene, the apartment bristled with activity. Members of the forensics squad moved through the hallways, carrying evidence bags, cameras, and site-mapping equipment. It was their job to photograph the apartment, dust for prints, and search the premises top to bottom for anything resembling a clue. The work would continue well into the next day before it was complete.

Reg Cleak was standing by the entry when Kate arrived. He offered a polite smile, but she could see that the day's labor had tired him. The lines on his face were cut as deeply as a relief map, and his cheeks hung like saddlebags from his jaw.

"Hello, Reg," she said, squeezing his arm. "Fighting the good fight."

"As ever, boss." Cleak ventured a smile. "If you'd care to follow me."

He walked across the foyer and turned into the kitchen, holding the door for Kate. "I had the team case the joint for anything that could have served as the murder weapon. You know, something hard and heavy. They had a go at the lamps, the odd statuette, tools, kitchen utensils, to see if there was any hair or tissue. Hit someone that hard, you're likely to take a little something with you."

"Anything turn up?"

Cleak sighed. "Do you think I brought you in here to sample the custard pudding? Have a look." He opened the freezer door, revealing shelves stocked with frozen meats, precooked meals, and ice cream.

"Hit him with a bag of frozen peas, did he?" asked Kate.

"You're not far off." Cleak kneeled to open a storage drawer at the bottom of the compartment. When he stood back up, he was holding a bottle of vodka sheathed in an ice collar. "Ever seen one of these?"

Kate shook her head. "I drink mine warm, or with a couple of ice cubes if I'm lucky."

"Go ahead, you can hold it." Cleak handed over the bottle. "There were two. Evidence took the weapon."

"The weapon? You mean he hit Russell over the head with a bottle of Russian vodka?"

"Not Russian, Polish. Anyway, we found no fewer than three blond hairs embedded in the ice. They're off to the lab for DNA testing, but I reckon we'll have a match."

Kate replaced the bottle in the freezer and closed the door. "Not the first place I'd look for a weapon," she admitted. "He knew his way around, didn't he?"

With a nod, Cleak motioned for her to follow.

"That isn't the half of it. The chute was used for laundry back when the building was a hotel," he explained. "Made of Manchester steel. Hasn't rusted a bit since it was built a hundred years ago. There's an access door on every floor. When the new owners renovated the place, they walled over the chute and patched up the doors."

The two police officers were kneeling inside Robert Russell's walk-in closet, staring down the beam of a flashlight into a gaping square cut out of the wall. The missing piece of drywall was en route to the lab for fingerprinting and analysis.

"He came up from the basement," said Cleak. "Did a nifty job of patching up the wall down there, too. Took his time."

"You're telling me he managed to climb five stories inside this steel coffin?"

"A regular Spiderman."

Kate peered into the bottomless chute, wondering what kind of person had the skill, or the guts, to climb up something so narrow and so dark. It seemed to drop forever. Suddenly her breath left her and she grew dizzy. Yanking her head clear, she stalked out of the closet.

"You okay?" asked Cleak, following close behind.

"Fine," she managed. "It's nothing. Don't like tight spaces. That's all." She bit her lip until the pain forced her fears back where they belonged, then she said in a stronger voice, "So the killer started here and made his way to Russell's office. Let's see how he did it, shall we?"

Methodically they retraced the steps the murderer had taken eighteen hours earlier. In every room Cleak pointed out the location of the various security devices: motion sensors, thermal detectors, pressure pads. They ended up in Russell's clean room of an office ten minutes later.

"How long do you reckon it took him to neutralize this system?" Kate asked.

"Never mind how long," said Cleak. "We're still working on how. The setup is supposed to be undefeatable."

"Aren't they all?"

Once in Russell's office, Kate's eyes jumped to the plasma screen. "What about her? Any luck tracking down our mystery woman?"

"None, I'm afraid," said Cleak. "We've flagged the cable provider, but they want a warrant from the Home Office before even starting to look at who sent that message. Even then it's an uphill battle. If Russell took measures to hide his tracks, it will be nigh impossible to track her down. At least in the short run."

"Dammit," said Kate. "We've got to find her. She's all we've got. Lord knows, she may be in danger herself. Russell might not be the only one on their hit list. Pros, Reg. We're up against some very nasty individuals. Government-trained thugs."

"Individuals? I thought we were looking for just one."

"Hardly." Kate left the office and headed down the hall at her usual breakneck pace. As she walked, she explained what she'd learned about Russell's work at Oxford Analytica. "He was poking his nose where he shouldn't have been, little Lord Russell was. This operation was planned down to the last detail. They had access to building plans, a schema of the apartment's security system, everything. I wouldn't be surprised if there weren't at least three men involved. One to watch the building, one to cover Russell, and the murderer himself. Pros, Reg."

Cleak stopped at the front door, breathing hard. "Would you slow down a sec? You're giving me a coronary. Where are you going in such a rush?"

"Building security," called Kate over her shoulder.

"But we already looked at the tapes," protested Cleak. "We came up empty-handed."

Kate was waiting inside the elevator as Cleak managed to sneak past the closing doors. "We didn't look closely enough," she said.

Building security was located on the second floor of One Park. It was a cramped room dominated by a multiplex of video monitors built into one wall and, despite the ordinance prohibiting smoking, reeking of tobacco. Kate stood with her back pressed to the rear wall, her eyes dancing between the sixteen live feeds. Reg Cleak stood to one side. To the other stood the building manager and the chief of security.

"The reason we missed him earlier is that he was already here," said Kate as they waited for the first of the disks to be loaded and synched.

"I'm afraid there's no camera in the basement," said the chief of security. He was a former infantry officer with a bristly mustache and a slight limp, which he made sure everyone knew he'd acquired at Goose Green in the Falklands. "We never thought there was a need. There's no access to it from the street. The only way in is via the elevator or the stairs, which are already covered."

"Precisely," said Kate. "I'd like to start with the disks monitoring the elevators and stairwells. Let's have a look at the last loop prior to Russell's murder, beginning last night at midnight."

The chief of security found the corresponding DVDs and slid them into the machine. A wide-angle view of the elevators filled the main screen. A time code ran on the bottom left-hand corner. Kate asked that they sync the disks with cameras in the lobby and the carpark. In this manner they could ascertain whether someone had entered an elevator on a high floor and failed to exit at the lobby or the garage.

At that time of night, most traffic involved residents returning to the building after an evening out. The residents could be seen crossing the garage or lobby, then appearing in one of the elevators. At each sighting, the building manager called out the person's name. "That's Sir Bernard," or "That's Mr. Gupta."

The flow of traffic slowed after one a.m. They ran the DVD at accelerated speed, pausing only when a figure appeared onscreen. When the time code showed 0225, the time of Russell's death, and every individual viewed onscreen had been accounted for, the chief of security asked if they'd like to take a break.

"Keep it running," said Kate. "If he got out through the basement, he had to come back up afterward."

They continued viewing the disks. To her consternation, there was no sighting of a man entering the elevator on any floor, basement through eleven, from 2:20 in the morning until Detective Ken Laxton's arrival at 3:15. At 3:17, they watched as the well-coifed detective entered the elevator and stood beside a woman with auburn hair. It took Kate a moment to realize that something was out of whack.

"Hold on," she said sharply. "Who's she?"

"You mean Pretty Kenny?" said Cleak, chuckling as he rubbed his eyes.

"I mean who's the lady accompanying him in the lift?"

"Don't know," said the security chief. "Not a resident, I can tell you that much. I'd have remembered."

Kate exchanged glances with Cleak. "Where in heaven's name did she come from at three-seventeen in the morning?"

"I imagine she must have driven into the garage," said the security chief.

"I didn't see anyone drive in, did you, Reg? Rewind it."

The security chief froze all screens, then rewound the loop showing the parking garage. Kate was right. No automobile had entered the garage. "Go back to the elevator. We must have missed her getting on."

They backed up the disk and watched as Ken Laxton walked backward out of the elevator. The unknown woman remained inside, which meant that she was there when Laxton had gotten on. The frames went back further. Eleven seconds earlier, at 3:16:45, the door opened again and the woman retreated. "She got on in the basement," said Kate.

Reg Cleak pursed his lips, as if he were uncomfortable accepting everything that went along with Kate's conclusion. She thrust her hands in her pockets and turned away from the screen. "But how did she get in?"

The chief of security shook his head. "We checked our log and accounted for all visitors these last four days."

Kate considered the information. "Get me the disks covering the garage."

It took them another hour, but they found what they were looking for. At two o'clock the previous afternoon, Russell had pulled his Aston Martin DB12 into the garage, parked in his reserved space, and walked to the elevator. Five minutes later the garage lights dimmed. And five minutes after that, the Aston Martin's trunk sprang open. Out climbed a woman in fashionable attire, slinging a leather bag over a shoulder. The bag appeared to be the right size to heft the tools required to cut through the basement wall and patch it up again afterward. The light was too dim, however, to get a good view of the woman. She crossed the garage briskly, keeping her face angled away from the camera.

Kate studied the woman as she entered the elevator and rode up one floor to the basement. Never once did the intruder lift her face so that the camera might get a good look at her. A pro, Kate reminded herself. Maybe more than that.

"She's our 'man.' "

13

Frank Connor did not like England. The food was lousy, the weather was dismal, and the place was more expensive than God. The English liked their beer warm and their roast beef cold. Worst of all, they insisted on driving on the wrong side of the road. Twice he'd nearly been run over after forgetting to look to his right before crossing the street. Draining the last of his Coke, he chomped on an ice cube and watched as the quilt of green pastures and rolling foothills rose up through the gathering dusk to greet him. It was only after the wheels touched down and the jet drew to a halt that it came to him why he disliked the country so. It wasn't America.

A car and driver from the office waited on the tarmac at Stansted Airport, 48 kilometers northeast of London. Connor deplaned and handed his passport to a waiting official. The pilot had radioed Connor's details ahead. A cursory check was made of his passport to confirm his identity and he was waved through. No one inspected his luggage.

"And so?" asked Connor as he climbed into the front seat.

"She's here," said the driver, a bluff, slope-shouldered Scot, steering the car onto the motorway.

"Did you get a visual?"

"No, but your boy Ransom's up to something. He put the dodge on us."

"Explain."

"He checked in to the hotel at eight this morning. Took a run around the park at lunch, then spent the afternoon in his room. At six he came downstairs for a cocktail party. Did a little mingling. Had a few beers. He's a civilian, and it shows. He didn't give neither me nor Liam a look. After thirty minutes, he made a run to the WC. We couldn't get too close, so as not to spook him. When he came out, he was with one of the docs at the conference. Tall gent. Distinguished. The two of them ducked into a conference room down the hall. We weren't suspicious right off. After all, Ransom had been acting normally until that point."

"And?" asked Connor.

"After about five minutes, the doc comes out, but Ransom doesn't."

Connor winced, then reminded himself that this was what he had wanted. A sign, even if he was unable to capitalize on it. "Where did he go?"

"The only way out of the room was a window that dropped him onto Park Lane. We got a man outside and around front in time to spot Ransom heading down Piccadilly. He was pretty far off by then. We caught him going into the Underground three blocks down the road. That's where we lost him."

"Where he 'put the dodge on you'?"

"It's a zoo in there," the Scot protested. "It was rush hour. We've only got two warm bodies to do the job, not a saber squadron."

Connor grunted. He could add another reason that he hated this country. They couldn't follow anyone worth a damn. "It's all right," he said consolingly, because it was his policy always to encourage his men. "I'm sure you did your best."

Division's agents were drawn from all four corners of the intelligence world. Some came out of the Army's Special Operations Command and had previously qualified as Navy SEALs, Green Berets, Rangers, and the like. Others transferred laterally from the Defense Intelligence Agency, from the Office of Consular Operations at State, or even from the Secret Service. Finally, there were those who drifted in from foreign shores. One of Division's best-kept secrets was that it contracted international operatives off the freelance market: foreign-trained intelligence agents who had lost their billets by dint of budget cuts, ideological disagreements, misbehavior, or any combination of the above.

"Where is he now?"

"He strolled back into the lobby without a by-your-leave at eight o'clock. But it was like we were watching a different man. Before he'd been calm, real loosey-goosey. This Ransom was very jittery indeed. Kept looking over his shoulder as if someone were about to sneak up behind him and put a round into the back of his head. I overheard him tell another doc that he'd gone for a walk in the park because he was jet-lagged. For two hours? Load of crap. Something had him spooked."

Or someone.

It was after ten when Frank Connor passed Marble Arch and drove down Park Lane. He craned his neck as they passed the Dorchester. "Did you find the other doctor?" he asked. "The one who led him to the conference room?"

"Negative. He disappeared into thin air. He was **not** a civilian."

"So she's working a team."

"It looks that way, boss." The driver glanced sidelong at Connor. "But for who?"

"That's the question, isn't it?" Connor stared at the glittering lights of the porte cochere, the richly liveried doormen, and the succession of beautiful people parading in and out of the revolving doors. He pulled a crumpled notepad from his jacket and wrote, "Nightingale in London." "Nightingale" being the last operational designation for Emma Ransom.

"Where to, Mr. Connor?"

"Notting Hill. There's someone I need to talk to."

14

Ka-tink.

Jonathan heard the noise and awakened instantly.

He bolted upright in bed, eyes open, ears straining to pick out the slightest sound. It was his habit to sleep with window and curtains open. Light from the full moon dusted the room with a silvery hue, casting sinister, elongated shadows. He saw nothing to alarm him and heard no further sounds. Throwing back the covers, he slid out of bed and walked to the door. It was closed, the lock secured, but the brass chain he'd fastened before going to sleep was dangling free, swaying ever so gently.

He turned back toward the bed, his senses pinched taut. He was not sure if someone had actually entered the room or if he'd tried to gain entry and failed. Jonathan turned on the lights. The bedroom was empty, so he walked toward the salon and ducked his head into the spacious sitting room. Again he saw no one. A warm breeze blew into the room, ruffling the curtains.

Ka-tink.

His glance fell to a side table where the curtain had harmlessly knocked a cut-glass vase against the wall. He moved the vase out of the way of the offending curtain. Relaxing, he put a hand to his chin and asked himself if he really had fastened the chain earlier. Maybe. Maybe not. He'd been tired, and more than a little stressed.

Just then, from close by came the hollow ring of a glass being set on a hard surface. He felt a presence behind him. Immediately he reached for the vase. He heard a footstep and thought, **This is it. They know I've seen Emma. They've come for me.** But before he could raise the vase, before he could spin to see who was behind him, a firm hand cupped his mouth and drew his head forcefully back.

"Ssshhhh. I'm not here." She spoke in the lowest of whispers.

Familiar lips lingered against his ear. The hand lessened its grip. Jonathan turned, seeing Emma standing with her fingers to her mouth. He signaled his understanding and waited, motionless, as she circled the room, waving a small rectangular instrument close to the walls, the lamps, the television, and the telephone. She found what she was looking for behind an equestrian print, and in the bathroom attached to the back of a vanity mirror. She dropped the electronic listening devices into a glass and filled the glass with water from the sink. Then she closed the bathroom door and crossed the room to him.

She was dressed in black from head to toe. Black jeans, a black T, and black flats. Her hair was gathered into a ponytail, her cheeks flushed, her face unadorned with makeup. She ran her hand across his bare chest. "I told myself I wasn't going to do this."

"Do what?"

She kissed him with her eyes open, then stepped back and peeled off her shirt. Never dropping her gaze, she unfastened her brassiere and let it fall to the ground, then stepped out of her jeans.

"How did you get in?" he asked.

"I have a room key."

Somehow the notion didn't surprise him. "And the chain?"

"That's a parlor trick. I'll show you someday."

"I'll bet," he said. A parlor trick, just like her ability to field-strip a pistol blindfolded. "I thought we were going to see each other tomorrow."

"Lack of discipline. No excuses, sir." Emma lay on the bed, entangled in the sheets. "This is going to be harder than I thought."

"What is?"

"What I have to tell you."

Jonathan turned on his side. He looked into his wife's eyes, cataloguing the flecks of amber in green. "Here I am," he whispered. "Tell me."

Emma ran a finger across his cheek. "I'm leaving."

"You mean for another five months?"

"Longer."

"You're sure? How do you know?"

"Because I have to go away."

"You already went away," he said. "You said you

were going to work things out and that we'd see each other when it was safe."

"I hoped it might work that way."

"How long are you talking?"

"I can't say . . ."

"A year? Two?"

"Yes . . . I mean, I don't know. A year, at least. Maybe longer. Maybe forever."

Jonathan studied her features, seeking out the secret places where she hid her doubt. But he saw only steadfastness: the same resolute, stubborn woman he'd fallen in love with. "There has to be another way."

"There isn't. We both know that."

"Stop talking as if I have a say in this. It's your decision. It's your damned life." He threw back the sheets and left the bed.

"Not anymore it's not," said Emma. "I traded it in ten years ago."

"For what?"

"Duty. A sense of belonging. The need to contribute. The same thing we all sign up for."

"You did all that," he said, turning, approaching her with a hand extended. "You did more than that. The government should be grateful."

Emma lowered her gaze. "Division caught hell for the operation. Congress wanted to shut them down, but the president's given them one last chance."

"Another chance? Is he crazy?"

"I told you," said Emma. "Division is like the

Hydra. Cut off its head and ten more grow in its place. Division has its uses. The president knows better than to limit his options."

"Have you spoken with them? With Division?"

"You're joking."

"I just mean—"

"What do you mean?"

"With all your contacts, I thought you might find a way to explain why you had to disobey your orders. They'd have to understand."

"I'm rogue, Jonathan. I didn't just disobey orders, I went completely off the reservation. I tried to take down the whole ship. That makes me the enemy."

"But you stopped a passenger jet from being shot down."

"But nothing. Besides, **you** saved the plane. The first time I show my face, I'll get a bullet in the head. I thought I'd explained that to you. You think I'm living like a war criminal for the fun of it?"

"I'm sorry. I'm sure I don't know half of what you've been through."

"No, you don't." Emma drew a breath. "Look, the new man running Division is a complete bastard. His name is Frank Connor. He's not one of us. I mean, not trained in the field or any of that. His whole career he's been behind a desk, and now he's making up for lost time. God knows how they chose him. He's smart enough to realize that his overseers won't let him lift a pinkie until he takes care of me."

"Are those his guys downstairs?"

"Probably."

Jonathan sensed that there was more. "What happened, Em? Has he already tried? That scar on your back—what's it really from?"

"Does it matter?"

"Of course it matters."

Emma stood and faced him. "Then, yes, Jonathan, he's already tried. It's what we do, remember? We target enemies. We find them, we follow them, and when we're good and ready, we take them out. The only difference is that this time it's me wearing the bull's-eye."

Jonathan nodded. He wanted to reach out and hold her, but he knew better. "Where were you?"

"Rome."

"What were you doing there?"

"Seeing old friends, Jonathan. At least, I thought they were my friends. I was wrong. Anyway, there I was in the Borghese Gardens, standing on a corner, waiting for a ride to dinner. I broke every rule in the book. I was alone without backup in a city I didn't know well. For ten minutes my guard was down. And that's when they came at me."

"Jesus Christ, Emma."

"Blakemore likes his knife," she said offhandedly as she fingered the livid scar. "He forgot I knew that. I got away with twenty-seven stitches and a lacerated kidney. Guess I'm lucky."

"But how did they find you?"

"It was you."

"Me?"

"You called. It was in April. They had your phone in their system."

"But that's impossible. I bought that phone in Nairobi. No one called me except my colleagues at camp."

"I told you. They have eyes and ears everywhere."

"But it was just the once . . ."

"That's all they needed. They got my number, my GPS coordinates. They engineered a phony meet. They used the name of an old contact. Someone they knew I would trust. As I said, I broke every rule."

"I'm sorry." Jonathan sat down, crestfallen.

"It's not your fault. It's mine. I should never have kept the phone. The fact is that I wanted you to call. I wanted you to tell me that you had to see me. The hard part about running is that after a while you get tired. You forget that they're there even if you can't see them. You get lazy. Or, worse, sentimental."

"And him?"

"Blakemore? He's dead." Emma said the words without emotion. It was her agent's voice, the one she used when she talked about her work, businesslike and matter-of-fact, as if there was nothing out of the ordinary about a man putting a knife into your side and you killing him in the ensuing struggle.

Jonathan looked on as Emma rubbed a finger across the scar. He saw a faint smile trace her lips. Where the hell did that come from? he wondered. A sense of victory? Survival? Revenge?

"I can go somewhere," he said. "I can hide. After a couple of years, they'll give up."

Emma shook her head but said nothing.

"There has to be a way," he continued.

Emma walked to him, put a hand on his shoulder, and looked into his eyes. "Do you have any idea what it took to see you this evening? Can you even begin to imagine the risks I ran to get into this room tonight? Sure, I may know my way around a locked door, but I can't outguess every goon in town. You know what the first thing is that they teach you? In every op, you only get one chance: your first and your last. I've used up my nine lives, Jonathan. I'm running on faith. What I did tonight was just plain stupid. The problem is that I knew it all along and still I did it. I had to see you. You're dangerous, Jonathan. You're my poison." Emma let go of him and walked toward the window. She stood, framed by the dawn sky, the curtains billowing gently around her bare legs. She turned to look over her shoulder and smiled sadly. "Emma Ransom died tonight."

Jonathan stood behind her and wrapped his arms around her. He had mourned her once. He knew the misery that came with the loss of a spouse. But somehow this was worse. The idea that Emma was out there alive somewhere and that he could not see her was too much. A profound sadness settled on him.

They stood that way for a long time, watching as the sun warmed the trees in Hyde Park and the horses and their riders appeared along the serpentine trails, listening as the impatient, mechanized sounds of the city rose around them.

Emma's phone rang. Without a word, she freed herself from Jonathan's arms and found her phone. She checked the incoming number, then looked up at him. In an instant her disposition had changed. Her eyes stared at him with abandon, as if he were a stranger or, worse, the enemy.

Emma turned away and walked into the bathroom. She did not answer the phone until she'd closed the door behind her. When she came out two minutes later, the transformation was complete. She was no longer Mrs. Jonathan Ransom. She was the woman he had discovered went by the call sign Nightingale, a former operative for the United States government, and now a fugitive at large.

"I've got to go," she said, gathering up her clothes in her arms.

"Who was that?"

"It doesn't concern you."

Emma sidestepped him, but Jonathan quickly blocked her path. "Where are you going when you leave here?" he demanded.

"Get out of my way."

"In a second. First tell me where you're going."

Emma lowered her eyes and began to walk around him. Jonathan grasped her arm. "I asked you a question."

"And I gave you an answer. It doesn't concern you. Please, Jonathan—"

"You didn't come here to say goodbye to me. You're on assignment or whatever they call it. You have it written all over you. One second you're Emma—I mean, my Emma—the next you belong to them. Who was that on the phone?"

"Let go of me, Jonathan."

The words were spoken crisply and with an absence of emotion that angered him that much more. Jonathan yanked her toward him, causing her to drop her clothes to the floor. "I want to know where you're going."

Suddenly the world was in motion. His feet were rising, his head was rushing at the carpet, and his arms were searching for something to grab on to. He landed on his back, the wind knocked out of him.

Hastily Emma scooped up her clothing and walked into the bathroom. The door slammed and he heard the lock engage.

Jonathan struggled to his feet and lumbered toward the bathroom. If she thought the matter was finished, she was mistaken. He was through letting her dictate the terms of their relationship. She couldn't just pop in and pop out of his life whenever she felt like it.

Emma's cell phone lay on the carpet, half hidden beneath the sofa. Evidently it had fallen from her clothes when he'd boorishly tugged her toward him. He glanced at the bathroom door, picked it up, and hit the send button. The number of the incoming call appeared on the screen. A text message was attached and it read: "Package ready for pickup. ETA 11:15. Parking arranged. LT 52 OXC Vxhl. Meet WS 17:00."

He accessed the call register and scrolled through the calls she'd received. He saw the same number again, and others listed as "restricted." He thumbed to the second page and saw a familiar international country code: 33, for France. He didn't recognize the city code. He scrolled down and saw that the call had been made a week ago.

A loud noise came from the bathroom. Hurriedly Jonathan returned the phone to the floor and busied himself dressing. Emma emerged a moment later, looking distressed. "Where is it? Where's my phone?"

"I have no idea."

"Bullshit. You took it."

Jonathan repeated his denial, but Emma wasn't listening. She marched past him and grabbed the phone from where he'd put it beneath the sofa. "Tell me you didn't take this and I'll believe you."

"I didn't take it," lied Jonathan.

"Thank you," said Emma, softening. "Believe me, it's better this way."

Jonathan stared at her, not answering.

"I've decided to tell you where I'm going," she said.

"Why the change of heart?"

Emma approached him, cocking her head. "I don't want us to part on bad terms. That was a friend who called me. Someone who's helping keep me safe.

He's set it up for me to leave the country this morning. I'm catching a flight from City Airport at ten. I'm going to Dublin. I won't be staying long. From there, I don't even know myself."

"I guess I'll have to be happy with that." But in his mind, he had a dozen other questions. What was "the package"? Whose estimated time of arrival was 11:15? What did LT 52 OXC mean? And finally, who was Emma supposed to meet "at WS at 17:00"?

Emma stared at him from beneath her brow. It was her way of showing that she wanted peace. She put her arms around his neck and kissed him. "I love you," she said. "No matter what you may hear about me in the future, no matter what people say, you must always believe that."

Jonathan put his arms around her and hugged her to him. Finally Emma pushed herself away.

In silence, he watched her gather her things and leave without saying goodbye.

15

For eight years Jonathan had lived in the dark. For eight years he'd been married to a woman he'd loved and trusted but in fact didn't know the first thing about. All too frequently he had watched as Emma left on last-minute trips with vague destinations. If Emma said she was taking a night train to Mombasa to pick up a load of quinine, that was what she was doing. If she needed two days in Venice for some R&R with a friend, she had his blessing. He never questioned her. His faith was absolute.

And then, five months ago, he had discovered that it was all a lie. Not only the trips to Mombasa and Venice, but all of it—her name, her past, her devotion to bringing medical care to those who needed it most. Since the day he met her, Emma had been working as an agent of the United States government, and Jonathan had been her unwitting, unsuspecting cover. Time did not heal this wound, even by degrees. If anything, time worsened it. Jonathan was not suspicious, but he was prideful. Standing with his back to the door, he decided that eight years was enough.

He waited a minute after Emma had left the

room, then went into the hall and took the elevator downstairs. In the lobby, he immediately saw Dr. Blackburn—the real Dr. Blackburn—and Jamie Meadows and a host of other well-fed, prosperous physicians gathered by a coffee station in a far corner. If his watchers were also present, he saw no sign of them. There was no OBG in a blue tracksuit looking his way. No shady characters keeping a hand to their earpiece, monitoring his progress through dark sunglasses.

Even so, Jonathan skulked around the perimeter of the lobby, head down, keeping to the walls. He was due to give his speech in a little over two hours, and if anyone saw him, they'd be worried. He hadn't shaved or showered. Dressed in jeans, desert boots, a navy blazer pulled over his old Basque sheepherder's shirt, he looked like the kind of bad element the doormen were paid to keep out.

He passed through the revolving door and hit the street. He craned his head left and right, hoping for a glimpse of a woman dressed in black with her hair pulled back severely from her forehead and up in a ponytail. He failed to see her, but he wasn't disheartened. He didn't imagine that she had walked through the front door when she had come to visit last night, and he didn't imagine she'd left that way at the height of the morning rush. He headed to his left, circling the building, and came to the service area. Delivery trucks idled in the garage as workers unloaded crates of beer, boxes of fresh produce, and freshly laundered towels. A set of stairs led down to the employees' entrance. He glanced over the railing. The door was shut. Wheeling, he studied the backstreets for the likely avenue Emma had taken. One road ran parallel to Park Lane and was flanked by mews houses. Another ran eastward into the heart of Mayfair, but dead-ended after a few blocks. Twenty-five meters to his right, an alley ran down toward Green Park. It was in this direction that he'd been instructed to walk last night. He jogged down the pavement, training his eye for swaths of black.

He stopped at the first corner. As he waited for a car to complete a left-hand turn in front of him, Emma materialized as if out of thin air a hundred meters up the street. On closer examination, he observed that she'd emerged from a boutique. Some instinct or reflex caused him to retreat into a doorway, and at that moment she turned and glanced behind her. He held his position. Waiting, he noticed that he was sweating and that his heart was beating faster than it should.

He counted to five, but before setting out, he shot a look up the street behind him.

One block back, a tan Ford Mondeo idled at the curb. The morning light struck the windshield full on and reflected off the driver's shiny blue tracksuit. One official bodyguard licensed to carry firearms, according to Emma's furious description. He caught another figure in the passenger seat and maybe one in the rear. Jonathan's watchers in the flesh.

They'll follow you to get to me.

He returned his attention to Emma. She was keeping close to the storefronts, never looking back as she neared the intersection with New Bond Street.

It was then that he made a decision.

Stepping onto the sidewalk, he continued in his wife's direction. At the next light he waited patiently for the signal to change. It wasn't necessary to look over his shoulder to check if the Mondeo was there. The sideview mirror of a cab idling next to him did the job astonishingly well. Jonathan was picking up the tools of Emma's trade.

The signal changed in his favor. He entered the intersection, but halfway across he darted to his right and regained the sidewalk. He looked for a store to duck into, somewhere he might disappear for a minute or two. But the street was lined with private residences. Door after door was locked. He checked behind him. Caught in traffic, the Mondeo hadn't yet made the turn. Across the street, Jonathan spotted a newsagent's shop. There might just be time . . .

He dashed into the oncoming traffic, dodging the fast-moving cars, ignoring the horns and the squeal of brakes. Reaching the far sidewalk, he flung open the door to the newsagent's, setting a chain of bells tinkling madly. He bent low behind a wall of magazines. A moment later he spied the Mondeo speeding past. Still breathing hard, he watched until it disappeared from sight. Only then did he leave the store.

"Where the hell is he?" shouted Frank Connor from his position in the backseat of the Mondeo.

"I don't see him," said the driver. "Do you, Liam?"

The rangy dark-haired man in the passenger seat shook his head.

"Turn around," said Connor, shifting his considerable bulk so that he could peer out the rear window. "He's in one of those shops. He couldn't have gone anywhere else."

"I can't just yet," said the driver, indicating the steady stream of oncoming traffic.

"Screw the traffic," retorted Connor. "Make a U-turn."

"It'll cause an accident."

"Just do it. Now! There's a break!"

The driver whipped the car around, keeping one hand firmly pressed down on the horn. The sudden turn tossed Connor against the door. He glanced up in time to see a white van skidding toward them. There was a squeal of brakes, a cacophony of horns, followed by the sickening crunch of metal impacting metal. The collision threw Connor to the other side of the car, and he struck his head violently against the window. The Ford came to a halt and he pulled himself upright.

"I told you," the driver was shouting. "I knew there was no way we could make the turn. Crap!"

"You were too slow," said Connor. "You got no reflexes. You had plenty of time."

"Like hell!"

"Forget about it," said Connor.

The man named Liam pointed at Connor's head. "You're bleeding, Frank."

Connor drew a hand across his brow and looked down at fingers red with blood. He asked for a handkerchief and held it to his forehead, then climbed out of the car. Already traffic was snarled in both directions. An irate woman was walking up the road, berating him for being "a demon of a driver," and "some kind of idiot." Connor pushed her out of his way and stalked to the sidewalk. He looked up the road toward the intersection where he'd last seen Jonathan Ransom, but it was hopeless. Ransom was gone.

Connor told his men to take care of the mess, then started up the road. He should have known better than to rely on his own depleted resources.

It was time to bring in reinforcements.

New Bond Street was a commercial thoroughfare famed for its high-end retail outlets and tony art galleries. At 9:30, pedestrians crowded the sidewalk. Jonathan zigged and zagged through the onslaught of people, searching for his wife's auburn hair. **It's impossible,** he said to himself. There were simply too many people. Oxford Street was two blocks away, and he knew that if he didn't spot Emma soon, he'd lose her for good.

He started to run, knocking into men and women, slowing only to stand on his tiptoes and gaze ahead. A hundred meters farther on, he pulled up. It was no use. The sidewalks were growing more crowded, not less. He put a foot into the street and stood exposed, canvassing the cascade of bobbing heads and shoulders.

There . . .

It was Emma. She stood on the far side of the street at the end of the block, one foot in the road like him, a hand raised to hail a taxi.

Jonathan looked to his right. Spotting a cab with its fare light on, he signaled for it to pull over. The cab docked at the curb expertly. Jonathan leaned into the passenger's side window. "Make a U-turn. I need to follow a cab going in the opposite direction."

"Can't turn here, gov. 'Gainst the law, isn't it?"

Jonathan threw a fifty-pound note onto the seat. "Emergency, **isn't it**?"

"Hop in," said the cabbie. "Which car is it you'd like me to follow?"

"Turn around and I'll tell you."

Jonathan hauled himself into the backseat, all the while keeping an eye pinned on Emma. As the cab negotiated a U-turn, he was afforded a perfect view of his wife climbing into a maroon taxi with a T-Mobile placard affixed to its doors.

"That's the one," said Jonathan. "And keep your distance."

They followed Emma's cab without incident to a home in Hampstead, a well-to-do neighborhood in the northern reaches of London. The driver was born to subterfuge. Effortlessly he maintained a safe distance behind Emma, never going closer than four car lengths. In a city where taxis nearly outnumbered private cars, he was invisible. Taking up position at the rear of a line of parked cars at the end of the block, they watched as Emma paid off her cab and walked to the side of a modest mock-Tudor-styled home, where she entered through a side door. Jonathan checked his watch. It was after ten. Emma had officially missed her flight to Dublin.

He had another concern. He was due back at the hotel in little more than an hour to deliver his keynote address. If he left now, he might just make it back in time, but he would have to shower and shave in record time. Blackburn and his associates had spent a lot of money to fly him to London and put him up in the five-star luxury to which they believed he was entitled. Jonathan didn't want to disappoint them. And yet he could not make himself leave.

Just then the garage door opened, and all thoughts about rushing back to the Dorchester vanished. Jonathan leaned forward, his eyes trained on the gray BMW sedan pulling out of the garage and turning in their direction.

"Get your fare light on," he commanded as he flung himself flat onto the rear seat.

"Already done."

"Is it her?" Jonathan asked, still lying low.

"Bingo, gov. It's her."

"Then what are you waiting for? Get moving."

It took Emma exactly thirty minutes to reach her destination. Her route took her south, back through Hampstead to Bayswater Road, where she cut through Hyde Park toward St. James. She drove slowly, more cautiously than was her habit. His Emma—or the real Emma, as he liked to think of her—was an Indy car driver in search of a track. She had only two speeds, fast and faster. This one braked for yellow lights instead of flooring it to make it through, signaled religiously, and rarely changed lanes. The implication was clear. Operational Emma, or Nightingale, could not afford to be stopped by the police.

From St. James it was a maze of narrow residential streets, constantly turning left, then right, but always keeping toward the Thames. Afraid to be seen, Jonathan shouted for the driver to lag behind, and two or three times they lost all sight of her. Luck, however, was with them, and after a tortured span of five or ten seconds, they spotted her again.

She parked in a space on Storey's Gate Road. It was a narrow two-way street bordered by attached buildings dating from the late nineteenth century. All were five stories high, hewn from an identical batch of gray Portland cement, and constructed as part of a single ambitious project to gentrify the area. Only afterward did Jonathan remark on the perfect timing of the departing motorist, or recall that the car pulling out of the space had been a Vauxhall, the same car mentioned by code in the text message on

Emma's phone. At that moment, he simply attributed it to Emma's good fortune.

"What now?" asked the cabbie as they stared at the BMW from a distance of a hundred meters. Emma's silhouette was distinctly visible. She sat behind the wheel, as stationary as a statue.

"We wait," said Jonathan.

16

It was past seven a.m. when Kate Ford returned home and closed the kitchen door behind her. "Good Lord!" she muttered as the scent of spoiled milk assaulted her senses. She flipped on the light and immediately identified the culprits: a bowl of half-eaten muesli and a quart of milk stood on the table exactly where she'd left them some twenty-six hours earlier. In her rush to get to One Park, she'd forgotten to clean up after herself.

Hurriedly she flung open the windows and waved the foul-smelling air out. Unlike Lord Robert Russell, she did not enjoy the benefits of central air conditioning. East Finchley was much farther from Park Lane than 20 map kilometers. Sighing, she dumped the cereal down the sink and followed it with the clotted milk. It was not how she'd envisioned coming home after her first day back on the job.

Upstairs, she turned on the shower. When it grew hot, she undressed and threw her suit and blouse into a pile on the floor. It was off to the dry cleaner for both. She didn't like the idea of paying ten quid to have them cleaned and pressed, but she liked the idea of not smelling to high heaven. She took care climbing into the tub. The water was hot and the pressure was strong enough to peel paint, which was how she liked it. She washed her hair, then soaped her body, running a loofah over her arms and legs. She was careful to avoid the scar above her hip. A few weeks earlier, when she'd first come home from hospital, it had bulged like a swollen leech. The bullet had entered from the rear, just above the spleen, leaving barely a clean hole, and then blasted through the other side like a sledgehammer through rotting wood. Hollowpoints did that. The doctors had been unanimous in pointing out that it was a miracle that the splintered round had not nicked an artery or caused greater internal damage.

Kate remained under the showerhead until every last drop of warmth had been bled and the nozzle ran as cold as a Scottish stream. And then she stayed longer. She stood beneath the jets until her skin prickled with goose bumps and her flesh went numb. The numbness helped her deal with the silence. If she was frantic to towel herself dry, she didn't notice that there was no radio blaring, no clumsy male hands clanking the breakfast plates, no East End baritone ordering her to hightail it to the car so they could drive in to work together.

A mirror hung on the wall, and she caught sight of her body, thinner now than it had ever been. She stared at her biceps, which looked taut and ropey beneath her pale skin, at her pelvis, so sharp and fragile, and at her scar. "The bullet destroyed one of your ovaries," the surgeon had explained with maddening sympathy. "It also tore the lining of the uterus. To control the bleeding, we had to remove the uterus in toto. I'm so sorry. We did everything we could."

He'd never mentioned the baby, though surely he'd known. Six weeks along was hardly enough for it to show. Maybe he'd been waiting for her to ask. Or maybe he thought Kate didn't know herself and hoped to save her further anguish. She never knew if it was a boy or a girl.

She touched the scar and felt a jab inside of her, sharp as a spear. Gasping, she caught her eye and stared at the frightened woman bent double in the mirror. **Cry,** she told the reflection. **No one can see you. You've been strong. You don't have to prove how tough you are. It's time.**

The pain went away. Kate stood up straight. Dry-eyed, she turned away from the mirror and wrapped the towel around her.

Someone was knocking at the back door.

Still in her towel, Kate hurried downstairs and ducked a head into the kitchen. She was surprised to find a tall, fair-skinned man in a dark suit standing there with his hands in his pockets, as if he belonged there. "I think your milk's gone bad," he said.

"Who the hell are you?"

"Graves. Five. I apologize for letting myself in. I'd

been knocking awhile, and I was afraid that your neighbors were getting curious."

"Five" for MI5, the country's national security and counterterrorism apparatus, better known as the Security Service. She should have known it by his posture. He looked as if he had a steel rod in place of a spine.

"What branch?"

"G Branch." G Branch handled counterterrorism in all countries except Northern Ireland. Kate peered out the front window. The curb in front of her home was empty. "Where's the blue Rover?" she asked on a hunch, remembering the car that had been parked inside police tape at 1 Park Lane yesterday morning.

"Parked it down the road. Think you might like to get dressed? They're waiting for us at HQ. Traffic's a bugger this time of day."

Kate took a longer look at the man who'd let himself into her home. He was fortyish, tall and spare, with thick blond hair cut more casually than she would have expected. He wore a navy pinstripe, clearly Savile Row, with the requisite inch of cuff showing, and a striped necktie that hinted at service in some elite outfit or another. His black wingtips were of the sleekest order and polished to a paratrooper's exacting standards. But it was his eyes that captured her attention. They were diamond blue and near holy in their intensity. They were the same eyes she'd seen yesterday evening gazing at her from the offices of Oxford Analytica.

"You have a first name, Mr. Graves?"

"Yeah," he said. "Colonel."

MI5 has its headquarters in Thames House, an imposing block-long building situated (as to be expected by the name) on the banks of the River Thames in the Millbank section of London, overlooking Lambeth Bridge. Graves's office was on the first floor, down the hall from the director. Kate, the born striver, was suitably impressed. It was a corner office, decorated with fashionable modern furniture. Picture windows offered a stunning view over the south side of the river.

"Sit down," said Colonel Graves. "You know why you're here. It's about Robert Russell. Or, to be more accurate, what he was working on."

"I was made to understand he didn't work for the Security Service," said Kate, taking her place on a low-slung fawn-colored sofa. A chrome-and-glass coffee table faced her. There was an ashtray brimming with cigarette butts alongside copies of various law enforcement journals.

"He didn't," replied Graves. "Not knowingly, at least. You spoke with Ian Cairncross. He told you about Russell's interest in TINs—trusted information networks. You know . . . experts he'd assembled to gather information about this or that subject. Let's just say that Lord Russell was a member of my TIN."

"Looks like he was a member of quite a few."

Graves nodded. "At the time of his death, Russell had pieced together information indicating that some sort of attack or plot was being planned on London soil. We're viewing his murder as validation that he was correct. Accordingly, we've ramped things up a bit."

"Why did you wait until now?"

"You mean why didn't we bring in Russell earlier? It's a question of resources, DCI Ford. At any time we're keeping tabs on a few dozen plots in various stages of planning. It's a matter of separating the chaff from the grain." Graves reached into his jacket for a packet of Silk Cuts. "Smoke?"

Kate declined.

He lit one and exhaled gratefully. "I'm supposed to say something about the Official Secrets Act now. You know, ask you to swear not to divulge any information you may learn as part of this investigation. Word is that you're a good egg. We don't need to have you sign anything, do we?"

"Is this the part where you're going to admit that Five was maintaining some kind of surveillance on Russell without a warrant?"

"Something like that."

"I'm a policewoman," said Kate. "Not a civil libertarian. I'm sure our interests mirror each other."

"Good." Graves picked up a remote control from the coffee table and aimed it at a flat monitor on the wall. It was a SMART Board, an interactive high-definition monitor hooked up to the office's central computer network. The face of the tired, mousy housewife Kate had seen the previous morning in Russell's flat appeared. All eyes focused on the screen as she spoke to Russell about Mischa, Victoria Bear, and the "hush-hush" meeting set to take place at 11:15 this morning—a little more than an hour from now.

"Know what it means?" asked Kate afterward.

"Not a clue. There are a hundred Mischas in the Russian embassy alone, and that's not counting the scourge of them that have taken over the West End. A delegation from the Kremlin is visiting, but they're in Whitehall today, holed up with the Navy. I think they're safe for the moment."

"That sounds rather hush-hush, doesn't it?" asked Kate, quoting from the video message.

"Actually, it's a matter of public record. No Mischas among them. Just a few Ivans, Vladimirs, and Yuris. Oh, and a Svetlana."

"And Victoria Bear?"

"We've run the name through all our files and drawn a blank. Our boys in decoding are having a go at it as we speak."

"Have you been able to draw a bead on the woman? Russell's source? Frankly, I'm worried about her. If Russell was killed for what he knew, why not her?"

"We're trying to locate her. It's not so easy. The way our system functions is that we grab everything going into Russell's in-box, as it were. That doesn't mean we know where it came from. Tracing it back to its source is trickier. We brought you in to see if you've turned up anything in the course of your investigation that might shed some light on this."

Kate suspected Graves knew more than he was letting on. She'd long heard that Five kept a roster of spies inside the Met. "Robert Russell was killed by a woman who gained entry to his flat from the basement and shimmied up an old laundry chute to a closet in his master bedroom. Once inside, she defeated the alarm system, knocked him unconscious with a bottle of frozen vodka, then threw him over the balcony to make it appear a suicide. It was our good luck that he landed facedown. Otherwise, we'd never have suspected a thing. It goes without saying that the woman is a professional. She knew her way around Russell's flat, so we can assume she had access to building plans, including his home security system. It's my guess that she was working as part of a team, and that her partner or partners were keeping tabs on Russell."

Graves leaned forward, elbow on his knee. "How do you know it was a woman?"

Kate took a disk out of her jacket. "We have a visual."

"May I?" asked Graves, rising from his chair. He handed the disk to a deputy, who placed it in the DVD player. A moment later the image of the auburn-haired murderer taken by One Park's CCTV camera filled the screen.

"Not much to go on," said Kate. "She did an outstanding job keeping her face away from the camera."

"A pro, as you said."

Just then there was a loud knock on the door. Reg Cleak entered breathlessly. "Sorry I'm late," he said, crossing the room and taking a seat next to Kate. "I'd just nodded off when a big bloke showed up at the back door. Nearly scared the missus half to death."

Introductions were made, but Cleak was barely paying attention. "Just got off with the boys in Automobile Visual Surveillance. They weren't able to get a line on the car all the way from Windsor, but they came darned close."

"Where did Russell go after leaving his parents' house?" asked Kate.

"To his club in Sloane Square for about an hour."

"That only takes us to one a.m.," said Kate. "Where did he go afterward?"

"Hold your horses, boss. I'm getting to the interesting part. From his club Russell drove to Storey's Gate. We've got stills of his car parked on the sidewalk for over an hour. Don't ask me what he was doing."

"Storey's Gate? That's not far from here." Graves instructed his deputy to bring up a map of London on the SMART Board. A moment later a city map appeared, with a circle indicating the location. Storey's Gate was a short, narrow two-way street running east to west about a half-mile from Buckingham Palace and St. James's Park.

"Do you see what I see?" asked Kate, standing and walking to the screen.

"What is it?" asked Cleak, but Graves was already nodding.

Kate guided her finger along the map down Storey's Gate Road and turned a corner onto a broader thoroughfare. It was labeled "Victoria Street." "There's our Victoria," she said.

If she expected Graves to show some surprise, she was disappointed. He remained nailed to his seat, smoking his cigarette ruminatively. "So it's a place," he said. "Not a name. Now what?"

But Kate wasn't finished. Sliding her finger up Victoria Street, she came to a rectangular gray outline commonly used to denote a government building. "This is a ministry building. I believe it used to be the Department of Trade. Can you tell me who's housed there now?"

Graves snapped his fingers and his deputy clicked on the interactive map. A photograph of the building appeared, and under it the name of its current occupant. "Department of Business, Enterprise, and Regulatory Reform, formerly Trade and Industry."

"Business, Enterprise, and Regulatory Reform," said Kate. "B-E-R-R."

"Bear," said Graves in the same calm voice.

Cleak screwed up his face. "I'd call it 'brrr.' "

"And if you were foreign, like the person who gave

Russell's girl the clue?" asked Kate. " 'Bear' sounds right to me. Bear on Victoria Street," added Kate. **"Victoria Bear."**

"I'll be a monkey's," added Cleak, eyes wide, fidgeting in his chair, the only person in the room not above showing some emotion.

"Bring up a list of the building's tenants," commanded Graves.

A moment later, a list of all government agencies having offices in 1 Victoria Street appeared. They included the Office of Employment, the Economic Development Agency, the Bureau of Competitiveness, and the Office of Science.

"Get on to Diplomatic Security," Graves continued. "See if any foreign dignitaries are slated to visit any of the agencies on the list. Then contact BERR's chief of security. Tell him to lock down the place until we arrive. We'll be over in ten minutes."

"What about traffic?" asked Kate. "Shouldn't we block off all roads leading to the building?"

"If we locked down traffic every time we had a threat, London would go out of business in a fortnight." Graves looked at his assistant. "Get the demo boys over there. Can't hurt." He stood and faced Kate. "I take it you're joining me."

Kate, Graves, and Cleak took the elevator to the ground floor, where Graves's Rover had been brought round and stood waiting, engine idling, doors open. Kate climbed into the front seat next to Graves, while

Cleak slid into the back. The blast barrier was lowered and Graves accelerated onto Horseferry Road, where he quickly became enmeshed in traffic. The Rover advanced slowly, making it through one signal, then another. Kate glanced at the clock: 11:03.

"Got a flasher?" she asked, referring to a portable siren.

"Afraid not. We're more in the preemptive line of things."

The traffic light changed and Graves pulled across the intersection. After traveling 50 meters, he came to another halt. Victoria Street was less than two kilometers away. In reasonable conditions, the drive would take three minutes. As it was, they were looking at upwards of twenty.

Graves was on the phone with his assistant. "No foreign parties visiting BERR today," he said to Kate, relaying the news as he received it. "The minister is in Leeds. Everything's business as usual."

The car inched forward.

Kate noted that Graves's cheeks were flushed and that he was batting his hand against the steering wheel. "Maybe we should walk," she suggested.

"Forget it." Graves studied the road in front of him, his blue eyes no longer so divinely certain. Suddenly he swung the car into the oncoming lane of traffic. The road was clear for 30 meters. He floored the Rover, keeping his palm on the horn, until a lorry forced him back into his own lane.

Again they came to a dead halt.

The clock read 11:06.

Five minutes later they reached the intersection of Victoria Street. Graves turned right and sighed with relief when he observed that traffic was flowing nicely. He accelerated to 80 kilometers an hour, rocking in his seat, mumbling, "Come on." The light turned red and he braked hard.

"There it is," said Kate, pointing to a modern office building 300 meters along the road.

"Thank God," registered Cleak from his post in the rear seat.

The light turned green, but the traffic didn't move. The driver of the vehicle in front of them opened the door and put a foot on the pavement. Kate got out of the car. "They're running a temporary road block," she said, sticking her head into the cabin. "Someone's coming through. Raja from Whitehall or a visiting dignitary. I thought you said there was nothing scheduled for the area."

"I said nothing was scheduled inside the building." Graves threw open the door and climbed out. He had his cell phone to his ear, but Kate couldn't make out to whom he was talking.

Just then she caught sight of the first car in the motorcade barreling out of Storey's Gate and turning in front of them onto Victoria Street. It was a black Suburban, windows tinted, riding low to the ground. An armored vehicle moving at speed.

"Who's in town?" she asked Graves. "Looks like the bloody president of the United States."

Graves was shaking his head. "I've got nothing on this," he said, his calm suddenly in short supply.

Somewhere in the distance Kate caught the sound of a man shouting. Over the roar of the passing motorcade she couldn't make out what he was saying. It sounded like he was calling someone's name. One thing was for sure: he was worked up.

"Do you hear that? Something's wrong."

"Where?" asked Graves, only half listening. He was conducting a running skirmish with the office, demanding to know what foreign dignitary was in the city and why he hadn't been informed about it.

Kate stood on her tiptoes, craning her neck in an effort to locate the source of the shouting. About 300 meters up the sidewalk, she caught sight of a dark head running toward them. The head bobbed up and down. Visible one instant, gone the next. It belonged to a white male. Graying hair. Blue jacket. More than that she couldn't tell.

A second Suburban shot into the intersection, followed by a trio of Mercedes sedans, all black, all with windows similarly tinted to prevent unfriendly parties from identifying their occupants. A miniature flag flew from the antenna of the lead Mercedes. She recognized the blue, white, and red tricolor of Russia.

She checked her watch. It was 11:15.

Mischa, she thought.

17

Seated in the rear of the cab, Jonathan watched Emma climb from the BMW and walk away from the car. He had his money ready, and as soon as Emma had gone ten steps, he passed the cabbie two fifty-pound notes. He waited another moment, his eyes fixed on his wife as if there were a cable connecting them, then opened his door and set off down the sidewalk. He kept close to the buildings, slowing now and again to keep some pedestrians between him and his wife. "Natural cover," she'd called it, explaining her work to him.

Emma continued down Storey's Gate for exactly one block before stopping at the intersection of Victoria Street. The light changed. Pedestrians on either side of her crossed the street, but Emma remained where she was.

Jonathan hung back, watching. Any second now, a car was going to pull up, Emma was going to climb in, and that would be that. He would never see his wife again. He turned, looking for a cab, but for once there were none to be seen. He balled his fist and pounded his thigh. He should never have abandoned the taxi.

It was almost 11:15. Dr. Blackburn would be frantically searching for him at the hotel, wondering where his keynote speaker had disappeared to. He imagined Jamie Meadows pounding on the door of his hotel room, asking if everything was all right. Jonathan put them out of his mind. He could give his talk tomorrow.

It was then that he saw a motorcycle policeman zip past him, and all thoughts about the conference vanished. The policeman continued to the intersection of Storey's Gate and Victoria Street, where he stopped his bike, dismounted, and blocked off all eastbound traffic. Quickly the road emptied of vehicles and grew curiously calm. Jonathan was put in mind of the eerie silence that precedes an avalanche.

By now a group of pedestrians had surrounded Emma. Even so, he could see her clearly, standing with a cell phone to her ear, gazing intently in front of her.

Behind him, he heard the hum of a powerful engine. He turned in time to see a flash of black, and a Chevrolet Suburban zipped past him, then another identical to it, close behind. Both were followed by a fleet of jet-black Mercedeses. Three in all. He saw a flag fluttering from one of the cars. The red, white, and blue of the tricolor shimmered in the bright sunshine. It took him a few seconds to guess the country. Not France, not Holland **. . . Russia.**

It hit him then. He knew why Emma was waiting at the corner.

Lebanon. Kosovo. Iraq. She had told him about

her work in those places. Invariably it involved the kidnapping or assassination of a high-ranking figure deemed unfriendly to the cause—the cause being the security and well-being of the United States of America. It was no coincidence that she was standing on this particular street corner at the precise moment that a motorcade ferrying Russian officials across London was passing.

Emma had come to London to kill someone, or, as he'd once heard her refer to it, "to secure a political objective."

All this passed through Jonathan's mind in a second.

He began to run, shouting her name. He wasn't sure why he was doing it. Emma had taken pains to explain why her actions were necessary, and in every case he'd come to share her views. It was a common misperception that aid work is a liberalizing force. In fact, time spent in impoverished countries, caring for the poor, the sick, the downtrodden, had the opposite effect. Jonathan had no tolerance for the corrupt and powerful who furthered their gains at the expense of their countrymen. It didn't matter what country. He didn't believe in second chances, either. The fact was that most of the people who ended up on Emma's list had it coming. But this was different. This time he was involved. This time he **knew.** To watch and do nothing, to stand still and bear mute witness—it was asking too much. He would not be an accomplice to murder.

"Emma!"

The last Mercedes drove past. Jonathan's voice was drowned out by squealing tires, the aggressive roar of so many powerful engines. The motorcade shot down the street, only now coming abreast of the gray BMW.

The car.

The parking space conveniently available.

The text message on Emma's phone was emblazoned on his memory. "Package ready for pickup. ETA 11:15. Parking arranged. LT 52 OCX Vxhl. Meet WS 17:00."

The BMW was the package. The attack was set for 11:15. It was a Vauxhall car that had vacated the space.

"Emma!"

Finally she turned toward him, and in the instant before the explosion, their eyes met. And as the blast wave hit him and lifted him into the air and threw him with astonishing force through the windshield of a Range Rover parked nearby, he registered only the ferocious explosion and inside it the image of Emma's condemning eyes.

He had never seen her more angry.

18

The first thing Kate noticed was the silence. She didn't think, **Oh, I'm alive. What the hell just happened?** She knew that she was alive because her throbbing head told her so, and the sharp ache in her ribs wouldn't let her forget it. And she knew that it had been a car bomb. She had seen the flash of light, the incendiary star burning to orange, before the blast wave knocked her to the pavement. But she hadn't expected the silence. It was as if the entire city were holding its breath.

Gradually she became aware of the tinkle of glass falling to earth and the groaning of distressed metal. Her vision cleared. The first thing she saw was a line of burning cars. Every automobile parked within 20 meters of the bomb was on fire. They must have exploded instantaneously, she thought to herself, because she'd heard only the one bang, and then she wondered if maybe she'd been knocked unconscious for a moment or two.

She picked herself off the pavement, aware of an ache in her chest. "Christ," she mumbled. "We've stepped in it this time. Can you believe this, Reg?" She looked over her shoulder for Cleak, but didn't see him anywhere. "Reg? You all right, then?"

He lay on the ground next to the car. His eyes were open and fixed, as if he were staring at the sky. A piece of metal protruded from his forehead. It was a four-inch bolt.

Kate dropped to her knees, putting a hand to his neck to check for a pulse. There was none.

Nearby, Graves stood with his phone to his ear, speaking entirely too calmly as he instructed his subordinates to get a bomb response team to Victoria Street and Storey's Gate, and only as an afterthought to "send some ambulances. Plenty of them." He hung up and looked at her, then at Cleak. "He's dead. Help me secure the blast scene."

"You're hurt." She pointed to his cheek.

Graves appeared peeved by the comment. He touched his hand to his face, and when it came away bloody, he swore, then took a handkerchief and pressed it to the wound. "Get on to SO15," he said, referring to Special Office 15 of the Metropolitan Police. "Have them issue an evacuation notice for the area."

Kate rose, her ribs beginning to hurt in earnest. Gingerly she opened her jacket and saw a streak of blood on her blouse. The fabric was torn, and through it she could see a gash. Looking closer, she spotted a hole in her jacket where a bolt or a nail had passed, grazing her. A few centimeters to the right and she'd most probably be dead.

She leaned against the car door, transfixed by the hellish tableau. The bomb had been detonated as the third and last Mercedes had driven by. It appeared that the blast had lifted the automobile into the air and driven it against the wall of the building. The car sat on all four tires, crumpled, ablaze, already a husk. Barely ten meters in front of it, the second Mercedes lay on its side. Two bodies lay half in, half out of the front windscreen. It was also on fire, and the flames darted like snakes' tongues through hundreds of perforations in the car's skin.

Nails, thought Kate, glancing at Cleak, feeling the ache of her own wound. They had packed the car like a suicide bomber's vest.

The lead Mercedes had crashed into a lamppost. She noted that the airbags had deployed and that there was some motion inside. The rear door opened. A man crawled out and fell to the ground, his face bloody.

Closer to her, the chassis of the two SUVs that had provided escort were also riddled with punctures, their tires exploded, windows blown out. All of their doors stood ajar, and big, barrel-chested men in dark suits were tumbling out, several brandishing compact machine guns, and rushing toward the lead Mercedes. Already two bodyguards were pulling a second man out of the rear seat.

Graves ran across the intersection, past the Suburbans, and advanced on the lead sedan. He pushed his way past the bodyguards, calling out his name and identifying himself as a policeman. Kate followed close behind.

"Who was in the motorcade?" Graves asked.

"They wanted me," said the bloodied man. He lay on the pavement, propped up on an elbow.

Graves knelt down next to him. "What is your name, sir?"

"Ivanov. Interior Minister Ivanov."

Kate knew the name, if not the face. Ivanov was one of a half-dozen men rumored to be candidates for the Russian presidency. "Stay there," she counseled him. "An ambulance will be here shortly."

Ivanov lay down.

The whine of approaching sirens filled the air. In the space of thirty seconds, Kate counted five cars approaching from all directions. Silence no more. Graves broke off from the Russian interior minister and walked toward the second Mercedes. Flames shot from the interior. Inside the inferno, the driver remained strapped in his seat. He had been beheaded by the blast. The two men who had been ejected through the windscreen appeared to be dead, too, as did a body slumped in the rear seat. It was difficult to be certain because of the fire.

There was no question about the sedan having been the target of the blast. The interior seemed to have been obliterated. The chassis was grotesquely bent. There was little left inside it except the remnants of the seats.

"Who was in the other cars?" Graves asked one of the Russian bodyguards.

"Mr. Witte and Mr. Kerensky, Interior Minister

Ivanov's assistants. And Mr. Orlov, our ambassador to Great Britain."

"What about Mischa?" Kate asked, referencing Russell's video message.

"No Mischa."

"Yes," said Kate. "He was part of the visiting party."

"No," replied the bodyguard, more vehemently. "No one named Mischa is traveling with us."

The first police cars arrived. Officers ran to assist the injured, but Graves signaled for them to come to him. "Get tape around the perimeter. These buildings are being evacuated, and I don't want every Tom, Dick, and Harry to muddle the evidence. Once you're done, you can tend to the injured."

Kate stepped away from Graves and began heading up Storey's Gate, past the site of the explosion. Just before the blast she'd heard a man yelling some kind of warning. Strange, but she'd forgotten about it until Graves had mentioned the need to preserve evidence. She recalled seeing a cap of graying hair, a navy jacket.

By now men and women were streaming out of the buildings on both sides of the road. In case of terrorist attack, city law called for the mandatory evacuation of all buildings and residences in the area. Many hurried up the street, anxious to escape. Others lingered, exhibiting a morbid curiosity about the blown-up vehicles and the fate of those inside.

Kate walked against the tide. Victims of the blast

lay on the sidewalk. Most seemed to have superficial wounds: bloody noses caused by the concussion of the blast, ruptured eardrums, cuts inflicted by flying glass, shock. She paused to let them know that help was on its way, then continued her search.

Graying hair. Navy jacket. She saw no one who fit the bill.

There was a crater where the bomb had gone off. The car itself sat twisted and in flames 3 meters away. As she passed it, she raised a hand to ward off the ferocious heat. Black smoke rose into the sky, mixing with dust and debris, burning her eyes and making it difficult to see. She held a hankie to her mouth, but even then the air was hot and choked with soot. She began to cough.

Another Mercedes lay burning 10 meters up the street. Suddenly a man fell out of the vehicle and began to crawl away from it. A halo of flames surrounded his head. Clothing hung in tatters from his arms and chest, but his back appeared to be flayed to the bone. She heard a voice yell, "Lie down" and saw another man running to his assistance, throwing a jacket over his head and extinguishing the flames. The Samaritan had graying hair, and the jacket he'd used to put out the flames was a navy blazer.

Kate radioed Graves. "I'm halfway down Storey's Gate. Get over here. I've found the man I was looking for."

Within seconds Graves was by her side, two policemen in tow. "Where is he?"

"That's him. Kneeling next to the injured man."

Graves shouted instructions, and one of the policemen ran forward and threw the man to the ground.

"Don't touch him!" shouted the Samaritan, his words clear, the American accent pronounced. His face was covered in blood, but he sounded strong and in control of his wits. "He has third-degree burns all over his body. Get a poncho and cover him up. There's too much debris in the air. You have to protect the burn or he'll die of infection."

Kate knelt beside him. "What's your name?" she asked.

"Ransom. Jonathan Ransom. I'm a doctor."

"Why did you do this?" she demanded.

"Do what?"

"This. The bomb," said the woman. "I saw you shouting at someone back there. Who was it?"

"I don't—" The man bit back his words.

"You don't what?"

For a long moment, the man didn't answer. He stared past her, and for a minute she thought he had fallen into a state of shock. Finally he looked at her. "I don't know," he said.

Then he laid his head down on the pavement and closed his eyes.

19

From Division's office in Lambeth, south of the Thames, Frank Connor heard the blast and immediately turned on the television. A bulletin cut into programming within five minutes. A still photograph of the Department of Business, Enterprise, and Regulatory Reform was displayed as a reporter offered the first sketchy details of a car bombing near Victoria Street, in the heart of London. A rattled eyewitness followed, describing the blast.

Connor watched intently, popping open a can of Coca-Cola and sneaking glances out the window. It wasn't long before he caught the plume of smoke drifting above the skyline. He knew about explosions, and this one was a monster.

One of the desk girls entered the room. "I've tracked down Hubert Lorenz," she said. "He's available, but he's asking for one hundred thousand pounds."

Lorenz was a German bounty hunter known in the trade for his precision and reliability.

But Connor didn't answer. If anything, he drew nearer the television, his eyes transfixed by the pictures now being beamed live from the scene. The camera panned over several mangled automobiles and lingered on bloody victims lying on the sidewalks. The reporter announced that seven people were confirmed dead and at least twenty injured. Connor was surprised the numbers weren't higher.

"I've got him on the line," continued the assistant in her aggravating north-of-England accent. "He's not someone who likes to be kept waiting."

"Yeah, yeah, just hold on." Connor turned up the volume. The reporter announced that the target of the attack was thought to have been Igor Ivanov, the Russian interior minister, and added that Ivanov had been taken to a nearby hospital, where news of his condition was expected at any minute. "And?" Connor whispered to himself, like a bettor with an interest in the game. "Is he dead or alive?"

"Mr. Connor, what do I do about Mr. Lorenz?"

Connor spun in his chair. "Tell him to fuck off! Can't you see I'm busy?"

"Excuse me?"

"You heard me. Get out. I'm fuckin' occupied!"

The assistant beat a quick retreat.

Connor rose and opened the window. By now the smoke had spread into an ominous black pall that enveloped Big Ben and covered a good portion of the sky. Helicopters flitted low over the skyline. The wail of sirens sounded from every direction. Once again London was under attack.

And Frank Connor knew who was responsible.

Seated alone in the former linen closet that served as her office, Connor's assistant hung up the phone and crossed the German's name off the list of surveillance experts she had prepared for her boss. Suddenly she noticed that her hand was shaking and she put down her pen. Never once in five years had she heard Mr. Connor swear. At all times he'd been respectful, polite, and decent. In her diary she had called him a "nice bloke," which to a working-class girl was high regard indeed. The outburst had shaken her. But it wasn't the epithets that left her stunned and feeling weak in the knees; it was the savagery of his tone and the rage in his eyes. For a moment she'd felt certain he was going to harm her.

Overcome, she sobbed and rushed to the ladies' room.

20

"How many people?" asked Jonathan.

"Seven dead, so far," said the woman, whose name was Kate Ford, a detective chief inspector for the Metropolitan Police. "Two dozen wounded, several critically. You're in quite a bit of trouble."

"Actually, you're in more than that," said Graves, who'd introduced himself as being from the counterterrorism wing of MI5. "As it happens, you are currently being viewed as an accomplice to seven counts of murder, as well as conspiracy to commit a terrorist act on British soil."

Jonathan stared into the hard, expectant faces. He lay in a camp bed with metal rails at his feet, rough sheets, and a green woolen blanket. A portable sphygmomanometer sat near his head, next to an IV drip delivering a clear solution that he guessed to be either glucose or saline into his left arm. There was no television, no second bed. Just a guard at the door dressed in army greens, with a submachine gun hugged to his chest.

From London, Jonathan had been transported in a blacked-out ambulance. He'd ridden alone, except for the company of a police officer who'd told him to "shut it" every time he'd started to ask a question. Ten minutes before arriving, the ambulance had stopped and the driver had come into the rear bay and supervised the draping of a black hood over Jonathan's head. Only when Jonathan had been installed in his bed had the hood been removed.

That was three hours ago.

"Where am I?" he asked.

"Someplace quiet and out of the way," said Graves. "Someplace where we can have a heart-to-heart discussion about this morning's events without too many prying eyes and ears."

"We need to make sure that this is getting through to you," said Detective Chief Inspector Ford.

"Oh, it's getting through," said Graves, stepping closer. "Dr. Ransom is a clever man. No doubting that. Well, then, Dr. Ransom, let me begin by saying that there's very little you can tell us that we do not already know. Namely, that you arrived yesterday morning on a Kenya Airways flight from Nairobi, that you've come to attend a medical conference and are staying at the Dorchester Hotel, and that you're planning to leave in two days' time." He paused. "All we want from you is an honest accounting of what you were doing at Storey's Gate this morning."

"We have a tape of the bomb going off," said Detective Chief Inspector Ford. "In fact, we have three or four views of it going off from a variety of angles."

Graves propped a portable DVD player on

Jonathan's bedside table. He hit the play button and the screen filled with a long shot of Storey's Gate. Directly in the center of the picture was the gray BMW Jonathan had followed from North London. A few seconds passed and the driver's door opened. Emma stepped out and walked toward the intersection of Victoria Street. Jonathan watched as she took up position at the crosswalk and stayed there as the light changed and the pedestrians around her left her side. The motorcycle police escorts arrived and blocked traffic. The first SUV came into the picture and zoomed around the corner. Then the second, followed by the pack of Mercedeses. Suddenly there was a flash. When the screen came back into focus, it showed smoke and flames billowing from the BMW. One of the Mercedeses lay on its side; another had crashed into a lamppost. But Jonathan didn't spend time studying the wreckage. He was too busy staring at the intersection, looking for Emma, wanting to be sure it was really she whom he'd seen.

"She's gone," said Graves, as if privy to his thoughts. "Your wife, I mean. Emma Rose Ransom. That is who you were looking for, isn't it?"

Here it was, then, thought Jonathan. Truth or fiction. Confess or deny. The moment he had to decide whose team he was really on. **Tell them everything,** Emma had instructed, twelve hours and a thousand years ago. **They know it anyway.** If only it was that easy. He weighed the facts as he knew them. Emma had knowingly planned and executed a car bombing that had taken the lives of seven people and grievously wounded many more. She had lied to him about her purpose for being in England. She had made him an unwitting accomplice to her deeds. All this against the loyalty a husband owed his wife.

"My wife's dead," said Jonathan. "She died in a climbing accident in the Alps six months ago."

"So we've heard. When we were checking you out, we found a warrant for your arrest issued by the Swiss Federal Police in February. They sent over your file. It contained a photograph of your wife, presumed dead in a climbing accident, February the eighth of this year. Which makes her turning up in London a few days ago doubly strange."

Days ago? Jonathan was unable to keep himself from reacting to the news. "That's impossible," he managed woodenly. "She's dead."

"Is that right? Why don't we see about that? These pictures were taken in London thirty-six hours ago." From a folder, Detective Chief Inspector Ford spread a series of photographs across the blanket covering his lap. They showed an elegantly dressed woman with auburn hair standing inside an elevator. In all of them, the woman's face was lowered and it was hard to get a good read on her features. Still, it was glaringly obvious to Jonathan that the woman was Emma.

The police officer picked up one of the photographs and compared it to a picture blown up from one of the outdoor CCTV cameras on Victoria Street. "Is that or is that not your wife?"

"I'm not certain," said Jonathan.

Ford set the pictures taken in London next to Emma's passport picture, which had been provided by the Swiss authorities. There was no denying that it was the same woman. "And now?"

"It looks like her," said Jonathan. His head throbbed. He was too fatigued to keep up the pretense.

"So we may assume that she is alive?"

Jonathan said nothing.

Ford picked up the photographs. "Does the name Robert Russell mean anything to you?"

"No," said Jonathan. "Should it?"

"He was murdered yesterday morning. The first picture we showed you of your wife came from a surveillance camera in his building. We have evidence implicating her in Russell's killing."

The DVD was still playing, showing the BMW exploding from a different position up the street.

"One second she's there," said Graves, pointing a finger at the screen. "Bang goes the car, and the next, she's gone. A bit spooky, actually. Where'd she go? She was too far away to get vaporized by the blast. Look closely. DCI Ford is just across the intersection. You can see her before and after. But your wife's disappeared. We still can't figure it." He turned off the machine. "So what were you trying to do, Dr. Ransom, running down the street like that?"

Jonathan didn't answer.

"What?" demanded Graves.

"I was trying to stop her."

"So you knew there was a bomb?"

"No, I just—"

"Admit it," said Graves. "You just said that you were trying to stop her. What happened? Have a last-second change of heart? That it? New to this kind of thing, are we?"

Jonathan stared at Graves. "I didn't know anything about the bomb," he said.

Graves came closer. "We have reports that you were extremely anxious upon your arrival at Heathrow. Set off all kinds of bells and whistles. Sounds to me as if you knew exactly what she had planned."

"That's not true," said Jonathan. "I only found out Emma was in London last night."

"Come on," said Graves, suddenly assuming a comradely manner. "Stop lying to us. Surely you knew about it. You were helping her at every turn. Did you smuggle in the explosives? Swipe some plastique from your rebel buddies in Africa? Was that your part of the job? Later you can tell us how you managed to sneak it past our boys. Right now we're more interested in why you and your wife wanted to blow up the Russian interior minister. Who exactly are you working for, Dr. Ransom?"

Jonathan recalled the white, red, and blue flag flying from the car's antenna. The interior minister could count himself lucky to be alive. Emma didn't fail often. "I don't know anything about the Russian or about the bomb. I was invited to London to give a speech at a medical conference. I'm not working for anyone."

"Then what were you doing at the exact location where the attack took place?"

"I already told you. I was trying to stop her."

"Stop a dead woman from carrying out an attack you didn't know was going to take place?" Graves continued relentlessly. "Please, Dr. Ransom, listen to yourself. Don't insult our intelligence."

Just then Jonathan heard a boom far in the distance and its echo drifting over the countryside. He was familiar with the sound of heavy artillery. He fingered the rough wool blanket. They had him tucked away at an army base. He was outside the system, and he knew all too well the kinds of things that happened there. If he ever wanted to get out of here, he was going to have to cooperate. Emma had been right. He must tell them everything.

"Emma worked for the U.S. government," he said. "She was an operative for an organization called Division. It's part of the Defense Department, but don't bother looking it up. It doesn't exist. At least, not officially. Something happened in Switzerland last February. A mission that went wrong . . . Actually, Emma made it go wrong. Several of Division's men were killed, including its leader. It was better that we pretended she was dead."

"Why's that?" asked Graves.

"Emma knew that Division would come after her. She had to hide. I only found out that she was in London last night. I was at a reception in my hotel for the conference and Emma sent someone to tell me she was here. She arranged for us to meet at an apartment on Edgware Road."

Kate Ford asked for the address, then shared a look with Graves. "And why did she wish to see you?"

"To say goodbye. She wanted to let me know that it was getting too dangerous for her. She couldn't risk making contact with me in the future. She came to my hotel at four this morning. She got a call before she left my room. I sensed something wasn't right. You know, that she was up to something. I asked her why she was really here and she told me to mind my own business. I didn't know it was an operation, or that it had anything to do with any Russians. I thought it was something to do with her keeping safe. Staying one step ahead of them. Anyway, it didn't matter one way or the other. All I cared about was that she was leaving. I couldn't stand the thought of never seeing her again. When she left the room this morning, I followed her. She went to a house in Hampstead and picked up the car there."

"Do you have an address?" asked Ford.

"No, but if you take me there, I can probably find the place."

Graves shot Ford a disbelieving glance. "Go on," he said.

"After that I followed her to Storey's Gate. She stayed in the car for a while, and that confused me. But as soon as I saw the motorcade I knew. With Emma there aren't any maybes. That's why I was shouting at her. I didn't want her to go through with it."

"So it's your word that you didn't know anything about her plan to assassinate Igor Ivanov until you reached Storey's Gate?" Ford pressed.

"Of course I didn't know," said Jonathan more confidently, now that the truth was in the open.

"I think I've heard enough," said Graves, snorting as if he wasn't having any of it. "The Americans have never heard of your wife. We checked with Langley first thing. We wanted to give them a chance to 'fess up, as it were. You being an American. They denied it absolutely. Never heard of Emma Ransom. Don't know a thing about a plot to kill Ivanov. Shocked. Angered. Offered their help, and I believe them. They'd never even consider carrying out that kind of an attack on our soil. I've got contacts at the FBI, too. Your wife's name drew a blank again. The only vaguely truthful thing you've told us so far is that she was in Switzerland last February, but you want to know something? The British passport she was traveling on was a phony. And now you want me to believe that she worked for some secret spy shop you called . . ." Graves prompted Jonathan for the name.

"Division," said Jonathan.

"Division," repeated Graves, "that either is or isn't a part of the United States Department of Defense. And that she was some sort of operative traipsing around Europe and pulling jobs. I'm sorry, Dr. Ransom, but we have a word over here for that kind of story. Bollocks."

"Believe what you want," said Jonathan. "I'm sick of this."

Graves shook his head in disgust. "I don't know why I shouldn't throw you to the wolves."

Jonathan sat up, ignoring his pounding head. "Because I am not involved. Can you get that through your thick head?"

Graves stepped closer to the bed. "We put that shirt you were wearing through one of our fancy machines. It said that there was enough explosives residue on it to set off a dozen scanners. At some point in the past twenty-four hours you've been in direct contact with plastic explosives."

"That's impossible." But even as Jonathan said the words he knew that it **was** possible—that somehow it was Emma's doing.

Graves went on. "As it stands, you're an accomplice to murder and guilty of conspiracy to commit a terrorist act. You've admitted that it was your wife we saw on the tape. We have pictures of you at the scene moments before the attack. Add to that the explosives residue on your shirt and you won't last a morning at the Old Bailey. The only pity is that we don't execute scum like you anymore. We just let them rot in prison. Now tell us where we can find your wife."

"I can't."

"You can't or you won't?"

"I don't know any more than you."

Jonathan sank back onto the bed. It was over. He was going to jail for a very long time.

The policemen came back into the room an hour later. It was evident from the start that their demeanor had changed. Not the woman. She was as stiff and upright as ever. But Graves appeared more relaxed, determined as ever, but looser, as if he'd come upon a new and guaranteed way to make Jonathan talk.

"Listen closely," said the man from MI5. "I'm not saying I believe one word of what you told us. However, I made it a point to speak with a man you might know. Actually, he's an old friend of mine. Marcus von Daniken, from the Swiss Service of Analysis and Prevention. I see the name rings a bell. Anyhow, seeing as how he and I both do more or less the same job, I gave him a shout and asked if he knew anything about your wife. Told him she was involved in today's business and that I had you in custody. He might have let slip a few things that I'm fairly certain others wouldn't want to get out.

I'm not saying I know anything about an attack on an El Al jetliner or an organization called Division. For the record, I don't, and that will never change. But von Daniken did tell me one thing. Do you know what that is?"

Jonathan shook his head.

"He told me that you were a tenacious SOB. And that you moved hell and high water to discover what your wife was up to. Given those facts, and given some other complexities that we are not at liberty to reveal, I'm going to ask you to do something for us."

"What's that?"

Graves sat down on the edge of the bed and took his time crossing his arms and getting comfortable. "There's a reason that we're out here in the country at Hereford instead of downtown at Scotland Yard," he said. "Once you're named as a suspect, I can't come within a mile of you. A criminal act has taken place. Innocent people are dead. Someone has to pay, and you were involved. It's an enforcement matter, pure and simple. Even as we speak, my friends over at SO15 are baying for your blood. But I've talked to my boss, and he's talked to theirs, and all things considered, we've decided it's best that this part of the investigation remain under my purview a little longer. For now, there are to be no charges filed against you. Technically, you're a free man."

Jonathan stared into Graves's eyes. He was capable and smart and more than a little ruthless. Jonathan knew better than to trust him. "So what is it exactly that you want?"

"You're going to lead us to her," said Graves with a valedictory smile. "You're going to help us find your wife."

21

His name was Sergei Shvets and he was chairman of the Russian Federal Security Service, or FSB, the successor to the much vaunted and feared KGB. Seated in the copilot's seat of the Kamov helicopter, he watched with impatience as the calm waters of the Black Sea whisked below him. He was a sturdy man with dark, sunken eyes, a bulldog's jowls, and a spray of silver hair. He was fifty years old. In Russia, he looked his age. In Paris, New York, or London, people thought him sixty. Though it was cool inside the cockpit, beads of sweat dotted his forehead and upper lip.

"How much longer?" he asked the pilot.

"Five minutes."

"Good," said Shvets, checking his watch. For some meetings, it was wise not to arrive late.

Ahead, sprawled across a 150-kilometer crescent of shoreline, lay the city of Sochi, and behind it, rising out of a pink mist, the snowcapped spine of the Caucasus Mountains. Sochi had long been the chosen summer resort of Russia's Communist leaders. Like those leaders, the town was staid and orthodox, almost ashamed of its bourgeois subtropical climate.

In the past few years, however, the city had undergone a spate of development. The country's newly minted elite arrived in loud, bejeweled masses to revel in Sochi's abundant sunshine and outdoor cafés. Luxury villas had sprung up along the seafront, each more grandiose than the next. Roads meant for ZILs and Ladas were clogged with Mercedeses and Range Rovers. Sochi was christened Russia's Saint-Tropez.

But of late the president had given his countrymen a new reason to flock to Sochi. In 2014 the Black Sea resort would host the XXII Winter Olympic Games.

Shvets counted the number of cranes on the skyline and stopped at fourteen. It was the same number as the last time he had visited. As the helicopter swooped low over the city, he observed that several of the building sites appeared deserted, or in some cases abandoned altogether. Sochi, like the Rodina, lived and died according to the price of oil. He had little time to consider this. By then he'd spotted his destination and was pulling himself upright in his seat, wiping his brow, and tightening his necktie.

Bocharov Ruchei, the president's summer palace built in the 1950s, was situated on a wide swatch of lakefront several kilometers south of the city. The helicopter landed in a grass field adjacent to the palace's office wing. A waiting shuttle delivered Shvets to the rear of the president's quarters. As he walked toward the entrance, he noticed a shadow above him. He glanced up. Snipers from the Interior Ministry were positioned on every rooftop of the complex. The president was frightened. This was a new development.

Once inside, Shvets was led to an elevator and ushered two floors belowground to the president's shooting range. An aide offered him noise suppressors. Shvets placed them over his ears before passing through the glass doors that led into the range itself. Back to the wall, he watched the president fire round after round into the blackened silhouette of a United States Marine.

Finally the president turned and motioned for Shvets to approach. "Well?" asked the president.

"Ivanov is alive, but in intensive care. I have no word yet about his prognosis. Ambassador Orlov is dead, along with several of his staff. The police have no one in custody. Details are still sketchy, but it's clear that this was no homegrown operation. The attack required expert planning, execution, and intelligence."

The president struggled with the pistol's safety. He possessed none of his predecessor's facility with weapons, nor his love of violence. By nature he was weak but cunning. A weasel, with a weasel's razor-sharp teeth. He was also smart. He knew that Russia demanded its leader to be a strong man and he was determined not to disappoint.

"Orlov was a good man," he said. "I know his family. We will make sure he receives a state funeral."

He finally snapped the safety into place and gazed up at his visitor. "Did we not have any indication that something was in the air?"

"None," responded Shvets. "Given Ivanov's history, it's difficult to know the motive. If ever there was a man with an abundance of enemies, it is Igor Ivanovich."

"True, but I am certain this is not about Igor Ivanov."

"Oh?"

"If Ivanov's enemies wished to kill him, they could find a way to do it in Moscow with far less trouble." The president dropped the clip from his pistol, and Shvets saw that it was the antique 1911 Tokarev custom built for Czar Nicholas II, rumored to be the very weapon that had killed him and his family. Even from several steps away, he could see the jeweled Romanov eagle embedded in the pistol's pearl handle.

"No, this was not an attack on Ivanov," the president went on. "This was an attack on our country. An attempt to strike while we are weak."

Shvets thought of the abandoned worksites he'd viewed flying in, the buildings left half finished. He did not refute the comment. The country was in a lamentable condition, and everyone knew it.

For the past ten years the Russian economy had expanded at an average annual rate of 7 percent. Growth was due entirely to the exploitation of its vast natural resources: timber, gold, diamonds, natural gas, and most of all oil. Proven reserves stood at

80 billion barrels—seventh largest in the world—with experts certain that another 100 billion barrels remained to be discovered. Production had increased from 6 million barrels a day in 2001 to 10 million barrels a day in the past year. This increase, along with the stratospheric rise in oil prices over the same time, had resulted in a bonanza of cash. At its peak, Russia was earning well over $1 billion a day from oil exports alone, or over 65 percent of the country's gross domestic product.

Since then the price of oil had utterly collapsed, and it showed no signs of rebounding. The stock market had shed 80 percent of its value, and foreign direct investment had dried up entirely. Worse still, the ruble was down by half against the dollar in the past three months alone.

The country was in free fall.

"Do you know why I sent Igor Ivanovich to London?" the president asked.

Shvets admitted that he did not.

"I sent him to meet with a consortium of European petroleum companies in the hopes of winning back their confidence so that they might consider investing with us once again. In the past we were arrogant. We did not keep our promises to our business partners. Our demeanor was predatory. We wanted everything for ourselves. It's no wonder that they fled. I'll admit it was my fault, but what's done is done. It was Ivanov who showed me that I was wrong. Without help from the West, we will never be able to bring back oil production to its former level, let alone increase it. With my blessing, he extended an olive branch to the major petroleum producers. It was not a popular decision."

"Oh?"

"The men who run our domestic oil operations aren't anxious to cede even one ruble to others. They've grown fat and lazy. They've lost the ability to separate their own well-being from that of the motherland's."

Shvets knew them well.

Before moving into the private sector, all had spent their careers with the KGB. One had served an assignment as station chief in Mozambique. Another had been second secretary at the United Nations. A third had acted as a double agent nestled inside the Russian embassy in Madrid, pretending to be America's greatest source. And Shvets had headed Directorate S of the KGB, in charge of clandestine operations, everything from running covert agents abroad to conducting industrial espionage on Russia's behalf to planning and executing acts of terror on foreign soil.

They were a brotherhood of spies.

And as such, none was to be trusted.

Shvets knew why the president had posted snipers around his compound.

"Do you believe that one of them had something to do with the attack on Ivanov?" he asked.

"I said no such thing." But the president's sour

expression conveyed a different message. "Igor Ivanovich is a friend. He is also a patriot, which is more than I can say for the others. You will bring the state's fullest resources to tracking down and punishing his attackers."

The president hugged Shvets and kissed his cheeks three times, as was their custom. "And Sergei," he said, holding the spy at arm's length. "If, by God, they are Russian, I shall carry out the sentence myself."

22

In London, Interior Minister Igor Ivanov lay sleeping in his bed in the intensive care unit of St. Catharine's Hospital. One IV delivered a glucose drip to his arm. Another administered hourly doses of pentobarbital to keep him in an induced coma. A cuff monitored his blood pressure. Clamps on his fingers measured his blood oxygen. His face—or what was visible of it beneath his bandages—was colored a violent, multihued purple. Gashes on his forehead and cheek had required a total of ninety-nine stitches. He was not a handsome man to begin with. He would be less so upon his discharge, should he survive.

"Do you know who he is?" asked the nurse in charge, a soft-spoken brunette named Anna.

Dr. Andrew Howe, chief of neurology, finished entering the patient's vital signs on his chart. "Ivanov? Some sort of diplomat, isn't he?"

"He is a monster."

"Say again?" asked Howe, taken aback by the vitriol in the woman's voice.

"At home we call him the Black Devil."

Howe put down the chart and took a closer look at the nurse's name tag. Anna Bakareva.

"Where's home?"

"Grozny, Chechnya," she said. "I left many years ago, when I was eleven. But I remember Ivanov. He led the troops who sacked the city."

Howe was a former military man himself, a surgeon attached to the Royal Scots Guards, and he remembered hearing about the atrocities inflicted by the Russian army during their attack on the Chechen capital in the mid-1990s. It was a grim business.

The nurse had large black eyes that never left Ivanov. "His soldiers came to my neighborhood looking for one of the resistance leaders. When they could not find him, they rounded up all the men from my building and the buildings up and down the street and took them to the soccer stadium. They took old men, young men. It didn't matter. Seven hundred in all. They took my brother, too. He was ten years old." She stopped and pointed at Ivanov. "He personally shot every one of them."

"I'm sorry," said Howe.

"Will he live?" the nurse inquired in a tone inappropriate for a caregiver.

"Too soon to tell. Not much damage apart from the cuts and bruises. No broken bones. No internal bleeding. It's the brain I'm worried about. He got knocked around pretty well inside his car."

Howe knew a few things about cerebral trauma. A few years back, he'd done a tour in Basra, in southern Iraq. Improvised explosive devices, or IEDs, were the most frequent cause of injury. During his time he'd seen over two hundred cases similar to Ivanov. So soon after the initial trauma, it was impossible to make an accurate prognosis. Some patients regained full control of all their faculties. Others persisted in a vegetative state for weeks or months. Others never woke again at all. Most, though, fell in between, suffering some form of lasting impairment, anything from a faulty short-term memory, to loss of their sense of taste and smell, to more serious neurological disorders.

"His MRI came back negative," said Howe. "When the swelling goes down, we'll know more."

The nurse from Chechnya nodded. It was apparent that the news displeased her.

Howe left the room and walked directly to the aid station, where he made sure that Nurse Anna Bakareva would have nothing further to do with the care of Igor Ivanov, the Black Devil. He did not believe that she would do anything expressly to harm him. She might, however, forget to administer a painkiller or inadvertently dose him with the wrong medicine. It was not a risk he was prepared to take.

23

Hunched in the backseat of Colonel Charles Graves's Rover, Jonathan watched as the country lanes of Hereford gave way to two-lane roads and the rolling hillocks yielded to asphalt plains. Finally they gained the M4 motorway and made a beeline for London. A police escort led the way, lights flashing, siren muted. Another followed, practically riding their bumper. It was after six, but the fierce sun showed no signs of calming. Inside the car, the air conditioner blasted everyone with a torrent of humid, lukewarm air.

Technically Jonathan was a free man. Graves had said so, after all. But Jonathan had no illusions about the truth. He was a prisoner, and he would remain one until he brought them Emma's head. If he dared think otherwise, all it took was a look at the uniformed policemen seated on either side of him or the electronic bracelet clamped around his left ankle.

"It's a military model," Graves had pointed out as he'd fixed it to Jonathan's leg, purposefully notching it too tight. "We developed it for the bad boys in the tribal lands of Pakistan. Its signal can pinpoint you to within a meter of your position, no matter where you stand on God's green earth. And if you try to take it off, it'll snap your leg in two."

At that, Graves had chuckled, but his eyes left Jonathan wondering whether he was joking or not.

The interrogation had begun in the hospital and continued as he'd had his skull X-rayed for a possible fracture or concussion (none), while he'd changed back into his street clothes, and up to the present moment. Graves and Ford rode up front and took turns peppering him with questions. What time had he gone to the cocktail party? When did the fake Blackburn make contact? Had Jonathan ever seen him before? (And here Graves was quick to insist that meant as long as he'd been with Emma.) What route did Jonathan take from the Dorchester to the tube? What was the address of the flat he visited on Edgware Road? Did he see anyone else before Emma arrived? What kind of car did she use to drive him back to the hotel? And, most important, did Jonathan have any clue whom Emma might be working for?

Jonathan spat out the answers dutifully, but as the questions began to encroach on more private matters, he grew wary. Where did Emma grow up? Were her parents living? If so, where? And what about her schooling? Did she have friends in London? For these were matters that even he was unsure of.

Until five months earlier, he'd thought she'd been born and raised in Penzance, at the southwestern tip of England, and was a graduate of Brasenose College, Oxford. A richly embroidered childhood history fell in between, replete with loyal dogs, skinned elbows, deceased parents, and even a wayward older sister named Bea whom Jonathan had actually met on three occasions. All of which was a complete and utter fabrication. A Gobelin tapestry of falsehoods. A Potemkin life.

Emma hadn't been born in Penzance but in Hoboken, New Jersey. Her father was not a schoolteacher who had perished in a fiery car crash but a colonel in the United States Air Force who had dropped dead of a heart attack at fifty. Her impeccable English accent came from the eight years her father had been stationed at Lakenheath Air Base in Suffolk. As for college, she'd managed three years at Long Beach State in California, which was about as far away from Oxford as you could get, both literally and figuratively. Her real name wasn't even Emma, even though she'd decided to keep it because it was how Jonathan thought of her.

Still, he did his best to answer. He gave them what he knew, even if he knew it was incorrect.

But even as Jonathan complied, he was conducting his own private interrogation. He harbored no doubt about Emma's fate should he succeed in finding her. In short order, she would be questioned by MI5, turned over to Division (in the guise of the CIA, the DIA, or any other overt intelligence agency), questioned again, and then "disappeared." "Disappeared," meaning shot, hanged, or, as Graves had so eloquently put it earlier, "drawn and quartered and left for the crows." If Division had wanted Emma dead before, they'd be twice as firm in their intentions after the attempt on Igor Ivanov. There were only two sides in this game. If Emma wasn't working for them, she was working for the enemy.

Outside, the sights grew familiar as they reentered London. They drove past the Victoria and Albert Museum and Harrods before making the turn onto Park Lane.

Despite the lies that had gone before, the dissembling and the duplicity, Jonathan knew that he still loved Emma. They had had eight years together. He believed that for the most part the woman with whom he'd shared his life and his love had reciprocated his feelings. He had no proof. Just his heart. In the end, that's all there was anyway.

He looked at Graves, sitting so stiffly in the front seat. **The enemy,** Jonathan thought, with a viciousness that alarmed him.

He would not deliver her to the executioner.

On the other hand, Jonathan had no intention of spending the rest of his life inside a British jail. He would not play the martyr, either.

Not even for Emma.

At 6 p.m. sharp, the Rover pulled into the Dorchester's drive and stopped in front of the entrance. A plainclothes officer opened the door and stood by as Jonathan was ushered out. There were more police in the lobby, effectively lining his route to the elevator. Graves led the way, with Ford one step behind.

"Quite a welcoming committee," said Jonathan. "Where do you think I'm going to go?"

The elevator arrived. Graves took hold of his arm and guided him inside. "You'll go where we tell you," he said.

Outside his door, another plainclothes officer waited. Seeing Graves, he whispered a respectful "Sir."

Jonathan's suite was a hive of activity. It appeared as if a search of the room had been completed and everything was being put back as it had been. Graves dismissed the last officers and shut the door. Jonathan opened his wardrobe and noted that his clothes hung much more neatly than before. "Did you find anything?" he called over his shoulder.

"Take a shower and put on some clean clothes," barked Graves. "You've got ten minutes."

"Where are we going?"

"You'll find out in due time."

"I thought you wanted me to help you find Emma."

"Oh, you will. Now do as you're told."

Jonathan walked into the bathroom, closed the door behind him, and turned on the shower. Steam began to fill the room. He took off his shirt, then gazed down at the bracelet on his ankle. He opened the door to Graves and Ford standing a few feet away, engaged in a heated discussion.

"Now what?" asked Graves, looking his way.

Jonathan pointed to the bracelet. "Is this thing waterproof?"

Graves shook his head, then approached. "I should make you shower with one foot out the door." He fiddled in his pocket for a key, then, kneeling, unlocked the bracelet. "I hear if you keep it on long enough the epidermis begins to fuse with the steel. The docs have to cut it away from the leg. You know anything about that?"

"I don't."

Graves stood, bracelet in one hand. "This is the last time it comes off until we bring your wife into custody. Are we clear?"

"Thank you." Jonathan began to close the door, but stopped halfway. "Colonel Graves, just what makes you so sure Emma's still in England?"

Graves looked at Ford, then back at Jonathan. "All in due time, Dr. Ransom. Now get cleaned up."

24

"Emma Ransom is our prime suspect in Lord Robert Russell's murder," said Kate Ford. "We have evidence that she was at the scene of the crime. No other person could have gained access to his apartment. This case belongs to homicide."

"It's a counterterror matter now, DCI Ford," replied Graves. "Foreign nationals have been killed, including several high-ranking diplomats. The Russians are screaming their bloody heads off for us to take action. Igor Ivanov is a prime contender for the presidency in two years' time. If he dies, it will sour relations between our countries for years to come. This isn't a simple murder. It's a national incident."

"Be that as it may, homicide needs to stay involved."

"Out of the question. If you don't like it, take it up with the PM. The Cabinet Office Briefing Rooms are sitting right now. Because the bomb went off so close to Whitehall, they're trying to decide if it was an attack against government or simply a one-off to take out Ivanov. The home secretary is considering asking for an evacuation of all government offices in Westminster. It's far beyond homicide."

"I brought this case to you," said Kate, slowly and clearly. "I have every right to stay involved."

"As I recall, I contacted you. It was me was standing in your kitchen this morning."

"Because of the work my team had accomplished. You knew I was onto something and you wanted my help."

"I'd say things have changed considerably in the past twelve hours."

"But Jonathan Ransom can't help you. Can't you see that he was telling the truth?"

"Actually, I can't. All the plastic explosives residue we found on his clothing must be blinding me. After Ransom gets cleaned up, we're going to make a tour of the spots where he claimed to have met his wife. If he isn't more forthcoming, I'm taking him back to Hereford to have a full and frank exchange of views with some of the lads from the regiment."

"You're going to beat it out of him? That will get you precisely nowhere."

"We would never touch him, and you know it. But we might do our best to scare him." Graves peeled back the window sheers. "You see, DCI Ford, I think our doctor is lying," he said, gazing out over Hyde Park. "I'm convinced that he knows precisely where his wife has run to. I've got this theory: the reason Ransom was running toward his wife wasn't to stop her from blowing the bomb. It was to make her blow it more quickly."

"What do you mean?"

"Ivanov was in the first Mercedes, not the third. Ransom saw him as he passed by and was trying to warn his wife to blow the device earlier."

"The windows on those cars were dark as night," retorted Kate. "No one could see through them. Ransom couldn't have known who was in what car."

Graves turned, his arms crossed. "I think we're finished here."

But Kate stood her ground. "It's the murder angle that will get you to Emma Ransom before Ransom and all of your intelligence snooping."

"Will it?" Graves spoke over her shoulder as he walked to the door.

"We must find the woman who sent Russell the video transmission. It was her source that tipped off Russell about Victoria Street. That means her information came from within the organization that was planning the attack. I'd wager somewhere close to the top. It's all that nonsense about TINs, trusted information networks. If we can find out where she got the tip, we'll know who gave Emma Ransom her marching orders. The woman holds the key to this."

"But we'll never find her. The odds of tracing the message back to its source are nil. I'm sticking with Ransom. You know the saying, 'A Yank in the hand . . .' " Graves paused, his fingers curled around the doorknob. "In the meantime, you're free to pursue the case as you wish, but it will be independent of my office. We run Jonathan Ransom ourselves." He opened the door to the hall. Two plainclothes officers ducked their heads around the corner. Graves waved the all-clear.

"What about Reg Cleak?" asked Kate.

"Who?" Suddenly Graves remembered, and his face hardened. "Oh yes, I'm sorry about your partner."

"When I leave here, I am going to his home. I plan on telling his wife that I'm personally assuming responsibility for finding the individuals and the organization or government responsible for his death. It would help my investigation immeasurably if I could add Five's resources to my own."

"Goodnight, DCI Ford."

"For Reg's sake," argued Kate.

Graves moved his face closer to her, so that she could see the brown flecks in his blue eyes, and the conviction behind them. "This is the black world, DCI Ford. We don't do favors."

25

Jonathan stayed in the shower until Graves threw open the door and told him to get the hell out. The intelligence officer stood a body's length away, watching Jonathan dress, murmuring "Hurry it up" and tossing the monitoring bracelet from one hand to the other. Jonathan took his time, resisting the proffered underwear and pants until he was good and ready. He shaved and combed his hair, then left the bathroom to find a clean shirt.

But all the while he was sending himself the same message. Emma wasn't finished. The bombing was just another step along the way. It didn't matter whom she was working for, or why, or whether their objectives were justified. He knew, and that was enough. Her acts of crime had become his. In the eyes of the law and his own, he was Emma's lifelong accomplice. There was only one way to clear his name. He must stop her. He must find Emma before the authorities did.

It was then that he noticed that the suite was empty but for the two of them.

"Where's Detective Ford?" Jonathan asked, unsettled by the silence and isolation.

"Detective Chief Inspector Ford was called away."

"So I can get changed out here?"

"And about time," muttered Graves. "Get a shirt and a jacket. Come on, then."

"Will I be coming back?"

"That depends on you."

Jonathan looked at Graves, at the bulge under his left arm that was undoubtedly a pistol, at the electronic bracelet clutched in his hand. He noticed for the first time that Graves was actually smaller than he, and thinner without the armor of his suit. His hands were slim and manicured, almost ladylike. He also noticed the dark circles under his eyes and the slackening of his earlier ramrod posture. It was a look Jonathan recognized all too well. He'd seen it countless times glancing in the mirror after a day and a night in surgery. Graves was exhausted.

Jonathan went about his business with a newfound alacrity. It was just the two of them. Outside there were more. There'd been two on the door when he'd entered. No doubt there were a half-dozen posted downstairs, too. There would be more joining the group wherever he might travel. But for now . . . for these next few minutes, there were just the two of them.

Jonathan grabbed a button-down from the closet and put it on. He took a windbreaker, too, and threw it over the back of a chair. It was still warm outside, but he wasn't thinking about now. He was thinking about six hours from now, or twelve, or, if there was any luck remaining on his side of the ledger, longer. He snatched his wallet off the dresser and slipped it into his back pocket, then grabbed a pair of socks out of the drawer.

Graves was pacing like a guard dog, cell phone to his ear. "And what did the ERT find in Hampstead? Nothing? Impossible! My man said the car was parked there. Saw it with his very eyes. Check again. There's got to be some residue inside the garage. Any cameras on the street? Then ask the neighbors—**someone** had to see them going in and out of the house. The owners were on vacation. In Immingham? No one takes a vacation in Immingham."

He snapped the phone closed and glared at Jonathan. "Seems to be a hole in your story, Doc. Problem with that residence north of town where you claim to have seen your wife grab the car. I'm wondering whether I should deliver you forthwith to the Inquisition or if I should follow my hallowed rule book and offer you a second chance to come to Jesus."

But for all Graves's urgency, Jonathan affected not to notice. He stood with his back to Graves, head bent, groaning.

"Did you hear me?" said Graves.

Still Jonathan didn't answer. Like a blind man, he reached out a hand and probed until he found a chair, then felt his way to sitting down in it.

"What is it, then?" asked Graves, more with irritation than with curiosity.

"There's a problem," said Jonathan, sotto voce.

"You're right about that," said Graves, hovering nearby. "Your story isn't checking out. And we're going to clarify it right now."

"I mean with my head. It's killing me."

"Hell do you mean?"

"Something's wrong. I don't know what it is. I've got a terrible headache." He gasped. "I'm having trouble with my sight. Could be dehydration or a concussion."

"You'll see fine soon as we get you some fresh air. Drink some water and you'll be good as new." Graves knelt at his feet and fumbled with the monitoring bracelet. "Give me your leg. Either one. Your choice."

Jonathan moaned and extended his left leg. Graves slipped the metal cuff over his ankle and snapped it closed. He gave it a tug to make sure, then leaned back on his haunches. "There, now. Open your eyes. Can you see me all right?" He lifted his chin to look Jonathan straight in the eye.

And that was when Jonathan kicked him.

He kicked hard with his right foot, striking Graves's jaw precisely where he'd aimed, an inch or so below the ear, where the mandible met the skull. Graves tumbled onto his back, stunned. Before he could react, Jonathan fell onto his chest, a forearm pinning his neck to the carpet, the fingers of his right hand pressing against Graves's carotid, stanching the flow of blood to the brain. Graves thrashed. He threw a wild punch that glanced off Jonathan's cheek. And then, like that, he was out. His eyes rolled back into his head. He expelled a breath of air and his body went limp.

Six seconds had passed.

Jonathan kept the artery blocked until he was certain that Graves was unconscious, then climbed to his feet. A mirror hung on the wall, and he found himself staring at a wild-eyed man fighting for breath. **There's no other way,** he told himself.

Kneeling once more, he dug inside Graves's jacket for the key to the ankle bracelet. He found it and unlocked the cuff. Then he removed Graves's wallet and his phone. His hand brushed against the butt of Graves's pistol, but he decided against taking it. A criminal takes a gun. An innocent man leaves it. Standing, he hurried to the door. A peek through the spy hole showed not one but two plainclothes officers standing to either side of it.

Just then Graves's phone rang. Jonathan dashed into the bathroom and closed the door. The name on the screen read Director General Allam. He took it to mean the director of MI5. Yanking a towel off the rack, he stuffed the phone into its folds. Four interminable rings later, it went silent. He ran back to the door, but the guards had not budged. Graves still lay immobile. He would remain unconscious anywhere from three to ten minutes. There was nothing Jonathan could do to lengthen the period, save suffocate him. He disliked Graves enough to carefully consider the idea.

Jonathan crossed the room and opened the sliding doors that gave onto the balcony. He went to the railing and leaned his head over. He stood eight stories aboveground, approximately 60 meters above the hotel's main entrance. Each balcony was protected by an awning. The one below was at most a meter beneath his terrace. Technically, it was not a difficult descent. He was an experienced alpinist. He'd downclimbed sheer faces offering holds the width of a table knife more times than he could remember. He reminded himself that he'd also had a rope and harness securing him in one form or another to the rock and that on any number of occasions he'd slipped. This time there was no margin for error.

Dusk was falling. The sky had tempered to a tame violet. Traffic on Park Lane was a dense, slow-moving braid. Below in the courtyard, a steady stream of taxis and automobiles passed beneath the porte cochere. There were too many heads milling about to count. **Just don't look up,** he ordered them.

He slipped on the windbreaker and stuffed Graves's wallet and phone into the pockets. As an afterthought, he raised Graves's pants leg and cuffed the electronic bracelet around his ankle. The key went down the toilet. Then Jonathan returned to the balcony and deftly climbed over the railing.

He knelt.

He grasped the terrace with his fingertips.

He lowered one leg until it touched the top of the awning.

Then his actions grew fleet and agile. Freeing one hand, he reached down to locate the steel rods that constituted the awning's support. Stretching, he slipped his fingers beneath the flap and wrapped them around the bar that formed the awning's horizontal support. Then, as quickly as he could, he freed the other hand and did the same. All ten fingers now clutched the bar. At that instant, he kicked his legs free and swung out and down. The awning groaned, but held. He landed his feet on the narrow railing of the seventh-floor balcony.

He gazed into the window. No one was there. Drawing a breath, he lowered himself to the terrace and repeated the motions until he reached the sixth floor. Sweat burned his eyes and creased his palms. It wasn't the heat so much or the exertion, but the mental stamina required to guard against the smallest mistake. He felt no anxiety, nothing that he could label as fear. The world had shrunk to the 2 meters above him and the 2 meters below.

Stretch. Grip. Drop your legs. Land just there. Breathe.

Jonathan's every energy focused itself on the calculus of coordinating mind and body to hoodwink gravity. As he gained confidence, he moved more rapidly. He made it to the fifth floor, then the fourth, and then he was standing on the pebble-strewn roof of the porte cochere. Four minutes had passed. He ran to the side of the rooftop, bounded the waist-high rail, lowered himself off the edge, and dropped to the ground.

He landed next to one of the frock-coated doormen, who jumped in surprise. Flushed, Jonathan patted him on the shoulder. "I'm a hotel guest. Can you get me a taxi?"

"Certainly, sir. Where to?"

"Heathrow."

A two-pound coin secured the bargain. The doorman blew his whistle and waved up the next taxi in line.

"Heathrow, sir?" asked the driver.

"I've changed my mind," said Jonathan. He chose the busiest place in London at this time of night. "Piccadilly Circus. Take me to the bottom of Shaftesbury Avenue."

"Right-o." The taxi peeled out of the drive and turned down Park Lane. They'd gone half a mile when Graves's phone rang. This time Jonathan answered. "Yes?" he said.

"Ransom," said Graves softly, "you've made a serious mistake."

"Maybe."

"I'll give you one chance. Come back this second and our deal's still on. Help us find your wife and you'll go free. Otherwise, all bets are off."

"How is that a deal? I wasn't involved in the bombing. What you're talking about is blackmail."

"Call it what you like. It is what it has to be."

"You said you heard about Division. Then you know what I said about her is true."

"I heard a rumor. It doesn't change a thing."

"Who told you? Was it someone named Connor? Frank Connor?"

"I can't reveal that."

"If you want my help, you'd better."

Graves pounced on the invitation. "So you do know where she is?"

"I didn't say that."

A pause. "And I already told you. It was my oppo at the FBI. Sorry, no names, but it wasn't Connor. What exactly did your wife do?"

"Division used to be headed by Major General John Austen. You might have read about him. The American general killed in a car crash in Switzerland last February."

"I recall something about that. Not just Austen, but several officials with him. There was some hint that it might have been a terrorist plot."

"It wasn't any plot and it wasn't a crash. Austen wanted to bring down an El Al jet to fire up tensions in the Middle East. Emma stopped him."

"You mean she killed him."

"I mean she saved five hundred lives." Jonathan didn't elaborate. It had been his finger on the trigger that had ended Austen's life. "Her actions prevented a war, but no one cares about that now. All they care about is the fact that Emma disobeyed orders. That she broke ranks. Nobody in Washington wants to congratulate her. They want to kill her."

"That's absurd."

"Is it?"

For once, Graves was silent.

"What my wife did today was terrible. I can't make an excuse for her, except to say that we both know she's acting on someone else's orders. But I'm sorry, Colonel Graves, I'm not going to help you find her."

"What can I do to entice you? Money—is that what you want?"

"Nothing . . ." Jonathan bit back his words. Graves had to know he wouldn't betray his wife for money. The offer was as ridiculous as it was insulting. Graves was trying to distract him, to keep him on the line.

Jonathan glanced out the rear window. One hundred meters back, he caught sight of a police car. As he entered Piccadilly Circus he saw another, this one approaching from Regent Street, lights flashing, but no siren. Suddenly its strobes died. In Jonathan's anxious state, he was certain that the policeman had been told not to draw attention to himself. And if there were two so far, there had to be more on the way. It was Graves's phone. Jonathan had forgotten that MI5 would be able to track it just as easily as his ankle bracelet. He had set his own trap.

He slapped his palm over the phone. "Pull over here," he ordered the cabbie.

"I thought you wanted to go to Shaftesbury Avenue."

"Right here!"

"You still there, Ransom?" asked Graves in his silky voice.

"Goodbye, Colonel."

"You're a dead man."

"Not yet."

Piccadilly Circus at 8 p.m. on a warm summer's evening was as crowded as Times Square on New Year's Eve. Giant neon signs clung to the surrounding buildings, bathing the street in a glowing iridescent light. Jonathan paid the cabbie and stepped onto the sidewalk. The fast-moving crowd engulfed him instantly. He moved with the throng, crossing at Coventry Street and heading north, all the while watching the two police cars converging on the congested square. At that moment another police car drew up alongside him. Its window was down and he could hear the hiss and crackle of its radio and a voice blaring orders. "Suspect has left the cab and is on foot. Set up emergency blocks at Coventry, Piccadilly, and Shaftesbury. All available officers to Piccadilly Circus. Subject is a white male, thirty-eight years of age, six foot tall, graying hair, last reported wearing a white shirt, jeans . . ."

Jonathan didn't wait to hear any more. He slunk into the crowd, turned, and walked in the opposite direction. He ducked into the first store he came to, a tourist emporium selling everything from T-shirts to Princess Di bobbing heads. Racks of clothing filled the store. He selected a black T-shirt and a **Les**

Mis baseball cap. He paid and immediately put on both the shirt and the cap. There was nothing to be done about his blue jeans.

In the short time he'd spent in the store, the police had moved in en masse. Roadblocks were in the course of being set up at all arteries emptying into Piccadilly Circus. A van had appeared at Regent Street and was disgorging uniformed officers. Horns blared. Traffic ground to a halt.

Back on the sidewalk, Jonathan kept close to buildings, attaching himself to knots of pedestrians. He slipped from group to group, searching for an escape route. As if taking its cue from the stationary automobiles, the pedestrian traffic slowed. An anxious mood stirred the crowd.

Jonathan spotted a pair of policemen, fluorescent orange bibs on their chests, coming toward him, their eyes searching every face they passed. He looked over his shoulder and counted no less than four peaked caps. Not knowing what else to do, he stopped where he was and turned his attention to the nearest store window. It belonged to a currency exchange firm. The teller was open for business. A line extended from the customer window. He stood at the back, hands in his pockets, eyes to the fore. He imagined the policemen coming closer and felt the hairs on his neck stand on end.

A slight older man stood in front of him, counting coins from a change purse. Jonathan took a step forward, bumping into him forcefully, causing him to drop his change. Coins tinkled onto the pavement.

"I'm sorry," said Jonathan as he crouched down to help the elderly man pick up his change. "That was clumsy of me. Let me help you."

"Thank you," mumbled the man in accented English.

Jonathan trained his eyes on the pavement as he picked up the stray pound coins. From the corner of his eye, he observed two pairs of polished black boots stride past. When the policemen had gone, he stood and handed the man his change. "Did we find it all?"

The man counted his coins and nodded.

The line moved forward. Jonathan stepped to the window and exchanged one hundred dollars for pounds. After completing his transaction, he continued down the street, hugging the buildings.

A few feet ahead he spotted the sign for the Underground. He descended the steps into the station. If anything, it was more congested than the street. The depot spanned the width of the intersection above them. Two officers scouted the turnstiles, searching for the six-foot male in white shirt and jeans, with graying hair. He bought a ticket, then timed his passage until the policemen were busy on the far side of the station.

He passed through the turnstile and made a beeline for the nearest tunnel. Bakerloo Line north. It was the same train he'd taken the night before. As he progressed through the tiled passageways, the foot traffic grew sparse. Suddenly he was alone, with only the echo of his heels for company. He descended a last flight of stairs to the platform. The train arrived ninety seconds later.

Five minutes after that, Jonathan got off at Marylebone station.

He was a free man.

26

Twenty-five Notting Hill Lane was an Edwardian two-story town home painted robin's-egg blue, with dormer windows upstairs and a black lacquered front door replete with a brass knocker. It was nine-thirty, and night had fallen as Jonathan climbed the short flight of stairs and struck the heavy ball three times. Almost immediately the door opened, causing Jonathan to start.

"Hello," said a little girl with black hair done in pigtails.

"Is your daddy home?"

"Jenny, whatever are you doing? You're supposed to be upstairs in bed." A plain, dark-haired woman in sweatpants and a cardigan sweater hurried to the door. Jonathan recognized Prudence Meadows from the cocktail party the evening before. "Hello," he said. "Is Jamie here?"

"Oh, hello, Jonathan. No, Jamie's not back from hospital yet. Would you like to come in?"

"Do you expect him soon?"

"Any minute. Do come in. You can wait in the living room until he gets home."

Jonathan stepped inside and Prudence Meadows

shut the door behind him. She asked him to wait a moment while she tucked her daughter back into bed, and disappeared up the stairs. Jonathan walked across the foyer, ducking his head around the corner and looking at the living room. Pictures of Meadows and his family decorated a side table. There was a leather couch and an ottoman with a hand-knitted blanket thrown across it. Toys and stuffed animals littered the floor.

"Can I get you something?" asked Prudence Meadows as she came down the stairs. "Coffee? Tea? Something stronger, perhaps?"

"Some water, maybe. Thanks."

She passed by him, slowing as she caught sight of his face. "What happened to you? You're all scratched up."

"I was in an accident today."

Prudence Meadows stood on her tiptoes, touching her hand to his cheek as if she were an admitting nurse. "Goodness. Are you all right?"

"Just a little shaken."

"Was that why you missed your speech? Jamie called from the hotel and said the place was in an absolute uproar. He wanted to contact you, but he didn't have your number."

"Something like that. It's complicated." Jonathan followed her into the kitchen and took a seat at the counter. Prudence handed him a glass of water and he drank it down. Without asking, she prepared a plate of biscuits and fresh fruit and set it before him.

A snifter of brandy came a minute later. "Thought you might need something with a little bite to it," she said. "You look rather done in."

"You could say that." Jonathan took a sip of the strong liqueur, letting it relax him. "You have a nice home," he said.

Prudence smiled. "And you? Jamie said you had a wife but hadn't settled down in any one place."

"The job keeps us moving from place to place. There's no time to put down roots."

"Must be exciting," she said. "All those foreign locales."

"Sometimes."

"No children?"

"Not yet." Jonathan checked the clock. It was nearing ten. He finished the brandy and stood. "I should be going. It's late."

"Don't be silly. Jamie would positively kill me if he found out that I'd let you leave without seeing him. Have some more brandy while I give him a call and find out where he is." She refilled his glass, and with a smile walked out of the room.

Jonathan made a circuit of the kitchen. There were kids' drawings on the fridge and an agenda spread open. From afar he could hear Prudence speaking with her husband. Glancing down, he flipped a page back, then another. A severe black line inked across the page caught his eye. The day before, a dinner engagement with a "Chris and Serena" had been crossed out. In its place were the words "Dorchester, 6 p.m. Cancel 4 p.m. surgery."

"He's on his way," called Prudence. "Should be pulling into the drive any minute. In fact, I think I hear him."

From the back door came the sound of an automobile. The engine cut and a door slammed. A few moments later, Jamie Meadows stepped inside. "Jesus, man, look at you. What the hell happened?"

"Can we talk?" said Jonathan.

Meadows kissed his wife. "We'll be upstairs in the study, Pru. Be a dear and bring me a little something. Ham sandwich would be nice. Lots of mustard. The hot stuff."

Meadows led Jonathan to a cozy wood-paneled study on the second floor and pointed to a high-backed captain's chair. "Sit," he commanded. "Speak."

With a sigh, Jonathan sat. "I need a place to stay."

"Thought you were at the Dorchester."

"I am. I mean, I **was.** I checked out."

"You're serious? And you want to stay here? Don't get me wrong, you're welcome. Stay as long as you like. It's just that I don't think a trundle bed in the kids' room is an even trade."

"Something's come up."

Meadows refilled Jonathan's glass. Setting down the decanter, he pointed to the cuts on Jonathan's face. "You look like you were in a fist fight and you lost."

"It's a long story."

"Out with it. It's me, Jamie. I've got enough skeletons for two closets." He offered a sneaky grin as consolation. "Not a woman, is it? I know some of you aid docs. You've got a warm gal stashed in every port."

"Not exactly."

"It's not Emma, is it? You're not hiding from your wife?"

"I'm hiding, but it's not from Emma. It's from the police."

"Stop having me on. What's up?"

Jonathan leveled his gaze at his friend. "I'm not kidding."

Meadows's face dropped like a stone. "For real? The police?"

"You heard about the car bomb today?"

"Bloody savages," said Meadows. "London's not safe to walk in any longer."

"I was there. That's where I got these cuts. Flying glass. Debris. In fact, you could say I was part of it."

"You're joking." But there was no mirth in Meadows's voice.

"I wish I were."

"What were you doing there?" asked Meadows. "I mean, why . . . how?"

"I can't tell you. Believe me, you don't want to know. It wouldn't be safe."

"Safe? You're on the run from the police and you come to my house where my children are asleep. Don't tell me about safe. If you're dragging me into something, I want to know what it's about."

"I can't. It's not just about hiding from the police, either. There's more to it than that." Jonathan stood and made to leave. "I'm sorry I came. I see now that I shouldn't have. I wasn't thinking."

Meadows lumbered to his feet. "Wait just a second. You haven't been arrested, have you?"

"No," said Jonathan. "Not officially."

"You didn't set off that bomb, did you?"

"Of course not."

"I'm not harboring a bloody serial killer?"

Jonathan couldn't stop from smiling. "No. You're good there."

"All right, then. Offer holds. You can stay as long as you like. But I'll have to tell Pru. Not all, mind, but at least some of it. You can have Frannie's room. Don't mind sprites and unicorns, do you? She's going through the fairy stage. Bed might be a tad short, but at least it's soft."

"The couch downstairs is fine," said Jonathan, standing.

"Wouldn't hear of it. Can't have the best surgeon I've ever known busting his back on that monstrous contraption. We've got to take good care of those magic hands. Keep them in good stead until they can save some more lives."

"Thank you, Jamie. I can't tell you what this means to me."

"But what are you going to do?" asked Meadows.

"Right now? I'm going to sleep."

"I mean tomorrow or the next day. You can't run forever."

"You're right about that."

"Then what?"

Jonathan threw a hand on Jamie's meaty shoulder and gave a pat.

Magic hands.

The words hit him like a hammer. Emma had used the same words to describe his surgical skills last night.

It had to be a coincidence, he thought, looking into Meadows's eyes. Surely it was a common enough expression. But no amount of mental cajoling, no calls on camaraderie or loyalty could fool him. A surgeon might have gifted hands or supple hands or healing hands, but "magic hands"? He'd never heard the expression before.

Jonathan stared harder at Meadows. Now that he thought of it, the mention of his magic hands wasn't the only coincidence. Jamie's first posting with the National Health Service had been in Cornwall. Emma's cover story had her growing up in Penzance, also in Cornwall. Jamie had been up at Oxford. Emma claimed to have graduated from there, as well.

And what about the agenda downstairs? Prudence Meadows had said in no uncertain terms that they had been planning to go to the medical conference. Yet according to the agenda, they'd had a dinner engagement with Chris and Serena scheduled. An engagement obviously canceled at the last moment.

There is no such thing as coincidence. It was practically Emma's mantra.

"This way to Fairyland," said Meadows. "Come, good Oberon."

Jonathan followed him into the bedroom. After saying goodnight, he waited a few minutes, then crept into the hallway. The corridor was dark and silent. Meadows had gone back downstairs. His voice could be heard talking urgently on the phone in the kitchen. No doubt he was calling Division, letting them know he had Emma Ransom's husband in captivity and asking for instructions.

Jonathan padded into Meadows's study. By the light of the desk lamp, he searched for a weapon. His eyes landed on a letter opener. It was long and sharp, with a carved ivory handle. More of a dagger than an office tool. He picked it up.

Silently he descended the stairs.

Meadows was sitting at the kitchen table. He looked up abruptly. "You scared me."

Jonathan approached cautiously, the letter opener pressed against his leg. "Who were you talking to?"

Meadows tried on a smile. "Oh, that . . . nobody."

"Who, Jamie?"

"My nurse. Have a special case in the morning. I'd just remembered that we needed some extra meds."

"You said I had magic hands."

Meadows considered this, confused. "Did I?"

"Emma used the same expression when I saw her yesterday. I was wondering how it came up between the two of you."

Meadows peered at Jonathan, mystified. "The two of us? Me and Emma? It didn't. I've never met your wife."

"I just thought it was an odd coincidence. I mean, I've never heard it put that way before, and then here you are talking on the phone about me. It was about me, wasn't it, Jamie?"

"Of course it wasn't. I told you, it was my nurse."

Jonathan went on. "What time is it in Washington, anyway? Let's see . . . it must be just about five in the afternoon. All the staff still at their desks? Emma said Division works twenty-four/seven. Lights always on."

Meadows was shaking his head. "I wasn't talking to D.C. I was talking to my office."

"At eleven o'clock?" Jonathan registered his disapproval. "I'd grade your story as weak, Jamie. Not up to Division standards."

Meadows smiled uncomfortably. "What the hell is this 'Division' you keep talking about?"

"You tell me. After all, you've been there long enough. I am curious: did they bring you in before Oxford or after? Did you point Emma in my direction? That's one thing I've always wondered about."

"Would you stop this nonsense? Actually, Jonathan, you're frightening me."

"What did they want you to do? Keep me here until they show up? Kill me or just follow me?"

"Kill you?" Meadows's eyes widened. "I think you'd better leave. You were right. It isn't safe."

"You worked in Cornwall," said Jonathan.

"At Duchy Hospital. So what?"

"That's near Penzance, where Emma said she was

from. At Oxford, you were at Brasenose before medical school. So was Emma. And then there's the matter of the couch."

"The couch?"

"I guess that's just good tradecraft. You couldn't let me sleep there. It's too near the front door. I could up and go without your knowing it. You needed me upstairs, where you could keep an eye on me until your friends come."

A sheen of sweat had popped out on Meadows's forehead. "Friends? What friends? Jesus, Jonathan, get a grip! It's me, Jamie, you're talking to."

But Jonathan wasn't listening. He knew about Emma's training. It was all about cover. He glanced toward the front door. "Are they coming now?"

It was then that Meadows discovered the letter opener. "Don't do it," he said, his voice rising. "Whatever it is you have in mind. Don't. I'm not with Division. I've never met Emma. Swear on my children's lives. Whole magic hands thing—coincidence. Something I must have heard somewhere. Pure chance." He was rising from his chair, hands in front of his body. The sweat was coming now, gathering in his bushy eyebrows and sliding down his pink cheeks. "Pru!" Meadows began to call, but Jonathan was around the table and on him before he could get the name out. He clamped a hand over Meadows's mouth and pressed the tip of the letter opener against his neck. "Quiet," he said.

Meadows nodded furiously.

Jonathan lowered the blade, then removed his hand from Meadows's mouth. "I need some money."

"In my wallet. It's on the counter by the key basket. Take whatever's there. Should be several hundred quid. Take the ATM card, too. PIN's one-one-one-one. Please, no lectures. It's too easy, I know already. You can have my car, too. It's a Jag. Fast as all hell. I won't call the police. Not right away, anyway. I mean, later I'll have to. Insurance and all that. The thing cost a fortune."

Jonathan found the wallet and counted the bills. The total came to five hundred and seventy pounds. He snatched the car keys. "The one out back?"

Meadows nodded. "You didn't have to do this, you know. You could have just asked."

"Maybe, but then . . ." Jonathan caught himself. There was something in Jamie's eyes that wasn't right. The man was genuinely frightened. Jonathan knew with a sudden and complete confidence that it wasn't an act. "You're not with Division, are you?"

Jamie Meadows shook his head.

"You don't know Emma?"

"Never had the pleasure."

Jonathan sighed. Suddenly he felt very tired. "Will you wait until tomorrow to call the police about the car?"

Meadows waved off the question. "I'll wait a week."

"I'll pay you back for the cash."

"Whenever. Take your time."

Jonathan nodded, turning toward the back door. He advanced one step, then stopped. There remained a last, nagging issue. "What about the conference? Why did you tell me that you'd been planning on going for so long?"

"It was my idea," said Prudence Meadows, from across the room. "Couldn't have you thinking we'd only just learned you were in town. You'd have become suspicious."

She stood at the base of the stairs. She was wearing silk pajamas, and in her right hand she held a pistol.

27

"Pru, what the hell are you doing?" asked Jamie Meadows.

"Shhh, darling. We don't want to wake the children." She was screwing a fire suppressor onto the snout of the pistol. Finished, she held it at arm's length, pointed squarely at Jonathan's chest. "It was me Jamie heard. I was the one who commented on your magic hands. It was something Emma told me years ago. She never did stop bragging about you."

"What are you talking about?" Meadows continued, if anything louder than before. "What the hell is that you're holding?"

"Jonathan, do you want to tell him? Might as well, since you've seen fit to tell him so much besides."

"Your wife works for Division," said Jonathan, never taking his eyes from Prudence Meadows. "They're trying to find Emma and kill her."

"Nonsense," protested Meadows, as if he weren't staring at his wife six meters away, brandishing a semiautomatic pistol. "Pru? Tell him. It's all a mixup. What is this Division you're talking about, anyway?"

"It's an intelligence shop run by the Americans,"

said Prudence. "We have MI6. They have the CIA. Division's just smaller and a bit more secret."

"I don't get it," said Meadows.

"She works for the same organization that Emma did," said Jonathan. "They undertake covert operations around the world to advance American security concerns. Mostly they kill people."

"Couldn't have said it better myself," remarked Prudence, advancing a step. She looked at her husband. "I might add that we only kill people who need to be killed."

"I've never seen you before, have I?" asked Jonathan.

"I'm a desk girl. I run things in our London office. Or used to, I should say. After Emma's stunt, they practically shut us down. Moved things to Lambeth. **Lambeth!** But no, we haven't seen each other before. We can't all be like your wife. Just as well. I'm a bum for languages. I've got my English accent. That's good enough."

"Your English accent?" said Jamie, perplexed. "You're from Shropshire. Of course you have your English accent."

"Don't count on it," said Jonathan.

Pru glanced at her watch, then went on. "Someone spotted you entering the country yesterday morning. The boss called and offered me full reinstatement if I could bring you in. Even a pay raise. We're all very anxious to find your wife."

"You've got it all wrong, Pru. He just wants to get

out of England," argued Meadows, on Jonathan's behalf. "Go ahead, tell her. The police want him, but it's a mistake."

"Be quiet, Jamie," said Jonathan. "I need to speak to your wife."

"Did you meet her?" asked Prudence Meadows. "Is that where you went last night when you skipped out of the cocktail party?"

Jonathan didn't answer. He saw Prudence check her watch again and guessed that others were on their way. It was imperative he leave as quickly as possible.

"So what did you have planned next?" Pru went on. "Hooking up with Emma down the road somewhere? It won't be easy with every intelligence agency and cop shop on your tail. I don't think a one-way ticket out of here is going to help much. It's time to come in. Message to Jonathan: Division wants to help."

"Is that what they told you to say?"

"Frank Connor's word. You can ask him yourself. He should be here any minute."

She closed the distance between them, moving with unsteady steps. Jonathan raised his hands in a gesture of surrender and nonaggression, and as she came into the light, he saw that she wasn't as cool and collected as she sounded. Her eyes blinked constantly and she was drawing each breath as if it might be her last. But then, like she said, she was office staff. Emma took care of the fieldwork.

"You're right," said Jonathan. "A one-way ticket wouldn't be much help. But I don't think talking to your boss is going to make things any better."

"Of course it would," pleaded Meadows. He was on his feet, coming round the table, shaking his head as if this whole thing were just a friendly misunderstanding. "Talking always helps."

"Stay there, dear," said Pru.

But Meadows kept coming.

"I said stop!" Prudence shouted.

Meadows froze. "Damn it, Jonathan," he said. "They only want to talk to you."

"No, Jamie, they don't. They want me to tell them where my wife is and then they're probably going to kill both of us."

"Pru, is that true?" asked Meadows.

"No, Jamie. We have no intention of harming Jonathan. We just want to talk to him."

"See, Jonathan? You must believe Prudence."

"I'm sorry, Jamie, but I have to leave now." Jonathan looked directly at Prudence. "I don't know where my wife is. Tell that to Connor. I asked where she was going, but she wouldn't tell me."

"I can't allow that," said Pru. "Just stay where you are. It will only be another minute."

Meadows was standing by a pillar that separated the kitchen from the living room. His expression said that it was all too much for him. The gun, the confession that his wife was a covert intelligence agent, the strain of the standoff. Anger was the only refuge left to him. "Wait a second, Pru," he said. "Are you really going to hurt him?"

"Sit down, Jamie, and mind your own business."

"I will not," said Meadows, gathering steam and courage. "Jonathan's a friend. I don't care what it is you do or whom you work for. We'll have to sort that out later. As for now, you're going to put down that gun and allow Jonathan to leave."

The pistol coughed, and a chunk of plaster flew from the pillar a foot from Jamie Meadows's head.

"Stay there and shut up, darling. We'll talk about this later."

But the shot only seemed to spur Meadows on. "I don't give a damn, Pru," he went on heatedly. "Are you going to shoot him? Are you going to shoot me, too? Don't be ridiculous."

"Jamie, just stop!" she said.

"You stop!"

Prudence aimed the pistol at her husband. "I said stop, dammit."

Meadows pushed Jonathan out of the way and lunged for the gun. There was another cough, and Meadows collapsed to his knees. "Pru," he said feebly and without blame, as if the victim of a random accident. "You shot me."

"Jamie?" she said.

Meadows slid to the floor. Blood streamed from the corner of his mouth. Jonathan knelt and rolled Meadows onto his back, first clearing his air passage. Opening his shirt, he saw a neat black hole pulsing blood an inch above the sternum. If the bullet hadn't pierced the heart itself, it had nicked a coronary artery. "Get me some towels," he said. "Call an ambulance."

Pru looked down at her husband. "I didn't pull the trigger," she mumbled. "I couldn't have." Then, to Jonathan: "Do something."

"Just call an ambulance!"

Pru rushed into the kitchen and called emergency services.

Jonathan pulled the blanket from the ottoman and used it to wipe away the blood. He pushed his index finger into the hole, feeling for an artery he could stanch.

"Keep trying," said Meadows, struggling to raise his head. "Don't worry about the pain. I can't feel a thing. The bullet must have hit the spinal cord."

"It's a little slippery," said Jonathan, angling his index finger through muscle fascia into the thoracic cavity. "Let me just try on this side."

"Got it?"

"Not yet."

"Don't give up."

Jonathan leaned closer, eyes narrowed. "Hang in there. I'll get it clamped in a second."

"I know you will." Suddenly, Meadows went into spasm. His body heaved. His head bolted forward and dark arterial blood pulsed from his mouth. "Jon . . . help me."

"Lay back, Jamie. We can do this." Jonathan lowered Meadows to the floor, took a steadying breath, and recommenced his blind search for the nicked artery.

"Christ, the girls," said Meadows. "They're so young."

"You just worry about yourself. Hang tight. We'll have you at a hospital in no time. Understand?"

"It's just . . ." Meadows's words trailed off.

"Stay with me!" Jonathan inched his finger to the right and felt a current of blood. Probing more deeply, he located the source of the internal bleeding. "There," he said. "I've got it. Now lay still."

"Thank God," whispered Meadows, his eyes meeting Jonathan's. "That's a good chap, Ransom. It's true then."

"What?"

"Magic hands. You do have them." Then he gasped and went still.

Jonathan watched as his friend's pupils dilated and his face drained of color. The change was immediate and dramatic. Gingerly, he removed his finger and sat back on his knees, gazing at the still form.

Pru returned to the living room, her eyes darting between Jonathan and her husband's corpse. "What happened? How is he? **Jamie?**"

"He's dead," said Jonathan.

"What? But the ambulance is on its way. They said three minutes. It can't be." Prudence laid the gun on a side table, knelt and placed a hand on her husband's cheek. "Jamie," she whispered close to his ear. "Come on then. Hold on for a little longer. The ambulance is almost here. Division will understand. You're my husband. They have to."

"I'm sorry," said Jonathan.

"No, it's not possible," the woman protested. "He can't be. I didn't . . . I mean it was an accident."

The room grew quiet, the odor of gunpowder fouling the air.

"You did this," said Prudence, after a moment. Her eyes were wet with tears, but her voice remained flat. "You killed him. You and Emma."

"No," said Jonathan, tiredly.

In an instant, she was on her feet, her hand reaching for the pistol.

Jonathan reacted instinctively. There was a flash of silver, a thud, and a sharp intake of breath. He picked up the gun and moved back a step.

Prudence Meadows stared in horror at the letter opener pinning her hand to the side table, but she made no noise. Her eyes met Jonathan's. In the distance, an ambulance's siren wailed.

"Jenny," she called upstairs to her older daughter, with unnerving calm. "Wake up! There's an intruder and he's shot Daddy!"

Jonathan ran out the door.

Five minutes later, he was driving Jamie Meadows's Jaguar along the A4 out of London.

28

Officially it was called the Telephone Information Unit of the London Metropolitan Police, but everyone on the force knew it as the Aquarium. The Aquarium was located on the third underground floor beneath a government building in Whitehall. The building, a dignified assembly of red brick and mortar, might have been designed and constructed in the seventeenth century by a pupil of Inigo Jones, but the Aquarium was strictly twenty-first century. Instead of brick there was stainless steel, and instead of mortar, fiber optic cable. Thousands of miles of it ran through the walls and under the floors and into the warren of cubicles and bullpens and soundproofed conference rooms that covered an area the size of a football pitch. It was the Telephone Information Unit's job to eavesdrop on the telephone conversations and e-mail traffic of some five thousand people deemed "persons of interest" by Her Majesty's government.

Kate Ford hurried along the elevated walkway that ran the length of the Aquarium. A pane of soundproof glass separated her from the work area. Every 20 meters there was an exit and stairs that descended from the catwalk to the floor. It was past eleven at night, but the floor bristled with activity. In the digital world, there was no day or night.

She stopped at the third doorway, passed her identification card through the reader, waited for the green pinlight, and applied her left thumb to the biometric scanner. Ironically, security increased once you'd been granted admission to the building. She descended the stairs. The warren was so complex that the walkways that crisscrossed the giant floor had all been given names. She passed pennants denoting Belgravia and Covent Garden, stopping at Pimlico.

Tony Shaffer slouched at his desk, keyboard on his lap as he tapped instructions into his computer. "Oh, hey there," he said, coming to attention. "Just finishing a little something."

"Hurry it up," said Kate, finding an empty chair and rolling it to Shaffer's cubicle.

Shaffer was young and unshaven, with a head of unruly black hair. "I've started working on the info you gave me," he said.

"Any luck?"

" 'Fraid not."

Kate frowned. Upon leaving the Dorchester, she'd phoned Shaffer to request that he start tracking down the IP address and location of the woman who'd sent Russell the video message yesterday morning. "Name and address check out?"

"No problem there," said Shaffer, with an air of apology that made her nervous. "Robert Russell was duly registered with British Telecom and Vodafone. I have the number of every phone and cable line running into his apartment at One Park. Theoretically, it's just a question of tracing the traffic that came through Russell's pipe."

"Then why the long face?"

"Russell's info is blocked. Can't get to it."

"How's that? I was at Five this morning. They've had a clamp on Russell's numbers for weeks. They'd even made a copy of the transmission."

"Five's the problem. They have a filter on the node running into that part of the city. Essentially, they're capturing every bit of communications traffic in Mayfair, whether they have a warrant for it or not. Russell's just the tip of the iceberg."

"Did you request copies of the traffic to his flat?"

Shaffer nodded. "I did, but they refuse to share it. Fed me a line about national security taking precedence over a local investigation."

"A homicide investigation, thank you."

"I told 'em. Didn't cut me any slack."

Kate leaned forward, pinching the bridge of her nose. "The woman's the key. She's the human connection. It was her source that gave Russell 'Victoria Bear.' She's the one who can tell us who's behind the bombing."

"You'll need to file a request with the Security Service, but I wouldn't hold my breath."

"I thought this was the age of improved cooperation."

"That **is** improved cooperation. Believe me. Before, Five wouldn't even take my call." Shaffer scratched his head. "Don't you have any other way of finding your Joe? You said it was a video message. Did you do an ambient sound analysis? Sometimes they can find the craziest things. Radios playing in another room, church bells ringing miles away, all kinds of stuff that can help you pinpoint the location of the sender. Then you can reverse-engineer the whole thing. Narrow it down to a few square miles, identify the local cable node, and see who in that area was sending messages to Russell."

"And how long will that take?"

"Days, maybe a week—provided, that is, that they get to you. Queue's about sixty days as it is."

"Thanks for the tip, Tony."

"Sorry I couldn't help."

"No worries." Kate patted him on the shoulder and made her way to the stairs. Ambient sound analysis, she thought to herself. There had to be an easier way. She shook her head. Church bells, of all things.

Just then she remembered something about the video message, a detail she'd noted but had dismissed as more grasping at straws. She stopped in her tracks. It was probably nothing, but . . .

She ran up the remaining stairs and threw open the door before getting hold of herself. No running allowed, she reminded herself. Never let them see you bothered.

Setting her chin against the world, she strode down the walkway and out of the building. She needed to review a copy of the video transmission. She was going back to Thames House, Graves be damned!

29

"Keep the lights off!" shouted the besotted voice.

Kate advanced into the recesses of the office on the first floor of Thames House. Squinting, she made out a shadowy form slumped behind the broad desk. "You all right, then, Colonel Graves?"

"What do you want?" The words slurred in a messy polysyllabic swamp.

Kate ran her hand along the wall and flicked on the lights. The room blazed to life. Graves raised a hand to ward off the glare, staring at her hatefully through bloodshot eyes. There was a bottle of whisky on his desk and a cut-glass tumbler filled nearly to the lip.

"I couldn't reach you. Your assistant said I might find you here."

"Remind me to sack him."

"What's all this, then?" Kate indicated the bottle and the glass and his generally lamentable state.

"Why, nothing, DCI Ford. Everything's hunky-dory. All quiet on the western front. You may return to your troops forthwith."

"I thought you'd be halfway to Timbuktu by now. You and your trusty Yankee bloodhound."

"Ransom? You mean you haven't heard?" Graves's throaty laugh echoed through the room, a single forlorn bark.

Kate advanced tentatively toward the desk. "What is it?"

"He's gone."

"Gone? Did you hand him over to the Americans? Did they admit to knowing him after all?"

"The Americans? 'Course not."

"Then what?"

"He escaped."

"He did what?" Kate asked, certain that Graves was engaging in some sort of twisted practical joke.

"Skedaddled. Went over the wall. He is no longer in police custody. Wipe that damn look off your face. Are you having a problem understanding me?"

Kate fell into the chair facing Graves's desk. She was furious. Monumentally angry at whatever act of incompetence had allowed a suspect to escape from police custody. "When I left, you had him locked in his room with enough guards to protect the pope. What exactly happened?"

"Chap climbed down the building. Off the balcony and right down the façade. Apparently it's not as hard as it looks." Graves pushed his chair back and stood. "You didn't tell me he was a climber," he said, circling the desk menacingly. "I only just got that part. If I'd been so apprised, then perhaps I would have put two and two together. Not as dumb as some of the boys upstairs think, actually."

"So you're blaming it on me?"

"No," admitted Graves. "This one's all mine. When you take off a prisoner's cuffs and let him wander around the room as if he's the Prince of Wales and you're his valet, then you don't have anyone else to blame. My fault entirely." He leveled a finger at her. "You may now mention something about my being an arrogant bastard who deserved to be hoisted on his own petard. I yield the floor to the member from Hendon."

"Not my style," said Kate.

"Funny, it's mine," said Graves, almost cheerily. "Or should I say it was."

"You sacked, then?"

Graves shook his head as if it were the furthest thing from the truth. " 'Course not. They tend to be diplomatic about this kind of thing. The director will wait a week or so, so as not to draw any more attention to the matter than necessary. Still, it's a matter of time. You don't let the prime suspect in a car bombing that took seven lives, including some very important, very nasty Russian diplomats, slip through your fingers. Not when you have him under lock and key. **Sacked?** I'll be lucky if I'm not crucified."

"I'm sorry."

Graves rolled his eyes. "Christ, a sincere one." He picked up the glass and swallowed a mouthful of whiskey. "What are you doing here, anyway?"

"Trying to find the woman who contacted Russell."

"A nonstarter. Didn't your buddy Tony Shaffer tell you that over at the Aquarium?"

Even now Graves had to let Kate know that he was one step ahead of her. "He said Five wouldn't cooperate."

"Better than admitting we were flummoxed," said Graves. "Russell's got that message routed through ISPs all over the globe. Before coming to England, it passed through France, Russia, and India. It would take a month to track it down." Suddenly he guffawed. "The woman's probably a pro, too. The baby was cover."

Kate twisted in her chair to follow Graves as he ambled around his office. "Do you have a copy of her message handy?"

"Sure, but I can tell you that my best men have given it a thorough going over and come up with exactly nil."

"Would you mind playing it?"

Graves opened the AV cabinet and activated the DVD player. A moment later the intercepted message began to spool.

"Stop there," said Kate, halfway through the woman's speech.

Graves froze the image. Onscreen, the woman had bent forward an inch or two to quiet her baby. One of her hands brushed the infant's cheek.

"Look at the ring," said Kate, pointing to the woman's outstretched fingers.

"What about it?"

"It has a coat of arms. I think it may be a university ring."

Graves increased the size of the image and the woman grew larger, her hand positioned in the center of the picture. Kate stepped closer to the monitor. "That's an Oxford ring, if I'm not mistaken."

"How the hell do you know?"

"Because I wanted to go there desperately."

Graves studied the image for a few seconds, then spun and walked back to his desk. "Christ, you just may have something."

In the space of ten seconds, his gait had regained its authority. His posture was its once rigid self. He plucked the phone from the cradle and put it to his ear. "Roberts," he said, the slur a bad memory. "Get down to archives. Find the Oxford University yearbooks for . . ." Graves lowered the phone.

"The last twenty years," said Kate.

"The last twenty years and bring them right up." He set down the phone. "Drink?" he said.

Kate shook her head. "Better not. Still recovering."

Graves perched himself on the edge of the desk. "That was you who blew the Kew Strangler arrest, eh? Tough going."

"We had him IDed, with enough evidence to put him away for life. Our profiler said he was docile except when acting out his fantasies. We walked up to his front door as if he was any other Joe. We even rang the bell and introduced ourselves. I didn't think there would be a problem. I've arrested twenty murderers. None of 'em made a peep. Gentle as lambs when we brought them in. We got complacent."

"The chap who was killed—a detective chief superintendent, wasn't he?"

"Billy Donovan. He was my fiancé."

Graves winced. "I'm sorry."

"The Met tried to force me to retire," explained Kate. "They don't like embarrassments either. I told them to shove it. I wasn't going out like that. They stuck me on night shift and look what happened. I've got my second chance."

"I don't think the director general is so forgiving."

"You've got seven days. It takes that long just for the paperwork to get started. We can prove both our bosses were wrong."

Graves lifted his glass. "On that inspirational note, DCI Ford, cheers and fuck the lot of you!"

Kate put her hand on his arm. "That's enough charity for tonight."

Graves yanked his hand loose. He glared at Kate, then turned and set the glass down on the desk. "Ransom's dirty. Von Daniken said the same thing. Ransom's too skilled to be an amateur. And don't you say he's just scared."

"I disagree. He was too close to the blast, for one. And why would he run down the street shouting like a madman at his wife? If he were a pro, he would have managed to alert her more discreetly. He had to know we'd get it on tape."

"That's what bothers me," said Graves. "It's her behavior that doesn't make any sense."

"How so?"

"We know she's a pro, whether she used to work with the Americans or not. We learned that at Russell's flat. Someone had to teach her how to defeat that security system. Then you have the car bomb. It's no easy task to assemble that kind of device and get it into central London without being spotted. But what does Mrs. Emma Ransom do with all her training and supposed years of experience? She stands on that street corner plain as day through two cycles of the traffic signal and practically stares into the camera as she blows the bomb. She wanted us to see her." Graves slapped his leg in a sign of frustration. "To tell you the truth, the behavior of neither of them makes a lick of sense."

"Him I understand," retorted Kate. "He told us that she'd surprised him at the hotel. He knew what she'd done in the past. He put two and two together and realized she was up to something here in London."

"And now?"

"And now he's trying to save her."

"You've got to be kidding!"

"What would you do if it was your wife?"

"I'd have chosen a bit more carefully," said Graves.

Just then Roberts knocked and entered the office. He was followed by another man, and between them, they were carrying the requested university yearbooks. Graves took the topmost yearbook and compared the shield on its spine to the one visible on the monitor. The two matched. "Set them on my desk," he directed.

"Anything else, sir?" asked Roberts.

"An urn of coffee and two cups, sugar, cream, the works. Anything else you can think of, DCI Ford?"

"If you can find a chip shop that's open, I wouldn't mind a piece of cod."

"Wrapped in newspaper?" said Graves, with the hint of a smile.

"Newspaper would be fine," answered Kate sternly. She was in no mood to be Graves's newly appointed buddy.

"You heard the lady," barked Graves. "Fish and chips. Get me some, too. I'm starved. Now get out of here."

"Yes, sir," said Roberts with a sharp nod.

"Good," said Graves, settling down at his desk. "That's taken care of. Now let's get to work. We've a helluva lot of faces to look at."

30

"Keep your eyes on the ground," shouted Den Baxter, chief of the London Metropolitan Police's Evidence Recovery Team, as he walked up Storey's Gate. "The pieces are all here. No one better even think of going home until we find them!"

It was eleven o'clock. The sun had slipped below the horizon ninety minutes earlier. Across London, the curtain of night had fallen. Everywhere except Storey's Gate.

Along Storey's Gate, it was as bright as midday. Up and down the 500-meter band of pavement, from Victoria Street to the west to Great George Street to the east, tall halogen work lamps illuminated the area where the car bomb had been detonated twelve hours earlier. There were over one hundred lamps in all, each with a brash 150-watt flood trained on the asphalt. Half again as numerous were the members of the Evidence Recovery Team, or the ERT, as it was better known. Clad head to toe in white Tyvek bodysuits, they swarmed up and down the street with the single-mindedness of army ants.

"Chief, over here!"

Baxter circled the husk of one of the burned automobiles and hurried toward the sidewalk, where a man stood with his hand raised. Baxter was a fireplug of a man, with flaming red hair and a boxer's broken nose. A thirty-year veteran of the force, he'd arrived at the scene shortly after the first responders—the initial police, firemen, and paramedics called in to deal with the casualties. It was his job to locate, preserve, and catalogue any and all evidence having to do with the blast, and he carried it out with a zeal bordering on the fanatical.

"What've you got?" he asked.

The man held up a jagged piece of metal the size of a pack of cigarettes. "Bit of treasure. Piece of the car that went up. Got a nice dab of residue."

Baxter examined the hunk of metal, quickly spotting the blackened crust on one corner. A scrape of his thumbnail revealed a field of white powder beneath the surface. He walked to the mobile command center at the corner of Victoria Street. The rear doors were open, and he climbed inside. "Got a present for you."

Two men sat inside at an elaborate bank of instruments. Using a cotton swab, one freed a dab of explosive and prepped it for testing. One of the machines at his disposal was a Thomson gas chromatograph–mass spectrometer capable of analyzing the chemical composition of every commercially manufactured explosive compound known to man, and plenty that were homemade, too.

With an admonition to inform him as soon as any results were received, Baxter jumped out of the van and looked to see where he might be of some use. Twelve hours on the scene and he was still as charged up as a bantam cock.

When he arrived at 11:35, barely twenty minutes after the blast, his first task had been to clear the scene of casualties and establish a secure perimeter. His fellow officers were often his worst enemy. In their haste to help the injured, they stomped around the scene with little regard for evidence. It was three hours before all casualties were cleared from the scene, and another two before the last uniformed policeman had been escorted off-site. Only then was Baxter able to begin his real work.

The perimeter of a bomb site was established by the size of the blast area. The majority of car bombs employed one form or another of plastic explosives which, when detonated, expanded at a rate of nearly five miles per second. Baxter grew angry when he saw movies where the hero outran a fireball emanating from a detonation. Not likely. Thankfully, Storey's Gate was a narrow street. The blast wave had ricocheted between the buildings, dissipating rapidly, and remained largely confined to its length.

Next Baxter gridded out the area, assigning 20-by-20-meter squares to teams of five men each for examination. Every square inch of the site was photographed, and all debris was studied with an eye to determining whether it was or was not evidence. If so, it was marked, photographed again, catalogued, and bagged.

The ERT looked for two things in particular: elements of the bomb itself—namely a detonator, circuit board, mobile phone, and the like; and any materials coated with a residue of the explosives. A bomb's architecture spoke volumes about the bomb maker: his training, education, and, most important, his country of origin. Ninety percent of terrorist devices were made by individuals with prior military experience, and many bomb makers (inadvertently) developed a signature that gave them away as surely as Picasso's script at the bottom of his paintings.

Blast residue indicated the type of explosive used, and often where the explosive was manufactured, and even when. Determining whether a bomb utilized Semtex, C-4, or one of a dozen more arcane explosives was a crucial first step in tracking down the identity of the assailant.

"Boss!" A whistle from the interior of the van drew his attention.

Baxter arrived in record time. "You have a result?" he asked breathlessly.

"Semtex," declared the technician. "From the home factory in Semtin." Semtex was a common plastic explosive manufactured in Semtin, Czech Republic.

"Taggants in good condition?"

"Taggants" referred to chemical signatures placed in the explosives denoting the place and date of manufacture.

"Check. We sent them over to Interpol for analysis."

"And?"

"The Semtex used in the bomb came from a shipment sold to the Italian army. Here's where it gets interesting: the Italians reported the shipment hijacked en route to a military base outside Rome in late April."

One of Interpol's lesser-known responsibilities was to maintain an up-to-the-minute database of every batch of explosives manufactured from legitimate explosives concerns around the world and to keep track of where and to whom they were sold.

"How big was the shipment?"

"Five hundred kilos."

"Ask Interpol if any of the same batch has shown up somewhere else. Oh, and good work."

Baxter climbed out of the van and headed back up the street into the glare of the lights. The Semtex was just one piece of the puzzle. He'd need many more before he could begin to make heads or tails of the bomb and, more important, the bomber.

"Evidence," he shouted to his men. "I want some bloody evidence!"

It was nearing midnight, and Den Baxter's day was just beginning.

31

It took Kate and Graves three hours, but finally they found her.

Her name was Isabelle Lauren, and she had studied at Balliol College, Oxford, from 1997 to 2000.

"Funny," said Kate. "Robert Russell wasn't even up at Oxford when she was there."

"Was he teaching?"

"Not till 2001."

Graves shrugged. "I suppose it doesn't matter how they knew each other. Just that they did."

"Mmm," Kate agreed. "Still, I'm curious."

Graves closed the university yearbook and rang up his assistant, giving him Isabelle Lauren's name and requesting that all pertinent personal information be on his desk within thirty minutes, beginning with a current address and phone number. When he'd finished, he set the phone down and glanced up at Kate. "I suppose it's too late for an apology," he said.

"An apology for what?"

"For this morning. I'm sorry for barging in on you like that. I tend to get carried away."

"Your manners need improvement, no doubt," said Kate. "But that's not what bothered me."

"Oh? What was it, then?" Graves hurried to ask. "That I didn't want to cooperate?"

How was it, she wondered, that someone so smart could be so damn stupid? The answer came to her at once. Men. The inferior species. "You still don't get it, do you?"

The phone rang before Graves could answer. Motioning for her to give him a second, he picked it up. "What is it now?" Suddenly his face fell. "Oh, excuse me, Detective Watkins. I was expecting another call. Ransom? He did what? Good Lord!"

"What?" Kate put her head close to his, trying to listen, but Graves immediately walked away, nodding and grunting and mumbling "yes" over and over again. Finally he said, "I'm with DCI Kate Ford. It's important that she hear what you have to say. I'm going to put you on speaker. Go ahead."

"The woman's name is Prudence Meadows," explained a deep voice. "Jonathan Ransom shot and killed her husband two hours ago."

Graves exchanged a glance with Kate that said he'd been right all along.

"There's no question whatsoever," Watkins continued. "Ransom and her husband were at university together years ago. The woman and her husband visited with him only last night at a reception at the Dorchester. According to Mrs. Meadows, Ransom came to the door of their home in Notting Hill at approximately nine-thirty. He demanded to speak to her husband. She said he looked agitated, but she let him in anyway. The two men retired upstairs for an hour. During that time she put her children to bed and then went to her bedroom to read. At ten forty-five she heard raised voices coming from downstairs. She went to see what was going on and found Ransom holding a gun on her husband, shouting that he wanted money and the keys to his car. Dr. Meadows refused. An altercation ensued, and Ransom shot the man dead."

"Go on," said Graves. "Then what did Ransom do?"

"Mrs. Meadows tried to call the police and he put a dagger through her hand into the table to stop her."

"Didn't he try to kill her, too?" asked Kate, staring hard at Graves.

"No. Just left her like that, then took the keys to the car and fled."

Kate shot Graves a perplexed look. "Can we speak with Mrs. Meadows?" she said.

"Not right yet," responded Watkins. "She's in surgery for the hand. You can have a go at her tomorrow morning."

"Right," said Graves. "Anything on the car Ransom stole?"

"Not yet, but we're looking."

"Cover all the airports and the ports along the coast."

"Already done."

"Of course it is. Thank you again for getting in touch so promptly." Graves hung up. He raised a hand to stop Kate before she could begin. "I know what you're going to say. If Ransom killed the husband, why did he leave the woman alive?"

"It must have been an accident. He's not a killer."

"You keep saying that, and the people around him keep dying."

The phone rang again. It was Roberts, who stated that Mrs. Isabelle Lauren's primary residence was in the city of Hull, in the northeast of England. Graves requested that an aircraft be made ready and told Kate to meet him early the next morning at Thames House for a briefing prior to departure.

As she walked to the door, he called, "You never did tell me what bothered you so much."

Kate looked over her shoulder. "You really want to know?"

"Couldn't sleep if I didn't."

"What bothered me, Colonel Graves—"

"Call me Charles."

"What bothered me, Charles, wasn't that you came into my home unannounced and took it upon yourself to march into my kitchen."

Graves set his hands on his hips. "What the hell was it then, DCI Ford?"

"Kate."

"Okay . . . Kate."

"I saw your Rover yesterday morning at One Park. What really pissed me off was that you arrived before I did, and you didn't tell me. It was my crime scene. I don't like to be second to anyone."

32

The Peninsular and Orient ferry Princess of Kent, 179 meters in length, 40 meters from sea to smokestack, and 33 in width, with a draft of 22,000 tons and capable of carrying 500 automobiles or 180 trucks, along with 2,000 paying passengers, sat moored at the dock of the Dover–Calais terminal, ready to commence boarding in twelve minutes and thirty-seven seconds, as noted by the enormous digital clock arrayed on the neighboring warehouse. It was 6 a.m. The sun had come up a half-hour ago, and though the temperature was no more than seventy-five degrees, there wasn't a lick of wind, and it was already uncomfortably humid.

Jonathan snaked through the idling trucks. Drivers milled outside their cabs, smoking, exchanging trade tips with one another, or just stretching their bones. He was studying the size of the cabs, the addresses of their owners (usually noted on the driver's door), as well as the rigs' home country plates. As important, he was determining whether the driver was at the wheel waiting to guide his rig aboard the ferry or somewhere en route to or from the ticket office.

He eyed a Peterbilt cab belonging to the freight

forwarder Danzas and piloted by a M. Voorhuis of Rotterdam, Holland. The cab would be perfect, offering ample room to hide a fugitive eager to reach the European continent. Better yet, it belonged to an established freight company. Customs and immigration checks were carried out upon landing in France. Inspection was supposedly random, but he knew that vehicles registered to the established companies were rarely selected.

A man he assumed to be Voorhuis stood on the running board, smoking. Next to him, resting her head on his shoulder, was a frizzy-haired woman, all jeans, black leather, and skull rings. But Rotterdam wasn't any good, and three was definitely a crowd.

Eleven minutes.

A Volvo FH16 carrying a Cat backhoe out of Basel, Switzerland, gave Jonathan momentary hope. The cab had a rest area behind the driver's seat, and the Swiss plates meant free passage across borders. Even the driver looked okay, a middle-aged schoolboy wearing a silver cross around his neck. It was the biblical scripture airbrushed on his cab's side panel that was the problem. If push came to shove, there would be no doubt that he would offer up a prayer and scream for the police. Besides, Switzerland wasn't far enough south.

It was then that he saw it. Situated above the ticketing office stood a regulation highway-sized digital billboard, and on the billboard was a color photograph of Dr. Jonathan Ransom. A scroll running beneath the picture read, "Have you seen this man? His name is Dr. Jonathan Ransom and he is wanted for questioning in association with the London car bombing of 7/26. Ransom is six feet tall, approximately 180 pounds, and is thought to be armed. Do not attempt to approach him on your own. If you have any knowledge of his whereabouts, call . . ." A London number followed.

Despite the heat, Jonathan felt a chill along the back of his neck. All he had in the way of a disguise was a watchman's cap to cover his graying hair and a pair of wraparound sunglasses. It wasn't much, but for the moment, no one could match him to the man on the billboard. He stared at the picture of himself. It was the same photo used in the convention's brochure. There was no longer any chance of bribing his way onto a truck. He'd have to sneak aboard.

The clock ticked down to ten minutes.

Ten minutes to find a way out of England.

Jonathan rubbed the sweat out of his eyes and kept moving.

The parking lot was a modern-day stockyard, with eighteen-wheelers and double-rig juggernauts taking the place of longhorn steers and grass-fed cattle. The random blare of an industrial-strength air horn was as disconcerting as the lowing of ten thousand frightened cattle, and the billowing exhaust every bit as noxious. If you couldn't see the English Channel pressing down on three sides of the lot, you wouldn't imagine that you were anywhere within a hundred miles of the sea.

Jonathan came to the end of a row and moved down the next. He'd left London at the wheel of Meadows's Jag. He'd found the car around back, exactly as Jamie had said. It was a risk, but then everything was. He'd driven until three, then pulled off the motorway in Canterbury to rest, but he'd been too wired to sleep.

It had been five when he arrived at the ferry. After checking the morning's schedule, he'd driven to the outskirts of town and parked on the fourth floor of a long-term garage. He'd even gone so far as to steal a tarp from a nearby Mercedes and throw it over the Jag.

Another horn sounded. Longer and louder. At the rear of the lot, a boom dropped, effectively prohibiting any further entrants. Jonathan stopped, leaning against a fender to scan the assembled armada of trucks. There were rigs from Germany, Belgium, France, Sweden, and Spain. Where was Italy?

Jonathan's logic was straightforward, if problematic. Emma claimed to have been attacked in Rome. By the look of the scar, the wound had demanded immediate medical attention, if not a convalescence in the hospital. Somewhere there would be a record of her admittance. He was sure she hadn't used her own name. He could rely on a picture and his own expertise in dealing with hospital administrators. That and something else.

His work provided one last arrow in his quiver. Years back, an Italian physician had joined the Doctors Without Borders mission in Eritrea on the horn of Africa for a three-month rotation. (This short stay was more the rule than the exception. Most doctors who gave their time to DWB did so temporarily. Stints normally lasted between three and six months.) The doctor's name was Luca Lazio, and if Jonathan wasn't mistaken, his practice had been near the Borghese Gardens in Rome.

There remained one small problem. Jonathan and Lazio hadn't parted on the best of terms. In fact, a broken nose might have been involved somewhere along the line. But Lazio owed him. Of that, there was no doubt. Lazio owed him big.

Either it was Rome or it was nothing.

A shrill whistle followed the horn, and there was a thunderous, knee-shaking rumble as the drivers fired up their engines and shifted the drive trains into first gear. One by one, the rigs boarded the ferry, advancing up a wide black iron ramp and disappearing into a murky netherworld for the ninety-minute traverse.

Panicked, Jonathan began to jog through the rank of trucks.

And then he saw his chance.

On the rear flank, the driver of an Interfreight lorry was only now climbing down from his rig and rushing toward the ticket booth. He held a phone to his ear, and his red cheeks and vocal responses made it apparent he was engaged in a quarrel. Jonathan edged closer to the truck. He couldn't see the plates yet, but it no longer mattered. Anywhere was safer than England. He rounded the back of a gleaming chrome monster hauling natural gas and pulled up. The driver had disappeared inside the ticket office. His cab sat 12 meters away. The morning sun reflected off the windscreen, making it impossible to ascertain whether or not someone was riding shotgun. It was then that he spotted the license plate. Black, rectangular, with seven white numerals following the prefix "MI."

"MI" for Milano.

He had found his chariot.

Jonathan approached the truck at a confident clip. He climbed onto the passenger-side running board and pulled at the door. It was open, and he swung inside and slammed it behind him. No one was inside. Keys dangled from the ignition. A GPS monitor dominated the dashboard, and cigarettes overflowed from the ashtray. The radio was playing, filling the cabin with saccharine Italian pop.

There was a curtain behind the seats. He parted it to reveal two single beds side by side, unmade, with clothing strewn across the blankets. In place of girly mags, there was a pile of newspapers—French, Italian, and English, issues of **Der Spiegel** and **Il Tempo,** and a volume titled **History of Stoicism. Great,** he thought, **the truck driver as intellectual.** He glanced over his shoulder. The driver had emerged from the ticket office and was hurrying back to the truck, the phone still clamped to his ear.

Jonathan wedged himself between the seats and

pulled the curtain closed. Gathering a ball of clothing, he lay down on the far bed, arranged the blankets over him, and covered himself with the wrinkled (and sweat-stained) garments. He'd just set his head down when the door opened and the cab rocked with the arrival of the driver.

The truck lurched ahead. There was the spark of flint, and then a hint of tobacco as the driver fired up a cigarette. All the while he talked. He was Italian, a southerner by his accent. He was speaking to a woman, probably his wife, and the subject was grave. She had spent too much for a new mattress when the family needed a new water heater. Civil war was imminent.

There was a thump, the truck descended a ramp, and then came a hollow knock as the truck advanced across the ferry deck. It drew to a halt. Jonathan waited for the driver to descend and avail himself of the myriad pleasures aboard ship. The travel time across the channel was one hour and thirty-three minutes, and the brochure he'd read mentioned plenty of duty-free shopping, several bars and restaurants, and even an Internet café.

But the driver didn't budge. For the next ninety minutes he remained on the phone with his spouse, whose name, Jonathan learned, was Laura, and who apparently had at least three dimwitted brothers who owed the family a great deal of money. He did not stop smoking the entire time.

The ferry docked according to schedule, at 8:30. Ten minutes passed before the truck moved an inch, and another ten before its wheels rolled onto solid ground. Again the rig stopped. This would be customs and immigration, Jonathan knew. He reminded himself that he was riding in a brand-new eighteen-wheeler with chrome pipes belonging to a worldwide freight company. It was the other guys that got searched: the independent contractors, the start-up freight companies, the drivers whose vehicles were in poor condition. Still, it wasn't only his imagination that the line was moving at an agonizingly slow pace. Over and over the driver mumbled under his breath, "Come on. What the hell is the problem?"

Sixty minutes passed.

The truck advanced, only to stop yet again. But this time there was a bone-rattling shudder as the driver put on the air brake. The window was lowered and Jonathan overheard the exchange.

"Where are you coming from?" asked the customs inspector.

"Birmingham," answered the driver, in respectable English.

"License and manifest, please."

The driver handed both over. A few minutes passed as the paperwork was studied and returned.

"Pick up anybody on the way?"

"No. Against company rules."

"See anyone trying to hitch a ride near the coast?"

"It was dark. I see no one."

"You're sure? Man about six feet tall, dark hair, maybe a little gray, an American?"

"I'm sure."

"So you don't have anyone back there in your cabin?"

"You want to look? Come on, then, I show you."

The inspector did not respond to the offer. "And you never left the truck alone?"

"Never!"

The heartfelt lie boosted Jonathan's hopes that he was with the right driver.

"Where you going to?" continued the inspector.

"Berlin, Prague, and Istanbul. It says so on the papers. Come on, mister. I'm in a hurry."

A thwack on the door as the inspector patted the truck goodbye. "Off you go."

Not daring to move, Jonathan listened from his blind bivouac as the truck gained speed and the ride smoothed out, and he was transported across the fertile plains of northern France toward Berlin and Istanbul.

33

Frank Connor showed up at St. Mary's Hospital, Praed Street, Paddington, at 11 a.m. sharp. To his credit, he brought a bouquet of flowers, a tin of chocolates from Fortnum and Mason, and the latest Jilly Cooper novel. He was dressed as befitted a visit to an ailing relative, in his gray Brooks Brothers suit that was loose around the shoulders, tight across his back, and didn't stand a chance of covering his impressive gut. His coarse gray hair was combed neatly, even if the rabid humidity had made a wreck of it.

On the opposite side of the ledger, Connor had been drinking since the night before, when he had missed capturing Jonathan Ransom by a mere ninety seconds and learned that Prudence Meadows had shot and killed her husband in the bargain. Despite a shower, a change of clothes, and a handful of Aqua Velva for each mottled, sagging cheek, he still reeked of alcohol and cigars.

Connor took the elevator to the fourth floor. There was no air conditioning (another reason he detested England), and by the time he strode to the nurses' station his shirt was soaked through. He gave his work name, Standish, and claimed to be a relative. The duty nurse confirmed that his name was on the family list and showed him past two officers of the Metropolitan Police waiting to interview Prudence Meadows as soon as she was able.

Once inside the private room, it didn't take Connor long to lose his temper. He'd been on a short fuse since missing Ransom at the hotel two nights before, and the sight of his injured, feckless employee set him immediately on edge.

"Where is she?" he asked, tossing the flowers onto a side table and dumping the book on her patient's tray.

"He doesn't know," Prudence Meadows said, her eyes fixed straight ahead.

"Bullshit," said Connor, who by now had categorically abandoned his resolution against profanity and even forgotten that he'd ever had one. "He was with her for two hours the night before and they shacked up in his hotel room yesterday morning. What do you think they talked about—the weather?"

"All I know is that he wants to get to her before the police do."

"So he's going to track her down? How?" Prudence didn't answer, and Connor slammed his hand down on her meal tray. "How?"

Prudence looked at Connor, but only for a moment. "Ask him. He did it before."

"Where was he headed? He must have given you some clue."

"I have no idea."

"You sure? You haven't gone soft on me because of your husband, have you? You still know where your allegiance lies, right?"

Prudence turned her face toward Connor, her cheeks flushed. "My allegiance ended three months ago, when you fired me!"

"You're wrong there, sweetie," Connor fired back. "We're just like those assholes in Belfast. Once in, never out. I'd suggest you bear that in mind."

Prudence turned away and stared out the grimy window.

Connor circled the bed and blocked her view. "How did the surgery go?"

"Successful, as far as I know."

"Yeah, what'd they do?"

"Realigned some bones, repaired some nerves. I was too drugged up to get most of it."

Connor reached over and grabbed her hand, lifting it up and examining it.

"Don't!" said Prudence.

"Hurt much?"

"Stop! You'll tear the stitches."

Connor dropped the hand onto the bed. "I'll do worse than that if you don't tell me everything that happened last night. And I mean the real version."

Prudence clutched her hand to her chest, whimpering.

"Anytime you're ready," said Connor.

With a fearful glance, she took a drink of water,

then related the events of the past evening as accurately as she could remember. She was an intelligent woman, and her account was close to verbatim.

"You're forgetting one thing," said Connor, when she'd finished. "If you shot your husband, why didn't you shoot Ransom, too?"

"You told me that he had to be taken alive. I was following your instructions."

"You qualified with that pistol. You could have shot him in the leg or taken off his big toe. Hell, I don't know. Either way, we'd have Ransom. Instead you broke down and called an ambulance."

"I was in shock," she retorted.

"You failed your training," said Connor, examining the IV and the machinery monitoring her respiration and blood pressure.

"My husband was dead. What did you want me to do?"

"I wanted you to follow orders. If you'd waited five more minutes, we could have cleaned everything up ourselves. I hope you have your story straight for the police."

"I do."

"You better."

Connor moved closer to the bed, bending at the waist and bringing his face close to hers. "One slip-up—one mention of who you work for—and I'll know. I'll see to it that your British passport doesn't hold up under too much scrutiny. I'll make sure the authorities get a look at your past. You'll be deported inside of ninety days, and I don't think that your husband's family will stand for your girls going with you. It's not so nice in that shitty little republic you come from. There's always one war or another going on there."

"Get out," said Prudence Meadows.

But Connor didn't budge. "I wonder what your girls will do when they find out that it was you who killed him."

"Get out!" she screamed.

A nurse entered the room. Seeing the patient's agitated state, she ordered Connor from the room. He made a show of resisting, yanking his arm clear and calling the nurse a few choice names before allowing himself to be escorted to the elevator. The policemen were on their feet at once, asking if they could be of assistance. But by then Connor had quieted down. Still, they'd noticed and made a point of referring the incident to their superiors, a report of which landed on Charles Graves's desk the next morning.

The nurse, too, filed a detailed report in the hospital log.

On the street, Connor's belligerence vanished. He had done what was needed. No more, no less.

34

Before earning her promotion to detective chief inspector, Kate Ford spent three years with the Flying Squad, the elite undercover unit of the Metropolitan Police charged with preventing armed robberies. The Flying Squad took its name from the cars originally assigned to the unit in 1918, two Crossley Tenders that had belonged to the Royal Flying Corps. Cockney rhyming slang transformed "Flying Squad" to "Sweeney Todd," and today everyone on the force simply called it the Sweeney.

It was an exciting time. Nights spent lying in wait for armed criminals, days staking out banks and jewelry shops. High-speed chases. Lots of banging heads and plenty of arrests. There was even the occasional gunplay, though Kate had never actually shot anyone herself. But one thing she'd witnessed time and time again was the criminal's habit when cornered of climbing to the top of whatever house or building he was hiding out in, in the hope of escaping. Some hid in the attic. Others made it all the way to the roof. It didn't really matter where they went, just that they kept moving up. Motion lent them the momentary and illusory notion that they still had a chance of getting away. Hope died hard.

"That Skye?" said Graves, seated next to her in the twin-engine Hawker business jet. "Never been here. Now I know why."

"Me neither," said Kate. "Bit bleak. Don't you think?"

Graves didn't respond. He was too busy playing with his cell phone. All during the flight he'd been waiting for an update on Ransom's whereabouts, striding to the cockpit every ten minutes to inquire if Thames House had radioed in. Now, with the landing strip in sight, he could find out for himself.

As the plane made its final approach, Kate stared out the window at the desolate landscape. The land was flat, scarred, and windswept. Little grew except gorse and heather. Away to the north there was a flat, sandy beach, and beyond that nothing but the sea stretching endlessly toward the horizon.

Isabelle Lauren was just like the others. Instead of cowering beneath the eaves of her home in Hull, she'd fled north, to the roof of her country. The Isle of Skye, off the northwestern coast of Scotland.

Poor Isabelle, thought Kate. Even here there was nowhere to hide.

The plane dropped and the wheels struck the tarmac. As soon as the ladder had been lowered, Graves rushed down the stairs, phone to his ear. Following a step behind, Kate was treated to a string of profanities. "What is it?" she asked, tapping him on the shoulder.

Graves raised a hand, signaling for quiet. "Have you gotten on to the French police?" he asked. "And send a note to Interpol while you're at it. Have them blast an e-mail to every federal, state, and local police force on the continent. He can't get far." He ended the call and turned to Kate. "They found the car Ransom stole from the Meadowses' place parked in a long-term garage near the Dover ferry. They're canvassing the dock, but so far no luck. No one matching his description bought a ticket. We're taking the CCTV films into custody to have a look for ourselves."

"How many destinations do ferries out of Dover serve?"

"Too many," said Graves. "Boulogne, Calais, Dunkirk. Boats left to all three before nine this morning."

"It's a quick drive from London. If I were Ransom, I wouldn't want to hang around too long. What's the first boat of the day?"

"P&O to Calais at six-fifteen," said Graves. "Next one to Boulogne at seven. Have you ever ridden on one? It's quite a show. Hundreds of trucks and private vehicles. He could have hitched a ride with any one of them. Who knows where he's going?"

"I do," said Kate. "He's going to find her."

The drive to the Skye Tavern and Inn took twenty minutes. Kate and Graves went inside, showed their identifications at the reception counter, and asked for Isabelle Lauren. They were told she was on the third floor, room 33. Graves asked their local police escorts to wait in the lobby, and he and Kate walked up the stairs to the third floor.

Isabelle Lauren had not been difficult to find. She was listed in the directory. A call to her home in Hull was answered by her mother, who revealed without the least prodding that her daughter had run off to parts unknown, leaving her infant daughter in her care, a favor she was none too happy to render. Call number two went to the Inland Revenue, which duly provided Isabelle Lauren's social insurance number. Call three went to the Nationwide Credit Bureau, which replied that Miss Lauren possessed four charge accounts with the larger credit card companies. The fourth call went to American Express, which e-mailed a list of her most recent charges. Most prominent were a second-class British Rail ticket to Inverness, a charge to Hertz auto rental, and a two-hundred-pound hold placed by the Skye Tavern and Inn. The fifth call went to said Skye Tavern and Inn, which confirmed that Lauren had indeed checked in and was at that moment upstairs in her room, watching the in-house cable movie channel.

Five calls. Forty-seven minutes.

Kate knocked and stepped away from the door. "Police, Miss Lauren," she announced. "We'd like a word."

A pretty brown-haired woman opened the door. It took a moment to realize that this was the mousy-haired mother after she'd had a shower, exchanged glasses for contact lenses, and put on clean clothing.

"I'm Bella Lauren," she said. "Would you mind showing me some identification?"

Kate proffered her warrant card and a look at her identification. "We've come from London."

"I'm glad it's you," said Bella.

"Who were you expecting?" asked Kate.

"Pretty much the opposite. Come in, then."

Kate and Graves entered the hotel room. It was large and neatly furnished, with windows looking over the ocean. Kate took a place on the couch, with Bella next to her. Graves paced.

"May I ask how you found me so quickly?" Bella asked.

"We were at Robert Russell's apartment when you made your last call."

"But Robbie promised me that no one could ever track our messages."

"He was telling the truth," said Kate. "Despite our best efforts, we haven't been able to track where the message came from. His web security was quite elaborate."

"Then how?"

"Your university signet ring," explained Kate. "When we studied the transmission, we observed that the ring bore the Oxford crest. We found your photo in the yearbook."

"And from there? It was my ma, wasn't it?"

"Your mother was no help," said Graves. "But next time you decide to run and hide, I'd caution you not to be so free with your credit card."

"But they're not allowed to share that data. It's private."

Graves gave her a look to suggest that that wasn't remotely the case.

"Have you come to protect me, then?" she asked. "It wasn't a suicide, you know."

"We're taking the view that Lord Russell's death was a homicide," agreed Kate. "But we have no reason to believe that you're in any danger. Just in case, we're leaving you with two policemen for the next several days."

Graves cut in. "If you don't mind, we've traveled quite a long way to ask you some questions."

"Certainly." Bella clasped her hands, the picture of cooperation. "How can I help?"

"To begin with, what can you tell us about yesterday's attack on Igor Ivanov?"

"Who?" Bella looked between them, confused.

"Igor Ivanov," Graves repeated. "The Russian interior minister who was attacked in London yesterday."

"Oh, yes. Now I know," came the annoyed response. "Why are you asking me about him?"

"You alluded to the attack in your message," said Kate. "You informed Lord Russell that someone named Mischa had come to London for a meeting that was scheduled to take place at eleven-fifteen yesterday morning. You even gave a clue as to the location. **Victoria Bear.**"

"But I've no idea what Victoria Bear means. I told Robbie as much."

"He knew already," said Kate. "He visited the site shortly before he was murdered. It referred to the headquarters of the Department of Business, Enterprise, and Regulatory Reform, at One Victoria Street—the precise location of yesterday's attack against Ivanov."

"But Mischa isn't Russian," said Bella.

"He isn't?" said Graves.

"Not he. **She.** Mischa's a woman. Her name is Michaela Dibner. She's German. She works for the International Atomic Energy Agency. It was Mischa whom Robbie and I were afraid for. Not Igor Ivanov."

Graves looked at Kate, who appeared to share his consternation. "I think it best if we start from the beginning," he said. "How did you come to know Lord Russell?"

"We were friends," said Bella. "Colleagues. We met six years ago at an event at Chatham House, a think tank in London. Mostly they work on national security issues. They publish papers, give talks, organize symposiums, that kind of thing. At the time I was with British Petroleum, working as an engineer designing rigs and other power installations. The talk that night was about the true level of world oil reserves. He bought me a drink and chatted me up a bit. He was very charming."

"And what did he want to know?"

"Nothing. Actually, he gave **me** a bit of information. He told me that there might be a new field worth exploring in the North Sea. He didn't tell me how he knew, just that it might be worth our while to stake a claim to a certain quadrant in international waters."

"And was it?"

"Do you mean was there oil there? Quite a bit. But at the time oil was going for forty dollars a barrel. At that price, it was too cheap to be extracted profitably from such a difficult spot. The boys in exploration didn't want to touch it."

"But the price went up," said Kate.

Bella smiled knowingly. "That's why BP has a rig up and running on those exact coordinates."

"That's some information," said Graves.

"Five billion euros' worth."

He whistled under his breath. "And so?"

"And so," Bella continued, "when Robbie asked for my help, I gave it."

Graves crossed his arms, assuming the inquisitor's stance. "What exactly did he want to know?"

"He wanted me to put him in touch with some of my contacts at the IAEA," responded Bella Lauren, answering his stare with one of her own. "I left BP years back. I design nuclear plants now. He said he had information for them."

"What kind?"

"He was worried about an accident at a power plant. A **nuclear** plant. He wasn't specific as to what kind of accident or where, but he seemed to believe that something might happen soon."

"In your message you said, 'Seven days isn't long enough for them to unpack their bags,' " said Kate, hoping to prod her. "That soon?"

Bella nodded. "It's scary, I know. He asked me lots of questions about security measures and that kind of thing. I put two and two together. If Robbie wanted to talk to the IAEA about a possible 'accident,' and he was interested in how well or poorly guarded the plants were, then I just assumed he had wind of something bad. I mean glow-in-the-dark, hair-falling-out-of-your-scalp-in-handfuls bad."

"So you put him in contact with the IAEA?"

"Yes."

Kate consulted her notepad. "You also asked him if you needed to leave. Did he ever indicate that the 'accident' might occur on British soil?"

"Never. I can't think it was, or he would have warned me."

"Can we talk about Mischa?" inquired Graves. "What exactly does she do for the IAEA?"

"She's director of S&S at their headquarters in Vienna. That's the Department of Nuclear Safety and Security. She'd come to London to meet with the UK Safeguards Office. They help manage security protocols for the EU."

Graves exhaled loudly, then turned away and planted himself by the window, where he stood gazing at the sea. "Safety and Security," he said, his voice wrung out. "They're the IAEA's watchdogs."

"What do they do?" asked Kate.

"A lot of things," said Bella. "They set up procedures for safeguarding plants, of course. Handle vetting of employees. Standardize training of plant workers."

"And watch over the illegal trafficking of radioactive materials," added Graves from across the room. "It's up to them to make sure that no one is selling weapons-grade uranium on the black market."

"Is that what you think Russell was worried about?" asked Kate. "A weapon?"

"If it were a weapon, Robbie would have gone directly to the police. I know that much. This was different."

"How?"

"He was primarily interested in learning how people got into and out of the plants. Who was granted admission, who wasn't. If all vehicles were searched. If the plants maintained paramilitary forces to protect them. I couldn't answer half of his questions. He was upset that he wasn't able to figure things out. That's why he was so desperate to speak with Mischa Dibner."

Graves crossed the room and sat down facing Bella Lauren. "But how did Russell come to suspect an attack in the first place?"

"It's what he did. He gathered information."

"Yes, but from whom?" asked Graves.

"Who told him about Victoria Bear?" pressed Kate.

Bella Lauren looked up. "I don't know, and I

knew better than to ask. All Robbie said was that he'd been asking questions where questions weren't appreciated. He told me not to worry. He said he'd done everything he could to make sure he was safe, but with these people there was always some danger."

"Just who in the world are 'these people'?" demanded Graves.

"I don't know," said Bella, looking into her lap. "But whoever they are, they killed him."

35

Den Baxter's day was picking up.

At 9 a.m. a section of the axle bearing the vehicle identification number of the BMW housing the explosives was found. The VIN was sent to BMW Headquarters in Munich, Germany, together with a second, different, and presumably false VIN recovered from the engine block the night before, to determine where and when the car had been manufactured and sold. Both numbers were also forwarded to Interpol headquarters in Luxembourg to be checked against a registry of stolen vehicles worldwide.

At ten, the Laser Transit Surveying team completed their initial mapping of the crime scene. Using an electrodigital theodolite, a telescope mounted within two perpendicular axes—the horizontal, or trunnion, axis and the vertical axis—the team plotted the grid points of all evidence, creating a three-dimensional picture of the crime scene. Among other things, the electrodigital theodolite measured the volume of the bomb crater, compared it to the distance and location of the blast debris (including the scattered remains of body parts), and determined the weight and distribution of explosives used in the device.

Initial measurements indicated that 20 kilos of plastic explosives had been packed into the BMW and that a significant amount of unmixed cement used as a tamping agent had ensured that the charge was directed into the passing vehicle. Conclusion: the device was hand-tailored to destroy a specific target while causing limited collateral damage. As such, Baxter could assume with a high degree of certainty that the bomb maker had at some point received an advanced course in military explosives training.

At eleven, Interpol called back to report that the BMW had been reported stolen from Perugia, Italy, three months earlier. From Italy, the car had been shipped to Marseille before entering the United Kingdom in Portsmouth. It was the firm of Barton and Battle LLC, registered automobile importers, that had cleared the stolen vehicle two weeks before and released it to the custody of a Mrs. K. O'Hara, resident of Manchester.

And at twelve, Baxter received a call on his two-way radio that would significantly alter the pace and direction of the investigation.

"Boss, this is Mac. Have a minute?" Alastair McKenzie was one of his up-and-coming stars, a twenty-four-year-old bloodhound with glasses like Coke bottles and intuition that couldn't be taught. "I found a little something at the site."

"But we already covered the crater," said Baxter, playing devil's advocate. "We didn't find spit."

"I decided to have another look anyway," said McKenzie. "Thought I'd give the Microviper a go."

"Of course you did, lad. That's why I love you. Stay put. I'll be right there."

Baxter dumped his piss-warm coffee into the trash and hurried down the street. He found McKenzie standing waist-deep in the blast crater. In his hand, the gangly policeman held a metallic cable running to an aluminum suitcase that sat open at his feet. At one end of the cable was a miniature camera that broadcast its images on a high-contrast screen set inside the suitcase. The device was called a Microviper, and was in fact a portable, nearly indestructible microscope capable of magnifying images up to 1000X.

"Have a look," said McKenzie. "I found a piece of something fused to the underside of the asphalt. I've got it up on the screen."

Baxter hopped into the crater and knelt by the Microviper.

"It's a circuit board," said McKenzie, pointing to the jagged piece of sky-blue plastic filling the screen. "Part of the phone used to detonate the bomb. I found other pieces here and there. I scanned them all and rearranged them so they fit together. Mind you, some pieces are still missing, but I think we're getting somewhere."

"Are those the serial numbers?"

"Four-five-seven-one-three," said McKenzie. "We're missing a few at the beginning. That piece must have been obliterated. Sorry 'bout that."

"Got a maker?"

"Not yet. We need to send it to the lab. They can run it against their samples for similarities."

To each phone a circuit board, and to each circuit board a serial number. Further study of the circuit board's architecture would pinpoint the manufacturer. From there, it was a matter of tracking down where all phones carrying circuit boards with the last five digits 45713 had been distributed. The goal was to ascertain where the phone had been sold, the SIM card or phone number assigned to it, and, if you were lucky, the name of the villain who'd purchased it. It was no different from following a wounded animal back to its lair, thought Baxter.

"I want you to deliver all the pieces you've tagged and bagged to the lab," he said. "Stay on them until they come up with something, then call me. Doesn't matter what time."

Baxter stomped off toward the mobile HQ. For the first time in twenty-four hours, he had a smile on his face. It was an ugly, pained smile, but nonetheless, it counted.

Den Baxter had the scent of his prey.

It was only a matter of time until he found them.

36

The truck had come to a halt. Jonathan lay still, listening to the hiss of air escaping the brakes and the low-throated rumble as the engine quit and died. The window was open and Jonathan could hear the growl of cars and trucks arriving and departing around them. He waited for the driver to climb from the cabin, but the man remained stubbornly at the wheel, arguing with his dispatcher over a change in his routing. To Hamburg now, farther north than Berlin.

Jonathan edged the blanket from his face. Blinking back the light, he raised his head in order to catch a glimpse of the outside world. He needed to situate himself on a map. They'd been driving for over two hours at what felt like a rapid speed, and he estimated that they'd traveled 200 kilometers at the very least. From his position behind the driver's seat, he spied the corner of a Shell Oil placard, and beyond it a highway sign offering the distance to Brussels as 16 kilometers. Aachen, in Germany, was another 74, and Cologne, 201. The distances reinforced his impatience. All were too far in the wrong direction. With a full tank, the driver could make it another 600 or 700 kilometers before having to refuel.

Jonathan's hands twitched with the need to move, yet he forced himself to remain still. He couldn't afford a confrontation with the driver. Not here, where a dispute would be witnessed by dozens and the likelihood of a policeman's being nearby was high. He would have to keep hidden longer.

Just then the driver ended his call. But instead of climbing down from the cabin, he turned in his seat and lunged toward the bunk. Jonathan yanked the blanket over his head and held his breath as forceful hands searched among the books, magazines, and papers littering the bed. Finally there came a grunt of satisfaction as the driver found what he was looking for: a logbook barely an inch from Jonathan's head.

The driver's door opened and he descended from the cab. Jonathan threw off the blanket and sat up. Gasping, he crawled across the bunk to the passenger door. In the side mirror, he watched the driver unscrew the gas cap, insert the fuel nozzle, then move to the rear of the truck, where he knelt to check the tires' pressure.

This was the time.

Jonathan moved into the front seat, and opened the passenger door and jumped to the ground. Parked adjacent to him, no more than 2 meters away, was a Peugeot sedan painted with the orange-and-blue insignia of the Belgian police. An officer sat at the wheel. Another uniform was standing nearby, pumping gas and blocking passage toward the front of the truck. Jonathan hesitated, his hand still on the door, then walked in the opposite direction. A moment later the driver rounded the rear of the truck, effectively boxing him in. He looked at Jonathan and said loudly in Italian, "Hey, what are you doing?"

Jonathan approached, smiling. He was aware of the policemen's gaze and knew that he held their undivided attention. The driver was a grizzled man, fifty or more, and in bad humor after the drawn-out arguments with his wife and his boss. Jonathan thought of the academic tomes, the newspapers. The driver was an intelligent man, to be sure. Only the truth would do.

"I hitched a ride in your truck from England," he answered, his Italian fluent, if workmanlike. "I apologize. I should have asked, but I was afraid you would say no, and I couldn't take that chance. I'm broke and I'm trying to get to Rome to see my girlfriend. I saw your plates, so I took a chance."

"I'm going to Hamburg."

"Yeah, I heard. That's why I thought I'd get out here." Jonathan let his eyes gesture at the police. **"Prego, signor."**

"Where are you from?" the Italian asked in a quieter voice.

It was the defining question. Funny that a man effectively without a country should have to answer it. "America."

Out of the corner of his eye, Jonathan saw a

policeman approach. **"Ça va, monsieur?"** he asked the driver.

The driver sniffed, his eyes never leaving Jonathan's. **"Tout va bien,"** he responded finally.

"Vous êtes certain?"

"Oui." The driver knelt and unscrewed the tire pressure gauge. As Jonathan passed, he glanced up. "Your Italian's not bad for an American," he said in English. "Now get lost."

"Thanks."

Jonathan continued toward the kiosk. With each step he expected the police to call out. They would ask to see his identification papers and discover that he had no passport. They would take his driver's license instead, and ask him to sit inside the police car while they checked him out. That would be that.

But the policemen said nothing. Jonathan was still a free man. For the time being.

Inside the kiosk, Jonathan purchased a razor and shaving cream, two oranges, a salami sandwich, mineral water, a toothbrush and toothpaste. The kiosk was part of a larger shopping gallery that spanned the highway. There was a Mövenpick restaurant and a clothing store, some tourist shops, an electronics shop, and several tobacco vendors. He passed from one to the next, purchasing a new pair of pants, a button-down shirt, a windbreaker, and a baseball cap. There was a single-user bathroom. It took him ten minutes to cut his hair and shave it down to a stubble. At last the gray was gone. He applied a self-tanner to his face, careful to blend it naturally with the lighter flesh tones of his neck and chest. Finished, he found a pay phone and called for a taxi.

Fifteen hours had passed since his escape from Graves. He had no doubt that his name already figured high on every fugitive watch list across Europe. But he knew enough about law enforcement, and more about governments and bureaucracies, not to be overly concerned. It would take awhile for his information to be forwarded to hotels, car rental companies, airlines, and the like. At some point Graves would see to it that his credit cards were frozen, too, but all that was in the future. Jonathan guessed that he had a window of twenty-four hours to get where he needed to go.

He arrived at Brussels airport an hour later. And thirty minutes after that he was signing the papers to rent a mid-size Audi sedan. The clerk slipped the car keys across the desk. "One last question, sir."

"Yes?" replied Jonathan.

"You do not plan on driving the car to Italy, do you?"

"Is that not permitted?"

"Of course it is permitted, but we would insist on a higher rate of insurance. Alas, there is much theft there. Rental cars are a prime target."

"How can you tell which one is a rental car?" asked Jonathan.

"By the license numbers. In Belgium, all rental car

plates begin with a sixty-seven. It is the same with each country."

Jonathan digested the information for future use. Then he answered the clerk's question. "No, I don't plan on going to Italy," he lied. "In fact, I'm going to Germany. Hamburg. I've heard it's lovely."

"I wish you a safe journey, Dr. Ransom," said the clerk.

Jonathan nodded and left the counter. Emma had taught him well.

37

"Five days. We don't know where, when, or how. Only that Robert Russell suspected an impending attack of some kind at a nuclear plant and that he was the nearest thing we have to a seer." Charles Graves walked briskly across the tarmac toward the waiting aircraft, hands buried in his pockets. A fitful wind blew off the ocean, flinging sea spume into the air. It was nearly two in the afternoon, and despite a clear sky and brilliant sun, the air was chill.

"I do know one thing," said Kate.

"What's that?"

"We've been wrong all along."

"About what exactly?"

"Everything."

Graves pulled up. "I'll grant you we've been a step behind, but I wouldn't say we've been wrong."

"Really? Then tell me this: who was Emma Ransom after? Ivanov or Mischa Dibner?"

"Ivanov, obviously. And I have a car bomb packed with twenty kilos of grade-A Semtex to prove it."

"But didn't Russell think the attack was going to be against Mischa Dibner? I mean, she was the one he'd spoken to about it."

"His intelligence was incomplete. Happens all the time. He missed one this time. So what?"

"What if we're both wrong? Remember the clue 'Victoria Bear'? Maybe that was the target. The Department of Business, Enterprise, and Regulatory Reform. That's where the UK Safeguards Office is housed and where the emergency meeting with the IAEA was scheduled to take place."

"And Interior Minister Ivanov? How do you explain his timely arrival at the scene?"

"I can't," said Kate. "I'm not there yet. Let's stay with Mischa. She was inside the building at the time of the blast, but she didn't stay there. She couldn't have done."

Graves nodded, his eyes saying that he was beginning to see where Kate was headed. "How so?"

"The law. In case of a blast or a terrorist act, the law calls for the mandatory evacuation of government buildings in the vicinity. You saw Victoria Street five minutes after the car went up."

"A bloody debacle. Looked as if half London worked inside those buildings."

"Exactly. And I'm willing to wager that Mischa and her team from the IAEA were among them."

"Do we know that for certain?" Graves was no longer doubting, but playing devil's advocate.

"No." Kate spoke slowly and with great care. She was walking on quicksand and she knew it. "What if Emma Ransom just wanted to force Mischa and her team out of the building?"

"And the attack on Ivanov was the means to do it?"

"Precisely."

"Which means there must have been something pretty valuable inside that she wanted to get her hands on."

"Something that Mischa and her team from the IAEA had brought with them."

Graves pulled his cell phone from his jacket and placed a call. "Get me Major Evans, Department K."

Kate stayed at Graves's side. Department K of MI5 was in charge of protective security for all government offices in the British capital.

"Hello, Blackie. Charlie Graves. Listen, I've got you on my cell's speaker. A bit windy here, so if you could speak up, it would help. I'm with DCI Kate Ford of the Met. We're tracking down a lead on yesterday's bombing. Quick question. Anything odd come up during or after the evacuation of our people at One Victoria Street? Department of Business, Enterprise, and Regulatory Reform? Theft of some kind?"

"You could say that," came a clipped upper-crust voice. "All hell's breaking loose down here. During the evacuation someone got into the offices of the nuclear safeguards people and nicked some high-grade stuff."

"Can you give me some more detail?"

"Officially, some briefcases and travel bags were lifted from a meeting room on the third floor."

"Did they belong to the team from the International Atomic Energy Agency?"

"How the devil did you know? The meeting was supposed to be very hush-hush."

"Go on, Blackie. What was in those briefcases?"

"Take me off speaker," said Evans.

Graves deactivated the speaker. Kate watched with alarm as his face grew taut. He thanked his colleague and hung up.

"What is it?" demanded Kate. "You look as if you've seen a ghost."

"No one gives a damn about the briefcases and travel bags that went missing. It's what was inside them. Someone made off with several laptops belonging to the members of the IAEA's Safety and Security Division."

"Emma Ransom."

"Who else?"

"So why the concern? Precisely what was in the laptops?"

Graves swallowed hard and fixed her with a doleful gaze. "Bloody everything."

38

Lev Timken was not a man that you would care to observe making love. To begin with, he was obese. He was also short, ugly, and as hairy as a Mingrelian bear. But these unappealing physical attributes were nothing compared to his primal grunting. In the throes of passion, the man produced a gut-curdling bark that would make a horny elephant seal blush.

"Can't you turn down the sound?" demanded Sergei Shvets.

From his position in the backseat of his BMW stretch sedan, Shvets enjoyed an unimpeded view of the advanced communications center built into the dashboard. At that moment the monitor was displaying a high-definition picture broadcast from Timken's bedroom. "Sound and light," as the men in Directorate S called it. Shvets had installed similar surveillance systems in one hundred apartments around the city. It was necessary to keep an eye on your adversaries.

His driver obediently lowered the volume.

"Christ, look at him," said Shvets. "I believe that I'm doing the women of Moscow a favor. He has enough blubber on him to supply a village with oil to last a Siberian winter."

"And enough fur to make a dozen coats."

Shvets was parked across the street from Lev Timken's apartment building on Kutuzovksy Prospekt. The building dated from the 1930s, when Stalin was on his quest to westernize Moscow, and it would not have looked out of place off the Étoile in Paris or the Kurfürstendamm in Berlin.

Timken had made his fortune in the halcyon days of the '90s, a KGB colonel in charge of weapons procurement and production. When the Communist Party ceased to exist, he claimed ownership of a raft of factories producing everything from bullets to bombers and sold their output to the highest bidder, usually budding African despots in need of a competitive advantage to oust their rivals from power. In short order Timken traded his uniform for a business suit and departed Army Southern Command in the unglamorous city of Minsk for the private sector and a shot at the big time in Moscow, or "the Center," which was how Russians referred to their nation's capital.

His fortune secure, he moved laterally into politics. A native of St. Petersburg and a former judo champion (weren't they all, these days?), Timken allied himself to that other son of the north, Vladimir Putin, and rode the diminutive former spy's coattails to power. It was a meteoric rise. A seat in the Duma. An appointment to the cabinet. Then the move to counselor, and a voice in making the really big decisions.

For the past three years Timken had served as first aide to the president, where his primary function was to hold hands with the myriad Western oil companies brought in to modernize Russia's aging infrastructure and exploit the nation's vast oil reserves. His work had met with so much success that he was a front-runner to succeed the president when he stepped down in two years' time.

"What did we give her?" asked Shvets, eyes drilling the monitor.

"Cyanide."

"We still use that?"

"Nothing works as quickly. Once the scent fades, it is almost impossible to detect in the blood. It will appear that Timken had a heart attack. Who will doubt it?"

Shvets angled his head to better view the writhing coils of flesh. "How will she administer it?"

"You do not wish to know."

"Go ahead."

The driver explained briefly. For once, Shvets had no comment.

Since the eleventh century, Mother Russia had been a land ruled and divided by clans. Stretching over eleven time zones and incorporating over fifty ethnic minorities, Russia was simply too large a landmass for one man, or one family, to govern. Ivan the Terrible relied upon his feudal lords to see his will carried out. Peter the Great, on the caste of noblemen called Boyars. Each granted his supporters large tracts of land in exchange for fealty, and in doing so united their aims with his own and guaranteed their loyalty.

It was no different in the twenty-first century.

On the surface, Russia appeared as monolithic as ever. The new, modern Russia was a Western-style democracy boasting a popularly elected president and a bicameral legislature. But appearances were deceiving. Just below the surface, the country was a caldron of competing interests. In place of warlords, there were mafia chieftains. In place of Boyars, there were CEOs. Land was no longer the favored asset, but money, preferably shares of large corporations built on the plundering of Russia's vast natural resources: oil, natural gas, and timber. And knee-deep in the intrigue was the nation's intelligence service, the FSB, fighting with everyone else for the president's favor.

Russia was, and would always be, a country ruled by clans.

Rapacious was the head that wore the crown, and no one was more so than Sergei Shvets, chairman of the FSB. Shvets had long ago set his sights on the pinstriped ermine of the Kremlin. Nothing short of the presidency would do.

On this cool, rainy morning in Moscow, three men stood in his way. One lay comatose in a London hospital bed. Another was touring a natural gas facility in Kazakhstan and was due back later that night. The third, Lev Timken, first aide to the president, was about to die.

Shvets watched as his agent uncoupled herself from Timken and placed her head between his legs. Timken's mouth fell open, and Shvets could hear the man's howls even with the volume turned off. Timken arched his back, his eyes bulging in ecstasy. The woman raised her head from his lap and kissed him on the mouth, lifting a hand to massage his cheek.

Shvets shuddered, imagining the capsule entering his own mouth, his teeth gnashing down on it and releasing the poison into him.

Timken pushed away the nude woman and struggled to stand. The woman remained on her knees, watching as Timken collapsed to the floor and lay still.

Sergei Shvets tapped his driver on the shoulder. "Yasenevo," he said.

He looked out the window as they drove.

One down.

Two to go.

39

The Ristorante Sabatini sparkled like a gem beneath the cloudless Roman night. Rows of tables dressed with white tablecloths bathed in the glow of fairy lights strung overhead. Across the Piazza Santa Maria, the façade of the Basilica di Santa Maria dominated the square. At 11 p.m., the open-air restaurant was packed. Boisterous conversation mingled with the chink of cutlery and the bustle of waiters rushing to and fro to create a convivial, energetic atmosphere.

Yet even among the ranks of satisfied diners, one group appeared to be enjoying themselves more than the others. There were eight persons in all, three men and five women. The men were tanned and elegantly attired, by age and comportment successful professionals. The youngest was forty-five, the oldest sixty, but all were boyishly exuberant in the Italian manner. The women were much younger, barely out of their teens, and beautiful, notable for their sharply tipped, decidedly un-Roman noses and generous, proudly displayed breasts.

A waiter snaked through the crowd and handed a note to the man at the head of the table. "Dottor Lazio, from a friend at the bar."

Accepting the note, Dr. Luca Lazio tried at first to read it without glasses, failed, and then fished a pair of bifocals from his silk blazer and tried again. Lazio was a fifty-year-old Apollo, his feathered hair a shade too black, his chin a shade too tight. His green eyes quickly abandoned the note and turned toward the interior of the restaurant, where the bar was crowded with clients. Making his apologies, he rose and walked inside.

Seated at the bar, Jonathan watched Lazio approach. Though exhausted, he felt a surge run through his body at the sight of the man who might be able to get him a step closer to Emma. He rose from his stool, and Lazio stopped dead.

"Not who you expected," said Jonathan.

Lazio wrinkled the note between his fingers. " 'An old friend' is not exactly what I would have called you."

"You're still practicing." It was a statement, a reminder of a service rendered.

Lazio shrugged, acknowledging the debt. "I haven't had a drink since we saw each other last. I thank you. Again." Lazio reached out to give Jonathan a belated hug and a kiss on each cheek.

Lazio was one of the corps of doctors who revolved in and out of the missions run by Doctors Without Borders around the world. Six years earlier he'd worked under Jonathan's supervision at a camp in Eritrea. When several of Lazio's patients died of suspicious causes, Jonathan discovered that the Italian doctor had been operating while drunk. He had suspended the doctor pending an investigation. In the meantime, word leaked to the local tribespeople. A mob got up, captured Lazio, and was very nearly successful in administering a punishment of its own. Jonathan had intervened and personally shepherded Lazio onto a plane back to Rome. Grateful for his life, the Italian had promised never to drink again. Given all the circumstances, it was the best outcome Jonathan could expect.

"I'm glad to see you're recovering," said Jonathan.

"What are you doing in Rome?" Lazio searched up and down the bar. "And where is Emma? I thought you two only took vacations in the mountains."

"We make an exception now and then," said Jonathan. He didn't add anything about Emma.

"If you don't mind my saying, you look like you could use some mountain air yourself."

Jonathan glanced at himself in the mirror behind the bar. He'd been driving for hours and his eyes were sunken, rimmed with circles. "I'm fine."

"And so," said Lazio, "tell me, is this a coincidence?"

Jonathan finished his beer, then shook his head. "I called your wife and told her it was an emergency. She told me where I could find you. Apparently she thinks you're with some fellow doctors from the hospital."

Lazio glanced back at his friends. "I am." He shrugged. "What about you? Still working for peanuts?"

"I'm back in East Africa. Kenya this time."

"Is that why you're here? To remind me of what happened?"

"I'm here to ask a favor."

Lazio found this amusing. "What can I do for the great Dr. Jonathan Ransom?"

Jonathan moved closer to Lazio, close enough to smell his cologne and see the roots of gray beginning to poke from his scalp. "It's about Emma. She was here a few months ago and had an accident that required surgery. I need to know which hospital treated her."

"What happened?"

"She was mugged and stabbed."

"Emma? I'd thought of her as someone who can take care of herself."

"She can. Usually."

Lazio fingered the chains at his neck. "So why are you asking me this? Surely she remembers where she was treated."

"Emma and I aren't together."

Lazio considered the request. "Fine," he said at length. "I'll help you find the hospital that took care of your wife. It shouldn't be difficult. I'll make some calls in the morning." He motioned toward his table. "Why don't you join us? The sole is fabulous."

"I need to find out where she was treated now," said Jonathan. "Tell your friends you have an emergency. They're doctors, right? They'll understand."

"You're asking a lot."

"We're just beginning here."

Lazio exhaled loudly. "All right, then, but I have to use the men's room."

"Sure," said Jonathan, putting a hand on Lazio's shoulder. "But give me your wallet before you go."

"My wallet?" protested Lazio. "I don't think so."

Jonathan dug his fingers into the soft flesh, allowing a measure of his hate for the man to slip through. Lazio grimaced and handed Jonathan his alligator billfold.

"Two minutes," said Jonathan. "Be at the front door." He watched Lazio slide through the crowd, the picture of elegance and good manners. Then a very different image of Lazio came to him. He saw the doctor being dragged along a dirt road by an angry mob armed with machetes and clubs. He saw Lazio crying out for someone to help him, his wonderfully groomed hair a mess, his face clawed, his shirt hanging in tatters. The Italian hadn't been so suave and polished then, thought Jonathan.

He opened the wallet and studied the image on the driver's license. He looked at the dancing eyes, the easy smile, the facile expression. He was looking at a fraud.

Jonathan jumped off his stool and elbowed his way through the crowd in a rush toward the bathroom. He paused at the entry and gently opened the door.

"He's here, I tell you," came Lazio's voice from inside a stall. "**That Dr. Ransom.** The man wanted for the bombings in London. No, I am not crazy. I know him. I am a doctor, too. We worked together. He is the same man I saw on the news."

Jonathan kicked open the stall, grabbed the phone out of Lazio's hands, and severed the connection.

"Leave me alone," shouted Lazio. "You have nothing on me. You can't make me help you. What have you done? You are a terrorist."

Jonathan shoved him against the wall. Lazio's head snapped against the tile and a stunned look came into his eyes. "Listen to me," said Jonathan, fingers curled around Lazio's collar. "I had nothing to do with what happened with the bombing in London. Nothing! Do you understand? And I have plenty on you. Five patients died under your care because you were too drunk to do your job."

"That was years ago," retorted Lazio. "Ancient history. I've been sober ever since. No one pressed charges then, and they won't now. Are you going to bring a bunch of Africans to the stand? Where's your proof? I'll deny it, and that will be that. And who are you to be telling me what to do? I saw your picture on the television. You're a wanted man."

Jonathan released his grip and Lazio fell back against the wall. He was right, of course. No one would help. It was only then that Jonathan realized that he could never go back to work, for DWB or anyone else. This wasn't a case of malpractice in a forgotten corner of a Third World country. It was a terrorist act against a ranking government dignitary, an act that had taken seven lives. Innocent or guilty, he would be forever tainted by his mere proximity to the crime.

He decided then that if he were a criminal, he'd better start acting like one. Slipping a hand behind his back, he freed the pistol he'd taken from Prudence Meadows and jabbed it into Lazio's gut. "Last chance."

For the first time Lazio appeared genuinely frightened. "Okay, okay, I'll help," he said.

Jonathan rammed the pistol further into the man's belly. "Did you tell the police where you were?"

Lazio shook his head. "I didn't have time."

"Is that the truth?"

Lazio nodded violently.

"Okay, then, we're going to walk out of here," said Jonathan. "You're going to take me to your car, and from there we're going to drive to your office. If you help me out, we'll be finished by morning. I'll disappear from your life and you'll never see me again. Do we have a deal?"

"Yes. Deal."

Keeping a hand on Lazio's arm, Jonathan led the doctor out of the restaurant. Clusters of youths stood on the sidewalk, smoking, laughing, arguing. Mopeds zipped by. "Which way is your car?"

Lazio looked in both directions, hesitating.

"Which way?" asked Jonathan.

Lazio pointed to a silver Ferrari parked illegally 10 meters up the street. "That's it."

"Of course it is." Just then Jonathan heard the

siren. He looked over his shoulder. Across the piazza, a Fiat belonging to the Italian carabinieri pulled into the square, slowing to a crawl as pedestrians scattered. He looked at Lazio. Of course the man had lied.

Lazio yanked his arm free and began to run down the street. Jonathan slipped on a cobblestone, regained his balance, and started after him. He caught him after ten strides and threw him against the wall of the basilica. "Go ahead, then. Shout. This is your chance. If you're so sure no one will care about what you've done, yell for the police."

Lazio's eyes darted here and there, but he remained quiet.

"In your car," said Jonathan. "Or I will shoot you. Right here. Right now."

"Okay," said Lazio. "In that case, we'd better hurry."

40

Luca Lazio's private practice was located in a three-story travertine villa in the Parioli district, adjacent to the Borghese Gardens. In contrast to Trastevere's pulsing nightlife, the neighborhood was sleepy and peaceful, the winding, leafy streets split between businesses and residences.

Lazio unlocked the door and showed Jonathan inside. "So what's it all about? You didn't get your picture all over CNN for nothing."

"It's a mistake," said Jonathan.

"A rather large one, it seems."

Jonathan followed Lazio past the reception desk and through a maze of hallways. Lazio was a dermatologist, and his practice looked more like a day spa than a medical office. Everywhere there were potted plants and posters of men and women with tight, radiant skin, advertising the benefits of one laser treatment or another.

Lazio reached the end of the hall and flipped on the lights to his private office. "Is it to do with her?" he asked, tossing his keys onto his desk. "Emma?"

"Something like that." Jonathan exchanged glances with the Italian, sensing that Lazio was holding something back. "Did you know?"

"Know what?"

"About Emma. What she was doing."

"She was working with you, no?"

Jonathan waited a moment, searching Lazio's features for a sign, some indicator, but saw nothing. "It's better if you stay out of this."

"I'll take your word for it." Lazio sat and powered up his computer. "So, my friend, what are we looking for?"

Jonathan came around to his side of the desk. "Emma told me she was hurt when she was here last."

"A knife wound, you said?"

"Yes. I'm certain she would have gone to an emergency room. I want to find out where she was treated and by whom. Can you access a hospital's admissions records?"

"There is no central registry of patients, but I'm friendly with the chief of surgery at all the major hospitals in the city. If I pass them Emma's name, they will be able to tell me in a matter of minutes if she was ever a patient. Emergency room admission, you say . . . let's see . . ."

"Emma didn't use her name."

Lazio stopped typing and glanced up. "Excuse me?"

"She wouldn't have been admitted under the name Emma Ransom," said Jonathan. "She would have used something else. Try Eva Kruger or Kathleen O'Hara."

Eva Kruger was the name Emma had used in

Switzerland, while posing as an executive at an engineering firm covertly manufacturing and exporting high-speed centrifuges to Iran for use in the enrichment of uranium. He knew less about Kathleen O'Hara. The name belonged to a false passport Emma had kept. One of her get-out-of-jail cards, she called it.

Instead of typing, Lazio rolled his chair away from the desk and gazed at Jonathan, saying nothing.

"She was an agent," Jonathan explained. "An operative. She worked for the United States government. Emma's not even her real name. I didn't say it would be easy to find her. If it was, I wouldn't have come to you."

"Was she involved in this affair in London? This bombing?"

It was Jonathan's turn not to speak. Silence was its own affirmation.

"So you're hoping to find her yourself?" asked Lazio. "Before the police do it for you?"

"Just look."

Lazio slid his chair closer to the desk. "So," he began, with a renewed gusto, "shall we say a foreign woman with a knife wound . . ."

"In the lower back." Jonathan indicated a spot above his left pelvis. "She said there was damage to her kidney. If that's the case, a thoracic surgeon would have been called in. I saw the scar. It was no outpatient procedure. And put down that she was allergic to penicillin."

"Do you have a picture I can scan and send along with the request?"

Jonathan took two photographs from his wallet. One was of Emma as he knew her. It showed her in jeans and a white T-shirt, a red bandana around her neck and sunglasses pushing her wavy auburn hair out of her face. The other was of quite a different woman. It came from a driver's license he'd discovered belonging to Eva Kruger. The photo showed a stern face, sleek hair pulled severely back from the forehead, heavy mascara behind stylish glasses, plenty of lipstick. But there was no mistaking the eyes. It was Emma, too.

Without comment, Lazio scanned the photographs into his desktop, then completed the messages and e-mailed them to his colleagues at the seven largest hospitals in the Rome metropolitan area. "Done," he said. "I'll call them in the morning to make sure they've received the message."

"Call them now," said Jonathan. "Say she's a relative or one of your girlfriends. I want an answer within the hour."

"Are you going to wave that gun at me again?"

Jonathan grabbed the Italian by the collar. "No," he said, yanking him close. "I'm not going to wave the gun at you. I'm going to ram it down your throat and pull the trigger if you don't do what I just told you."

"I believe you've made yourself clear."

Jonathan listened as Lazio placed call after call,

first apologizing then hectoring his colleagues to contact the hospital and perform a check of emergency room admissions. Lazio spoke in short rapid bursts, like a well-trained machine gunner, throwing in medical slang that all doctors tend to use too frequently. Jonathan had trouble following the conversation. He was fatigued, and his efforts to make sense out of Lazio's words only made him more tired.

"Espresso?" asked Lazio, after a time had passed. "It will keep you awake."

"Yeah," said Jonathan. "Sure."

Lazio rose and Jonathan shot to his feet.

"It is okay," said Lazio. "I am only going to the pantry down the hall. We have a refrigerator, too. Perhaps you would like something to eat."

"Just the espresso," said Jonathan. "Hurry it up."

"It will be a minute. That is all."

"Fine." Jonathan followed him to the alcove. Satisfied there was no way out, he walked up and down the corridor, shaking out his legs, trying to rouse himself. Lazio appeared quickly enough with two cups of espresso. Jonathan drank his in a gulp.

"More?" asked Lazio.

"Sure," said Jonathan. Then: "Thank you."

"You're welcome."

The two men returned to Lazio's office and the Italian resumed his calls. Ten minutes later, Jonathan had his answer.

"You were right," said Lazio. "She was here. She

was admitted to the Ospedale San Carlo on April nineteenth."

Jonathan slid to the edge of his chair. "The Ospedale San Carlo—where's that?"

"Close by. Also in the Parioli district."

"Go on."

Lazio motioned for calm. "A foreign woman with wounds consistent with those you describe was brought to the hospital by ambulance at nine forty-five in the evening and underwent surgery an hour later for a torn kidney. She stayed two days and was checked out against the advice of her physician. She possessed no identification and gave her name only as Lara."

"Lara?"

"Yes."

Lara. The name meant nothing to Jonathan. "What about a last name?"

"She gave none. She was listed as an NCP—a noncompliant patient. Fortunately for you, the nurse who admitted her is on duty this evening. She recognized the photograph of your wife."

"Which photo?" asked Jonathan.

"I don't know," said Lazio. "Does it matter?"

Jonathan said no. His head began to throb, and he closed his eyes for a moment. Lara. Where had she picked up that name? The thought came to him that it might have been someone else altogether. "What about the penicillin? Did the records say that she was allergic to penicillin?"

"I printed a copy for you to read." Lazio handed Jonathan a sheaf of papers and sat down on the arm of his chair. Line by line, the Italian ran through the documents, pointing out the time and date of arrival, the patient's height and weight. Emma had given her age as twenty-eight. She was in fact thirty-two. That also sounded like her.

When Lazio came to the details of the surgery, Jonathan asked that he read slowly. He was anxious to know the extent of the injury. The knife had penetrated three inches into Emma's abdomen, nicking the kidney and puncturing the wall of her stomach. The report noted that the patient had blood type AB negative and that during the surgery she had required transfusions totaling six pints of blood.

Six pints. Nearly two-thirds of her blood supply.

Jonathan put down the page. He was trained to listen dispassionately, but he'd never had to apply that emotional distance to his wife. "You're certain that she didn't provide a last name?"

"Absolutely."

"You said she checked out against the doctor's will? How did she settle her bill?"

"Someone paid it for her."

"Who?"

"I don't have that information. It says here that all charges were taken care of to the hospital's satisfaction."

Jonathan grabbed the papers out of Lazio's hands

and rifled through them until he came to the last page. The bill for Emma's stay totaled some twenty-five thousand euros. Over thirty thousand dollars. He breathed deeply, suddenly feeling hot, his throat thick and uncomfortable. Who in the world would have paid that kind of bill?

Lazio observed him with concern. "Are you all right? Would you like another espresso?"

"Yeah, sure," answered Jonathan distractedly. Something more important than espresso had caught his attention. He had come to a line at the bottom of the page listing the "Name of Responsible Party" who had checked her out. As Lazio had said, there was no name. There were, however, initials: "VOR S.A."

Lazio brought another espresso. Jonathan gulped it down, his eyes glued to the page. **VOR S.A.** "S.A." stood for **société anonyme,** the French equivalent of corporation. It was a business, then, that had paid. He set down the cup, then flipped back to the first page. There had to be more information. Something that could shed more light on the circumstances, something that would hint at the nature of the enterprise that had paid the staggering bill.

Under "Details of Admittance," it was noted that Emma, or in this case Lara, had been transported to the hospital by ambulance. But from where? He moved his finger across the line, struggling to make out the handwritten entries. Squinting, he made out the words "picked up patient at Civitavecchia at 2030."

"Civitavecchia," he said aloud.

Jonathan shook his head. Civitavecchia was an ancient port on the coast, nearly 80 kilometers from Rome. He knew the town because he'd been there on his honeymoon with Emma. An overnight stay en route to the airport. She'd insisted on visiting the historical seaside town, saying that she'd read about it as a child and had always dreamed of visiting.

Civitavecchia.

Where Emma had friends. Friends who no doubt predated her courtship with Jonathan.

He glanced up at Lazio, shielding his eyes from the overhead lamp's harsh glare. His face felt more flushed than before, and he was finding it difficult to breathe. He put a finger on his wrist, and was surprised to find his pulse racing. It was the fatigue. He was exhausted. That was all. He squeezed his eyes shut, forcing away the discomfort.

"Isn't there a hospital with a decent emergency room closer to Civitavecchia than this Ospedale San Carlo?" he asked.

"I imagine so."

"Which one?"

Lazio didn't answer.

"Which one?" Jonathan repeated. At that moment, a shiver passed the length of his spine and his eyelids clenched shut for a long, quivering second. He stood. There was a ringing in his ears and he was dizzy. Worse, he could barely breathe. In the space of five seconds, his airway had nearly closed. He was going into anaphylactic shock. He looked at the empty espresso cup. "You," he gasped, stumbling toward Lazio. "What did you do to me?"

Lazio backed toward the door. "Penicillin," he said. "You are allergic, too. I remember you were ill and we had to be careful what antibiotic to prescribe. Don't worry. I won't let you die. I have some epinephrine in the other room. As soon as you lose consciousness, I'll administer enough to keep you breathing until the police arrive."

"Get it now!" Jonathan pulled the gun from his belt, but dropped it to the floor. He fought for his breath. He had a minute, no more, before he'd lose consciousness. He collapsed against the desk, knocking a lamp to the floor. "A chair . . ." he wheezed.

Lazio hesitated, then rushed to put a chair behind Jonathan. As he did, Jonathan charged, striking the man in the chest and driving him into the wall. The jarring motion forced a breath of air into Jonathan's lungs, and before Lazio could react, before he could raise a hand to defend himself, Jonathan punched him in the chin.

Lazio slid to the floor, unconscious.

Jonathan stumbled down the hall. Whatever jolt he'd experienced was seeping out of him rapidly. He pushed open the door to a treatment room and yanked at the cabinets. Clumsily, he searched for a drug that would counteract the penicillin. Prednisone. Benadryl. Epinephrine. Where was the damn epinephrine Lazio had talked about? He found nothing of use. The room began to dim. He collapsed to a knee, then summoned his strength, stood, and willed himself down the hall and into the next room. Shaking hands clawed at a cabinet. He saw a word he recognized. Adrenaline. He grabbed at the box, knocking a dozen behind it onto the counter. He fumbled with the packaging, ripped off the cover, and freed the vial.

A needle. He needed a syringe.

He opened the top drawer. There. Plenty of needles. He tore at the paper packaging and flicked off the cap. He was moving by rote, his thoughts far away, drifting . . .

He forced himself to stay awake and focused his attention on the vial and the needle he needed to slip into it. There! Done! He extracted the plunger, desperately trying to regulate the amount of the hormone he needed. He had only one chance. Too little adrenaline would fail to counteract the penicillin. Too much would send his heart into violent paroxysms that would rupture his aorta. The problem was that he couldn't see clearly. His vision turned double, then tripled. He had no idea how much he'd taken into the syringe.

The world began to go dark.

Slipping. He was slipping . . .

He pulled at his shirt, wrestling an arm from the sleeve.

No time . . .

He fell and his head struck the floor. For a moment his vision came back. It was then that he plunged the needle into his jugular vein and depressed the plunger.

White.

The world exploded into a ball of blazing light. A spasm racked his body, arching his spine and locking down his lungs. A fire ignited inside his chest and shot upward into his head. It was a violent, searing heat that burned his eyes and expanded relentlessly inside his skull. His every muscle tensed. His heart thudded crazily, and he felt as though his brains were going to be expelled through his ears and eyes. He opened his mouth to scream, but no sound emerged. He remained frozen, his face contorted into a rictus of death.

And then it passed.

The pressure in his head subsided. The heat receded and he could see clearly. He drew a breath, his heart hammering inside his chest. He lay still as the pounding subsided. Finally he stood.

At once the imperatives of his predicament came back to him.

He hurried down the hall into Lazio's office. The floor was empty. Lazio was gone. He scooped up the hospital records, made his way back to reception and out the front door. As he came onto the landing, he heard the squeal of tires leaving rubber. He craned his neck and caught sight of a pair of taillights receding into the distance.

Jonathan gulped down the warm night air. He looked both ways, then turned left and ran up the street, away from the city.

Toward Civitavecchia.

41

Mischa Dibner, director of Nuclear Safety and Security for the International Atomic Energy Agency, Austria, sat alone at the head of the conference table deep in the catacombs of Thames House. Her hands were clasped on the desk, her posture without reproach. She was a fierce, pixie-ish woman with a helmet of henna-colored hair and a complexion as pale as a Kabuki mask, with shiny black marbles for eyes. Her record showed that she was fifty-six, a Hungarian by birth and German by marriage. But her English was an American's and hinted at long years spent in the United States.

Graves made the appropriate introductions. After inquiring as to her health and thanking her for venturing forth from her hotel so late at night, he got down to business. "What prompted your decision to visit London at such short notice?"

"We'd detected a problem with our security networks."

"What kind of problem?"

"Are you familiar with our work at Nuclear Safety and Security?"

"I've worked with some of your colleagues regarding pirated radioactive materials," said Graves. "Uranium, plutonium, the like. Until I learned about the stolen laptops, it had crossed my mind that that might have been the reason for your visit."

"I'm afraid not. The reason for our trip is more in line with another of our mandates that has to do with ensuring the safety of nuclear installations—both how they're run and how they're protected."

Kate looked at Graves, who returned her glance coolly.

"We're not worried about a physical attack," Dibner continued. "You could crash a 747 into the containment building of any plant in Europe and it would more or less bounce off. Absolutely nothing would happen. Short of a concentrated military assault with laser-guided munitions, we're safe. Even then, it would be difficult to provoke any large-scale release of radiation that would harm the civilian population. The reason for our trip has to do with cybersecurity."

"Hacking into a plant's control systems?" asked Kate.

"That's where the greatest risk factors lie. Think of each plant as a castle with four concentric rings of defense.

"To get from one ring to the next you must navigate through firewalls that get more and more impenetrable as you near the innermost ring.

"The outermost ring is the Internet. The second ring is the local area network—a firewall that protects the plant from outside incursions. The next ring is the most important. It's called the Plant Control System, or the PCS. Remember, all radioactive materials reside inside the reactor vessel, and it's there that the steam is generated to run the turbines and create energy. The PCS monitors all control systems to keep the process within safe boundaries. Every system is monitored by four separate computers, or four redundant systems. If two of these computers detect an operating error, they trip the safety systems."

"That's only three rings of defense," offered Graves respectfully.

"The fourth is the Reactor Protection System. And, should all else fail, there is the Engineered Safeguard System. By that I mean the actual machinery inside the plants that physically prevent an incident if the PCS were to fail. But it's the Plant Control System that has us worried."

"Has there been an incursion?" asked Kate.

"Not as such. But there have been attempts. All you need to know is that someone was able to get past a firewall at three different plants."

"Just how far past?"

"Far enough. We caught the incursion instantly. They never got close to being able to issue one command on their own. We have too many fail-safes in place. As a last resort, we can take manual control of all systems and thwart whoever is trying to break in."

"Any luck tracing where the hacker originated the attack?" asked Graves.

"None."

He continued: "Does that mean that you came to Britain because one of the compromised plants was in the UK, or was there another reason?"

"One of the plants was at Sellafield, though we'd like to keep that information under wraps."

"I see," said Kate. "So Robert Russell's communications with you had nothing to do with your trip?"

At the mention of Russell's name, Mischa Dibner's face fell. "Who told you about him?"

"Did you know that he'd been killed?" asked Kate.

"I saw it in the newspaper. I was disturbed."

Kate went on: "In the course of our investigation into his death, we came upon information that he had reached out to you. Is that accurate?"

"It was Russell who alerted me to keep watch for forays against our systems."

"Can you be more specific?" asked Graves.

"He said that he'd learned of a state-sponsored plan to get inside a plant and cause damage. He thought the target was probably in continental Europe, and he was most insistent that it would take place very soon. But he refused to hint at who was behind the plan."

"And why did you believe him?"

"Because in the past three months we've had over a hundred cyberattacks against our plants and he was able to name nearly every one. In my book, he'd established his bona fides. We'd planned on meeting yesterday morning to go over ways we could tighten our security."

"At One Victoria Street?" asked Graves.

Dibner nodded. "I didn't learn about his death until after the bomb against Ivanov."

"Ivanov was a decoy," said Graves. "The attack was a coordinated bid to force you and your team to leave the building and then steal the laptops while you were gone."

"That's impossible. No one apart from the six members of our team knew about the meeting."

"And your higher-ups?" suggested Kate. "I imagine you had to clear the visit with the director general."

"We'd never do anything of this nature without his approval."

Kate smiled understandingly. "How long ago did you float the meeting?"

"Seven days." Dibner sighed and seemed to shrink on the spot. "I see what you're driving at. Of course you're right. A good many people knew about the trip. Let me assure you both that I passed along Russell's warnings and that we've seen no unusual behavior anywhere to indicate that an accident is imminent."

"Until the laptops were taken."

Dibner swallowed hard as the realization hit home.

There came a knock at the door. An assistant entered, carrying a tray of coffees, and handed them around. Graves sipped his appreciatively. "Well, then, what do the laptops contain that would make them the object of such a well-planned operation?"

Dibner smiled ruefully. "Correspondence, field inspection reports, confidential country assessments, personnel information. I can't begin to imagine everything that is on them."

"Anything especially sensitive?"

"God, yes." Dibner looked up, her black eyes sunken deep in their sockets. "Several of them were holding emergency codes that allow the IAEA to circumvent every cybersecurity measure I described to you."

"What good will they do someone?"

"In theory, whoever possesses the codes can access the control room of any nuclear plant in the European Union without triggering an alarm. The codes were put in place to allow professionals to operate the plant from a safe distance in case of an emergency. But I wouldn't worry. As soon as we discovered the laptops were missing, we activated a kill switch, sending a command that effectively obliterated their hard drives."

"And how soon was that?"

"We were allowed back into the building at five p.m."

"Six hours," said Graves.

"More than enough time for someone to make a copy of the hard drive," said Kate.

"Even with the codes, it's impossible to precipitate an accident. Those plants are staffed with the best-trained engineers in the world. The moment they noticed something awry, they would take manual control of the plant. The final say will always remain in the control room. With men and women. Not with machines."

Graves pushed back his chair and stood. He helped Mischa Dibner with her coat and showed her to the door. Kate accompanied her down the hall. "Mrs. Dibner, why do you think someone would go to such an effort to get the codes if they really can't do any harm once they have them?"

"In this game, knowledge is everything," replied the director of Nuclear Safety and Security at the IAEA. "Maybe by stealing the codes, these people hope to gain an insight into current safety measures. Perhaps they just wanted to make us feel vulnerable."

The trio paused at the elevator bank. The doors slid open and Mischa Dibner stepped inside. "Remember this—if you want to hijack a nuclear plant, you can't do it from outside. You have to put someone on the inside. In the control room. And that, of course, is impossible."

42

Emma Ransom lay flat on her belly in the tall coastal heather, a pair of Zeiss night-vision binoculars to her eyes. Perched on the cusp of a sandstone bluff, she stared down at a complex of large buildings fronting the ocean some 800 meters away. There were three sets of buildings separated by intervals of 50 meters. From the exterior, each was identical to the next, so much so that it appeared that they were exact copies of one another. Each comprised two principal structures: a rectangular four-story building built of black steel set closest to the ocean, and, abutting it to the rear, a massive concrete block topped with a stout domed cylinder and a slim smokestack.

The complex was named La Reine. The Queen.

In technical jargon, La Reine was an EPR (evolutionary power reactor) or pressurized water reactor, capable of generating 1600 megawatts of electricity. In simpler terms, it was the world's most advanced nuclear power plant, a marvel of modern science able to provide energy to over 4 million inhabitants twenty-four hours a day.

To Emma, it was "the target." And nothing more.

Exchanging her night-vision binoculars for a camera equipped with a 1000-millimeter telephoto lens, she snapped off a dozen pictures. She was not interested in the buildings per se. She could download a hundred pictures of the plant from Électricité de France's website anytime she cared to. Instead she aimed her camera at the fences surrounding the complex. There were no pictures of these on the Internet. Set concentrically with 20 meters separating them, the fences were electrified and topped with razor wire. A stainless steel box was welded to every third fencepost. These, she knew, were self-powered security relays monitoring the hundreds of pressure sensors set in the ground at regular intervals around the plant's 3-kilometer perimeter. There was no way over or under them.

Replacing the camera in its bag, she traced the perimeter of the complex. She was dressed in black from head to toe. A microfiber cap concealed her hair. Nonreflective camouflage paint covered her face. Careful to maintain a distance of 100 meters from the outer fence, she reached the road that led into the plant. She knelt to listen for traffic. The air was still, the night frantic with the sawing of crickets. In the distance she heard an engine start up. A truck, she guessed, as the vehicle lurched through its gears. A Klaxon shattered the calm, and she heard the clatter of a gate sliding on its track. A moment later the truck drove past. It was a large flatbed rig, the kind used to deliver the uranium fuel rods that powered the reactors. Emma waited until its taillights had disappeared, checked back in the direction of the plant, then stepped forward. Just then a motorcycle rounded a curve, coming from the opposite direction. She threw herself into the grass, landing hard on her belly.

"Damn it," she cursed.

Like all nuclear plants, La Reine operated at full staffing and full capacity twenty-four hours a day. There were five teams in all. At any one time, two were on call and one was in training. The clock was divided into two shifts. The "front end" ran from 6 a.m. to 6 p.m. The "back end" ran from 6 p.m. to 6 a.m. Day or night, the plant was humming with activity. She could not afford to be careless.

When her heart had slowed, she peeked from the grass and looked in both directions. Certain that no traffic was approaching, she dashed across the asphalt and disappeared into the clumps of sea grass on the other side. Bent low, she continued moving for several minutes, raising her head every few steps to monitor her position.

It was not long before she spotted a low-slung building within its own fencing. Several jeeps painted olive green sat parked in front of it. This was the barracks. Every nuclear power plant maintained a paramilitary force of between seven and fifteen men. Most were former military personnel and were proficient in the use of automatic weapons and antitank guns as well as shoulder-held ground-to-air missiles.

Emma continued past the barracks, too. They were not part of her tactical considerations, and thus held no interest for her. She had no intention of waging a pitched battle against a superior force.

Reaching the far side of the perimeter, she was afforded her best view of the complex yet. In the moonlight, the domes atop the containment buildings glimmered like ancient temples. La Reine was a post-9/11 plant, meaning it had been built to the most stringent security specifications. The domes were actually two hulls of one-meter-thick steel-reinforced concrete—one inside the other, designed to withstand the direct impact of a fully fueled passenger jet traveling at over 700 miles per hour. Inside these domes was the reactor vessel, molded from a single slab of the strongest reinforced stainless steel in the world. Only one company in the world was able to manufacture steel of this strength: the Japan Steel Company of Hokkaido, formerly makers of the world's finest samurai swords. For all intents and purposes, the plant was indestructible.

At least from the outside.

Nuclear power plants operated on a simple proposition. Steam turned turbines and turbines powered generators. All you needed was lots of steam. That's where the nuclear part came in. The fuel needed to make the steam was uranium 235, and this isotope of uranium was fissile, meaning it emitted blazingly hot, lightning-fast atoms if given the correct environment to create a nuclear chain reaction. Put uranium in water, and pretty soon the water would start boiling like crazy and producing all kinds of steam. The steam then drove the turbine generator, which generated electricity.

It was as easy, or as monstrously complex, as that.

Uranium 235 was therefore the counterpart of coal, gas, or oil-fired boilers used to power the traditional smoke-belching fossil-fueled plants. And these days uranium was in large supply, and therefore cheap. Far cheaper than oil. That's why so many nuclear power plants were suddenly being built all over the world.

Not everyone thought that was a good idea.

In fact, there were some who would kill to prevent it.

From her pocket Emma pulled a handheld instrument—metal, heavy, colored yellow, with a viewfinder on one side and a lens on the other. The instrument was a portable theodolite, and it measured a chosen object's relative height above sea level. Putting the viewfinder to her eye, she focused on two separate points, one at the far side of the reactor building and the other at a point on the spent-fuel building approximately 15 meters away from it.

The fuel used to power the reactor took the form of long, slim rods of uranium (actually, hundreds of uranium pellets stacked on top of each other). The rods measured 16 feet in length and an inch in diameter, the width of a tube of Chanel lipstick or a Panatela cigar. They were grouped in square bunches, seventeen by seventeen, into a single fuel assembly unit. The rods stayed "hot" or "fissile" for four years. After that they were removed from the reactor vessel and transported a short distance aboard a miniature rail car through a tunnel into the spent-fuel building, where they were lowered into a pool of cold water and kept there until most of the radiation and heat had been bled out of them.

Emma checked the height readings from the two points and performed a calculation inside her head. The result pleased her. The plan was going to work.

Her task completed, she retraced her steps through the field and climbed the steep hillock. Her car was where she had left it, parked in a copse of ground oaks, covered by a profusion of branches. She cleared the foliage, threw her bag into a false compartment in the trunk, then climbed into the car. In a moment she was speeding down the highway toward Paris. The entire reconnaissance had taken her forty-five minutes.

Getting in was the easy part.

43

The director general of MI5 was Sir Anthony Allam. Allam was a career officer, a graduate of Leeds University who'd joined the Security Service directly after completing his studies. He'd done stints in all the major branches during his time: Northern Ireland, capital crimes, extremist groups, and most recently counterterrorism. He was a slight, unprepossessing man, with neatly trimmed gray hair, unfailing manners, and an ill-fitting suit. One of the meek who had little chance of inheriting the earth, no matter what the good book might say.

But looks were deceiving. One didn't rise to be head of Five without superior intelligence and more than a little of what his Welsh mother had called moxie. Behind the furtive blue eyes and the deferential smile hid a volcanic temper. Word round Thames House was that when Sir Tony, as he was known, was angry, you could hear him all the way to Timbuktu.

"You mean to suggest that Igor Ivanov was not the target?" said Sir Tony as he peered at Charles Graves.

"The bomb was a diversion. It was meant to precipitate the evacuation of the ministry building in order to steal some laptop computers that the visiting IAEA team had brought with them."

"You're certain?"

Graves looked at Kate. They nodded. "We are," she said.

"Interesting. Very interesting indeed." Allam leaned back in his seat. "But if you want me to go to the PM with this, you're going to need hard evidence. He's got himself convinced that it was the Chechens or some group pushing for democratic reforms in Russia. Rather likes the idea, too. Feels it takes him off the hook somehow."

"We've got evidence," said Kate. "May I?" She picked up the remote control and punched the play button activating the DVD player.

Graves narrated. "This feed is from the ministry building at One Victoria Street. Third floor, corridor seven, east. The camera covers the hall directly outside the conference room where the team from the IAEA and our lads from the Safeguards Authority were holed up."

"Is it in focus?" asked Allam as he slipped on a pair of glasses. "Half the time the lenses are fogged."

"Crystal-clear," said Graves. "We've got the woman going into the room at eleven-eighteen and coming out at eleven-twenty."

"Two minutes. She moved fast," said Allam.

"Yessir," said Kate. "She knew what she was looking for."

Onscreen a corridor appeared. It was a typical

government office building: linoleum floor, message boards on the wall. The color picture was grainy but in focus, as promised. A time code ran in the upper right-hand corner. At 11:15 the camera shook violently.

"There goes the bomb," said Graves.

Seconds later the first of the building's occupants began to file out of their offices. The trickle grew to a flood, and by 11:18 the corridor had emptied.

"Here she comes now. Keep your eye on the bottom of the screen. Can't miss her."

At 11:18:45, a figure entered the screen from the bottom left, moving against the current of workers, and walked directly to conference room 3F. The figure was moving rapidly, her face ducking the camera. Still, her attire was easily identifiable. Jeans. Black T-shirt. And, of course, there was the hair.

At 11:20:15, the door to the conference room opened and the woman stepped back into the hallway. She walked toward the camera, her head kept deliberately down, her face hidden in the shadow cast by her long auburn hair. Over her shoulder she carried an overnight bag.

"She's got the laptops in the bag," said Kate. "It's one of those collapsible ones that fold down to nothing when they're empty but are extremely sturdy."

Allam kept his fingers steepled to his chin, saying nothing.

"Now look at this." Graves replaced the disk showing footage from the closed-circuit television at

1 Victoria Street with another containing footage from the camera at the corner of Storey's Gate. The pictures showed a woman dressed in a black T-shirt and jeans standing at the crosswalk holding a cell phone to her ear. The lead SUV in Ivanov's motorcade crossed the screen, then the second. The woman stepped away from the curb and turned her back. At that moment the screen blanched. For two or three seconds, all remained white as the camera struggled to correct its exposure. When the picture returned, the woman was gone.

"It's the same woman," said Graves. "She's the one who stole the laptops. I'd wager on it."

"You know her?" said Allam.

"Her name is Emma Ransom."

"Ransom? Wife of the doctor whom you allowed to get away?"

Graves held Allam's eye. He'd been on the receiving end of Allam's temper twenty-four hours earlier and he'd be damned if he showed that it had fazed him. "According to her husband, she used to be in the employ of a secret United States government agency called Division. Something attached to the Pentagon. I spoke with my oppo at Langley. They deny it. Never heard of Division or Emma Ransom."

"They would, wouldn't they?"

"There is something else. When we first pulled in Ransom, he mentioned that his wife had thwarted some kind of attack in Switzerland back in February. I called Marcus von Daniken in Bern. Strictly off the record, he confirmed that there was some sort of dust-up involving a plot to bring down an El Al jetliner and that Ransom and his wife were up to their necks in it. No civilians involved, so they were able to keep it quiet. More than that, he wouldn't say."

Allam considered this. "Well, she doesn't look like a Chechen black-arse, that's for sure."

Graves frowned. "Which brings us back to the first question. Why was Ivanov visiting London in the first place? Everyone's been damned close-mouthed on the issue."

"With good reason. He came over to meet with some wallahs in our petroleum business. Wanted to get them jazzed up about restarting some old joint ventures to tap all that oil that's still lying under the ice in Siberia, modernize their existing infrastructure, that kind of thing. It's a sensitive topic, seeing as how the Russians chased all our firms out several years ago and pocketed their profits. The boys at the Foreign Ministry are viewing Ivanov's approach as a major policy shift on the Russians' part. Either their oil industry's falling apart and they're desperate for revenue or they've decided to rejoin the international community."

Allam sighed. "The question remains, however, just who Mrs. Ransom is working for."

"So far we have no clue," said Graves.

"Tell me more about what was on those laptops," said Allam.

Graves related Mischa Dibner's statement that whoever possessed the laptops could theoretically access override codes that would allow them to take control of a nuclear reactor somewhere in Europe. "There seems to be a time constraint as well," he added. "We're looking at the possibility of an incident within the next forty-eight hours."

"I see," said Allam simply. "There does seem to be one connecting thread between all this."

"What's that?" asked Kate Ford.

"Energy," replied Allam. "Ivanov's in town to talk about oil. You tell me that the bomb was a ploy to steal nuclear codes that may hasten an attack on a reactor in the next forty-eight hours. I don't think any of it is coincidence." The director general of MI5 removed his glasses and massaged the bridge of his nose. "Right now, we know of only one person who can tell us what it all means. Emma Ransom. What else do we know about her?"

"Next to nothing," admitted Graves. "Not who she works for, where she came from, or where she disappeared to. Only that she killed Lord Robert Russell and that she was here in London prior to that doing whatever she damn well pleased."

"You reckon they're in it together, Dr. and Mrs. Ransom?" asked Allam.

"I do," said Graves. "DCI Ford is of another opinion."

"Why's that?" asked Allam.

Kate went over Ransom's actions at the bomb scene. "He could easily have gotten away, but he stayed to assist one of the victims."

"Saved this fellow's life, did he?"

"No. The man died."

Allam raised his eyebrows. "How do you know Ransom didn't kill him? Maybe he strangled the man. After all, he shot someone else last night." Allam consulted the papers on his desk. "Another doctor. James Meadows. Harley Street surgeon. This Ransom sounds like a cold-blooded killer, if ever was."

"I don't have all the answers, sir," Kate continued. "But I'm convinced he's not a player in the bombing or the theft of the laptops. I can't explain why, except to say that it doesn't make sense."

"Doesn't make sense for an innocent man to run away from the police either, does it, DCI Ford?" Allam asked pointedly. Small stars of red had appeared in his cheeks, and he was sitting on the edge of his chair.

"It's my opinion that Ransom's trying to find his wife," she said firmly.

"Find her? I'd run in the other direction as fast as my legs would carry me." Allam coughed and sat back in his chair, momentarily appeased. "Any reason you think she might have gone to Rome?"

"Rome?" Graves narrowed his eyes. "Our last piece of intel puts Ransom in Belgium. He rented a car near Brussels airport."

Allam tapped his pen on a pink notepad in front of him. "I just received a call from the chief of the carabinieri. Your Dr. Ransom's causing all manner of problems over there. Assault, kidnapping."

"Kidnapping?" said Kate.

"Yes," said Allam. "And the Italians don't like it one bit."

Graves leaned on the director's desk. "Do they have Ransom in custody?"

Allam shook his head. "No, but they have the man he kidnapped. Another doctor. Apparently Ransom put him through the wringer, asking about that wife of his. It seems that she was in Rome, too, a few months ago, and didn't half enjoy herself."

"Oh?"

"I'm told she was attacked—mugged or something—and treated at a local hospital. Ransom wanted to know where exactly."

"When did this attack on Emma Ransom take place?" asked Kate.

Allam consulted a paper on his desk. "April."

Kate shot a glance at Graves and said, "The Semtex used in the car bombing was stolen from an Italian army barracks outside of Rome around the same time."

"She must have nicked the BMW from Perugia then, too," Graves added.

"Busy girl." Allam turned his gaze on Kate. "Ever been there?" he asked. "To Rome, I mean."

"On holiday. Years ago."

"Pack your bags. The both of you. I'll smooth the way diplomatically. Just remember the Italians have complete authority over the operation. It is their country, last I looked. Charles, sign a chit for one of the Hawkers. Put it on my budget." Allam returned his attention to the dossier on his desk, a sign of dismissal. Graves and Kate walked to the door. Suddenly Allam called out. "And Charles, I do rather hope your efficiency improves. I'm going to have to go to Downing Street with this news. The PM's going to be rather upset. No one likes more egg on his face. Especially a politician."

"What do you mean, **more** egg?" asked Graves, a hand in the doorway.

"So far we've failed twice. First, to protect a visiting dignitary against an attack. Second, to safeguard a sensitive government installation against theft. Nuclear secrets, no less. If a third failure leads to a nuclear accident, I'd think seriously about leaving the country. Permanently."

44

Sir Anthony Allam sat alone in his office listening to the ticking of his prize antique Asprey ormolu clock. The clock had belonged to his father, and his father before him, and so on all the way back to 1835, when Sir Robert Peel, modernizer of the London Metropolitan Police Force (hence the name bobbies), had awarded it to Detective Superintendent Aloysius Allam in recognition of his fifty years of service. Six generations later, the Allams had made a name for themselves as coppers on both sides of the Atlantic, and Sir Tony had the connections to prove it.

Feeling beneath his desk, he punched a button that indicated that he was not to be disturbed under any circumstance. Swiveling, he opened the sideboard that housed the director's line, a phone equipped with the latest in scrambling technology. These days it was as likely that your own brood was listening in as the enemy. He consulted his directory, then dialed an overseas number connecting him to a certain rather undignified suburb of Washington, D.C.

"Hello, Tony," said a rough American voice.

"Evening, Frank. How's the world treating you?"

"Fair to middlin'," said Frank Connor. "Yourself? It's a little late over there, isn't it?"

"You tell me. You didn't really think you could come for a visit without my hearing about it, did you? Enjoying your stay so far?"

Connor grunted. "Food's just as lousy as it was last time."

"Not having any success finding her either, I gather."

"Who?"

"You know who. Word is she went rogue on you."

There was a long pause, followed by a sigh of capitulation. "These damn field types. We get some of 'em so wound up they have no choice but to self-destruct."

"She looks rather composed to me," said Allam. "We've got her on tape detonating the car bomb that tried for Igor Ivanov."

"That was a terrible business," said Connor, without sympathy.

"Not yours, I trust."

"Come on, Tony. You know me better than that."

Allam left that comment alone. "Any idea who she's hired on with?"

"If I knew, I wouldn't be eating that soggy bacon of yours. Ivanov's got himself plenty of enemies. The man's a regular butcher. The Monster of Grozny, they call him. He's a freakin' war criminal. Word is he likes to get his hands bloody, and I mean his own hands. They say he threw that last journalist out of the window himself. You know, the guy in St. Petersburg."

"I heard the same thing. He's a devil, that one." Allam cleared his throat. "But here's the rub—my people have themselves convinced that Emma Ransom wasn't after Ivanov at all. They tell me that the blast was some kind of diversion to get into the offices of our British Nuclear Authority, the equivalent of your Nuclear Regulatory Commission, and make off with some laptop computers containing all kinds of sensitive codes. They believe that she may provoke some kind of incident or attack on a nuclear facility within forty-eight hours."

"In England?"

"Possibly. Possibly abroad."

"If there's anyone who could pull it off, it's her. You have your hands full. Me, I'm just looking to even up the scorecard."

"You made quite a scene at the hospital this morning. Was Prudence Meadows another of your agents who was wound too tight, or was it her husband?"

"No comment."

"Watch yourself, Frank. Remember, we're only cousins."

"I'll be on my best behavior."

"Thank you," said Allam earnestly. "Actually, this was meant to be a courtesy call. We received word that Jonathan Ransom is in Rome. It's our belief he's trying to find his wife. I can tell **he's** not one of yours. Leaves a trail a mile long and half again as wide. I'm sending a team down there to work with the carabinieri and see if we can run him to ground. I've a feeling he knows more than he's letting on. Anything you'd care to add?"

There was another lengthy pause, and Allam had the distinct impression that fat old Frank Connor was squirming in his chair. The mental picture made him very happy indeed.

"Are you free for lunch tomorrow?" asked Connor.

"I may be able to find an opening in my agenda."

"Good," said Connor. "Cinnamon Club. One p.m. Oh, and there's just one thing . . ."

"Yes?" Allam listened closely as Connor went on a lengthy discourse. It was all he could do to keep his temper from getting the better of him. "Very well, then," he said when Connor had finished. "I'll see you at one. But Frank—**Frank?**"

But there was no one on the other end of the line. Connor had already hung up.

45

Jonathan leaned his shoulder against the church's wooden door and was relieved to feel it open. Stepping inside, he paused to allow his eyes to adjust to the dim light. Candles flickered at posts around the building's interior. Moonlight streamed through stained glass windows lining the nave. He advanced down the aisle and slid into a pew. He didn't kneel, but laid his elbows on the bench in front of him. The church was still, the only sound that of his ragged breathing. Slowly calm settled over him. He was safe, if only for a few more minutes.

To his left was a chapel built into a side alcove. The altar was simple, adorned with a brocade cloth. A rough wooden crucifix hung on the wall behind it, with an elongated marble Christ.

Outside these church doors, the Italian police were combing the streets for Dr. Jonathan Ransom. He had to assume that they'd passed on news of his presence in Rome to their counterparts in London. At the same time they'd spread word to the local police forces in the vicinity. His capture would figure high on the priority list of every Italian policeman between Milan and Sicily.

Seated in the half-dark, Jonathan took stock of his position. He was not cut out for a life as a fugitive. He wasn't one to jump down his "rabbit hole," as Emma had called her escape hatch, and disappear from the world. Sooner or later he would be caught. The question was not if, but when. It was a matter of delaying the inevitable.

He unfolded the papers he'd taken from Luca Lazio's office. It was too dark to read, but he knew the words. A nicked renal artery had resulted in Emma's losing six pints of blood. She would have been delirious when she'd been transported to the hospital, perhaps even near death. In agony, drifting in and out of consciousness, she'd given her name as Lara. Not Eva Kruger, not Kathleen O'Hara, and not Emma Ransom—all well-known, practiced aliases—but **Lara.** And after the surgery, when asked for her last name, she'd refused it.

Jonathan could come up with only one reason why.

Lara was her real name. She had no alias to accompany it. Only the truth. And the truth she must keep hidden at all costs.

Jonathan rose and sidestepped to the center aisle. He spent a moment staring at the altar, gazing up to the ceiling and the oils depicting the Fall of man, the Resurrection of Jesus, and the Second Coming.

Turning, he made his way to the front door. A wind had sprung up outside, and somewhere it made its way through a crack in the church walls, sounding a high-pitched keening. He stopped to listen, hearing his own fear in the shrill wail. Suddenly the wind died, and he felt his uncertainty go with it.

He opened the door and went onto the street.

46

Frank Connor paid off the taxi and presented himself to the doorman at the Diamond Club in Belgravia. "Tell Mr. Danko that Bill from California is here. I'll be upstairs at the tables."

Connor paid the exorbitant entrance fee and walked upstairs. The Diamond Club was a privately licensed casino catering to wealthy Eastern Europeans who had made the move to London in a big way over the past ten years. The club was divided into three floors. The ground floor offered an elegant bar and restaurant. The second floor housed the casino itself. And the third floor was reserved for private gaming and management.

Connor took a place at a blackjack table in the center of the room. At 1 a.m., action was lethargic, with no more than two dozen players scattered around the floor. Connor ordered a whisky and began to play cards. After three hands, he'd lost two hundred pounds. He signaled to the floor captain and informed him that he'd like to see Mr. Danko. The captain nodded politely and continued on his rounds. Ten minutes and another two hundred pounds to the worse, Connor still didn't see Danko.

Enough, he told himself. He was done being polite.

Connor ordered a second whisky, loosened his tie, and began to really play. In ten minutes he was up a thousand pounds. In an hour he was up five thousand. He asked for a cigar, and when the captain returned with a Cohiba, Connor told him to tell Mr. Danko that unless he wanted to continue having a very unprofitable night, he'd better get his Bosnian butt down here faster than he could say Slobodan Milošević.

The captain left. To prove his point, Connor bet all or nothing on the next hand and drew an ace over king. Blackjack.

Danko showed up sixty seconds later. He was tall and slim, dark hair slicked back off his forehead, his Slavic stubble kept at an appropriate length, and he looked much too comfortable in a white dinner jacket.

"Hello, Frank. Long time."

"Sit down."

Danko dismissed the dealer and sat next to Connor. "What are you doing here?"

"I need your help."

"Look around you. I'm out."

Connor glanced around the casino before coming back to Danko. "I see the same guy. You know Rome. I need you to do a job for me there. Are your passports still in shape, or do you need me to run something up for you?"

Danko smiled, no longer so comfortable. "Frank, listen, I appreciate your interest. It's a compliment, I know. But I've moved on. I'm forty. Too old for that kind of work. Come on. Give me a break."

"No breaks tonight. Tonight is a break-free zone. Know what I mean? Now come on, get your stuff. You still keep that nifty rifle upstairs? Let's go on up to your office and I can fill you in on the details. Job pays ten thousand dollars."

"I make that much in a day here." Danko leaned closer, so that the smell of his cologne was ripe in Connor's nose. "I gave you seven years. Where's the American citizenship you promised? Where's the resettlement to California? You strung me along and then dumped me when you didn't need me anymore."

"I rescued your bony ass from an internment camp when you weighed ninety-six pounds. You owe me."

"Thank you, Frank, but I think that I've paid you back."

Connor considered this. "I can offer twenty thousand."

"Frank, it's time to go."

Connor tried to pull Danko closer, but managed only to knock over his whisky and spill it onto Danko's dapper jacket. "You may even know the target," he continued, undeterred. "Emma Ransom. Remember her?"

"No, Frank. I don't remember anybody or anything. That's how you taught us."

Danko lifted a hand, and two doormen were at the table a second later. "Take Mr. Connor downstairs," he said. "Help him find a cab."

"I'm still playing cards, you ungrateful Slavic piece of shit."

"Time to go."

Connor rose aggressively and one of the doormen grabbed him by the shoulders. Connor shook him off, then gathered his chips. Leaving, he flung a five-hundred-pound marker at Danko.

It missed.

47

They were trouble. Emma knew it at a glance.

The crew of Muslim toughs had rounded the corner just ahead and were headed straight for her, already whistling and calling out names.

"Hey, girl, you better watch out," one called out in Arabic. "Not safe for a Western girl all by herself."

"Maybe she needs somebody to protect her," added another. "A real man."

"Bitch!" said the last, as if ending the argument.

There were six in all, and they wore the urban attire popular among disaffected French youth: baggy pants, oversized athletic jerseys, gold chains. There was nowhere to turn, nowhere to run, even if she wanted to. She fumed. She was not in the mood for a confrontation. Not tonight. Not when she had the black on. Not when even the friendliest smile might set her off, let alone a bunch of terrorists in training. She cursed the boys at headquarters. You decide to set up shop in a **quartier louche,** you have to expect that this kind of thing might happen.

The **banlieue** of Seine-Saint-Denis, in the northeastern outskirts of Paris, was a neighborhood of immigrants. A neighborhood where the poor came and went. A neighborhood that the police avoided. It was past two in the morning, but the streets still had plenty of life left in them. Neon lights advertised an all-night falafel shop. A cluster of men stood nearby, smoking. Keeping her eyes on the gang of toughs, Emma pulled her shoulder bag closer to her body and kept walking. The bag contained her work clothes, the camera, her purse, and, of course, her weapon.

The gang circled her, following her up the street.

"We're talking to you, ma'am," another said, this time in French. "You visiting, or did you move in? I'm sure we haven't seen you before."

Emma kept her pace, rounding a corner. She paid their catcalls no heed. She knew what it was like to be young and ungoverned and wild, with too much time on your hands and not enough money. "Excuse me," she said, spotting her building, making to cross the street.

"Not just yet." It was the leader, if there was one. A homely boy of nineteen or twenty, Algerian by the look of his hawk nose and shadowy eyes. He stood in front of her, blocking her path. He wore a tank top, and his arms were enormous. She spotted a tattoo of a dagger on his neck. A convict. That explained the arms. He'd had plenty of time to pump iron in the prison yard.

"I said, 'Excuse me.' " Emma stepped around him, but he slid over to block her once more. She straightened up, sensing a tension that had not been there a minute before. "What do you want?"

"To talk."

"It's late. I need to get home."

"Why don't you come to my crib?" said the leader, moving in, getting into her space. "Just you and me. Don't worry, I'll have you home in time for morning prayer."

"That won't be necessary. You kids run along now." She was baiting them and couldn't stop herself. She had the black on. Tonight, no one gave her shit.

The others were moving in, too. She checked over her shoulder. The street was empty. No falafel joints or tattoo parlors here. Just dark storefronts. In the distance she heard the crash of a bottle breaking and a woman's hysterical laughter, giving way to a scream. Something clicked inside her.

"Don't be a hard case," said the leader. "Why don't you hang with us?"

"And you can give us your bag while you're at it," said another. "We'll deliver it to your room for you."

A hand reached for the bag and she yanked it away. "The bag stays with me."

"I'll decide that," said the leader. He stood inches away, his eyes close enough for her to see that one was half green and half brown. Then he made his mistake. He reached out and took her arm. Not forcefully, but firmly and with no mistaking his intent.

It was all the provocation Emma needed.

She hit him on the bridge of the nose, her knuckles extended. The blow was so quick that he didn't see it coming. It landed solidly and she felt the cartilage collapse, heard the septum break. He stumbled back a step, falling to his knees as the force of the blow registered, his nose broken, blood running copiously from his nostrils. She threw a kick into the chest of the man behind her, the one she'd sensed was the most violent of the group. It landed squarely on his sternum. He dropped like a sack of potatoes, winded, eyes looking as if they were about to pop out of his skull.

That's all it took. The others backed off.

Disgusted with herself, Emma crossed the street and entered her building.

It was a monument to anonymity, a ten-story HLM—**habitation à loyer modéré**—built forty years ago and untouched since. The lobby was stifling and reeked of hashish. Emma walked to the elevator and waited five minutes for it to come. The stairwell was across the foyer, but she knew better than to walk up five flights. She didn't care about the doped-up residents she might find. It was the stink of stale piss she hated. It reminded her of home and the past. And the past was the only thing that still frightened her.

The elevator arrived. She rode to the fifth floor. Apartment 5F was at the end of the hall. She had the key in one hand. The other was buried inside her bag, clutching a compact Sig Sauer P238.

Inside, she locked the door, taking care that the double bolt was secured. She dropped the bag on the kitchen floor, then knelt and dug out her pistol, checking that a bullet was chambered, safety on, before setting it on the counter. The place was a dump, just like the place she'd stayed in the night before, in Rouen. **Welcome back to the other side,** she muttered. Division would never have allowed a place like this. It wasn't the money. It was a question of security. To put an operation at risk because of a bunch of neighborhood hoodlums was beyond reckless.

And what about her own behavior? Picking a fight when she should have walked away. Reckless was just the beginning.

She opened the refrigerator. A stuttering bulb threw light on a plate of cheese speckled with mold and a quart of rancid milk she could smell from where she stood. She closed the door, swearing under her breath. The least they could do was put a little something in the fridge for her. Some yogurt, maybe a jar of pickles, even some mineral water. Even, God forbid, a bottle of wine. This was France, after all.

Her stomach groaned and she felt her muscles clench with hunger.

The memory hit her like a hammer.

A gangly girl in a torn woolen dress. Auburn hair cut short, uncombed and hopelessly tangled. Rebellious green eyes peering out from a face ragged with eczema. She was standing in the school kitchen, her hands held out for punishment. At her feet lay a fractured porcelain bowl and the fistful of gruel she'd scraped from the bottom of the pot. The black belt lashed her palms, and then it lashed other parts of her. And though her body cried out, it was her pinched, complaining stomach that hurt most.

Emma laughed at her mawkish sentiment. Others had had it worse. But somewhere inside her, she heard the name Lara, and she rushed to lock away the memory.

She made a tour of the flat, stopping in each room to listen at the walls. It was a formality. She could hear the voices of her neighbors without putting an ear to the chipped and barren concrete. Noise was good. Quiet was bad. Quiet meant fear. And fear meant the police.

She returned to the kitchen and searched through her purse for something to eat. She found a stick of gum and some allsorts she'd bought in London on the way to meet Jonathan. She emptied the licorice into her hand and ate it, piece by piece. She had to admit it. She'd picked a glamorous profession.

Just then there came a knock at the door. Emma passed through the kitchen, picking up the pistol. Three knocks followed. She put her eye to the spy hole and recognized the sullen disheveled figure on the other side. She opened the door. "Nice place you've got here, Papi."

"The flat isn't ours," he said, brushing past her. "It belongs to our friends from Tehran. Complain to them."

"I don't care who it belongs to. It's a risk to place a safe house in such a squalid **quartier.**"

"A risk, is it?" Papi straightened up, suddenly looking a little more like the career officer he was. "Seen any police cars around? Any prying eyes? I didn't think so. We couldn't be in a safer place, even if you did have to teach the local welcoming committee a lesson."

"You saw?"

"Of course I saw. You think I stay here?" He swung the large leather bag he was carrying onto the counter and rolled his neck, as if loosening his muscles. "What did you expect? A shiny ops center with analysts at their desks and a three-meter screen on the wall? You're part of my team now. We operate under the radar. Not too different from your former employers, though I dare say we're more ambitious."

"And the laptops?" asked Emma. "Did you decrypt the hard drives before they hit the kill switch?"

A smile twisted Papi's pale lips. Using both hands, he withdrew a sheaf of papers thick as a phone book from his bag. "Behold the Queen as only her intimates may see her." The papers landed with a thud. "Final construction drawings signed by the managing engineer himself. Downloaded directly from their innermost sanctum. Every hallway, every window, and every door. One hundred percent accurate."

Emma ran a hand over the detailed schemas, recognizing the outlines of the nuclear power plant she'd visited earlier that same night. "You're welcome," she said.

"Up yours, too," Papi mumbled.

For two hours they pored over the drawings, rehearsing the operation. They studied the security building Emma must pass through to enter the complex, her path to the reactor containment building, and, most important, the ways to get into and out of the spent-fuel building. They brought up the photographs Emma had taken earlier that night and studied them on Papi's own laptop, a sleek MacBook Pro. Like everyone else at home, he coveted American products.

Finally he talked about the placement of the explosives.

"You'll set two devices," said Papi. "The first carries a charge of two kilos of RDX with a dash of nitro to add a little oomph. Put it in the right place and it will blow a hole three meters in diameter out of the wall. That's more than enough to suit our purposes. The second is bigger. Three kilos of HMX. It's the latest and greatest. Ten times as powerful per cubic centimeter as Semtex. A bit unstable, though, so don't bang it about. When you set the timers, make sure that there is a differential of at least six minutes between the first and second blasts. We need that time for the water to drain." Papi turned over the drawings of the spent-fuel building and regarded Emma. "Give yourself adequate time to leave the premises. Once the water escapes the cooling tank, those rods will be shooting off more gamma rays than the face of the sun. When the HMX goes off, you don't want to be anywhere near the place. Any questions?"

"What about the inspector's credentials?"

"Right here." Reaching into the bag, he withdrew a packet and spilled its contents on the countertop. "Your name is Anna Scholl," he said, sorting through the identification cards and selecting an Austrian passport and driver's license. "Born Salzburg, 1975. Graduate of the Hochschule St. Gallen in Switzerland. You've worked for the IAEA for two years. You started in the administration department and were transferred nine months ago to Safety and Security, Inspections Directorate."

Emma studied the photograph inside the passport. It was her executive look. Short hair. Rimless glasses. Plenty of makeup.

"INSC's offices are located in La Défense. They'll check you at the entrance against her picture in the IAEA database. A man named Pierre Bertels will meet you at ten a.m. He runs their credentials department."

Emma studied the piece of paper. It read, "International Nuclear Security Corporation, 14 Avenue de l'Arche, La Défense 6, Paris."

"What about the real Anna Scholl?"

Papi's gray eyes flashed a warning. "She won't be a problem," he said stonily.

"Good," responded Emma, with equal dispassion.

"And you're sure this Bertels won't call Vienna to double-check?"

"As sure as I can be. His company doesn't work for the IAEA directly. Their clients are the power companies, not the regulatory bodies. The whole procedure shouldn't take more than an hour. I've brought you something to wear."

Papi took a garment from his bag and laid it on the kitchen table. It was a svelte black two-piece wrapped in protective plastic from the dry cleaner.

Emma picked it up and held it at arm's length. "If I cross my legs, you'll see my privates."

Papi stepped closer and put his hand on her waist. "I picked it out myself. Try it on."

"Later."

"I want to make sure it fits."

"Is that an order, colonel?"

"It's general now." Papi circled her, running a hand across her waist, letting it slide lower to caress her bottom. "I thought you might wish to oblige a superior officer."

"That was over a long time ago."

"It's over when I say it's over."

Emma spun and grasped his hand, folding it into a wrist lock. But Papi was strong and, despite his size, agile. He stepped clear of the lock, grasping her wrist instead, and slapped her across the face with his left hand.

"You've gotten stronger," he said, releasing her.

Emma's wrist ached, but she refused to touch it. "Don't do that again."

Papi snorted. "There is one more thing. Upon arriving at the plant, you will be issued a guest pass equipped with an RFID chip." RFID, for radio frequency identification device. "Sensors will track every step you take. The only person who can access your whereabouts without permission from the head office is the plant's chief of security. He'll have to be neutralized before you go in."

"What's his name?"

Papi frowned. "We don't know yet. All plant personnel are employees of Électricité de France, the utility that operates the nuclear grid. He'll have been vetted, just like you. Bertels should have his information on file. It's up to you to find a way of getting it." Papi walked lazily to the door. "I'm sure it won't pose too much of a problem. That's what we trained you Nightingales for, isn't it?"

He left the apartment smiling.

"Bastard," she said.

48

"I'm not going to Italy. I'm staying here. There's work to be done."

Charles Graves strode across the pale carpeting of his office on the first floor of Thames House and slipped behind his desk. Kate Ford followed steps behind, closing the door and pressing her back against it.

"I don't think Sir Tony will appreciate that," she said.

"Sir Tony wants results."

"Even if that means disobeying him?"

"Especially if that's what it means."

Kate took a seat opposite him. "What do you have in mind?"

"Those nuclear facilities aren't as safe as the IAEA would have us believe. Otherwise they wouldn't be in such a tizzy about the laptops." He opened his drawer and searched until he found a Met directory. "Remind me," he said, with a shake of his blond head, "wasn't Russell's home security system fail-safe, too?"

"You're saying the IAEA doesn't know what it's talking about?"

Graves stopped leafing through the directory. "I'm saying that if Emma Ransom went to all that trouble to get those laptops, it was for a reason. Something's up. Robert Russell knew it, and now we know it, too."

"And so?"

"I'm going to do what you suggested earlier. I'm going to find out just who Lord Russell's source is."

"The one who told him about the car bomb?"

"Is there another?"

"Have you gotten anything back from communications about his phone or Internet records?"

"Russell was better than any terrorist at keeping his trail clean. The only phone number we've got for him was used by friends and family. All strictly aboveboard. The devil probably kept a bag of SIM cards he interchanged for his private calls. Until we find one of them, we're out of luck. Same thing goes for his e-mails. Ah, there it is!" Graves located the page listing the Automobile Visual Surveillance Bureau, picked up the phone, and dialed an internal number.

"Graves. G Branch. I need everything you've got from Sloane Square three nights ago, between twenty-three thirty and one-fifteen. Target a four-square-block search area. Send the results to my personal in-box. How long? Make it an hour and a case of Guinness is yours."

"Russell stopped at Sloane Square after visiting his

parents' home the night he was murdered," said Kate.

"So he did." Graves rose and circled the desk, picking up his car keys and dropping them into his pocket. "The Windsor Club. Peers of the realm, bluebloods, that kind of thing. Like I said, stupid of me."

"Why stupid?" asked Kate, rising and accompanying him out of the office.

"Isn't it obvious? Russell met someone at the club who clued him in to what 'Victoria Bear' meant." Graves stopped at the door. Kate was standing barely a foot away. He noticed that she had a few freckles across the bridge of her nose and that her hair was naturally blond. Nice eyes, too. Something kind lurking behind all that steel.

"Good luck in Italy," he said. "Find him. Find Ransom."

And without a backward glance, he hurried down the corridor.

Alone. That was the problem, Graves decided as he drove through the streets of Westminster. Too much time on the job and too little time for himself. He was forty years old, married once, for all of two years. She'd kicked him out after he'd returned from a nine-month tour in Iraq during the first dust-up, in '91, or rather, she'd kicked out his suitcases, his football trophies, and his cockatiel, Jack. He had a scar and a medal to show for his efforts, but she wanted more. She wanted **him.**

Back then it had been the Parachute Regiment, with a stint at the SAS, the Special Air Service. Today it was Five. Both demanded the lion's share of a man's time, and he gave it willingly. Eagerly, even. He didn't know any other way. He'd thought about ditching it all. There were plenty of offers in private security these days. Big-money jobs hobnobbing with corporate bigwigs, helping this insurance company guard against fraud or that bank choose the most state-of-the-art alarm. But that's all he'd done: think about them. In the end, he didn't give a tinker's cuss about money. He made enough to see to his needs and to buy the occasional toy. It was about more than that, wasn't it? It was about something bigger. Christ, if he knew the word for it. It was about whatever it was that you felt when you got them before they got you.

He caught his eyes in the mirror and scowled. **Forget it,** he chastised himself. **Don't get all grandiose on me. A regular Edmund Burke. Just concentrate on your job. Find out what Emma Ransom was up to and do it fast.**

He turned the corner into Sloane Square and spotted his destination. Still, he was haunted by his sudden melancholy. He didn't expect anyone to understand.

Anyone except Kate.

An inconspicuous brass plate, its engraved letters worn to near obscurity, was all that noted the establishment at No. 16 Sloane Square. Graves pressed the Windsor Club's buzzer. A female voice answered, and he gave his name and occupation. "It's an emergency," he added. "Open up."

A buzzer sounded and he pushed open the door. The foyer was wood all around, light courtesy of a chandelier that had seen service with Nelson. The floor was scuffed and in need of polishing. Shabby chic for those too rich to be bothered.

"Colonel Graves, I'm James Tweeden, the club manager. How can we be of service?" He was tall but stocky, conservatively dressed in a navy suit and tie. His handshake was iron. Former military, guessed Graves, as Tweeden showed him into a deserted lounge.

"Always keep long hours?" Graves asked, unbuttoning his jacket and sitting down.

"Nothing fixed, really. We open at eleven in the morning. Keep the staff around as long as needed."

A waiter materialized and Tweeden waved him off before Graves could ask for tea.

"I'm here about Robert Russell. He was here two nights ago. I'd like to know whom he met."

"We don't discuss our members' activities," said Tweeden. "That's why the establishment is a 'private' club."

"What about your **ex-members**? Russell's dead."

"Same difference. It's the Russell family we're concerned about."

"All well and good. Under normal circumstances, I'd leave it at that, but something's come up. We've got pictures of his car parked just outside."

"Does this have something to do with his murder?"

"More than that, actually." Graves cocked his head and leaned in, whispering confidentially. "Look, Mr. Tweeden, you may keep late hours, but I don't. If I'm coming here at half-past one, it's because something serious is up. A question of national security. If you'd like, you can phone the director general." Graves held out his phone.

"I don't think that will be necessary."

"Who'd you serve with?" asked Graves.

"Grenadiers."

"Parachute Regiment, myself," volunteered Graves.

"Wankers."

"Look who's talking. Got to be a fairy to wear those bearskin caps."

The men shared a laugh. Tweeden motioned Graves closer. "Look, Colonel. This billet's a sweet bit of work. Remuneration's competitive. Members are a nice lot. Russell's father, the duke, saw my boy into Eton. The only things they ask of you are loyalty and discretion. When a member passes through these doors, he doesn't want the world following him."

Graves said that he understood. "This is between you and me. You have my word that it won't come back to bite you in the arse."

"All right, then," said Tweeden. "Guess a little chin wag won't hurt. But between us and us alone. Lord Russell was here. He arrived at midnight. I greeted him. He wanted a private room. He had a guest coming and he wanted to use the back entry . . ." A footstep sounded in the doorway behind them. Tweeden shot from his chair. Graves glanced over his shoulder and caught sight of a longish, bony face familiar to every Briton from the age of two up. One of a dozen or so men entitled to use the title HRH, His Royal Highness. The man's eyes looked Graves up and down, none the happier because of it. A second later he was gone.

The effect on Tweeden was immediate. "You'll have to leave now, Colonel," the club manager said icily. "I can't help you any further."

Graves rose. "Who was it?" he whispered. "Who did Russell meet with? Give me a name."

"Foreigner," said Tweeden. "Name you see on the football pages." Then, in a louder voice, for public consumption, "It was a pleasure, sir. My assistant will see you to the door."

"Come on," said Graves, taking hold of Tweeden's elbow. "One name. You can do that much."

Tweeden yanked his sleeve free. "Good evening, Colonel."

———

Graves dropped into the front seat of his Rover and slammed the door. "Damn it all," he muttered under his breath. He'd been a second away from getting the name, and then who of all people should show up? If he weren't a rationalist, Graves would think that the gods had something against him. He considered running home and packing a bag to join Kate. Her plane was set to leave at five. He might just have time to get an hour or two of sleep.

He felt his phone vibrate and saw that he had received an incoming message from the AVS, Automobile Visual Surveillance. He crossed his fingers. "If it wouldn't be too much trouble, Lord . . ."

He downloaded the message from his in-box into the car's command center. It was nothing James Bond–like, just a scratched-up color monitor like any other police car had these days. One after another, pictures taken from surveillance cameras in a four-block perimeter of Sloane Square appeared on the screen. He scrolled through them until he caught sight of Russell's Aston Martin DB12 parked in the same spot he now occupied.

Graves scrolled through the next few photos more slowly. A time stamp on the bottom corner indicated a lapse of two minutes between each picture. It would be sheer luck if he found anything. A Lamborghini passed by, then a BMW, a Mercedes, and an unmissable Rolls-Royce Phantom. He wondered if anyone in London drove a car costing less than a hundred thousand quid anymore.

The source of the pictures switched to the camera at the rear of the club. Graves sat up, remembering that Tweeden had vouchsafed that Russell's guest had entered via the back door. He scrolled through thirty or forty images before stopping abruptly.

It was the Rolls-Royce again: a black Phantom, the flagship of the brand. It had pulled up opposite the club's back entrance. Its passenger door was open, but no figure was visible. Tinted windows prevented him from seeing inside the vehicle.

Graves magnified the photo. The license was a vanity plate bearing the number ARSNL 1. Every soccer fan in London knew whom the car belonged to. He recalled the stack of sports magazines about the Arsenal Football Club he'd discovered in Robert Russell's flat. One more mystery explained.

He called in the plates to AVS, requesting all pertinent registration information. A name, phone number, and address were waiting when he arrived at Thames House nine minutes later. Not an HRH, exactly, but hardly a commoner either, at least not in the general sense of the word. Men and women whose personal fortunes exceeded a billion pounds constituted their own aristocracy, whether they were English or not.

Justice waits for no man, thought Graves as he picked up the phone and dialed the home number listed on the automobile's registration. He wondered how a billionaire felt about being roused at two in the morning. An angry voice picked up on the seventh ring.

"Da?" demanded the man nicknamed the Great White.

Graves had his answer. He didn't like it much at all. They weren't very different from us, after all.

49

Ghosts in the gathering light, the figures floated across the docks, gathering nets, hauling tackle, and coiling ropes as they fitted their craft for sea. It was not yet 5 a.m. and the port of Civitavecchia was wide awake. **The docks never sleep,** thought Jonathan as he trudged along the quai. He was tired and hungry and his pants were wet from sleeping on the grass in a field outside of town. To the north, intermittently visible through the patchy morning fog, lay moored the massive oceangoing ferries waiting to board at first light and deliver their passengers to ports in Corsica, France, and Spain. To the south, an armada of fishing boats bobbed inside the jetty, readying for another day's labor.

Jonathan bought a bag of warm roasted chestnuts and found a place to sit, anonymous among the passing seamen. The port looked neither familiar nor strange. Eight years had passed since he'd visited. It had been February, not July, the streets cold and empty, the town melancholy. Hardly a place begging to be visited.

Yet Emma had insisted they come.

"No one stays in Rome," she'd said. "It's much too

expensive. Civitavecchia is the real thing. You practically feel as if you'll run into Nero around every corner."

He knew now that her reasons were excuses. She hadn't come to escape the high prices or the tourists. In February, there weren't any. She'd come for the same reason that had brought her here three months earlier.

She'd come because she had to see someone. And he had a suspicion that that someone's name had the initials S.S.

He crunched on a chestnut, dredging up memories of their visit. Eight years was a long time, and he'd been too preoccupied with the last-minute change in posting that had cut short their honeymoon to play the eager tourist. He glanced over his shoulder at the cafés and coffee bars that lined the seafront. All were dark, awnings retracted, chairs stacked next to the door and chained to prevent theft.

And then he saw it. Large, colorful block letters unchanged since that day in February so long ago. He read the words, and it came back to him in a torrent. The quicksilver feelings of confusion, apprehension, and anger.

The sign read, "Hotel Rondo."

How was it that he had forgotten?

Emma threw her camera onto the table and collapsed on the bed. "So what do you think? Wasn't I right to suggest we come?"

It was four in the afternoon. Jonathan was drenched from an afternoon squall that had come in from the sea, taking them by surprise. They had made a tour of the ancient port city of Civitavecchia that would have exhausted even the most ardent sightseers.

"I think I've seen enough Doric columns to last me until I'm forty."

Emma punched him on the arm. "Be happy I only insisted on visiting the most important sites. Three hours isn't so much."

"Three hours? I thought it was three days." Jonathan watched as Emma peeled off her wet togs. First the jacket, then her blouse, the pants and socks. She turned, clad only in her underwear, which were sensible women's Jockeys. But on Emma, even a paper bag looked sexy.

"What are you looking at?"

"You."

"Why?"

"Because I think I deserve a reward. You know, for actually paying attention when you read all that stuff from the guidebooks."

"Do you, now?"

"I do indeed. Something that will make me forget that we could have been admiring the Sistine Chapel instead of all those ancient craphouses."

"You just like the sight of all those naked women."

"Michelangelo's eye for beauty was almost as good as mine."

"Really?" Emma gave him a look as if to say he was too arrogant by half. "Well, then, I think I can do something about that," she said, matching his tone and upping him one. "And I can give you your tour of the city at the same time."

"Interesting. I'm curious."

"Take a seat on the bed. And not too close. No touching the docent."

Jonathan jumped onto the bed and arranged the pillows behind his back as Emma disappeared into the bathroom. When she returned three minutes later, she had let her hair down, and the damp tresses fell onto her bare shoulders. A towel covered her chest, and she held one hand hidden behind her back. "Close your eyes," she said.

Jonathan complied.

"All right. Open them."

Jonathan opened his eyes. Emma stood at the foot of the bed, naked. One hand cover her pubis. The other held a polished red apple and was extended toward him. She was Eve from the Sistine Chapel.

"Adam never stood a chance," he said. "Where does the line for original sin begin?"

Emma snapped her fingers. "Close your eyes again."

Jonathan obeyed. This time when he opened

them, she had seated herself on a chair and sat gazing mournfully at Jonathan's wet patrolman's jacket arrayed across her legs. The emotion in her eyes caught him by surprise and struck a chord deep inside him. "You're Mary. I mean, the *Pietà*," he said.

"Very good." Emma sprang from the chair. "One more."

Jonathan closed his eyes a third time. When she asked him to look, she was standing on the same chair, one leg perched saucily on an armrest, her hands bundling her hair above her head. "*Birth of Venus*," he said.

"Wrong. It's in the Louvre."

"Caravaggio. Didn't he paint something in this town?"

"Strike two."

"I don't know. I'm a doctor. I spent all my time studying anatomy books, not art history. I give up."

Emma leaped onto the bed and snuggled next to him. "Emma Rose Ransom. Miss February. Your own private masterpiece."

Afterward, they lay in each other's arms. The rain had started up again and rattled their windows with a troubling intensity.

"Why Belgrade?" asked Emma. "Of all places. It's not fair."

"We're just flying into Belgrade. We're going to

Kosovo. That's a province in Serbia. It'll just be for a few months."

"But it's dangerous there. I've had enough of bullets and hand grenades for a while."

"The war's over," said Jonathan, propping himself on an elbow. "We're helping them get back on their feet. Half the doctors left the country. Besides, we're only there for three months, then we go to Indonesia as planned."

"They could have at least allowed us to finish our honeymoon. Everything's always a crisis. You'd think they could get along without us." Emma rolled off the bed and went into the bathroom. She emerged a few minutes later fully dressed. "I'm going out," she said. "You want anything?"

"In this rain?"

Emma peeked out the window. "It's not so bad."

"Compared to what—the Flood?"

"Aren't we biblical."

"Coming from Eve herself, I guess that means something." Jonathan chuckled, then threw off the blankets and stood. "Hold up, Mrs. Ransom, I'll come with you."

Emma came closer, kissing him. "Stay here. You look tired. Why don't you take a nap?"

"Nah, I'll get some air, too."

"Really," she insisted. "It'll be a bore. Do something useful. Reconfirm our flights. Better yet, find us a decent place for dinner."

Jonathan looked at Emma. He saw something in her eyes that he'd never seen before. She did not want him to join her. "Probably a good idea. I'll reconfirm the flights and book us a table at the best place in town."

"I want something decadent. Spaghetti carbonara with warm bread and butter, and zabaglione for dessert." She twisted up her face. "What do they eat in Kosovo, anyway?"

Emma went out. Jonathan took a shower and dressed. As requested, he reconfirmed their flights. According to the concierge, the best place in town was Trattoria Rodolfo. Jonathan was sure that the prices were sky-high, but what the heck? He didn't think he and Emma would be hitting any three-star eateries in the Serbian countryside.

Satisfied that he'd met Emma's expectations, he dug out his paperback and began to read. He checked his watch every fifteen minutes. When an hour had gone by, he put the book down and went to the window. If anything, it was raining harder than before, a veritable deluge. He smiled to himself. There he was, going all biblical again. Slipping on his jacket, he went downstairs.

"Scusi," he said to the concierge, "did you see my wife, Signora Ransom?"

The concierge said that he had. He came around from behind his counter and showed Jonathan the direction she had gone in upon leaving the hotel. Jonathan put on his baseball cap, then pulled his hood over it. Venturing onto the street, he made his way down the hill toward the port, hugging buildings and ducking under any available awnings. The rain was awful and the cobblestone streets were slick. He kept his eyes open for Emma, but after five minutes he'd had enough. He entered a kiosk to get some relief. He studied a carousel of postcards and picked out one of an amphitheater and another of the catacombs he'd toured that morning.

"Three euros," said the sales clerk.

Jonathan fished in his pocket for some coins. Waiting for change, he glanced out the window. Across the street, the doors to a hotel opened, granting him an unobstructed view of the lobby. It was a deep, dimly lit space with a polished wood reception counter and, oddly, a replica of an English phone booth stuck in the far corner. Walking across the lobby, deep in conversation with a man, was Emma. It was immediately apparent that they knew each other well. Emma rested a hand on his arm, and her attention was riveted on him. The man's back faced him, and all Jonathan noticed was the twill green raincoat and the matching trilby hat.

The next moment the hotel doors closed.

Jonathan stood for a moment, confused at what he had seen. At the same time, he recalled Emma's insistence that he remain in the hotel

room. Gathering up the postcards, he crossed the street, careful not to rush or to appear in any way upset. He was certain that there was a satisfactory explanation for why she had left the hotel to surreptitiously meet another man. But by the time he entered the lobby, Emma and the man with whom she had been so earnestly engaged were gone.

Jonathan checked the adjoining pub (that explained the phone booth), as well as the lounge and reading room, but to no avail.

Emma was nowhere to be seen.

Jonathan dropped the bag of roasted chestnuts into the trash and made his way up the narrow road toward the Hotel Rondo. He was walking quickly, a man in search of something. After so long, it was hard to remember exactly what he had seen that day.

Emma was in the room when he returned. As calmly as possible, he asked if it had been her inside the lobby of the hotel. She had replied that it hadn't. She had gone for a walk by the harbor. When he pressed her about it, she grew neither upset nor self-righteous. She simply replied that he must have been mistaken. And then she had given him a paperweight in the shape of an ancient Roman trireme that she'd purchased at a store they'd visited in the opposite direction from the Hotel Rondo.

That's where the matter ended. Jonathan believed her. The light in the lobby had been dim. The rain hadn't helped matters. He put it off to a case of mistaken identity. Never once in all the intervening years had he thought to question her story.

Until now. Until Emma had been picked up by an ambulance eight years later at this very address. Via Porto 89. Civitavecchia.

The address of the Hotel Rondo.

50

The Hawker business jet touched down at Rome's Leonardo da Vinci Airport at 8:33 local time. Under a pale blue sky, the plane taxied to an isolated terminal at the southern border of the 200-acre airport complex. A squadron of police vehicles formed a semicircle near the jetway. Descending the stairs, Kate Ford shook hands with the chief of the Rome police and a lieutenant colonel who headed up the Rome detachment of the carabinieri, or federal police. After an exchange of formalities, she was updated on the manhunt for Jonathan Ransom.

Photographs of Ransom taken upon his arrest had been forwarded to all local precincts. Prints of the picture had been distributed to foot patrols walking Rome's tourist areas—the Coliseum, the Forum, St. Peter's and the Vatican. Word that he had been spotted inside city limits was likewise transmitted to rail and transport authorities at Rome's four main train terminals. Police patrols were doubled at Leonardo da Vinci Airport, and at Ciampino, Rome's smaller commuter airport, located along the Greater Ring Road 15 kilometers east of the city.

"Have you instituted any roadblocks or traffic checks?" asked Kate.

"It is summer," explained the chief of police without apology. "Tourist season. Traffic is bad enough as it is. Without a confirmed sighting in a specific locale, there is nothing we can do."

"I understand," she responded, with a smile to smooth the waters. She motioned to the terminal. "Is the witness here?"

"Waiting inside. This way."

Kate followed the lanky police captain up some stairs into the building. The airport lay on the coast, and the tang of sea salt and brine and the freshening breeze invigorated her. Reaching the door, she paused to gaze out at the blue expanse. Ransom was close. It was odd, but she could feel his presence, even sense his desperation. They were both running.

After leaving Thames House, Kate had stopped by her home long enough to shower, pick up a change of clothes, and brush her teeth before dashing to Heathrow. In between briefings from Graves and updates from the Italian police, she'd managed two hours of sleep on a couch at the rear of the cabin. Now a gust of wind threatened her hair, and she rushed to clamp a hand to it. The motion made her think of Pretty Kenny Laxton, and she dropped her hand to her side. Barely three days had passed since she'd taken the call about the presumptive suicide at 1 Park Lane that had launched the investigation. In the interim the suicide had proven to be a murder, a car bomb had taken the life of her dear friend Reg Cleak and many others, and something infinitely more frightening was nearing fruition.

Inside the terminal, the group filed into an air-conditioned conference room. Dr. Luca Lazio sat alone at the head of the table, smoking furiously. Kate introduced herself. After establishing that Lazio spoke English fluently, she asked all officers except the chief of police to leave the room.

"That was a brave action you took, trying to stop Jonathan Ransom," said Kate, choosing a seat next to him, sensing he was comfortable in the presence of women.

"Not brave. Necessary."

"Weren't you afraid he might harm you?"

Pleased by her proximity, Lazio shook his head much too confidently. "I know Ransom. He waved his gun around a little, but I didn't think he would use it."

Kate hadn't expected Ransom to be armed. Strangely, she felt disappointed. "Even so," she went on, continuing to play up to Lazio, "what prompted you to take such bold measures? Why not just help him and let him go?"

"I saw what happened in London. Isn't that enough?"

Kate agreed that it was, though privately she thought there was more to it than that. "Did he admit his role in the bombing?"

"He said he had nothing to do with it. Of course he was lying."

"And did he give you any idea where he was going?"

"None. Unfortunately, I didn't see him depart from my office. When he discovered that I was trying to hurt him, he attacked me and I fell to the ground. He left me, I presume to find medicine to alleviate his allergic reaction. That was when I ran. You see, I'm not so brave after all."

An aide appeared, carrying a tray of espressos, and handed them around. The captain and Lazio took considerable time adding sugar and cream, each taking the moment to light a fresh cigarette. Kate looked on, struggling to conceal her impatience.

"You said that Ransom sought you out in order to find out some information about his wife," she asked. "Were you friends?"

"Not friends, but colleagues," replied Lazio. "We worked together years ago in Africa. I suppose I was the only doctor he knew in Rome. He told me that his wife had been attacked and injured in the city sometime in April. I tracked her down to the Hospital San Carlo, where she was treated for a knife wound."

This was the attack in April that Allam had mentioned. "Was it life-threatening?"

"Without question." Lazio talked for a while about the nature of the injury, the surgery performed, and the time needed to recover. "It was not easy to find her," he added. "She did not give her real name. Ransom said she was some type of secret agent or some nonsense. He had me check other names."

"Do you remember them?"

"Kathleen O'Hara and Eva Kruger, but they were of no use. That's the funny part. When she checked in, she gave a different name altogether."

"What was it?"

"Lara. Just Lara. She refused to provide a last name. For some reason this upset Jonathan."

The police chief explained that they had no record of any stabbing or similar assault during that time period, and that he'd sent three men to the hospital to keep watch for Ransom in case he went there seeking more information. With a smile, Kate told him that she appreciated his actions, and then she returned her attention to Luca Lazio. "Did Ransom have any idea who had attacked his wife?"

"None at all," said the Italian doctor. "He was very focused on finding her, and he was upset that I could not help more. If you ask me, he should be happy that she is alive at all. A woman who loses so much blood has no business surviving an hour's ambulance ride to the hospital."

"Is it normal to need one hour to reach a hospital in Rome?"

"Of course not," said Lazio, offended. "But she wasn't attacked in Rome."

"Then where?"

"Up the coast. I can't remember. It is written on the admittance sheet."

"Do you have that with you?"

"Ransom took it."

Kate ran a hand along the crease of her trousers. She'd done her homework on Lazio. Before landing, she'd reached Doctors Without Borders in Geneva and spoken with the woman who'd supervised the Eritrean mission where Lazio and Ransom had worked together. It took some prodding, but finally the woman had supplied some startling information about Lazio. The information went a long way to explaining why Lazio had probably been trying to kill Ransom with the overdose of penicillin, rather than merely render him unconscious. And why he was none too keen to see Ransom captured.

"You must have a copy on your computer," said Kate. "If you'd like, we can check from here." She stared into his eyes, letting him know in no uncertain terms that she knew all about him.

"Civitavecchia," said Luca Lazio. "That is where the ambulance picked her up. That's all I know."

Ten minutes later, Kate Ford was seated in the front seat of an Alfa Romeo belonging to the carabinieri, speeding up the highway. The ambulance company had provided the address where Emma Ransom, or Lara, had been picked up. Via Porto 89. It also listed the nearest establishment. A place called the Hotel Rondo.

"The drive will take thirty minutes," said the lieutenant colonel, a handsome olive-skinned man of thirty-five. "Maybe an hour, depending on traffic. Summer. You never know."

"Get your men there ahead of us," said Kate. "Block off all streets leading to the hotel. Make sure they have a description of Ransom."

"He is dangerous, this man? He has a gun, no?" **Dangerous.** Shorthand for asking whether the order be given to shoot Ransom on sight.

"We'd prefer him alive," said Kate. "He may have information that could save lives."

The lieutenant colonel placed a call to his counterpart in Civitavecchia and advised him that the man responsible for the car bombing in London two days earlier might at that moment be in or near the Hotel Rondo. "We are mobilizing our local brigade," he announced confidently upon hanging up. "We will have one hundred men on the streets within thirty minutes. We will shut down the area. If Ransom is there, we will get him."

Kate said nothing. She stared out the window at the whitecaps and the sailboats cutting through the blue water. Soon the road narrowed to two lanes. The Alfa Romeo slowed and came to a halt. Traffic was backed up in both directions. Drumming her fingers, she looked out the window. Across the street was a gated enclave with a sign reading "Regional Barracks Ladispoli; XX Artillery Battalion. Italian Department of Defense." Kate recognized the name with a start. It was from this barracks that Emma Ransom had hijacked the shipment of Semtex three months earlier.

Just then the car accelerated, and soon they were moving at high speed again.

Kate lowered her hand to her side and crossed her fingers for luck.

Ransom was close.

She could feel it.

51

The Hotel Rondo was closed for business.

Jonathan stood at the front door, gazing into the lobby where he had seen Emma those eight years before. The red English phone booth was gone, as well as the furniture and the potted plants. Even the reception desk had been ripped out. The hotel was a husk.

He tried the door anyway. Locked.

Disappointed, he turned and walked back down the street. A café around the corner was just opening its doors. He took a table near the window, and when the manager came, he showed him a picture of him and Emma together and asked if he might have seen her a few months back. The manager studied the picture long enough to be polite, then apologized and said that he hadn't.

"A coffee and some rolls," said Jonathan.

"Subito."

A busboy delivered the breakfast a few minutes later. Jonathan set the picture on the table and stared at it as he drank his coffee. The photograph had been taken five months earlier, in Arosa, Switzerland, the day before the climb that had ended in such disaster.

He and Emma stood close to each other on the ski slopes. She was smiling sunnily, her head resting on his shoulder. No matter how long he looked at her, he could not spot the artifice. He ran a finger over the image of his wife. Here was a woman who at that moment had taken upon herself the responsibility of preventing the destruction of a passenger airliner, and because of that, the outbreak of war, and she appeared as footloose and fancy free as a teenager on ski holiday.

He knew then that he was beaten. He was no match for her cunning. He'd been foolish to even try to find her. Worse, Emma knew it, too. **She'd known it all along.**

His fingers curled around the photograph and crumpled it inside his fist. The search was over. He had nowhere else to go. No more clues to follow. No trail, however faded, to trace. Emma had gotten her wish. She had disappeared.

Jonathan paid the bill and ambled outside. He looked up into the sky, considering what to do. Going back to work with Doctors Without Borders was out; so was returning to the camp in Kenya. The thought struck him that he might never be able to practice medicine again. He would need to reinvent himself. But as what? And where? He shrugged and began walking.

"Signore, per favore."

Reflexively, Jonathan quickened his pace.

"Yes, **you,** signore!"

Jonathan glanced over his shoulder and saw that it was the busboy from the café, the kid who had brought him his breakfast. He stopped and turned to face him.

"The woman you asked about. The lady with the beautiful hair. I see her."

Jonathan dug out the photograph. "Her?" he asked, flattening out the wrinkles. "You're sure?"

"She was here in April. She ate at the café every morning. She was German, I think, but her Italian was very good."

"Do you remember how long she was here?"

"Three or four days."

"Was she with anyone?"

"No, she always ate alone. Are you her husband or something?"

"Or something," said Jonathan. "It's important that I find her."

"Did you talk to her hotel? She was at the De La Ville. It is a few blocks up the road." The busboy smiled sheepishly. "I followed her one day when she left. I wanted to ask if I could buy her a drink." He lowered his eyes, signaling defeat. "I didn't have the courage to ask her name."

Jonathan patted the young man on the shoulder. "No apology necessary. Thanks for helping me out."

"She was a kind person. You know, decent. You could see it in her eyes. The first genuine girl I met in a long time. Before you go, can you tell me something?"

"If I can," said Jonathan. "Sure."

"What is her name?"

"Lara."

"Of course I remember Mrs. Bach," said the manager of the Hotel De La Ville, studying the picture of Emma and Jonathan on the ski slope. He was a short, fastidious man, dressed in an immaculate gray suit that contrasted with the lobby's seedy decor. "But who are you?"

"Her husband."

"Her husband?" came the skeptical response. "You are Mr. Bach?"

Bach. Another name to go with another identity. "Yes, I'm Mr. Bach."

"From France?"

"No," said Jonathan, taken aback. "I'm American, but my wife and I lived all over. Our last residence was in Geneva."

The manager looked at him a moment longer, then walked behind the reception desk and punched a blizzard of commands into the computer. "Your wife checked in on April fifteenth. She was here four days, then she disappeared. Not a word. Not a call. I phoned the police, but no one has heard of her. Is she all right?"

"She's fine. She had an accident while she was here and had to spend some time in the hospital. Do you still have her belongings?"

"I'm sorry, but I gave them to the other man who was here asking about her."

Other man? No doubt the same person who'd checked her out of the hospital. "Tall guy," tried Jonathan, fishing. "Dark hair."

"No, in fact he was short like me. And older, with gray hair. He said he was her husband, too, but I did not believe him. Mrs. Bach is far too pretty for such a rough man."

"What do you mean, rough?"

"He was not polite. A foreigner, but not like you. He paid the bill. Cash." The manager crossed his arms, his brows raised in some Mediterranean mixture of apology, sympathy, and camaraderie. Women, he seemed to be saying. They could never be trusted.

"Do you know where he was from?"

"He spoke no Italian, only English, but with an accent. Maybe British. Maybe German. I really couldn't say."

Jonathan sighed, bitterly disappointed. "Well, thank you anyway," he said, shaking the manager's hand, then feeling stupid for doing it. For some reason he needed that contact. Putting on his sunglasses, he headed for the door.

"I do, however, have an address," said the manager.

Jonathan spun and returned to the reception desk. "You do?"

"The man was very worried about your wife. He thought there might be other people inquiring about her. I got the feeling he did not trust her so much. Perhaps 'suspicious' is the better word. He asked me to contact him if anyone came to the hotel and asked about her."

"And you said you would?"

"For five hundred euros, wouldn't you?" The manager grew serious. "Do not worry. I will not tell him about you."

"Thanks," said Jonathan, not believing him for a second.

The manager went to his monitor and printed up a page with a phone number and the address Route de La Turbie 4, Èze, France.

Èze. A tiny medieval village carved into the mountainside overlooking the Mediterranean on the Côte d'Azur, a few kilometers from Monaco. Jonathan had driven through it, but never visited. It hardly seemed like a headquarters for a clandestine service that had employed Emma. Then again, he knew better than to be surprised.

Above the address was printed a company name: VOR S.A.

It was the same name given on the hospital bill.

52

"We tracked down the phone."

"You're sure?" asked Den Baxter of the Evidence Recovery Team.

"Oh, yeah. We've got it, all right. And there's more, boss. You'd best get over here as soon as you can manage."

Baxter checked his wristwatch as he ran up the stairs leading to the London Metropolitan Police's forensics laboratory. It was just shy of nine. It had taken the Met's team of technicians less than a day to piece together the fragments of the circuit board recovered at 1 Victoria Street and identify the make and model of the mobile phone used to detonate the car bomb aimed at Russian Interior Minister Igor Ivanov.

Twenty-one hours and forty-one minutes, to be exact.

Baxter kept track of such things.

Alastair McKenzie was waiting at the door to the lab. Baxter noted with pride that the man was wearing the same clothing as the day before. He smelled like last week's garbage, but so what? Cleanliness might be next to godliness, but it didn't do a thing to solve an investigation.

"Nearly killed myself getting over here," said Baxter, taking McKenzie's hand in his own and nearly crushing it. "Better be worth it."

McKenzie's answer was a tight smile and a direction to follow him.

Baxter entered a conference room and found a team of white-coated techs waiting. "Right, then," he said. "Let's hear it."

"Keep in mind that we had bugger all to start with," said Evans, the chief of the forensics squad. "Two grotty little remnants of the circuit board that Mr. McKenzie was kind enough to bring us, and that was it. We used a bit of epoxy to piece the board back together, cured it in the autoclave, and here's what we came up with." Evans handed Baxter a warped chunk of sky-blue plastic shaped like a wee pistol. "You can see the place for the screen, and here's where the microphone goes. What gave it away was the placement of the antenna feed pad. Only Nokia puts it there. We had a look at their manuals and straightaway saw that it was a model 9500S."

"Entry-level model," piped up one of Evans's assistants.

"Give 'em away free with a two-year subscription plan," said another.

"But what's most important," continued Evans, "is that the 9500S is brand spanking new." He took back the reconstructed piece of circuit board and held it up to the light for examination. "Problem was that we didn't have the entire serial number. Now, every circuit board gets its own number. Costs the manufacturer a penny more, but it keeps out the counterfeiters and helps law enforcement in the bargain. This particular board showed a 4-5-7-1 and a 3. We checked it against the prototype and saw that it was missing the first two numbers. Here's where we got lucky. I called my counterpart over in Helsinki and we conferenced the boys at Nokia. Turns out that very few of the phones using these new circuit boards have been sold as yet. In fact, the only buyer is Vodafone. The lads at the company were only too glad to be of service, provided we kept quiet about its being one of their customers who planted the bomb."

Baxter said he would do his best to keep the company's name out of the news, but if it came to trial, the circuit board would have to be admitted as evidence.

"Fair enough," responded Evans. "Here's where the story gets interesting. Vodafone's been selling the phone exclusively in the UK for the past two weeks. According to their records, phones manufactured with a circuit board ending in 4571 were sold in three metropolitan areas: Manchester, Liverpool, and London. My boys spent half of yesterday and all of last night calling every sales outlet and checking to see who did or didn't have phones with the serial numbers in question. Turns out that neither Manchester nor Liverpool has placed their wares on the shelves yet. That left London, where batches beginning with 12 through 42 were delivered. Because it's a new phone, the people at Vodafone were conducting what they called 'a soft rollout,' meaning they put a few on the shelves here and there to see if anyone liked the ruddy things. The warehouse manager looked round and confirmed that of batches beginning with the numbers 12 through 42, he still had 28 through 42. That means only batches 12 through 27 were gone. To make it short, we kept calling and narrowed down the place of sale of the phone used to detonate that bomb to three locations: Terminal Five, London Heathrow; the Vodafone store on Oxford Circus; and an independent sales agent in Waterloo Station."

"They still have them?" asked Baxter, who by now was perched on the edge of his seat, nearly driven mad by the wait.

"The store at Oxford Circus has all its phones with the serial numbers in question, and so does the sales agent in Waterloo Station."

"So our phone was sold at Heathrow," said Baxter.

"Five days ago, to be precise," said Evans. "A cash transaction, I'm sorry to say."

"The name? Was there a name?" He knew the answer. There had to be. Law required people to supply a name and identification when purchasing a mobile phone.

"Total nonsense, as was the address."

"Dammit." Baxter's heart sank.

"Still, we do have some news that might be of use," continued Evans.

"A number?" declared Baxter, rising out of his chair, fists clenched. "They sold the bloody phone with a SIM card, didn't they?"

"SIM" stood for Subscriber Identity Module. It was the SIM card that gave a mobile phone its number as well as recording all information about calls placed to and from that handset.

"Not one SIM card, Mr. Baxter. Three." Evans handed him a typed sheet.

Den Baxter grabbed it as if it were a lifeline. He thanked Evans profusely, then turned his attention to McKenzie. But instead of appearing happy, Baxter wrinkled his face in disgust. "We're done here, lad. Get home now and take a shower. You smell like a rubbish bin."

53

Jonathan ducked into the kiosk across the street from the Hotel De La Ville and purchased two newspapers, the **Corriere della Sera** and the **International Herald Tribune.** On its front page, the English-language paper carried a follow-up article about the London bombing. Jonathan was mentioned as an accomplice to the attack, but thankfully, there was no picture. The Italian paper carried a shorter article about the attack on an interior page. The latest Italian political shenanigans generated more than enough scandal to fill the headlines. Finished checking the papers, he tossed them into a trash can and headed down the main street, the Largo Plebiscito.

In the short time he'd been inside the hotel, the seaside town had sprung to life. Besides drawing visitors to view its ruins, Civitavecchia functioned as the main port of call for Mediterranean cruise ships visiting Rome. Earlier he'd counted no fewer than four liners docked in the harbor, and another three anchored at sea. It seemed that half the men and women crowding the street carried travel bags emblazoned with the name of one cruise line or another. Like mice fleeing a fire, they spilled out of hotels and tour buses and taxis and scurried toward the docks.

Threading his way through their ranks, Jonathan kept a sharp eye out for police. It was likely that Lazio had supplied them with a copy of Emma's hospital admittance form. A savvy investigator would surmise Jonathan's course of action and send men to scour the area. Jonathan paused, scanning the street. But it was far too busy to tell if anything was askance.

Ahead he saw the sign for the Hotel Rondo. Passing the hotel, he closed his fingers around the paper bearing the address of the man from France who'd rescued Emma from a Roman hospital and paid her hotel bill. VOR S.A. of Èze. But who was the man? And was he the same person Jonathan had glimpsed in the Rondo years ago? Jonathan had no doubt but that their relationship was professional. Why else would he foot her astronomical bills?

Apart from the address in France, Jonathan knew nothing more about him than that he was older, gray-haired, and spoke English with either a British or a German accent. Was he the person who had contracted her to carry out the car bombing? And if so, had Division's attempt on her life been an effort to stop her? Jonathan could assume that if he was the "friend" Emma had come to visit in the first place, then he, too, must be an enemy of Division's.

Still, one question held a key to all the others.

Who was Lara?

Somewhere in the distance he heard a tire squeal. A door slam. He stopped on a dime and searched up and down the street. He saw nothing to disturb him. Nerves. He wiped his forehead. Ahead, a sign pointed to the railway station. The nearest terminus to Èze was Nice, a seven-hour ride by train. He could not risk being cooped up in an enclosed space for so long. There had to be another way.

He continued walking down the hill, hoping to lose himself in the throngs along the docks. Rental cars were out. Hitchhiking was off the list. The only way would be to—

It was then that he heard the siren drawing near. It was close enough to make him jump, but before he could mark its distance, it cut off in midwail. He looked over his shoulder and noted a commotion two blocks down a side road. A man in a dark blue uniform and navy jodhpurs was pushing his way through the pedestrians. Two men followed him, hoisting a riot-control barrier. The men were carabinieri. Behind them came a squad of officers, moving authoritatively, submachine guns strapped to their chests, peaked caps pulled down low over the eyes.

Jonathan cut to the side of the street, taking up position near a coffeehouse. A line extended out the door, and he slid behind the waiting customers. He looked on helplessly as policemen positioned the barriers across the street. Their leader was speaking into a walkie-talkie, and it was apparent that he was coordinating his actions with someone else. Jonathan retreated along the street, hugging the storefronts.

Again he heard them before he saw them. A man's shrill voice barking commands. Then, the sighting of the blue uniforms.

Panic rose in his throat. Jonathan hesitated, not knowing which way to go. Finally he turned and began to jog back down the hill. Instinct told him to get to the docks, where he might lose himself in the masses. As he neared the bottom, a navy Alfa Romeo marked with police insignia drew to a halt 20 meters away. Several more police cars pulled in behind it. Jonathan glanced over his shoulder and saw a line of uniforms advancing toward him. Retreat was no longer an option.

There were no side streets branching off to his right or left, either. He looked down the hill. The main coastal highway ran directly behind the police cars. And across the four-lane motorway began the embarcadero, which skirted the sea as far as the eye could see to the north and south. Traffic was congested, a stuttering procession of automobiles and buses belching exhaust into the humid morning air. He stood frozen as policemen piled out of the cars and milled about. All the while the tide of tourists and pedestrians flowed around and past him.

What would Emma do?

Jonathan knew the answer immediately. There was really no other way.

Drawing a breath, he continued toward the police. He didn't lower his head. He didn't look away. He was wearing sunglasses, a baseball cap, and that was it. The front door of the Alfa Romeo opened and a svelte blond woman stepped out. She was dressed in a black pantsuit and white T, and she wore dark aviator sunglasses, but he knew her the moment he laid eyes on her. DCI Ford.

He watched as she scanned the crowd, flying right past him. Her head stopped and shot right back. She took off her sunglasses and, with less than 20 meters between them, locked eyes with Jonathan.

Jonathan darted a glance over his shoulder and saw a forest of blue uniforms, then he looked at Kate Ford and started to run. He ran straight at her, straight toward the Alfa Romeo, where at least three policemen were huddled in conversation, none of them paying either him or Ford the least attention.

"Ransom," she called, but her voice was weak, too full of surprise to elicit shock, let alone attention.

Jonathan brushed past her. And as he did, an ungoverned lick of anger flared inside him. He was incensed at the sight of her, enraged by her unexpected presence, unable to comprehend the reason for her tenacity. He'd told her he had nothing to do with the bombing. Why did she persist in thinking otherwise? Rashly, he tossed a solid forearm that caught her square in the chest and sent her tumbling onto the hood of the automobile.

He could only guess what happened next. He

wasn't going to stop and find out. Concerned about her well-being, the other police would gather around her solicitously, granting him a precious few seconds, a precious few meters. He did know that the jab had felt damned good.

"Ransom!" The voice was louder now.

Accelerating, he jumped the concrete barrier and ran onto the motorway, dodging the slow-moving vehicles and dashing to the far side. A long line of cars and trucks waited to pass through a manned gate and be granted admittance to the sprawling dockyard complex. He made to his right, skirting the line of cars and running past a guardhouse. A ship's horn blared long and loud. A hundred meters ahead, a jumble of passengers had begun disembarking from a liner. At the next dock, a platoon of cars was thundering up a loading ramp and into the belly of a ferry. Farther on, a train rolled on slowly, piled high with containers. Everywhere delivery trucks, mopeds, and taxis zipped back and forth.

By now sirens were wailing. In front of him. Behind him. He was breathing too hard to make sense of where anything was except the heart pounding madly in his chest. He caught a shadow behind him, a flicker of movement. Out of the corner of his eye, he spied a policeman running close behind. A blue uniform where no blue uniform should be. It was a younger man, thinner, fitter—a sprinter, judging by his hollow cheeks and perfect stride. Jonathan pushed harder, and for a few strides he was able to lengthen the distance between them, but that was no answer. Sooner or later the faster man would catch him.

Sooner was better.

Jonathan faltered and the officer was at his shoulder, an arm stretched to grab his collar. Jonathan leaned forward as if to get away, but the next instant he arched his back and threw an elbow behind him. The elbow caught the Italian squarely in the throat. The policeman flailed to a halt, clutching his neck before falling headlong to the asphalt.

Far ahead, two police cars mounted the curb and drove directly onto the embarcadero. The cars stopped, effectively barring his passage. Officers stood at the doors, guns drawn. Jonathan dodged left, legs and arms pumping, threading his way through the busy walkway and onto the broad quai that separated two cruise ships. As if in the eye of a storm, he'd reached a barren patch of dock, meaning that there were few people. Behind him was a mass of a hundred or so. Ahead were even more. But for once there were no blue uniforms anywhere.

Walk and no one looks twice at you, Emma had told him. **Run and you're a target.**

Against every instinct, Jonathan slowed to a walk. To his left, a gangway descended from a boat, and men and women were streaming onto the landing. To his right, stevedores pulled bags from the hold and arranged them in a neat row. A forklift honked and trundled past, carrying a large crate.

Jonathan headed to the edge of the quai. As he'd expected, a second landing about two meters down ran its length, accessed at intervals by ladders. This landing, he knew, was used by longshoremen and dockworkers to service the boats. Putting a hand to the dock, he hopped onto the landing and ducked his head beneath the foundations. A latticework of wood supported the quai. Water lapped at the barnacle-encrusted beams. Somewhere in the darkness, a rat stared at him. He started to run again, constantly checking behind him.

Then he saw it, and he knew it was what he needed.

Acting as cushions to protect the ocean liners' hulls when they docked were great man-sized buoys made from the same heavy black rubber as automobile tires. The buoys were 6 meters long, 3 meters tall, perfectly round, and hollow in the center. Jonathan grabbed hold of one end of the nearest buoy and swung inside it. Step by awkward step, he advanced until he had reached the middle. And there he sat for the next hour, listening as the sirens came and went and the voices of frustrated policemen echoed into his hiding place, until all of a sudden it grew quiet.

He still didn't dare to show his face on the dock.

Instead, he slipped out of the buoy and lowered himself into the sea.

The water was warm and filthy.

He took a breath and went under.

Kate Ford stood on the quai, hands on her hips, arms akimbo. Thirty minutes had passed since Ransom had made his mad dash across the highway and onto the embarcadero. Despite the efforts of over fifty policemen, no trace of him had been found. Even now searches of all the moored cruise ships were taking place. Patrol boats crisscrossed the harbor. She didn't have much hope.

"He's gone," she said.

The lieutenant colonel from the carabinieri shook his head. "It's not possible," he said. "We have him penned in."

"He swam," said Kate.

"But the ships," said the policeman, gazing up at the four-story superstructures to either side of him. "It is too dangerous."

Not when you don't have any other choice, thought Kate.

She turned and headed back to the main street. "Come," she said. "Ransom was here before us. He was looking for his wife. Someone must have seen him. Maybe someone spoke with him."

"Where do we start?"

Kate unfolded the hospital admittance sheet, running her finger to the entry that listed where the ambulance had picked up the injured woman who had given her name only as Lara.

"The Hotel Rondo," she said.

54

The offices of the International Nuclear Security Corporation were located on the twenty-seventh floor of a skyscraper in La Défense, Paris's bustling business district bordering the Seine. The company billed itself as a one-stop shop, capable of providing private businesses, government installations, and military bases with the "entire spectrum of security solutions." But as its name suggested, the company specialized in one area: the safeguarding and protection of nuclear installations.

With regard to a nuclear power plant, the company worked from concept through final construction, designing and implementing security measures governing everything from physical entry to and exit from a plant (alarms, cameras, biometric checkpoints), cybersecurity, in-plant employee location, force protection, and, last, the monitoring of all critical operations systems, including the storage of spent fuel. It was no exaggeration to say that nearly every major producer of power in the Western world relied on INSC to guarantee the safe and accident-free operation of its nuclear installations. To date, their trust was justified. No INSC-certified plant had ever experienced an outage, shutdown, or accident of any kind.

Emma Ransom was mulling this over as she crossed the broad plaza in front of the building. Nearing the entrance, she straightened her jacket and smoothed her skirt. The black suit was cut high on the leg and low in the chest, and the label graded it a cheap knockoff of Dior. It was Papi's taste. He had never favored the subtle approach; then again, he didn't come from a subtle country.

Her hair had been straightened, cut bluntly at the shoulder, and dyed a raven's black. She wore brown contact lenses and four-inch heels, because Anna Scholl had brown eyes and stood five foot ten in her stockings. As Emma opened the glass doors and walked into the air-conditioned mezzanine, she wasn't afraid of being spotted as a fraud. Rather, she was terrified of tripping on her stratospheric heels and falling on her inexpensively dressed ass.

"Anna Scholl," she said, slipping out the forged identification card that showed her to be a member of the safeguards and inspections staff of the International Atomic Energy Agency. "To see Pierre Bertels."

The guard examined her breasts long enough to see if they matched her identification, then noted her name on his register and called upstairs. "One minute. He'll be right down. In the meantime, wear this badge."

Emma slipped the lanyard and attached badge

over her head, then stepped aside. The specified minute passed, and then another, until ten minutes had gone by. Finally a tall, barrel-chested man passed through the turnstile. "Fräulein Scholl, I'm Pierre Bertels. How are you?"

Emma sized him up in a glance. Expensive navy suit. Contrasting brown shoes, polished to a mirror-like sheen. Gold bracelet hanging from a French cuff. A little too much gel for the fashionably short hair. Carrying an extra twenty pounds on a once-formidable frame, but God forbid you tell him. A slight limp he was trying to camouflage, probably from falling on the squash court, but which he'd try to pass off as an old war wound. And then there was the fresh indentation around the base of his left-hand ring finger, from which she was sure he'd removed his wedding band after admiring the photograph of Anna Scholl forwarded as part of her file. It all added up to a horny bull ten years past his prime and looking to prove that he still had the goods. All this she saw in the time it takes to blink.

"In a hurry," she answered, pouring ice water over his calculated warmth. "I'm due at Charles de Gaulle in two hours. May we?"

Bertels's smile vanished. "If you'll follow me."

Inside the elevator, he made a second attempt at conversation. "I understand you'll be spending some time in France. Any part of the country in particular?"

"That's confidential, as I'm sure you know. We

don't advertise our snap inspections. Especially after the incident in London two days ago."

"In London?"

Emma coughed and looked away. She had her confirmation that word about the stolen codes had not yet spread. As expected, the theft was treated as an internal matter to be settled between the IAEA and the power providers themselves—in France's case, Électricité de France. No outside firms were to be made privy. It was too big a secret.

"What happened in London?" Bertels persisted. "Was it the car bomb aimed at Ivanov? I had calls all day about it."

"I can't comment on that. Should they concern you, you'll be made aware of any developments sooner rather than later."

The elevator opened. Smoked-glass doors governed entry to the offices. Bertels placed his palm on a biometric scanner. The pinlight flashed from red to green. He stated his name. A second pinlight glowed green. There was an audible click as the lock disengaged. Bertels opened the door. "This way."

Emma took note of the enhanced security measures. A palm scanner coupled with voice-print analysis was new, and anything new was problematic. She followed Bertels down a busy hallway. The executive's office was large and neatly furnished, with a view of the Eiffel Tower and, beyond it, the Champ de Mars, Les Invalides, and Notre Dame.

"I've received your vitals from Vienna," said Bertels, taking a seat behind his chrome-and-glass desk. "I took the liberty of filling out the paperwork in advance. If you'd just read it over and double-check everything to make sure I haven't made any errors."

Emma slipped on a pair of reading glasses and brought the folder onto her lap. The form carried the logo of Électricité de France, the corporation that managed France's nuclear plants, and was labeled "Application for General Worker Identification Card." Within the industry, the card was known as a nuclear passport. With it, one was able to enter any facility without prior notification or escort. The nuclear industry was highly specialized. Engineers often traveled between facilities to practice their particular specialties. An engineer trained to power up and power down a plant could expect to visit ten plants in one year. A software engineer in charge of IT, more than that. It was too costly in terms of time and money for each individual facility to conduct its own background checks on each of its workers. Hence, anyone desiring to work in the French nuclear industry was vetted by INSC and issued a blanket clearance that allowed him or her admittance into any of the country's nuclear plants. Hence the term "passport."

A finger rose to her temple and tapped the arm of her glasses. With each tap, a miniaturized camera masquerading as a screw snapped a photograph that was wirelessly transmitted to a server at a destination that even she did not know. Her eyes skipped down the page, past her name, past her home address, phone, social insurance number, and details of her physical appearance.

"We are missing one piece of information," said Bertels. "It's something we've recently added."

"Oh?" Emma asked, not looking up as her heart skipped a beat.

"The names of your parents and their current address."

"They're deceased," she answered. "I'm certain that's part of my record."

Bertels consulted his papers. "Paul and Petra . . . am I correct?"

Emma glanced up sharply. "My parents' names are Alice and Jan."

Bertels met her gaze. "So they are, Fraulein Scholl."

Emma had been run through the interview by her controller ad infinitum. She recognized the question as impromptu and not a formal part of her background check. It was merely Bertels wanting to throw his weight around. She finished reading through the papers, then gathered them up and laid them neatly on his desk. "May we proceed? As I mentioned, my schedule is pressing."

"Just your signature."

"Of course." Emma signed, then stood up, glancing impatiently about the office.

Bertels led her first to have her photograph taken, then to have her hand contour mapped. Finally, a full set of fingerprints was taken. Emma inquired about the vocal print and was told that the system had only recently been installed at INSC's offices and that all plants relied primarily on palm scans.

Afterward, they returned to Bertels's office. "It will take a few minutes for the identification to be completed. May I offer you some coffee? Something to tide you over until you reach the airport."

"No."

Emma turned her back to Bertels and busied herself with a tour of the photographs displayed on his credenza. Several showed Bertels in camouflage uniform, a machine gun held at his side, in various tropical locales. Suddenly Emma gasped. "You were in Katanga?"

"Why, yes," said Bertels.

"My brother, Jan, was there, too. With the Légion Étrangère. Sergeant Jan Scholl. He served under Colonel Dupré."

Bertels rushed to her side and scooped up the photograph. "Really? I was there in '91 and '92 with the paras. Jan Scholl? I'm sorry, but I didn't know him. Of course I know Colonel Dupré. Your brother must be proud to have fought under his command."

"Jan's dead."

"In the Congo?"

She nodded and let her head fall, but only a little.

"I'm very sorry." Bertels placed a hand on her shoulder, and she allowed him to leave it there.

"Maybe a coffee would be nice," said Emma. "And perhaps some fresh fruit."

Bertels relayed the order to his secretary. The coffee and fruit arrived soon afterward. They ate companionably. Bertels went on at length about his real work at the firm, which consisted of directing force-on-force attack simulations at nuclear plants in France, Germany, and Spain. Another of INSC's primary tasks was to train the paramilitary troops stationed at plants to resist all manner of assault. To this end, Bertels supplied the weapons, the training, and the tactics.

Emma listened approvingly, but kept her interest strictly professional. When Bertels touched her arm to make a point, Emma drew it closer to her, making clear he was to desist. Her aloofness would only amplify a man like Bertels's attentions. She knew this from experience. "I don't suppose your job will be any easier with what happened," she said.

"What do you mean?"

"Can I count on you to be discreet?"

"As the Sphinx."

Emma weighed his pledge. "All right, then," she continued. "After the car bomb exploded in London, all British government buildings in the vicinity were evacuated. At the time, some of our people were holding a meeting with British officials. While they were outside the building, someone stole several of our laptops. We're not sure if anything's been compromised, but we can't afford to take chances. The laptops held key emergency command override codes."

"Override codes . . . you're not serious?"

Emma nodded, growing very serious indeed. "I'm telling you because I respect your work." And here, for the first time, she stared directly into his eyes. "I believe that you're a man who can be trusted."

Bertels said nothing for a few seconds, but Emma observed how he had raised his chin a degree or two and pushed his shoulders back, as if tasked with a queen's errand. "Your secret is safe with me."

"It's a disaster," Emma confided. "But it's something we're going to take care of swiftly."

"You'll need to change all the codes."

"And reprogram all security systems. Thankfully, we won't have to power down any plants."

"So that's the reason for the sudden trip," said Bertels. "You're checking to see if there have been any incursions."

"I can't comment on that, Mr. Bertels," said Emma, her tone now addressing him as a colleague and, therefore, an equal. "I can say, however, that the trip was sudden enough that I wasn't able to contact Électricité de France for the names of their security chiefs at the plants I'll be visiting."

It was protocol to inform security chiefs beforehand of an inspection. Security operated as an independent agency, one of the many checks and balances to guard against complacency and ensure that plants were run to the letter of the law.

"A surprise inspection, then? They'll be horrified."

Emma held his eyes, but said nothing.

Bertels took his cue. "A list of the plant security chiefs? That shouldn't be a problem." He was up on his feet in an instant. "Which ones do you need?"

"Without an okay from Électricité de France, you could get into trouble."

"Give me the names."

Emma rattled off the names of five nuclear facilities around the country. "And also La Reine. But if anyone finds out . . ."

"A flash inspection is the only way," said Bertels, brooking no criticism. "I can promise that your visits will be totally unexpected. It will do them good. Proactive is the only way to keep them on their toes."

"I'm glad we agree," said Emma.

Ten minutes later the names of all the heads of plant security, their business phones, e-mail addresses, and home and private information arrived in the form of a freshly burned CD. "Is there anything else?" asked Pierre Bertels.

"My identification would be nice," she said crisply.

"Of course." Bertels stepped outside his office and returned with an identification card attached to a red lanyard embroidered with the initials INSC. "Now you're official."

"This turned out to be more efficient than I'd imagined," said Emma. She made a show of checking her watch and being perturbed. "I must run. I will, however, be back in Paris in seven days. I may even have an evening free. I'd like to share the results of my inspections with you."

"That would be beneficial," said Bertels.

"Extremely," said Emma. "I'll know if you've alerted your cronies ahead of time. I have a very developed sixth sense."

Pierre Bertels swore his secrecy, saying it would be his job if Électricité de France found out he'd provided her information about its personnel without prior authorization. He gave her his private number and told her to call a day before she arrived. Emma promised as much. **"Au revoir."**

"À bientôt," answered Bertels.

After exiting the building, she crossed the grand promenade of La Défense, stopping at the railing overlooking the Seine. Her face took on a gray pallor. The memory of Bertels's lingering handshake sickened her. She turned her face to the sun, forcing herself to take long, slow breaths. All the while Papi's words echoed in her mind: **After all, it's what you Nightingales do best.**

Fixing her handbag over her shoulder, she set off toward the Étoile. And as she walked, her steps took on a marching rhythm. Her qualms passed. She slipped back into the protective shell of a trained government operative.

Emma hadn't stolen the codes to interfere with the functioning of a nuclear power plant. It was virtually impossible to defeat the myriad safeguards that governed their safe operation. She had stolen the codes to break into the IAEA's system and obtain a nuclear passport.

Slipping her hand into her pocket, she fingered the identification card.

Getting in was the easy part.

55

The Cinnamon Club on Great Smith Street was famed for its curry and its clientele. Located in the shell of the Old Westminster Library, the restaurant was an oasis of starched tablecloths and hushed conversations, a world far removed from the frenetic activities beyond its walls. Owing to its proximity to Whitehall, it had long been a favored haunt of MPs, civil servants with generous expense accounts, and visiting dignitaries.

"Location couldn't be better," said Connor as he scooted his chair back from the table to afford his girth some extra room. He had dressed for the occasion in his best suit, a three-year-old gray worsted that was missing only one button. His shirt, however, was brand-new. Pale blue and fashioned from the finest cotton-poly blend.

"You can still smell the cordite or whatever it is they use these days," said Sir Anthony Allam. "One Victoria is just around the corner. Place is still a mess. Blew out all the windows for three blocks. Luckily, the bombers used a shaped charge, or it would be much worse. I suppose we should thank them for that."

"Yeah, maybe you ought to throw them a parade," said Connor, his pouchy eyes peering over the top of his menu.

The waiter took their orders. Gin and tonic to drink and a Madras chicken curry for Allam. Hot-hot. Connor ordered the same without gusto.

"I appreciate your time, Tony, short notice and all."

Allam smiled politely. "My pleasure, though I have to admit this particular spot wouldn't have been my first choice. Too many eyes and ears."

"Exactly." Connor looked to his right and left, and appeared dissatisfied with his selection. "I don't see any unfriendly faces."

"Don't worry, they're there." Allam folded his hands on the table. He was a busy man, and his iron-clad gaze made it clear that it was time to get down to brass tacks.

Connor bent his head closer. "So Emma's been giving you a tough time."

"You might say that."

Connor offered a doctored version of what had taken place in the Swiss Alps five months earlier.

"And this is the first you've heard of her since?" asked Allam.

"We've been keeping tabs on the husband, hoping that he might lead us to her, but until four days ago he was doing his save-the-world thing down in Africa. Regular Albert Schweitzer."

"Are you saying that you haven't any knowledge about her actions in all that time?" Allam pressed.

"Not exactly," said Connor, with reluctance.

Allam pounced on the show of hesitation. "Oh?"

"Like I said, we'd been keeping tabs on her husband. A few months back he called one of her old work numbers. All lovesick. Had to see her." Connor shrugged. "He's an amateur. What do you expect? Anyway, we traced the call to Rome and got a team in place in record time. She got the better of us. Left our guy dead. Since then she's been off the grid."

"Until now."

Connor winced. "Yeah, until now."

"How could you let her get so out of control?" demanded Allam, his voice rising. "It reeks of irresponsibility."

"I told you, she went rogue. What she's doing now is her own business. I don't have the slightest clue who she's working for."

"Whoever it is, they wanted to kill Igor Ivanov and they did it on my turf. I'm surprised you have the gall to ask for our help. As far as we're concerned, the attack has your fingerprints all over it."

"What?" retorted Connor, drink and anger flushing his cheeks. "You think this was an American operation? Have you lost your mind?"

"Look at yourself, Frank. You're out of control. You're so blinded by your desire for retribution that you're putting yourself and your organization at risk. First you fly into my country without having the courtesy to notify me, then you make an arse out of yourself harassing Prudence Meadows in the hospital, and last night you dredge up that monster Danko and try to blackmail him into doing your dirty work. Word was all over town before dawn. The way you're acting, I wouldn't put anything past you. I think this is the right moment for us to formally cut the ties between our two organizations. From what I hear, Division isn't long for this world anyway."

Connor fought to find the right words, blinking madly. "Are you saying you won't help us find her?"

"I see you've finally learned how to speak English."

Connor chucked his napkin to the floor and stood abruptly, toppling his chair to the ground. "I should have known better than to ask a favor of our 'cousins,' " he said, wagging a finger in Allam's face for good measure. "Fuckin' limeys! You couldn't catch a tick if it was burrowed in your ass!"

"Good riddance," shouted Allam. He stayed absolutely still as Frank Connor stormed from the restaurant. It took all his discipline to remain seated while every head in the restaurant turned and stared at him.

"Don't worry, Frank," he said to himself. "The unfriendly faces are here all right. You just can't see them."

56

The plane was a Cirrus SR22, a single-engine turboprop capable of seating six with a top speed of 200 knots and a range of 900 kilometers. Mikhail Borzoi, chairman and sole owner of Rusalum, Russia's largest aluminum producer, majority shareholder of six of the country's ten largest commercial banks, single largest public patron of the Kirov Ballet (private patron to three of the company's leading dancers), and first counselor to the president, completed his preflight check. The pitot tube was free and clear. The stall flap was functioning nicely. The oil level was more than adequate, and the gas tank was filled to the brim.

"We're good to go," he called to his copilot before climbing into the cockpit and strapping himself into the left-hand seat.

Borzoi unfolded the map on his knee and plugged the coordinates of his flight plan into the Garmin computer. He was fifty-five years old, of average height and less than average build. Once long ago someone had said he was shaped like a pear, and the description still held true. But if he were a pear, it would be of the prickly variety. Mikhail Borzoi was not a nice man. Nice men did not control the world's largest producer of aluminum. Nice men did not amass a fortune worth some $20 billion, and that was after the stock market crash. Nice men did not rise from an impoverished childhood to stand at the president's side and be among the three candidates certain to take his place in the next election. Not in Russia. In Russia, nice men got trampled, chewed up, and spit out.

Borzoi radioed the flight tower and received his clearance to taxi. He had always dreamed of being a military pilot. As a youth, he'd attended the annual May Day parade in Red Square and gasped as the squadrons of MiGs and Sukhois and Tupolevs flew overhead. He had envisioned himself soaring high into the stratosphere and speeding back to earth. Those dreams ended at the age of ten, when the optometrist plunked a pair of hideous horn-rimmed spectacles on his nose. If he couldn't be a fighter pilot, he would settle for second best. He would be a spy.

Borzoi taxied to the end of the runway and turned his aircraft into the wind. Today's flight plan showed a quick 300-kilometer trip from Moscow's Sheremetyevo Airport to the town of Norilsk, where he maintained his largest smelting plant. Total flying time was calculated at one hour, thirty-three minutes. Weather was clear, with visibility of 10 kilometers. It was a perfect day to fly.

Borzoi powered up the engines, then released the brake and sped down the runway. At 120 knots, he rotated the wheels up. The Cirrus's nose rose and the small aircraft climbed magnificently, rising like a leaf in an updraft. Borzoi smiled, looked at his copilot, and said, "Doesn't this little devil just love to fly?"

The copilot did not respond.

When the Cirrus reached a height of one thousand meters above ground level, an explosive device containing fifty grams of high-grade plastique planted next to the gasoline tank automatically detonated. The Cirrus holds fifty gallons of high-octane aviation or test fuel. As Borzoi had earlier noted, the tank was filled. The explosion that ensued was monstrous. One moment the plane was climbing at a rate of two hundred meters per minute. The next it was a raging ball of flame.

The Cirrus cartwheeled and fell to earth.

There were no survivors.

The crash was ruled an accident and later graded "pilot error," though no details were ever provided.

Word of Borzoi's death reached Sergei Shvets less than five minutes later. The FSB was proud of its network of sources, and Shvets liked to brag that he was the best-informed man in the country. Upon receiving the news, he cast a dour face and professed his sadness. Borzoi was a friend of long standing and, of course, a fellow spy.

Privately, Shvets smiled.

Two down. One to go.

Only Igor Ivanov stood between him and the presidency.

57

Jonathan threw an arm over the gunwale and pulled himself into the skiff. He'd been swimming for two hours without cease. His neck ached. His shoulders burned. Worse, his stomach roiled with incipient nausea. Twice he'd come up for air only to find a patrol boat passing nearby. Both times he'd swallowed a mouthful of seawater in his hurry to disappear. He ran his hand over his face, skimming off a layer of oil and salt and effluents. Laying his head on the warm wooden slats, he let the sun beat down upon his face. He needed rest, but rest was a luxury he no longer possessed.

With a grunt, Jonathan sat up and took a long look at the shoreline. Here and there a couple sunbathed, a man walked with his dog. Up the beach, a trio of children labored over a sandcastle. By his reckoning, he'd covered 6 or 7 kilometers, much of it below the surface. Instead of drifting with the prevailing current, he'd headed north up the coast, battling a stiff tide all the way. Once clear of the harbor, he'd swum past the city's industrial quarter and farther still, until he reached a stretch of beach with waist-high grass and modest vacation homes tucked among scraggly pines. An irregular fleet of motorboats was moored 50 meters offshore, but all were covered with canopies. It was with no small joy that he'd spotted the skiff bobbing nearby.

A spasm racked his stomach, and Jonathan retched into the sea. Feeling better, he turned his attention to the outboard engine. It was a compact Mercury 75, similar to the auxiliary motor aboard the 16-foot Avalon he'd sailed along Maryland's Eastern Shore as a youngster. Unscrewing the fuel cap, he observed that the tank was half full, give or take. He returned the cap, then adjusted the choke. It would be best to wait until dark before stealing someone's boat, but waiting was not an option. At that moment, Kate Ford and her Italian colleagues were canvassing the tourist district in the vicinity of the Hotel Rondo, questioning shopkeepers, restaurateurs, and hotel managers about whether they'd seen or spoken with him. It was only a matter of time until they reached the Hotel De La Ville. Caution demanded that he assume they already had.

Moving fore, Jonathan untied the skiff, weighed anchor, then took his seat by the motor. He gave the cord a yank and the engine sputtered to life. To his fugitive's ears, the noise was as loud as a grenade. He guided the skiff out of the inlet north along the coast, keeping one eye on the shore. At any moment he expected the skiff's owner to run out of one of the matchbox houses, shouting for him to bring the vessel back. But no one so much as glanced in his direction.

In minutes his clothes had dried and the sun beat

hot on his brow. A weighted net lay in the bow, and he used the lead gumdrops to pin down the currency remaining in his wallet on the bench so that it might dry as well.

Gradually the character of the shoreline changed. The beach disappeared and was replaced by an endless jetty. The terrain grew mountainous, and slopes descended steeply into the sea, a succession of rugged cliffs curled around azure inlets.

Jonathan studied the coastline, looking for a place to put in. It was essential that he start to think aggressively. His respect for the law, and those who'd sworn to uphold it, was no longer appropriate. To a man in his position, the law was a hindrance. It was the law, be it in the form of Kate Ford, Charles Graves, or the blue-jacketed carabinieri who had pursued him across the docks in Civitavecchia, that sought to prevent him from finding Emma.

He grimaced, acknowledging a new and discomfiting emotion. No longer did he think of Emma as his wife, or even his friend. The events of the past forty-eight hours cast her in a cold, objective light, and for once he allowed her actions to paint her as she truly was. The portrait was unflattering. He forced himself to stare at this mental picture, to memorize its violent features and to put a proper name to her. Not Lara. Or Eva. Or even Emma. Something far more damning.

She was the enemy. And she had to be stopped.

But then what?

Jonathan did not yet have an answer.

Rounding the next point, he angled the skiff into a half-moon bay. There was no beach, not even a jetty, just rugged vertical cliffs that descended 20 meters into the water. At several points staircases cut into the rock ascended from private docks. A succession of seaview residences was built on the bluffs above them. Some resembled palazzos, others were stark and modern, and a sad few were uncared-for and dilapidated.

Circling back, Jonathan guided the skiff toward a recess in the wall, where he dropped anchor. Gathering his money and his wallet, he stripped to his undershorts, bundled his wallet and clothing into a ball, and swam to the dock, an arm held high to keep his possessions dry.

Once on the dock, he gazed at the house 30 meters above him. It was a weathered single-story residence, metal slats concealing its windows, a lonely flagpole standing sentry. To his eye, it appeared vacant, if not abandoned. He threw on his clothes, then climbed the stairs. An empty swimming pool fronted the home. He circled it, jumped a low gate, and came to the garage. Windows high in the wall offered a view inside. The garage was empty. No car. No bicycles.

Jonathan jogged up the road. In the distance he could hear the roar of speeding cars. In a few minutes he reached the highway. He looked north and south.

He ran north.

It was a yellow Ducati 350—a ten-year-old bullet bike with fat tires and a sparkling chrome muffler—and it sat in the center of a jammed parking lot servicing a beachside restaurant called the Coney Island. **Go figure,** Jonathan thought to himself as he moved purposefully among the cars packed cheek by jowl on the steaming asphalt. In America, every other restaurant was named after an Italian city. He couldn't count the number of Café Romas or Portofinos or Firenzes he'd been in. Now the Italians were getting into the act.

He walked directly to the bike and knelt down beside it. The car beside him was close enough to touch. No one in the restaurant could see him. Either the bike's owner would come or he wouldn't. It was that simple. Jonathan was done worrying about consequences.

Using his Swiss Army knife, he can-opened the cylindrical ignition housing clear of the chassis, then stripped the green and red wires that led to the spark plugs. A motorcycle's ignition wasn't like a car's. On an older model like this one, the key simply completed the connection between the spark plugs and the magneto. Jonathan twisted the wires together and thumbed the starter button. The bike roared to life. He climbed aboard, backed up the motorcycle, then accelerated down the aisle and turned onto the highway. Total time elapsed: two minutes. Emma would have been proud.

It was twelve-fifteen. The French border was five hundred eighty kilometers away. Jonathan slid into the fast lane, lowered his head, and gave the Ducati a little gas. The bike took off like a bat out of hell.

He planned on making Èze by seven.

58

Kate Ford collapsed on a chair outside a sidewalk café. "Impossible," she said, half to herself. "The man's not a ghost. He can't just have disappeared. He came here for a reason. He had to have spoken with someone."

The lieutenant colonel of the carabinieri took a seat next to her. He was handsome and suave, but she suspected he liked the flashy uniform a bit more than the job that went with it. "We have looked everywhere," he said, slumping his elegant shoulders.

"Not everywhere," said Kate. "We missed a few blocks back up that way."

"This is not a nice area," he said. "More for sailors. Many bars. It is a rough place. We go afterward. First a coffee."

Kate took off her jacket and fanned herself. "No, thank you," she said. "It's a little too warm for me." The lieutenant colonel offered a resigned smile, then signaled a waiter and ordered an espresso. Frustrated, Kate rose and started up the street.

Four hours had passed since Ransom had given them the slip. In that time, no fewer than sixty police officers had canvassed the sixteen-square-block area surrounding the address where the ambulance had picked up Emma Ransom. The Italian police were tenacious to a fault. To her eye, they had not missed a single store, hotel, bar, or café. She couldn't have hoped for more diligent police work in London. She wondered if Ransom had met with the same lack of success.

Reaching the top of the hill, she continued through the ever-narrower cobblestone streets, enjoying the shadows cast by the buildings lining her route. Many were old apartments, worn and unloved. She tried the doors but found them locked. A search of this area would require days, not hours. There were many bars, seedy establishments without names. So early in the day, they, too, were locked. Kate stopped inside a small market and showed a picture of Jonathan Ransom, then a grainy photo of Emma taken in London. Time and again she was met with a stony glare.

Kate leaned against a wall and pulled off one of her shoes to massage an aching foot. She sighed. There was little more she could do herself. She would task out the search to the Italian police and wait. She was not optimistic. Memory disintegrated quickly, the sight of an unfamiliar face quickest of all. Replacing her shoe, she began the walk back to the shoreline. But as she did she caught a sign out of the corner of her eye. It hung from a doorway, maybe 30 meters down the alley. Hotel De La Ville.

She shook her head and kept walking. As suddenly she stopped, ashamed of her pessimism. With renewed purpose, she retraced her steps and pushed open the door to the hotel.

At the front desk, she showed the manager the pictures of Jonathan and Emma Ransom and asked if he had seen either of them. The man did not answer immediately, but Kate observed a good deal of activity taking place behind his coffee-brown eyes. "Do you speak English?" she asked.

"Certo," he answered in Italian, as if insulted. "Of course."

"You've seen them, yes?" she suggested.

The manager began shaking his head slowly back and forth. His hand cupped his chin as his mouth curled into an expression of disapproval.

"What is it?" she asked. "Do you know this man?"

"Not sure."

Kate grasped his wrist. "Tell me the truth or I'll have the carabinieri in here in ten seconds checking the working papers of your staff!"

"He was here this morning."

Kate's heart skipped a beat. She nodded, urging him to continue. "Yes . . ."

The manager slapped the picture down onto the desk. "He is her husband," he said emphatically, as if correcting her from a misunderstanding. "He is **not** from France!"

The Aérospatiale Écureuil helicopter took off sixty minutes later from a police base in the hills above Civitavecchia. Kate adjusted the headphones and strapped herself tightly into the passenger seat. She gave the carabinieri a wave as the helicopter lifted into the air. Its nose dipped, the chopper banked over hard to the left, and in seconds they were skipping over the sea.

She looked at the pilot. "How long?"

"We'll fly a straight course," he explained. "The distance is six hundred kilometers. I think we can make it in three hours. If the wind is with us, maybe a little less."

Kate patched herself into the French National Police and requested that discreet surveillance be put on the address in Èze where she was certain that Ransom was headed. She needed their best men. She didn't want Ransom spooked if he got there ahead of her.

"And if we spot him and afterward he leaves?"

"Then take him down," said Kate. "But don't count on it. There's no way he can get there ahead of me."

Finished, she raised Graves on her cell phone. "Charles," she said, with much too much optimism, "we've got him."

59

Charles Graves stopped his car at the gate and reached his hand out the window to ring the buzzer. The gate was massive and imposing, with scrolled black iron bars and an ornate crest at its center. It had all the charm of a medieval portcullis. Something fashioned with great care and expertise to keep the Hun out. The gate shuddered and slid open, and he knew that somewhere hidden in the great banks of ivy covering the stone walls was a camera and that he had been identified and duly approved.

Graves accelerated down a well-tended lane surrounded on both sides by blazing flowerbeds and expansive lawns. He rounded a curve and the house came into view. He studied the hulking Palladian structure. "House" was the wrong word. "Palace" was more like it. And indeed, he remembered that the home had once been a summer residence for Queen Victoria. The papers had raised a stink when it was sold to the Russian billionaire three years back. Something about a czar stealing a queen's property.

Parked in a gravel forecourt was the Rolls-Royce Phantom Graves had glimpsed on the security tapes. And already descending the steps, hand raised in greeting, the trademark thatch of white-blond hair as gloriously unkempt as usual, was the man himself, Peter Chagall.

"Be careful," the boys on the Russian desk had warned him. "He smiles as wide as a shark and his teeth are every bit as sharp."

But Graves didn't need the Russian desk to give him a bio of Chagall. He knew it verbatim and had done ever since the day that Chagall had purchased Arsenal Football Club, the North London side Graves had pledged to every Saturday afternoon between September and May since the age of five.

Born in Siberia fifty-five years earlier, Piotr Chagalinsky was orphaned young and raised by his grandmother. A brilliant student, he obtained a scholarship to Moscow State University and subsequently graduated at the top of his class. After the obligatory stint in military service, he took a job with one of the USSR's largest oil producers. By twenty-seven he had risen to vice chairman, a rise all the more unbelievable because of his refusal to join the Communist Party. When the Berlin Wall came down and Russia's ossified government crumbled with it, Chagalinsky—by now rechristened Chagall—was in a perfect position to take advantage of it. He moved to modernize the oil company, boosting production while gobbling up smaller rivals and ensuring that a majority of the newly privatized company's shares ended up in his pocket. It was this propensity to swallow up his rivals, along with his shock of blond hair, that lent him his nickname. The Great White.

And then, five years ago, Chagall had up and sold

the company back to the Russian government for 10 billion pounds. The move was without warning and left many scratching their heads at the real reason for his departure. The next day he was on a plane to Britain. "I am finished with Russia and Russia is finished with me," he'd announced famously. But like so much else about Chagall, it was a falsehood. Chagall was Russian to the core. He would never be done with the Rodina, and his involvement with Robert Russell proved as much.

"Welcome!" called Chagall in his thick Russian accent, opening the car door before Graves could cut the engine. "Captain Graves. It is a great pleasure."

"Good of you to see me." Graves let the intentional demotion go without mention. Already he had his first clue that Chagall was in hot water. Billionaires did not curtsey to the police, not in Russia or in Britain.

"How could I turn down a request from the Security Service? I am a citizen now. A subject of the queen."

"Congratulations." Graves wondered how much a UK passport had cost him. The house had gone for 30 million pounds, his football team for 200 million. Whatever it was, Chagall could afford it.

"You're here about my friend Robert," said the Russian mournfully. "This I know. To tell you the truth, I had been expecting your call."

"Does that mean you have something to tell us?" Graves had no legal means of making Chagall cooperate. It was hardly against the law to meet with a man two hours before he was killed. If Graves wanted something out of Chagall, he'd have to trade for it.

"Perhaps," said Chagall. "But I was hoping that you had something to tell me."

"I might know a thing or two."

Chagall gripped his arm and led him around the side of the home. "How did they get to him?"

"Through the basement," said Graves.

"But he lived on the fifth floor. He had so much security—the alarms, the doormen."

"They used the building's old laundry chutes to move around without being detected."

"Who? This I must know."

"I can't share that information with you. The investigation is ongoing."

"Really?" Chagall shot him an inquiring look that might as well have telegraphed a bribe. How much did Graves want? Ten thousand pounds? Fifty thousand? One hundred?

"You'll know as soon as we make an arrest," said Graves.

"So it is soon?"

"We hope so."

Chagall led the way through immaculately trimmed topiary, the hedges cut in the shapes of circus animals: an elephant, a lion, a dancing bear. Here and there along the perimeter of the tall brick walls that surrounded the property, armed guards lurked in the shadows, cradling submachine guns as they made their rounds. In the space of five minutes, Graves counted three teams of two and six television cameras. The palace wasn't a home so much as a fortress. He said, "Tell me, Mr. Chagall, had you been friends with Lord Russell a long time?"

"Long enough. He was helpful."

"How so?"

"He did not believe. He was not fooled like all of you others."

"Fooled by what?"

"Look around you. You see the guns. My little army. What do you think? He was not fooled by **them.**"

They emerged from the topiary. A large farmhouse stood up ahead, with great green doors. The sound of an engine revving came from somewhere inside it.

"We have pictures of your car in front of Lord Russell's club the night he was murdered. After the two of you met, Russell drove to Victoria Street, the site where the car bomb attack against Interior Minister Ivanov took place. Do you have any idea why he might have felt compelled to go there so late at night?"

"Devils," said Chagall, with venom. "Evil men. You have no idea. They wear nice suits. They speak English perfectly so you think they are all right. Men you can deal with—like Mrs. Thatcher said about Gorbachev twenty years ago. But you are naive. Not these men. You cannot deal with them. Russia was born out of a swamp. For ten centuries we have struggled. Always the poor man of Europe. Ignorant. Superstitious. And now a miracle has come to save us. Do you know what that miracle is?"

"Oil?" ventured Graves.

"Oil," said Chagall. "Russia holds the second largest deposits in the world. Two hundred billion barrels. We used to pump over nine million barrels a day. But no longer. The men who control the oil companies would rather keep all the profit for themselves than split it with others. Instead of modernizing our drilling platforms with partners from the West, they allow the rigs to grow rusty. Instead of exploring for new deposits, they guard the old ones like jealous hens. The problem is that the men who have taken control of our country's natural resources are not businessmen. They are spies, and spies are paranoid and stupid. They look constantly over their shoulders, but never straight ahead. They say that they are patriots who bleed for Mother Russia. I have decided, Captain Graves, that there is nothing scarier than a patriot."

They had reached the farmhouse. The sound of the engine was louder now. Someone pumped the accelerator as voices called out instructions in Russian. Chagall opened a side door and entered. The farmhouse had been converted into a garage. Graves counted at least twenty automobiles parked under a canopy of heavy-duty floodlights. There was a Ferrari

Scaglietti and a Lamborghini Miura. A Maserati Quattroporte and a Mercedes McLaren SLR. A Porsche 911 GT and a Bentley Mulsanne Turbo.

Chagall stopped in front of a sleek gray two-door sports car. "The Bugatti Veyron. The most expensive car in the world. Do you know how much it costs?"

Graves smiled politely. "A bit more than my salary, I'd wager."

"Two million U.S. I will tell you something. If you tell me who killed Robert Russell, it is yours. No questions asked. My gift to you. What do you say?"

"Tempting."

"It is yours, then!" declared Chagall.

"I can't accept." Graves shook his head politely, as if awed by such a show of largesse.

"Hah!" shouted Chagall. "Another patriot."

Graves grew serious. "Why did Russell drive to One Victoria Street immediately after meeting with you? What do you know about the attack that took place there?"

Chagall busied himself with a chamois cloth, polishing the hood of a vintage black Ferrari Daytona. "Like yours, our investigation, too, is still ongoing," he said without looking up. "Perhaps we shall inform Her Majesty's government when we have accumulated more reliable information."

Graves stepped to his shoulder. "The attack on Interior Minister Ivanov was a decoy to force a mandatory evacuation of the government buildings in the vicinity so that someone could get inside and steal classified information."

"What kind of classified information?"

"Very classified," said Graves.

Skepticism clouded Chagall's features. "You mean they didn't wish to kill Ivanov? Nonsense. Everyone wants Ivanov dead."

"I'm only telling you what our evidence suggests."

"So what is this classified information that was so precious to them?" asked Chagall.

"You mean you don't know either?"

"Why would I drag my good friend Lord Robbie out so late at night if I already knew? We knew something was planned. We had word of the location, but we did not know what. Russell uses us and we use him. He often has better contacts in my country than I do. We were certain that he would know. All I can tell you, Captain, is that they are behind it all. The evil ones."

Graves knew who they were without having to ask. The FSB.

"Listen, Captain," Chagall continued. "I shall put you in touch with my source. He is one of them, too. But a good man. A face-to-face meeting. He will tell you what he knows. You will not be disappointed. In return, you must supply him with evidence of who killed Robert Russell."

"Is he here in London?"

"He is." Chagall threaded his way to the rear of the garage, where a car was being unloaded from a van. Graves took up position on one side of the ramp as a metallic blue 1964 Ford Shelby Cobra slid onto the floor. "My latest acquisition," said Chagall. "The car that beat Enzo Ferrari at Le Mans in 1964. It is my first American purchase. What do you think?"

Graves wanted to say that he'd give his right arm to drive it, but instead he settled for "It's very nice."

"And so?" Chagall asked as he climbed into the Cobra's driving seat. "May I tell him that you will give him the name?"

Graves smelled the leather, the new rubber. It was, he decided, the smell of power. "Deal."

Chagall's anxiety melted in an instant. Gone was his earnest, near-fawning demeanor. He was back to his arrogant self. "It is better that you hear it from the source. Otherwise, I do not think you will believe it. I will make the call immediately. You are free this evening?"

"I'll clear my calendar."

"Excellent." Chagall gazed up. "I have one last question, Captain. You said that Russell's killer entered his house through the basement. But the basement is also secure. I know. I nearly purchased a residence there. Tell me, please, how did they get in?"

Graves walked around the Shelby Cobra, tapping his fingers on the door. "They hid in the trunk of his car."

Peter Chagall's eyes opened wide.

60

"Frontière Française—2 km."

Jonathan slowed the motorcycle as he approached the French border. The highway split in two, the westbound lanes climbing a slight grade cut into the hillside, the opposing lanes hugging the strip of flat terrain adjacent to the coast. The early evening traffic was heavy, and after another kilometer he ground to a complete halt. Bracing the bike on his left leg, he gazed out at the sea. It had been his companion these seven hours, a beckoning blue expanse that led to his destination. Above his shoulder, the slope rose steeply. There were terraced houses and gardens, and clotheslines strung between olive trees. A breeze lifted off the sea, and he tasted salt and exhaust and the rich scent of warm pine.

The line of traffic shunted forward. He rounded a bend and spotted the broad shell-shaped building that housed the customs and immigration offices. Officers in pale blue tunics and legionnaire's caps sauntered up and down the line of vehicles, conducting a cursory check of passports and identity cards, waving the cars past. Jonathan had crossed borders inside the EU hundreds of times. To his worried eye, everything appeared calm, unrushed. Business as usual. He watched as a plain white van was guided into an auxiliary lane for inspection. The border officer signaled for the van to halt. The next moment a team of plainclothes men and women materialized as if from nowhere and swarmed all over it.

So much for business as usual.

Hurriedly he checked for an exit from the highway. There were none. The last was a kilometer back. He glanced over his shoulder, and only then did he notice a police car hidden behind the exit sign. He gave the bike a little gas and advanced another 20 meters. There was no way out.

Less than a minute later, he slid beneath the shade of the portico. He had his identity card ready. The card belonged to Dr. Luca Lazio. The photograph had been taken seven years earlier and was scratched and faded. An officer approached, checking Jonathan up and down. He raised a finger and motioned for him to drive nearer. "You," he said. "Stop."

Jonathan extended the card and the officer grabbed it from his fingers.

"Where are you coming from?"

"Milano," said Jonathan, because the motorcycle's plates were from the industrial northern city.

"Purpose of your visit?"

Jonathan had no bags with him, no clothing other than what he wore. "Visiting a friend in Monaco," he said.

The border guard studied Jonathan's face, then took another look at the card. "Lazio, eh?"

"Yes."

"A doctor?"

Again Jonathan said "Yes."

The guard shook his head and gave him back the identity card. "Figures. Only a doctor would be crazy enough to drive on the highway without a helmet. Not even boots." He waved him on. "Next time be more careful."

Jonathan gave him a thumbs-up and accelerated into France.

"Next!" shouted the border guard.

61

Another night. Another inventory.

Emma laid her work kit on the bed:

Ka-Bar knife
Duct tape
Pepper spray
Taser
Flexicuffs (two pairs)
Gauze pads (one box hypoallergenic)
Sig Sauer 9mm with muzzle suppressor
Two clips ammunition

She stepped back to assess the tools she would need that night. She spotted what was missing at once. She rooted around in her bag until her fingers clasped the rectangular metallic object.

Lock picks

There. It was complete.

She sat down and handled each item, making sure all were in good working order.

She sharpened the knife.

She folded down the lead edge of the duct tape for easy tearing.

She peeled off the protective layer of plastic from the pepper spray and depressed the nozzle. A tiny cloud of vapor appeared. She sniffed it and her eyes watered. She put the canister down.

She set the Taser for 10,000 volts and checked that the batteries were charged.

The flexicuffs were fine as was. Ditto the gauze.

She screwed the muzzle suppressor onto the pistol, fed a clip into the butt, and chambered a round. She let her hand get used to the weight of the gun, taking aim at imaginary targets around the room. Then she ejected the cartridge, dropped the clip, and unscrewed the silencer.

Picks oiled and sharpened as necessary.

She sat up straight and looked at herself in the mirror. She did not blink or breathe for a minute. Another test passed.

The doors to the balcony stood open. A cool breeze freighted with salt and brine carried from the sea, ruffling her hair. She rose and stepped outside. The room on the third floor of the Hôtel Bel-Air in Bricquebec near the Normandy coast offered a panoramic view over pastures, hedgerows, and beyond them, stretching to the horizon, la Manche. The English Channel.

She returned inside and replaced all the items in her work kit, which she slid beneath the bed. From her handbag she retrieved a map of the **département** and studied the grid between Bricquebec and La Reine. Running a nail over the map, she located the Rue Saint-Martin. It was denoted as a country road running in a straight line 4 kilometers between

Bricquebec and the neighboring hamlet of Bredonchel.

Emma grabbed her laptop from the desk and set it on the bed. Accessing the CD that Pierre Bertels of the International Nuclear Safety Corporation had provided earlier, she quickly located the address of M. Jean Grégoire, chief of security of La Reine. Navigating to Google maps, she entered the address 12 Rue Saint-Martin, Bredonchel, France. A picture of lush green countryside appeared. She zoomed down to an altitude of 100 meters. Though the image was blurred, she could tell that the home was a typical Normandy farmhouse, with a slate roof, two chimneys, and a clay bocce court in the back. She switched to street view and was granted a crystal-clear snapshot of the home taken from the front drive.

She returned to satellite view and noted that there were no other homes within 200 meters of 12 Rue Saint-Martin. This pleased her. Two hundred meters was officially defined as "shouting distance."

Emma changed into jeans and a T-shirt and washed up. Before going downstairs, she put a scarf around her hair and donned a pair of wraparound sunglasses. On the way to the door, she picked up her camera and attached the telephoto lens. The clerk at the front desk didn't give her a second look as she left.

The drive to the Rue Saint-Martin took twenty minutes. Signs pointed to historical names like

Bayeux and Caen, and more than once she passed small, immaculate cemeteries with hundreds of white gravestones, each with an American flag at its base. She knew little about these places or the battles that had raged on these fields. Her knowledge of the Second World War was centered on cities with names like Stalingrad, Leningrad, and Kaliningrad.

Nowhere were road names or street designations posted. She relied on the car's built-in navigation system to guide her. Reaching the fork for Rue Saint-Martin, she slowed to 30 kilometers per hour and rolled down both windows. There was only one house on the road. It was the house she had seen on the computer. The front door had been repainted, but otherwise it appeared identical. As she passed, she raised her camera and fired off a dozen pictures in rapid succession. She continued another kilometer before turning around and driving back the way she had come. Surely she wasn't the first tourist to become lost along these unmarked lanes.

She drove faster this time. As she approached she observed activity in front of the house. A girl with red hair jumped off her bicycle and dumped it on the lawn as she ran toward the front door. A blond boy, no more than three, followed her, shouting excitedly.

Emma did not slow. She kept her eyes ahead, even as her throat tightened. She had not known there would be children. A voice reminded her who she was and why she was there. It was Papi's voice, and it put steel into her heart.

Two additional subjects, she noted with a measure of dispassion that would do Papi proud.

She would need four pairs of flexicuffs.

62

Night was falling and the coastal air remained warm and scented with pine and jasmine. Jonathan slid down the hillside, spraying dirt and rubble, taking refuge behind an outcropping of rocks and boulders. Below him the medieval town of Èze clung to the mountainside, a collage of clay tile roofs and rustic masonry. A steeple breached its midst like an upturned dagger. Farther down, running like a ribbon along the hillside, was the Moyenne Corniche, continuing toward Cap Ferrat and the bay of Villefranche. A church bell tolled nine o'clock.

Jonathan dropped his rucksack to the ground and dug inside it for a pair of binoculars. He'd purchased the item, along with a cell phone, water, and other necessities, at the Hypermarché store in Menton, courtesy of Luca Lazio's credit card. Putting the binoculars to his eyes, he studied a villa perched on the opposing escarpment. It was small and old, fashioned from blocks of white stone, its chipped tile roof the same sun-bleached ocher as every other roof on the Côte d'Azur. Off to one side was a terrace surrounded by a metal railing. On the road below, a mailbox fronted the villa, with "58 Route de La Turbie" painted in white lettering.

Something moved on the terrace. French doors stood open, when a moment ago they'd been closed. A shadow floated inside the house. A man or woman. Instinctively, Jonathan pressed himself against the rocks. He remained still, eyes trained on the sheers billowing from the open doors. An enormous tabby cat wandered outside and plopped down beneath a wrought-iron table. Several minutes passed, and there was no further sign of the figure.

Jonathan slipped the new cell phone from his pocket. A single number was programmed into its memory. He punched speed dial and brought the phone to his ear. The call went through and began to ring.

Just then the figure appeared on the terrace. A man, Jonathan's age. Slim, medium height, with black hair and a complexion that begged for the sun. He was dressed in a dark suit and open-collared shirt. Both his clothes and his bearing were too formal for a summer's eve on the French Riviera. He was on the job.

"Allô," he answered. French spoken with a foreigner's accent.

"Is this VOR S.A.?" responded Jonathan, also in French. "I'd like to speak to Serge Simenon."

Jonathan had found VOR S.A. listed in an online registry of corporations domiciled in the Alpes-Maritimes. The name of its sole director was included, along with information stating that the company had been founded ten years earlier with a modest capital of one hundred thousand euros and that it maintained offices in Paris and Berlin. VOR S.A.'s principal business activity was listed as "international trade." It was, he decided, a suitably amorphous term for spying.

"Who is calling?"

"My name is Jonathan Ransom. Mr. Simenon knows who I am."

"Please hold the line." The accent betrayed the soft **t** and jagged **s** of Central Europe. But where? Germany? Poland? Hungary? Still peering through the binoculars, Jonathan watched as the man put him on hold and called another number. He spoke a few words, then his voice was back. "Mr. Simenon says he does not know you."

"Tell him that I've just come from Rome and that I know he paid Emma Ransom's hospital bill."

Silence.

"And tell him that I know exactly what Emma is planning to do," Jonathan added, with a certain recklessness, like a man who'd tossed his last chip onto the table.

Another click as Jonathan was put on hold. More conversation as the man on the terrace began to pace, his posture stiffer than it had been a minute before. Then the voice: "May I ask where you are, Dr. Ransom?"

"I'm in Monaco. Meet me at the Café de Paris in

fifteen minutes. Place du Casino. I'll be sitting at a table outside. I'm wearing jeans and a blue T-shirt."

"No need. We know who you are."

"Wait," said Jonathan. "Who are you?"

"I am Alex."

The call was terminated. Jonathan looked on as the pale, dark-haired man named Alex continued his conversation with Simenon. The exchange was brief, but even at this distance eventful. Several times Alex nodded his head with Pavlovian obedience. A man receiving his orders. He completed his call and put the phone away.

Transfixed, Jonathan observed him draw a pistol from the folds of his jacket, rack a round, then replace it. The man bent to pet the cat, then rose and disappeared inside.

A minute later, the door to a garage bay half hidden among the boulders and scrub 50 meters down the road from the villa opened. A white Peugeot coupe backed onto the road and roared down the hill.

Jonathan waited until the car was out of sight, then he waited two more minutes after that. Convinced that "Alex" intended to keep their appointment, he scrambled up the hillside and stuffed the rucksack and its contents into the motorcycle's saddlebags, straddled the bike, and navigated the winding road to the villa. He parked up the road, just beyond a bend. He did not bother with the stairs. Instead he jogged to the wall fronting the terrace and nimbly climbed the protruding stones. Five minutes after he'd hung up the phone, he was standing on the villa's terrace.

Oblivious to the intricate system of motion sensors installed throughout the villa, Jonathan entered the house. His presence activated a silent alarm. The signal did not go to the French police. Instead it directed a message to Alex's phone, and to another location more than a thousand kilometers away.

The villa was larger than it had appeared from across the hill. At first glance, it was a man's home. The furniture was sparse and modest. A high-end sound system held pride of place in the living room. There was a plasma-screen television and a leather recliner, and a framed poster for the 2010 World Cup. The kitchen was so immaculate as to appear unused.

Jonathan advanced from room to room, methodically pulling out drawers, scanning shelves, opening closets. Reaching the end of the hall, he found a door that was locked. Without hesitating, he backed up a step or two, then delivered a ruthless kick below the handle. The door didn't budge. Returning to the kitchen, he searched drawers for something useful, settling on a stainless steel meat tenderizer. He ran back down the hallway and attacked the lock with precise, brutal blows. The handle bent, then broke. The lintel splintered and the door opened.

It was a study decorated in a proletarian style. Metal file cabinets lined a wall. There was a map of Europe above the desk and an old Revox shortwave radio on a side table. The MacBook Pro on the desk, however, was decidedly more modern. The laptop was open, the screensaver showing a photograph of Earth floating serenely in space.

Jonathan sat down and hit a key. The screen flashed to life, flagged with dozens of icons. He noticed immediately that the letters weren't Latin but Cyrillic. Alex's accent wasn't Hungarian or Polish. It was Russian.

At first the symbols were incomprehensible. Jonathan spoke only a tourist's rudimentary Russian, picked up during a six-week teaching stint in Kabul, Afghanistan, shortly after the American invasion in the winter of 2003. As many Afghani doctors had been trained during the Russian occupation twenty-five years earlier, he'd been given the choice of Russian or Pashto. He chose the former.

Jonathan was more conversant with the Mac's OS X operating system. Moving the cursor to the Spotlight bar, which searched the hard disk's contents for designated keywords, he typed in "Lara," "Emma," and "Ransom."

A window opened and filled with the names of all files containing one or more of the keywords. Several had obscure titles, like "Report 15" or "Communication—February 12." But the fifth that appeared displayed the name Larissa Alexandrovna Antonova in capital letters.

Jonathan double-clicked on the file.

The screen lit up with a scanned copy of a typewritten personnel report. The name Larissa Alexandrovna Antonova appeared at the top of the page. "Born August 2, 1976." A black-and-white photo was attached to the upper right-hand corner. It showed a young woman, perhaps eighteen years old, with porcelain skin and eyes that dared the camera to come closer. The girl's hair was pulled into a bun, and the collar of a military uniform rode high on her neck.

It was Emma.

Jonathan felt nothing, which was worse even than disappointment.

A stylized header was emblazoned across the top of the paper. The words looked familiar. All the same, it took him nearly a minute to sound it out for himself.

Federalnoya Sluzhba Bezopasnosti.

Federal Security Service.

The FSB.

Jonathan continued reading, losing himself in the dense, monotonous text. He was unable to decipher many of the words, but those he understood were enough. He read while the clock chimed a quarter past the hour. He read as the Peugeot pulled into the garage bay carved out of hillside below and footsteps climbed an interior stairwell. He heard nothing. He noted nothing. The present had ceased to exist. He was lost in the horror of discovery. He had disappeared into the past.

Page after page he read, as every artifice was

stripped bare, every lie exposed, every falsehood revealed. It was Emma's secret history, and in a way his own. The sheer accretion of detail was numbing. Dates, places, names, schools, principals, classes, examinations, recommendations. And then a shift from academic to military. More schools, courses, units, fitness reports, political reliability, surveillance reports, promotions, and finally, and most interesting of all, operations.

There were photographs, too.

Emma as a schoolgirl, rail thin, with the worst eczema Jonathan had ever seen and a cast on one arm. Emma in uniform, an induction picture. But how old? Fifteen? Sixteen? Too young to serve, to be sure. Emma in uniform again, now with a rank at her neck, her skin cleared up, a proud jut to her chin. Older now, maybe eighteen, her face fuller, the eyes more confident.

Emma in civilian dress receiving a diploma, shaking hands with her superior, a portly gray-haired man twenty years her senior with terrible circles beneath his eyes. On the wall was a plaque bearing a sword and a shield, the symbol of the FSB. And on the photo, a stamped date. June 1, 1994.

And then other photographs, taken when Emma was unawares.

Emma on a parade ground, passing for inspection with a corps of female cadets, rifle at her shoulder.

Emma and a girlfriend shopping on a busy urban street.

Emma in her apartment, a glass of wine to her lips.

And still more photographs. Private ones. Photographs taken in the line of duty for purposes of extortion. Photographs that sickened him. All with the stamp "Nightingale" laid across the bottom in small black script.

Nightingale. It had been her code name with Division, too.

"You are surprised?" asked a soft, cultured male voice.

Jonathan jumped in his chair. He spun and saw Alex at the door, a pistol trailing from his right hand.

"Who did you think she worked for?"

"I didn't know," said Jonathan. "Not you, anyway."

"She's Siberian. Who else would it be?" Alex waved the pistol. "Stand up. Come with me. Don't worry. We don't want to harm you. You were good to Lara. We are not the kind who do not show their appreciation."

"If you want to show your appreciation, you can start by putting away the gun."

"A precaution."

Alex frisked Jonathan, and when he found no weapon, motioned for him to walk down the hall. "You would like some water, perhaps? Some cheese?"

"I'm good," said Jonathan. "You can tell me one thing. What do you have Emma doing?"

"You mean Lara? I thought you knew. Isn't that why you dragged me down to Monaco?" Alex nodded toward the living room. "Alarms everywhere. I wasn't gone ten minutes before I was notified."

"You paid twenty-five thousand euros to get her out of the hospital. It wasn't for nothing."

Alex answered with a cryptic smile.

In the kitchen he placed a phone call. He spoke rapidly. Jonathan was unable to comprehend a word. When he hung up, his face had hardened. "What did you read on the computer?"

But Jonathan had a question of his own. "Where's Simenon?"

"Please, Dr. Ransom. You are in my home. It is my turn to ask the questions. What did you read?"

"Nothing. I don't speak Russian."

"Really? Tell me, then, how did you teach the doctors in Kabul?"

Of course they knew about him, thought Jonathan. Their surveillance didn't stop with the pictures taken at Oxford. "Her personnel file," he admitted. "I just saw a few pictures."

"That is all? You are certain?"

"It was enough."

"Then we have nothing to worry about. You're sure you don't want anything? Take an orange. They are blood oranges from Israel. We must make a drive now." The Russian slipped his keys out of his pocket. "Stairs at the end of the hall. After you . . ."

"Gendarmerie. Ouvrez la porte." The forceful voice was followed by a series of violent raps against the door.

The Russian stepped past Jonathan, his eyes going to the door.

"Stay here," said Alex, as he advanced toward the entry.

The police knocked again. Louder this time.

Glancing around the kitchen, Jonathan picked up the first thing he saw that might serve as a weapon. It was a large cut-glass fruit bowl, and he rushed forward and brought it in a roundhouse against the side of the Russian's head. The agent staggered and fell against the counter. Jonathan brought the bowl down on the back of his skull, sending Alex crashing to the floor. And then, possessed by an animal fury, he struck the Russian again. There came an expulsion of breath. The body shuddered and was still. The Russian was dead.

"Police! Ouvrez la porte! Maintenant!" The pounding at the door increased in urgency, the voices demanding that he open the door.

Jonathan eyed the pistol. He'd left Prudence Meadows's gun in Rome, and he'd sworn never to touch one again. It was, he decided, a rash promise. He scooped up the pistol and ran down the hallway. The door to the stairwell stood open. A flight of stairs led steeply down to a dusky basement. He ran down several steps, then abruptly stopped. He gazed up. From where he stood, he could see the door to the office half open, and beyond it the laptop computer.

"Police! Ouvrez!"

Jonathan hesitated for a moment longer, then moved.

63

Kate Ford jumped from the Écureuil helicopter as soon as the skids touched ground. Head bowed, she ran to a small contingent of policemen gathered across the road. "Where is everyone?" she asked.

"At the house," called one of the men as he led her toward a Renault painted with the fluorescent orange stripes and white body of the French state police. "You're late. Come with me. I take you there. My name is Claude Martin."

Kate shook hands and introduced herself. "What do you mean, late? You were supposed to wait for me."

"Monsieur le Commissaire grew nervous. He will not permit Ransom to escape from us."

The barb cut deep. Ransom had escaped from the English. He'd escaped from the Italians. Monsieur le Commissaire intended to show that the French at least were competent. History writ small. "So Ransom is there?"

"We're not certain, but we found a motorcycle parked up the road."

Kate nodded and looked away, struggling to mask her disappointment. The flight from Italy had passed in a flurry of diplomatic wrangling. Calls had passed from the Met to the French National Police, from Five to the DST—the Directorate of Territorial Security, France's internal special forces—and then crisscrossed between the four of them. The French were wary about launching what they termed a wild goose chase to capture a foreign fugitive who most likely was nowhere near their borders. A full hour had been wasted debating the likelihood that Ransom could have covered such a long distance in so short a time. Another hour had passed discussing who would pay for the operation, England or France. It was finally decided that the police of the Alpes-Maritimes would coordinate the operation with the local brigade of the DST, to be flown in from Marseille. The bill would be settled later.

"How many men do you have in place?" asked Kate, feeling the knot that had been in her stomach during the entire flight from Italy tighten.

"We ordered two of our best men up to the house five minutes ago," said Martin, who by his shoulder boards was a corporal, and by his peach fuzz and hulking shoulders barely out of university. "We have a dozen more setting up a perimeter."

Kate wasn't sure she'd heard correctly. "I'd requested a tactical team from the DST. I thought this had been settled."

"I wouldn't know. We only arrived fifteen minutes ago."

"So it's just local?"

"So far, yes."

Kate didn't know why she was surprised. She wasn't in London calling out a team of her own to set up a blind on a suspected bank job. This was international, and international things rarely went smoothly or quickly.

"How far is it to the house?" she asked.

"Five minutes, but I get you there faster."

Kate climbed into the front seat. Martin left a yard of rubber on the pavement as he pulled away and attacked the road as if it were a Formula One track. "You said there was a motorcycle parked up the road, but did anyone get an actual sighting of Ransom?"

"I'm not certain, but I do not believe so. We are setting up a surveillance position across the hill, but it is getting dark."

The car negotiated a last hairpin turn and slammed to a halt. Parked on a steep section of pavement in front of them was a cluster of vehicles—a van, two police cars, and an unmarked sedan—but nothing that looked remotely like it belonged to the DST.

Kate left the car and hurried to a circle of uniformed policemen. In short order she was introduced to the chief of the state police and his lieutenants. There wasn't a woman in the bunch.

"We sent two men to the front door five minutes ago," explained the commissaire. "No one answered."

"Do you have a visual?"

"No," responded the commissaire. "But no matter. We have the residence surrounded. If he is there, we will get him."

Kate offered no reply. She'd said the same thing herself more than once and here she was all over again. "Do you have a phone line into the house? Let's call and see if anyone answers."

The commissaire shot her a black look. "It is too late for that." He motioned toward the hillside, where six uniformed policemen clad in Kevlar vests surrounded the house. Four of them were positioned near the front door; two more had climbed onto the terrace.

Just then there was a shrill whistle, and the team commenced its assault. The men on the stairs charged the entrance. The others went in through the terrace doors. A moment later came the explosive thuds of a Wingmaster blowing the front door off its hinges. Two muffled explosions followed: stun grenades, designed to immobilize any occupants. Smoke curled from the terrace.

Three minutes later a policeman appeared at the railing. **"Il n'y a personne là-dedans,"** he yelled down.

"What did he say?" asked Kate, looking from face to face. "I don't understand."

"There's no one inside," translated the commissaire. "**Merde!** Do you know what that means?"

Kate turned away, biting her lip white. She had come to know Ransom as a resourceful man. He had slipped through Graves's fingers in London, managed to escape England and to navigate as he pleased hither and yon across the European continent while being the subject of an international manhunt. But this was too much. Was Ransom a ghost?

"**Attention!** Someone is leaving!" one of the men shouted.

Fifty meters down the road, well behind the mass of parked vehicles, the door to an unnoticed garage bay stood open. Kate spun in time to see a white Peugeot burst onto the road and turn sharply down the hill. She had only a moment to glimpse the driver. It was a man with cropped dark hair and a tanned face, wearing a dark T-shirt.

For a split second he looked directly at her.

Ransom.

Kate ran to the nearest car and jumped in the front seat. The keys were in the ignition, and she fired up the engine. Martin, the blossom-cheeked corporal, climbed in next to her. "You can drive?" he asked.

Yes, she could drive. And she had two years on the Sweeney to prove it. "We'll find out, won't we?"

She dropped the clutch and spun the car through a tight U-turn. The car was a Renault sedan with a standard V6. Maybe 250 horses. If she kept the engine redlined, she might have a chance of catching him. Ransom was 500 meters ahead and gaining. She caught the flash of his brake lights before he disappeared around a bend.

"You know these roads?" she asked.

"I grew up in Beaulieu-sur-Mer."

"Where's that?"

Just then they rounded a curve. Kate was going much too fast. The rear wheel skidded off the asphalt onto the ribbon-thin shoulder. There was no safety rail. Another few centimeters and it was a sheer drop of 200 meters to the coast road.

"Down there," said Martin, pointing out the window, and she wondered if he was always this pale.

"Where can he go?"

Martin explained that the road led east toward Monaco and that there were very few side roads along the way intersecting this one. If Ransom selected one, he would reach a dead end within a kilometer. If he remained on the main road—if that's what you could call a strip of asphalt barely wide enough to accommodate two VW Beetles—he would arrive at an intersection where he could choose between the superhighway, a road leading into the high backcountry, or the main artery into Monte Carlo.

"How far is the intersection?" Kate asked.

"Eight kilometers."

There was a flash of light in her rearview mirror. She turned and glanced over her shoulder. A fleet of police cars followed her, strobes spinning. Two motorcycle officers peeled out from the ranks and slid into the opposing lane, rushing forward to overtake her. "No, you don't," she said to herself, jerking the car to the left and throwing her arm out the window to signal to the overzealous policemen to stay back.

"Call ahead. Have them block the road."

"No time."

"What do you mean?"

"The intersection is in the Principality of Monaco. I will have to speak with their police captain. It will take an hour at least."

"Have the chopper put down there instead. Tell him to block the turnoff lanes leading to the north. We can't allow Ransom to get onto the superhighway."

Martin radioed the request to his superior. "He is on his way."

Jonathan Ransom remained a half-kilometer ahead. The road leveled out and Kate could see its course, slaloming in and out of the mountain's contours. For once she had the advantage. She pressed the accelerator to the floor. The speedometer touched 140 kilometers per hour. The distance between the two cars narrowed.

Ransom braked, then swung around a bend, disappearing from view. The corporal threw his hands onto the dashboard. "Slow down!" he shouted.

Kate touched the brakes and spun the wheel to the left. The curve went on and on, and she felt the back end getting away from her. A jolt shook the car as the rear tires left the asphalt and skidded along the dirt precipice. Dust plumed into the air. "Blast," she said, slamming the gearshift into second and feathering the gas. The car found its line. Rubber gripped pavement and the car rocketed forward. Martin went from pale to transparent.

"There," he said, pointing to the intersection at the crest of the mountain. "That's the turnoff to the superhighway."

Foot to the floor, Kate leaned forward, as if willing the vehicle faster. Ransom was resourceful, no question. But he was not a better driver than she, and he did not benefit from a homegrown navigator. With unyielding determination, she closed the gap between her Renault and the white Peugeot.

Opposing traffic was light. Whenever Ransom came upon a car, he passed it recklessly. Kate followed his rule. At some point she'd decided that she wasn't going to slow down, whatever the reason. She rounded another bend and saw the ruins of an ancient Roman temple on the hilltop. A moment later she was passing through the village of La Turbie, one hand blasting the horn to keep all living souls on the sidewalk.

She could see the green-and-white road signs at the intersection ahead. Anything might happen once Ransom reached the superhighway. The risk of injury to him and to others would rise dramatically. She heard the sound of the helicopter's rotors passing overhead. A few seconds later she caught sight of the bird putting down on the crest of the mountain. It was apparent even from this distance, however, that he had left the right lane clear. Ransom could not get to the superhighway, but he had free access to the road leading down the hillside into Monaco.

Kate closed the distance to four car lengths. She

was close enough to see the back of his head, to glimpse his eyes in his rearview mirror. Ransom barreled over the ridge, approaching the intersection. His brake lights flared and the Peugeot slowed as he negotiated a path around the helicopter. Then, as quickly, the car accelerated, commencing the sweeping right-hand turn that led down the face of the mountain to the narrow, winding streets of Monte Carlo a few kilometers below.

Kate sped through the crossroads seconds later. Glancing out her window, she saw the roof of the Peugeot zip past on the switchback below. Her knuckles tightened on the steering wheel. "Can you shoot?" she asked Claude Martin.

"A little."

"Aim for the tires. I'll get you close."

The corporal drew his pistol and leaned out the window, using two hands to steady his aim. He fired four times in succession. Kate saw a puff of smoke pop from Ransom's rear left tire. The Peugeot veered to the right, coming perilously close to the road's edge before correcting its course. Martin ducked back inside. "Okay?"

"Okay."

The road took on a new character. The surface was smoother, well maintained. Guard rails ran along the exposed lane as it began a series of switchbacks, each punctuated by a tight 180-degree hairpin turn. Below, the buildings of Monaco crowded the hillside all the way to the sea.

"I can shoot him the next time he passes," volunteered the corporal. "Once he's in the city, we may lose him."

Kate considered her options. Part of her had grown convinced that Ransom knew more about Emma Ransom's activities than he had let on. He might even know how she planned to attack Europe's nuclear grid. If he perished, that knowledge would go with him. Still, in the end, Ransom was a fugitive. And a dangerous fugitive at that. He'd been given every chance to surrender and he had decided otherwise. "Shoot," she said.

She rushed the next curve and pressed her foot to the metal, needing to gain a few precious meters. She watched Ransom navigate the curve ahead. For a long stretch the Peugeot disappeared from view and she held her breath. It reappeared ten seconds later, speeding along the straightaway below them.

"Stop here," said Martin.

Kate braked and the car skidded to a halt. The corporal leaped out of the car. He was already firing, moving closer to the guard rail, the spent shells tinkling onto the pavement. Ransom's windscreen fractured into a thousand pieces and collapsed inside the driver's compartment. One of the front tires exploded. The car swerved, then straightened. Kate circled the front of the Renault. "Did you hit him?"

Martin lowered his pistol. "I don't know."

"Christ, no."

"What is wrong?"

Kate pointed.

The Peugeot was gaining speed, accelerating toward the hairpin when it should have been braking. The car began to swerve in earnest, as if a drunk were at the wheel. Or a man who was gravely injured.

"Slow down," whispered Kate.

The Peugeot hit the railing going more than 100 kilometers per hour. The car burst through the metal barrier as if it were a ribbon at a foot race. From her vantage point, the car appeared to travel endlessly into space. Then, as if an afterthought, its nose dropped, and it plummeted onto the rocky hillside. The car landed on its roof and tumbled over and over until it righted itself at the bottom of the ravine.

The flames began slowly, playfully, a tongue darting from the chassis, an innocuous wisp of smoke.

"Get in." Kate jumped into the driver's seat and sped down the road, negotiating two switchbacks until she reached the spot where Ransom had crashed through the guard rail. She slid down the hillside, her eyes searching for a sign of life. Suddenly there was a flash, a deafening blast as the gasoline tank exploded. She fell to the ground, singed by the wave of heat.

She got up slowly and neared the car, stopping when the heat forbade her. It was as close as she needed to be. From her position, she had a clear view of the man slumped over the wheel. He was badly burned by then, but there was no mistaking the dark shirt or the cropped hair.

She turned her back to the flames and climbed the hillside. Gazing down at the wreckage, she took her phone from her jacket and called Graves.

"Yeah," he said. "What's the latest?"

"Jonathan Ransom is dead."

64

The end of the cold war did not bring about an end to spying between the East and the West. After an initial thaw, relations between the United States and its NATO allies and the former Soviet Union grew as chilly as ever. Efforts to sow democratic reform in Russia failed. Plans to restructure the economy proved disastrous, resulting in the meltdown of the ruble in the late summer of 1998. Humiliated, broke, and smarting from its loss of international power, Russia vowed revenge. A new president was elected, a man from its security service who looked to history for inspiration. Russia had always needed a firm hand, and he was the man to provide it. Domestically, he quashed dissent. Abroad, he sought to win back his country's prestige. But this time there was something different, a serrated edge to relations that had been absent in the past. To quote an American expression, "This time it was personal."

No one noticed more than Charles Graves and his colleagues at MI5. In 1988 the Russian embassy registered two hundred employees. It was Five's guess that of these, seventy were graduates of the FSB Academy at Yasenevo. "Moscow Center hoods," in the parlance. By 2009 the number of employees at the new Russian embassy in Kensington Gardens had skyrocketed to over eight hundred, of which more than four hundred were thought to be trained spies. The sheer number made it difficult, nigh impossible, to identify who among them counted as ranking officers. And despite seeing its own numbers nearly triple in the same time, Five's internal shift toward domestic counterterrorism operations precluded it from conducting the degree of in-depth surveillance necessary to keep tabs on its former enemy.

So it was no surprise to Graves that he had never heard the name David Kempa, listed as a second secretary for cultural affairs at the Russian embassy, or to learn that he was in fact the FSB's ranking agent posted to London station. It was further news that the quaint townhome located at 131 Prince's Mews was actually an FSB safe house.

"Drink?" asked the Russian.

"No," said Graves. "I'm in a bit of a rush."

Kempa poured himself a tumbler of Stolichnaya, which he ruined by adding half a can of Red Bull. He was a youthful, kinetic man, with a direct gaze and shaggy brown hair. Dressed in a vintage Sex Pistols T-shirt and pencil-leg jeans, he looked more the diehard rocker than a government agent. Raising the glass in a toast, he said, "Chagalinsky tells me you know who detonated the bomb."

Chagalinsky. At least the old regime's anti-Semitism was firmly back in place.

"That's correct," said Graves.

"A name would be nice."

"In due time. Why did you pass Russell the message about Victoria Street? 'Victoria Bear' came from you, didn't it? What do you know?"

"Not much more than you. 'Victoria Bear' came from some notes scribbled on a paper we got out of Shvets's trash. The same paper had a list of active nuclear facilities in Western Europe. From that and other chatter we'd picked off the ether between Shvets and his soldiers, we surmised he was putting together some kind of attack against a nuclear plant. From all indications, it's going to happen soon. In fact, I'd wager we're too late. If we could have stopped them before the attack on Ivanov, we might have had a chance."

"Them? You just said it was Shvets's doing, and I believe you fall under that category."

"Yes and no. I'm FSB, but I had nothing to do with the operation. This one is Shvets's baby. Run by a splinter faction he controls himself. Something called Directorate S."

"Never heard of it."

"That's the idea."

"Do you know where the attack is going to take place?"

"If I had to hazard a guess, I'd say France. There's been a lot of activity moving through Paris in the last few days. Money. Vehicles. Residences taken out of circulation. I asked some questions, but I was shut down by Shvets's soldiers." Kempa swallowed another mouthful of his drink and chomped on an ice cube. "But if I were Shvets, I'd want to take out something new. Someplace everyone thinks is fail-safe. I'd do something to scare the pants off the entire world."

"What's the goal?" asked Graves.

"For Shvets? Everyone knows he has his eyes on the presidency. It looks to me like he's making his play. Lev Timken died yesterday. They say he had a heart attack while screwing his mistress. Mikhail Borzoi's plane went down this afternoon. That leaves Ivanov and Shvets as the only serious contenders for the throne."

"That may be Shvets's long-term goal, but I mean now. Today. What does he hope to get out of this?"

"To protect the goose that lays the golden egg."

"Oil?"

"Oil prices. They're already low, and everyone is worried about the West reembracing nuclear power. Shvets wants to stop this movement dead in its tracks. One accident is all it will take. The West will never build another nuclear plant."

"Another Chernobyl?"

"If you're lucky," said Kempa. "If you're not, something worse. Far worse."

"You're a barrel of good news, aren't you?" said Graves.

"No one ever came to a Russian for good news." Kempa gave a world-weary shrug before beckoning Graves closer. "If I were you, I'd look at how they might get in. To cause an accident, it will be necessary to physically penetrate one of the plants."

"You mean slip an operative inside?"

"Precisely."

"But the entire point of attacking Ivanov's motorcade was to find a way to steal the override codes."

Kempa scoffed at the suggestion. "The codes can do nothing, especially if the plants are on alert. Even if Shvets could manipulate the reactor controls, it would take an hour to create an accident. The control room would light up like a Christmas tree. There would be plenty of time to take back control of the commands."

"What are you suggesting?" asked Graves.

"If it were me, I'd take a shorter route. I'd use a bomb. It's cleaner that way—everything's tied off. When the plant goes up, no one's going to be able to get close enough to look for twenty years, give or take."

"But you can't get high explosives anywhere near a plant. They'd pick up the signature a mile away."

The Russian shook his head. He wasn't buying. "There's always a way."

Graves knew he was right. There had yet to be a security system created that couldn't be circumvented. Emma Ransom had skirted Russell's system, then devised a method to get into 1 Victoria Street. That was two strikes right there. Graves made a note to check how nuclear plant personnel were vetted. If Kempa was correct, there had to have been something on the stolen laptops' hard drives that made such surreptitious entry not only possible but undetectable.

"Now it's your turn," said Kempa. "Who blew the car bomb?"

"Her name is Emma Ransom. She used to be an operative for the Americans. A unit called Division." Graves handed him the photographs of Emma Ransom standing on the corner of Victoria Street and Storey's Gate. "She killed Russell, too. Know her?"

"Of course not."

Graves couldn't tell whether the Russian was lying or telling the truth. What he could tell was that the mention of Division had rattled him. "Russell believed the attack was due to take place within seven days. Don't you know anything more?"

"If I did, I wouldn't have had Chagall contact Russell," answered Kempa heatedly. "Russell disappointed me. I'd heard that he had excellent contacts close to Shvets. I was mistaken."

Graves smiled grimly. A Russian intelligence agent contacting an English civilian to spy on the Russian's boss, no less than the chief of the FSB. Matters were simpler before the Iron Curtain fell. "What about Ivanov?" he asked. "It was no coincidence he was at the precise location when the bomb went off."

"I'd have to agree. Shvets's office monitors all diplomatic visits. He may even have had a hand in arranging it. He must have thought he could kill two birds with one stone."

Graves ran a hand over his mouth. An attack against a nuclear plant in France. Activity in Paris. A team in place. He felt as if he had taken two small steps forward and one giant step back. He was tantalizingly close to learning the target, yet in actionable terms—and those were the only ones that mattered—he was hardly better off than he had been an hour ago. He thanked Kempa and asked that they keep channels open between them.

"Good luck, Colonel," said the Russian. "Please hurry. And remember—it's been six days since I contacted Russell."

65

Midnight.

The house on the Rue Saint-Martin was dark, except for a dim glow in an upstairs window. A nightlight, Emma guessed, in the children's room. Crouched behind the stone wall that ran around Jean Grégoire's house, she slid the balaclava over her face, taking time to adjust the eyes and mouth. Her knees ached.

She had held this position for an hour, keeping watch as the lights were extinguished one by one and Grégoire took a last walk around the garden, picking up a stray rake and righting his daughter's bicycle before enjoying a cigarette on the back stoop. He was a compact man with narrow shoulders and the beginnings of a paunch. An unassuming man to look at, except for his posture, which was ramrod straight and hinted at a military background. She pegged him as a fighter and made a note to take him first. The air hummed with the sawing of crickets. Somewhere close by, a swift stream hurtled past. Despite this, she'd heard the rear door close quite clearly and even the lock as it fell into place. A moment later Grégoire had opened a side window to allow the night air to cool the old cottage.

Emma checked her watch. Forty minutes had passed since the last light had gone out. It was a guessing game now. Some people enjoyed their deepest slumber immediately after nodding off. Others took ages to fall asleep. She could go now or later. The risks were the same.

In a single fluid motion, she rose and bounded over the wall. There wasn't a soul within a kilometer, but she ran to the house all the same and pressed her back against the wall. Training. A circuit of the cottage revealed no evidence of a security system. The back door was locked. Instead of risking her steel picks, she circled to the open window. The sill was at shoulder height. Freeing the screen, she propped it against the rock slurry that belted the cottage and peered inside.

The ground floor appeared to be a large, uninterrupted room with groupings of furniture defining its spaces. Closest, there was a television and a couch and two chairs. To the right was a dining room set. The stairwell rose in the center of the room, blocking her view. She guessed the kitchen was behind it, accessed by the back door, through which Grégoire had retreated after his cigarette.

Emma held her breath, listening.

The house was silent.

Taking a breath, she boosted herself onto the sill and swung her legs inside. The floor was wooden, aged, and warped. She shifted her weight from her left foot to the right. The floorboards groaned. Pulling off her shoes, she laid them by the window. The secret was to move fast. Everything had to happen quickly. There was no time for hesitation. No room for second thoughts.

She crossed the living room and mounted the stairs two at a time, careful to rise on the balls of her feet. In her right hand she held the Taser. In the left, flexicuffs. Precut strips of duct tape were laid across her forearm; her work bag was strapped snugly against her back.

She reached the top of the stairs and kept moving. The ceiling was low, the corridor short and narrow. A door stood open on either side. She remembered that the nightlight had been on the east side of the home—the right-hand side of the corridor. Grégoire and his wife slept in the room to the left.

She poked her head around the doorframe. Grégoire was sound asleep on his back, snoring quietly, his mouth open wide. His wife lay on her side, separated from her husband by several inches. Emma walked to his side of the bed, placed the Taser against his bare chest, and fired the 10,000-volt charge. Grégoire bucked, then lay still. The scent of burned flesh soured the air. Before he'd settled, she'd slapped a strip of tape across his mouth. Her left hand pulled down the blankets. She dropped the Taser and with both hands grasped his limp arms in an effort to secure the flexicuffs. One arm was pinned behind his back. She struggled to lift him. Grégoire's wife awoke and bolted upright in bed. Emma dropped his arms and reached for the Taser. The stun gun was not where she'd left it; she saw that she'd placed the duvet on top of it. The woman started to scream. Emma backhanded her across the mouth. Leaping onto the bed, she pinned Grégoire's wife down and taped her mouth. The woman was wiry and fit. A mother's fear amplified her strength. She shoved Emma violently, sending her sprawling onto the floor. Emma jumped to her feet, her vision blurred, her head throbbing. Grégoire's wife was sliding out of bed, working to pull the tape from her mouth.

Kill her.

Emma's hand dived into her bag. Her fingers closed around the pistol as her thumb dropped the safety. She thought of the little girl and released the pistol. With a cat's agility, she stretched out an arm and took hold of the woman's hair. She gave a single brutal tug, and the woman crashed to the floor. Emma dropped to a knee and brought her elbow onto the bridge of the woman's nose, immobilizing her.

Up again. Breathing hard now.

Emma found the Taser and rammed it against the woman's shoulder. Grégoire's wife shuddered, eyes rolling back into her head, saliva issuing from her mouth.

Panting, Emma stood, sweat streaming down her

back. She looked at Grégoire. Thankfully, he remained unconscious. She went to his side of the bed and cuffed his wrists. More tape bound his ankles. She returned to Grégoire's wife and bound her similarly.

In their room, the children continued to sleep. Emma stepped toward the boy, then halted. The nightlight fell upon his face, and she observed his long, graceful eyelashes, his unblemished cheeks. An angel's hair, she thought, looking upon his blond locks. Three years old. He would forget.

Then she heard a sound emanating from the parents' room. A grunt. The efforts of a man struggling to free himself. A split second later came a thud as Grégoire rolled off the bed and hit the floor.

Emma returned her attention to the boy. She moved quickly. Tape. Cuffs. She did not look at his terrified eyes.

The girl was awake. She sat up, staring at Emma. A vision from her worst dreams. A wraith in black. Tears fell from her eyes.

How old? Emma wondered. Six? Seven? Old enough to remember. Old enough never to forget. Emma wanted to say something, to tell her not to be afraid, that everything would be all right. It was a stupid thought.

Peeling off tape, she pressed it over the child's mouth and cuffed her hands.

Then Emma left the room, closing the door behind her.

She walked into the parents' bedroom and saw Grégoire struggling to his feet.

There was no time for mistakes.

Quietly she closed the bedroom door and reached for her pistol.

66

Charles Graves returned to his office in a state of agitation. He slid behind his desk and rang his assistant. "Get me Delacroix in Paris," he said, asking to be connected to his opposite number at the SDEC. "If he's at home, wake him up. It's an emergency."

"Right away, sir."

Graves put the phone down and loosened his tie. He felt uncomfortable, and not a little embarrassed at having to wake his colleague with so little information. He might as well shout that a tsunami was coming, but he didn't know precisely where along the French coast.

There were over seventy nuclear installations in France. Kempa suspected that the attack might take place against one of the newer facilities. That lowered the number to ten—if he was correct. An evacuation order would cause panic. France would never shut down its power grid on the basis of a rumor. Pride, as well as pragmatism, would force the French to brazen it out.

The phone rang and Graves picked up. **"Bonsoir, Bertrand,"** he said.

"Pardon me, sir, but it's Den Baxter, ERT."

"Yes, Mr. Baxter, how can I help?"

"We caught a break. Rather a large one, actually. We found a piece of the circuit board from the phone used to detonate the bomb. My men and I were able to establish the make and model and to track down where it was sold."

"Do you have a number?" asked Graves.

"Three, actually, sir. The buyer purchased three SIM cards at the point of sale."

"Go ahead, Inspector Baxter." With his heart lodged firmly in this throat, Graves dutifully wrote down each number.

Three phone numbers. They constituted the motherlode and also his last chance. Graves ran his eyes over the numbers, wishing he felt more confident. It was a simple question of backtracking, leapfrogging from one number to the next by tracing the call history. Best case, it would yield a web of accomplices leading back to the person who had planned the operation, either Sergei Shvets or one of his deputies. Worst case (and more likely), the numbers would constitute a closed loop, with each number having contacted only the other two numbers Graves possessed.

Graves called the security office of Vodafone. He was friendly with several of the men who worked there, and was pleased when a former messmate from the SAS came onto the line. Graves gave his friend the three numbers and requested a complete call history for each, with a specific charge to check if any had either placed or received a call two days earlier at 11:12 GMT.

The response came quickly. The first number had received but a single call in its entire working life. That call was logged precisely at 11:12 GMT. Moreover, the number had since been declared technically out of operation. For "technically out of operation," read: blown to smithereens. Graves made a star next to it. This number belonged to the phone used to detonate the bomb.

The second number on Graves's list corresponded to the SIM card that had placed that call. To place it in an operational context, it was the bomber's phone. This was the phone that the CCTV cameras on Victoria Street captured Emma Ransom holding at the time of the detonation.

"How much activity on this one?" Graves asked.

"Plenty. Forty or fifty calls."

Graves was surprised. "Where to?"

"London. Rome. Dublin. Moscow. Nice. Sochi."

"Hold it there. Did you say Moscow?"

"Several to Russia. A few placed to a cell number in Moscow four days ago. Another to Sochi the day of the bombing."

There it was. Confirmation that David Kempa had been telling the truth. Graves had no doubt but that Emma was contacting her controller, be it Sergei Shvets or another high-ranking hood inside the FSB. "Can you get me GPS coordinates pinpointing the locations of both parties for all those calls?"

"Right down to the city block."

"Do it."

"What about any calls to Paris?"

"I count four made to a landline inside the Paris area code."

"A landline? You're sure?"

The response was a curt "Hold while I get the address."

Graves drummed his fingers on the desk, confused. Continuing to make calls with a SIM card used in a bombing—a card purchased precisely because it was nearly untraceable—constituted a flagrant breach of protocol. It reeked of carelessness and amateurism, and did not for a moment fit with the sophisticated operation mounted to steal the IAEA's computer codes.

"The number is registered to a G. Bahrani at 84 Rue Jean Mathieu." There was a pause, then the man's voice notched up a tone and fairly bristled with anxiety. "Charles, you there? Wait a sec. Jesus . . . okay, we got it."

"What is it?" demanded Graves.

"We have a real-time call being placed to that address from one of the SIM cards you mentioned. The two parties are connected at this moment."

It had to be Emma Ransom, thought Graves. "Can you listen in?"

"Negative. I don't have that capability."

Graves swallowed his frustration. "Where's the initiating call coming from?"

"I can't tell that either. The call is running on

France Télécom's towers, so the incoming signal has to be located in Paris or somewhere nearby. Hold on a sec . . . the call was just terminated. Duration: thirty-one seconds."

"Get on to France Télécom. Ask them to compile a full list of all calls to that number and see how quickly they can isolate the caller's location. I'll have a warrant signed out by lunch. It's about the Victoria bombing. Top priority."

"Right away."

"Oh, and what about the last number I gave you?"

"That one? Virgin. Never used."

Graves suddenly had a terrible premonition. **Not used yet.** "Can you shut down that number? You know, deactivate it, so that it doesn't work?"

"I'm pretty sure that the boys in tech services can. It'll take some time to run the number through the system."

"How long?"

"Noon, latest."

Another twelve hours. Not good, but better than nothing. "Many thanks. I owe you." Graves hung up and rang Kate Ford. "Where are you?" he asked.

"Èze. Searching the house Ransom ran to."

"Whom does it belong to?"

"Officially it's the property of a small corporation called VOR S.A. The company registry lists a single director. His name is Serge Simenon."

"Serge Simenon. Sergei Shvets. Same initials, similar name. What do you think?"

"What are you talking about?"

Graves updated Kate Ford on his meeting with the Russian spy Kempa, as well as the information he'd received from Vodafone. "The cell is active, and its base of operations is in Paris."

"My God."

"Have you found anything there that ties into Russia?"

"There's a trove of papers in the office written in Cyrillic and a few CDs by Russian singers. Coincidence?"

"No way. Do you still have the jet?"

"On the runway at Nice."

"How soon can you get to Paris?"

"Three or four hours, if I hightail it. What are you planning?"

"A raid," said Graves. "We go in at first light."

67

The sun rose in Paris at 5:42 a.m. Driving into the city from Charles de Gaulle Airport, Kate Ford watched the first rays of light strike the dome of the Sacré Coeur high on the hill in Montmartre. Her car rattled over the Pont Neuf. The cool, pleasing scent of the Seine invaded the cabin, and she caught a glimpse of Notre Dame upriver. A moment later her view was obscured and she found herself speeding through a maze of drab, unloved streets. This was a different Paris, not the home of the Louvre and the Arc de Triomphe, but a dilapidated colonial outpost lined with Algerian coffeehouses, Middle Eastern cafés, and boutiques overflowing with West African clothing. As she progressed farther into the **banlieues,** the city darkened and acquired a hostile façade. Oil barrels black with soot, smoke from the past evening's fire still curling skyward, were not uncommon. A burned-out car lying on its side occupied one sidewalk. Dumpsters overflowing with trash lined more than one alley. Everywhere graffiti assaulted the eye.

The car rounded a corner and stopped suddenly. Ahead, the street was blocked with police vehicles. A dozen men moved purposefully, putting on vests and helmets, filling ammunition clips and checking weapons. Her driver, a sergeant from the Paris prefecture, led her across the street into a corner café where the mobile command post had been established. She found Graves standing over a table studying a set of blueprints, with several black uniforms on either side of him.

The police belonged to the Black Panthers, the nickname of RAID—Recherche Assistance Intervention et Dissuasion—an elite national squad twenty-four men strong on call 24/7 for exactly this circumstance.

"They're operating out of a one-bedroom flat on the tenth floor," explained one of the men in black assault gear, using the tip of his Ka-Bar knife as a pointer. "End of the hall. Apartments on either side. One way in, one way out. The building has two elevators, but only one is in service. The other is stalled between the fourth and fifth floors. There are two stairwells. We can put a team in on top, but the helo might scare the prey."

"Stick with the stairs," said Graves. "We want them alive. They may have vital information."

"Entendu."

Graves spotted Kate and stepped away from the table. "You made it."

"Had to scream at air control, but they came around. Looks like you were able to rouse the troops."

"I had Sir Tony get on the blower. He was upset, after the snafu on your end. I think they could hear his voice across the Channel unaided."

"Is she inside?"

"Have a look for yourself." Graves led her to an unmarked van parked outside. Inside the rear bay sat two officers in front of a bank of monitors and instruments. "We've got a surveillance post set up inside a building across the road. They have a couple of infrared cameras and a laser mike on the windows. We have identified two actives inside. Both are awake and moving around the flat."

"Early risers, eh?" Kate studied the largest screen. On it, displayed against a grainy gray background, the silhouettes of two figures could be seen walking back and forth between rooms. "Is it them?"

Graves squinted, as if he could will the fuzzy heat signatures into focus. "No visuals yet. They have the storm blinds down. But it could be. He's in town. So's she."

"Shvets is in Paris?" asked Kate, who'd received a full briefing and a temporary promotion to "Eyes Only" clearance en route from Nice.

"They call him Papi. I didn't know that. Quite the father figure. Rumor is he takes a personal interest in his more comely female agents."

Upon learning that Shvets had masterminded the car bomb at 1 Victoria Street and the theft of the IAEA's laptops, Graves's first order of business had been to share the news with Anthony Allam. A diplomatic dossier was established containing all facts tying Shvets to the crime. Besides going to the prime minister, the foreign minister, and the heads of MI6 and the Metropolitan Police, the information was passed to R Section, known within MI5 as the Red House.

"R Section tracks Shvets's position at all times," continued Graves. "They traced the tail number of his aircraft to Orly last night. Get this—the same plane landed at Luton Airport outside London the night before the bombing."

"So he's supervising this personally," said Kate.

"Oh yeah. This one's his, all right. Something he's running out of a shop called Directorate S. His locations correspond to calls placed from Emma Ransom's phone. Moscow, Sochi, Paris. Shvets's jet was in Rome two days after Emma Ransom was stabbed. We're getting a trace on the credit card used to pay the hospital bill right now."

"Her real name is Lara," said Kate. "She's a Russian, too."

"I guess so."

"Do you think Ransom knew?" she asked.

"I couldn't care less."

Kate pointed at the monitors. "What about sound? Can we listen in?"

"The storm blinds are making a hash of the lasers. We can't find a large enough section of glass to get a clear read." Graves tapped the technician on the shoulder. "Try the sound again."

The policeman flipped a switch and the van filled with the babble of television news, but the words were unintelligible. He played with his knobs and the din of the news diminished, replaced by fits and spurts of classical music. He fiddled some more and a woman's voice could be heard shouting something, then a man's voice in reply.

"What language are they speaking?" asked Kate. "Russian?"

"No idea. Could be anything."

At that moment the French police captain appeared at the door of the van. "We're ready." He looked at Kate. "You will join us?"

Kate nodded. The Frenchman issued a string of orders, and a moment later a deputy ran up, carrying a Kevlar vest. Kate took off her blazer and slipped on the vest in its place. Graves moved behind her, helping her tighten the straps. "You can stay here if you like. Safer."

"Right," said Kate, meaning there wasn't a snowball's chance in hell.

"That okay?" he asked, giving a final tug and pat on the back.

"Just fine, Colonel."

Around them the Black Panthers completed their final preparations, a corps of ninjas armed to the teeth. Graves adjusted his own bulletproof vest, then removed his pistol from his shoulder holster and chambered a round. "Know something?" he asked. "I've never fired this in anger."

"Even when you were in the military?"

"Even then."

Kate racked a round and thumbed the safety off. "Beat you there. I've taken down two bad guys."

"Killed?"

"Wounded."

Graves looked at her with a newfound admiration.

The police captain summoned his troops. "Everyone ready?"

68

Emma Ransom left the house on Rue Saint-Martin precisely at 5:45 a.m. She drove slowly down the country lane, her windows open, the air freighted with the smell of fertile earth and cut grass. She had dressed conservatively for the day's work, choosing charcoal slacks, a black blazer, and a white T. Her hair was pulled back into a ponytail and she wore little makeup. She did not carry a weapon. The only concessions to the job that lay ahead were the needle-nose pliers, Philips screwdrivers, and box of alligator clips that lay inside her purse. None of these items would be considered out of the ordinary for a trained inspector from the International Atomic Energy Agency.

After five minutes, she joined the D23 and headed in the direction of Flamanville. It was another sunny day, and she quickly put on a pair of sunglasses. She turned on the radio and listened to a patch of rock music, then switched it off.

She exited the highway at D4/Rue de Valmanoir, turning onto a feeder road that paralleled the highway. To her right, a vast wheat field swayed in the morning breeze. She continued for 10 kilometers, until she saw a sign that read, "La Reine 1 & 2. Restricted Entry. Authorized Personnel Only." She followed the sign onto a narrow two-lane road that ran straight toward the coast. Her eyes lifted to the hillside where she'd left her car two nights earlier and retraced the steps she had taken. Ahead she saw the line of the outer perimeter fence cutting the horizon in two and the guard post in the center of the road. Immediately she noted that something was amiss and her foot lifted from the accelerator. Parked on either side of the road was an armored personnel carrier with a 50-caliber machine gun mounted on its turret. Soldiers sat inside the hatches, watching the road like hawks.

With a hard-earned discipline, she laid out possible reasons for the elevated security presence. Pierre Bertels at the International Nuclear Safety Corporation had discovered she was not Anna Scholl but an impostor. The British police had tracked down Russell's source. Papi's plan had been uncovered inside the Kremlin and he had admitted everything. They all came down to the same thing: the operation was blown.

Applying the same cold logic, she parsed each possibility and discarded it in turn. Given Pierre Bertels's desire to bed her, it was doubtful that he had questioned her identity even for a second. Anna Scholl was safe. Second, even if the British police had tracked down Russell's source, they would have obtained no more information than Russell had. An attack was imminent, but the location was unknown. It could be anywhere in the world. And even if Papi's enemies in Moscow had discovered the plan, they would be unsure how to act, effectively paralyzed.

Emma studied the military vehicles and realized that they were there simply as a precaution because of the stolen laptops. If anything, the presence of armored vehicles with no supporting troops was proof that the plan was intact. If anyone had known, or even **suspected,** for that matter, that La Reine was the target, there would have been twenty armored personnel carriers at the guard post, not two, and an entire brigade of soldiers armed to the teeth.

Emma pressed her foot on the accelerator, harder this time.

She passed the armored vehicles and stopped at the guard post. "Anna Scholl," she said, handing over her credentials. "IAEA."

"Who are you here to see?"

"Flash inspection. Phone M. Grégoire, your chief of security."

"Wait here," said the guard, with more hostility than she would have liked. He took the identification card issued the day before by the International Nuclear Safety Corporation into his shed and phoned the main security building. Emma glanced to her left. The turret gunner was staring at her through a pair of reflective sunglasses. Emma nodded, but did not smile. The gunner's gaze never left her.

Several minutes passed. Emma lifted her hand an inch off the stick shift and held it steady. Her fingers hovered without the slightest tremor. Finally the guard returned. "Continue three hundred meters and park in the visitor lot on your left. Go into the central processing facility. M. Grégoire hasn't come in yet, but there will be someone else to look after you."

"I do hope so." Emma returned her identification to her purse, waited for the gate to open, then drove at a leisurely pace to the parking lot. On the way she glimpsed the paramilitary barracks to her left. Besides the jeeps and the trucks, there was a single police car belonging to the local gendarmerie. More proof that they had no idea La Reine was her target.

She parked and walked briskly to the central processing facility. Once inside, she showed her INSC "passport," and placed her hand on a biometric scanner to confirm her identity. The scanner confirmed her identity as Anna Scholl and she was directed to a metal detector, while her purse was placed on a conveyor belt and X-rayed. When the purse emerged, a guard sifted through its contents, examining the pliers and screwdriver and clips, along with her iPod, cell phone, lipstick, and other makeup.

"You're an engineer?" he asked, holding up the pliers.

"Inspector," replied Emma.

The guard replaced the pliers, handed her the purse, and wished her a good day.

An intense-looking middle-aged man wearing rimless glasses and sporting a 1950s brush cut waited on the other side of the barrier.

"Good morning, Miss Scholl. My name is Alain Royale, and I am M. Grégoire's assistant. He hasn't arrived yet, but I'm sure he'll be here any minute. He's never late. You can wait in his office while I have your site badge and key card made."

Emma followed the man upstairs into Grégoire's office. There were a large desk, some chairs for visitors, and a couch. Behind the desk was a bank of monitors showing two dozen locations inside the power plant. Emma recognized the main entrance, the control room, the reactor vessel, the outdoor loading docks, and, of particular interest, the spent-fuel pond.

"I'd like to get started right away," she said. "I'm sure you know why."

Royale nodded. "We received the alert at three this morning. Have you heard anything more?"

"Nothing. Naturally, you'll be the first to know when we do," replied Emma briskly. "Our security team is on top of the matter. What's important is that the individual plants take appropriate measures. I have some paperwork to do before I begin my physical inspection. Would you mind if I use M. Grégoire's office?"

"Be my guest."

Emma set down her purse on Grégoire's desk. "To get started, I'd like a delivery manifest of all fuel assemblies entering the plant and spent-fuel assemblies shipped out during the last powering-down cycle. I'll also need a list of where the spent fuel was sent and signed proof of its receipt."

Royale nodded again, his suspicious eyes never leaving her. "Coffee?"

"I'm fine, thank you."

Again the hard stare. "It will be ten minutes."

Emma nodded and Royale left the office. She sat down in the visitor's chair facing the desk and took out her phone. She counted to thirty seconds. On the dot, Royale opened the door and popped his brush-cut head into the office. "If the spent fuel was sent overseas, do you need customs forms?"

"That won't be necessary. Just the receipt showing time and date the delivery was made. Thank you, M. Royale."

Emma returned her attention to her phone. As soon as the door closed, she stood and placed her ear to it, listening as Royale's footsteps echoed down the hallway. She opened her purse, took out the pliers, screwdriver, and alligator cables, and slipped into the corridor. The door to her right was marked "Sécurité Visuele." She slid a graphite pick from her hair and jimmied the door.

Inside was rack upon rack of audiovisual equipment and DVD recorders. The room was unusually cool, with a steady current of air conditioning preventing the equipment from overheating. Two walls were taken up by a multiplex of monitors broadcasting live pictures from 150 locations inside the plant complex. Closer examination revealed that the monitors on each wall broadcast the same pictures. Or nearly the same. In fact, two cameras were positioned at every location. One belonged to Électricité de France, the company that managed the plant. The other was the property of the IAEA and served as an independent backup. As with every other system governing the safe function of a nuclear plant, redundancy was the watchword.

Using her phone, Emma accessed the schematic drawings showing the visual feeds into the central processing facility. One fiber optic delivered all the images from the IAEA's cameras. Another delivered the pictures from the plant's own cameras. It was essential that no one see her on her rounds inside the complex. To that end, she cut the cable delivering the feed from the plant's own cameras and spliced it onto that delivering the feed from the IAEA's cameras. A check of the monitors confirmed that the pictures mirrored each other perfectly.

Next she froze the image processor so that the pictures were no longer being broadcast live but showed only a single static moment. Emma ran her eyes over the monitors for telltale signs indicating that the picture was a snapshot. In only two of the monitors were there human beings. One camera was aimed at the security guard manning the post at the outer perimeter fence. As usual, he was seated inside his booth. He might sit like this for long periods at a stretch. Nothing odd there.

The other feed showed the reactor control room, where four men stood in front of a giant bank of instruments. This was more problematic. One only needed to study the picture for ten seconds to begin willing them to move. It wasn't natural for four individuals to stand frozen like mannequins. Still, there were 148 other monitors to study.

It came down to time. Emma couldn't risk resetting the pictures. It would have to do as it was.

Emma opened the door and returned to Grégoire's office. Hurriedly she dumped her tools back into her purse. A moment later the door opened and Alain Royale returned, carrying a pair of notebooks under one arm. "The manifests," he said.

"Put them on the table," said Emma.

Royale did as he was told.

"Still no word from M. Grégoire?" asked Emma.

Royale shook his head.

"I hope you understand that I'm not allowed to wait," said Emma, in a sufficiently authoritative voice. "I like my inspections to begin promptly at shift change. I can't have word getting out that I'm on site."

"I'm sure he'll be in any moment. I know he would want to say hello."

"We'll have ample opportunity to discuss my findings once I complete my inspection. In the interim, I'm sure he knows how to find me should he be so inclined."

Alain Royale handed Emma her site badge, instructing her to wear it around her neck at all times.

"And here is your key card. Swipe it downward quickly and the doors will unlock. Is there anything else?"

"No, thank you," said Emma, slipping the key card into her pocket. Out the window, she had a clear view of the large reactor dome, and beyond it the Atlantic Ocean. "This will be more than enough."

69

In London, sunrise came two minutes earlier, at 5:40 Greenwich Mean Time. In room 619 of the intensive care floor of St. Catharine's Hospital, the first shaft of light dodged the drawn curtains and fell squarely upon the brow of the sleeping patient. He was a hard-looking man, with tousled black hair, a Roman nose, and a dense stubble darkening his hollow cheeks. In repose he maintained a formidable presence, a coiled animal–like tension that gave the impression that at any moment he might leap from the bed and attack. Everyone on the floor knew of the man and his reputation. They were right to be frightened.

But the patient did not move. Even as the minutes passed and the sunlight grew brighter and slanted across his eyes, he did not stir. For almost ninety-six hours, Russian Interior Minister Igor Ivanov had lain in a coma. Though he bore no visible wounds, the examining neurologists all agreed that he had suffered a terrible trauma caused by the concussive wave of the bomb blast that had killed a number of his countrymen. By now the patient's vital signs had returned to normal. His blood pressure measured an admirable 120 over 70. His heart rate was an athlete's 58 beats per minute. His bloodwork showed his cholesterol to be below average and his testosterone to be far above it. The same physicians concurred that it was the patient's excellent level of fitness that had allowed him to survive such a heinous injury in the first place and kept him alive ever since.

A nurse entered the room and began her daily ministrations. She drew the curtains, lifted the patient's head and plumped his pillow, then checked his urine bag and made sure that his catheter was properly in place. As usual, she lingered on this last task a second or two longer than was necessary. She was a devout Catholic girl, and though she had worked in the hospital for over a year now, she had rarely seen such a gifted endowment. She smiled, ashamed of herself, but only a little.

It was then that the frighteningly powerful hand grasped her arm and she cried out meekly.

"Next time," said Igor Ivanov, his voice remarkably strong despite the hours of sleep, "please knock before you enter. And if you want to have a look, just ask."

The nurse covered her mouth and fled the room.

Ivanov set his head on the pillow and closed his eyes. The mild exertion had left him with a headache and surprisingly fatigued. Still, he could already feel strength returning to his limbs. In a few hours he would be bristling with impatience. He decided that by six o'clock that evening, he would be on a plane to Moscow.

The doctors were wrong about what had kept him alive and prevented him from drifting ever after in a coma's eternal netherworld. It was not his fitness. It was anger.

Igor Ivanov knew well and good who had done this to him.

And he wanted payback.

70

They formed lines on both sides of the hallway, each with six policemen clad in assault gear, backs to the wall, with Graves and Ford pulling up the rear. Black Panthers were permitted to carry weapons of their own choosing. The first man in line clutched a Benelli semiautomatic twelve-gauge shotgun. The second followed with a Heckler & Koch MP5 submachine gun. The strategy was blast and spray. And God help whoever was on the receiving end. The rest of them held pistols at the ready to fire on more precise targets.

The captain gave the signal to go forward. A policeman carrying a Remington Wingmaster ran down the hall and aimed the rifle at the door. The captain raised his gloved hand. His fingers counted down: five . . . four . . . three . . . two . . .

"Ready?" whispered Kate.

Graves nodded.

An earsplitting bang rent the hallway. The door careened off its hinges and slammed to the floor. There was a flash and a concussive change in the air pressure as the stun grenades exploded. One, then another. Smoke flooded the hallway. By now Graves was running into the apartment, his pistol extended, eyes watering. Someone was shouting, first in French, then in a language he couldn't understand.

"Arrêtez! Arrêtez! Bougez pas!"

Shotgun blasts fired in rapid succession. Graves's ears rang painfully. He registered the apartment in static frames. A run-down kitchen. A living room with threadbare furniture. The crate of machine guns. And another larger crate next to it, with the words "Property of Italian Armed Forces. Semtex-H. 50 kg." It was the Semtex that Emma Ransom had stolen from the barracks near Rome. He heard a scream. He turned a corner to see a slew of black uniforms tackling someone to the ground. It was a man with gray hair, and he struggled fiercely, shouting something in a language Graves recognized but at first did not understand.

A staccato burst from an automatic weapon forced Graves to spin and look behind him. Pieces of drywall scattered through the air, clipping his face and neck. He ducked instinctively. The policeman next to him went down, half his face blown away. Graves leveled his gun at a woman who stood facing him, an AK-47 held in her hands. He squeezed the trigger, but before he could get off more than one round, there was another blast and another, and the woman was blown across the room and slammed high onto a wall. Graves looked and saw the French police captain, the Benelli shotgun pressed to his cheek.

And then, louder than all that had gone before, silence.

Seven seconds had passed.

Graves walked to the woman. She was dead, effectively sawed in half by the shotgun's vicious barrage. He noted that a single bullet had pierced the center of her forehead. It was not Emma Ransom.

He walked into the bedroom.

A man lay facedown on the floor, his hands cuffed behind him. He was dressed in a gray suit; his hair was the color of steel wool. **It's him,** thought Graves. **Shvets.**

"Turn him over," he said.

A policeman rolled the body over and Graves swore very loudly.

At first glance, the man was of Middle Eastern extraction. He let loose with a violent protest in the suddenly familiar language. It was Farsi.

"He says they're Iranian diplomats," translated Graves. "You can find their passports in the bedroom."

A moment later another policeman emerged from the back room, clutching two diplomatic passports from the Islamic Republic of Iran. Graves opened the first. It identified the holder as Pasha Gozhi and stated that he was attached to the Foreign Ministry. "Mr. Gozhi," he said, "what are you doing with a crate of machine guns and plastic explosives in your apartment?"

"I wish to see the ambassador," he said. "I have

diplomatic immunity. You have no right to break in. Where is my wife? Anisha! Are you all right?"

Graves looked at Kate. "I can't believe this," he said. "We're royally screwed."

Kate placed a hand on his arm. "Maybe we'll get that reading on the location of the phone call Emma Ransom placed last night."

"Yeah," said Graves, without hope. "Maybe."

71

From his flat on the fourth floor of a building half a block away, Sergei Shvets watched in horror as the Black Panthers of the French RAID prepared to assault the Iranian safe house he'd used two nights earlier. There was no time to wonder how they had found it. A leak. A slip-up. A spy nestled close to his breast. A postmortem of the operation would locate the source. Right now, there was only time to act. Time to ensure that his months of careful planning did not result in unmitigated disaster. Reaching for his phone, he dialed a number to be used by him and him alone.

"What is it, Papi?" asked Emma Ransom.

"Where are you?"

"Inside the CPF. We're cutting it close. There was an extra security presence at the main gate."

"We had to expect as much once the Brits discovered the real reason for the bombing."

"Then why are you calling?"

"Nothing for you to concern yourself with. Just hurry and get the job done as quickly as possible. I'll be waiting at the airport."

"Keep the engines running."

"You have my word. Now go."

Shvets hung up the phone and scrambled into the bedroom, where he gathered his clothing and stuffed it into his overnight bag. Using a damp cloth, he rubbed down the lamps, light switches, the television remote control, and any appliances in the kitchen he might have touched. Satisfied that the flat was clean, he put on his coat, slipped his pistol into his waist holster, and put on his jacket. He checked his watch. It was nearly six-thirty.

Just then there came an eruption of gunfire from outside, a succession of bangs that crackled like a cap gun. Shvets hurried to the window. The uniforms were nowhere in sight, and a crowd had gathered on the corner. There was a burst of machine-gun fire, and a window shattered on the upper floor of the apartment building. People screamed as the glass rained down. Smoke escaped the window and drifted into the sky. Picking up his bag in one hand and his phone in the other, he headed to the front door.

"Yuri," he said, calling the pilot. "Get the plane fueled and ready for takeoff. I'll be there in an hour . . . Yes, I know it's early." He opened the door. "There's been a change of—" Shvets stopped in mid-sentence. "Jesus Christ," he said, looking at the man standing a foot away and pointing a pistol squarely at his face. "What are you doing here?"

"Hang up."

Jonathan Ransom pressed the pistol against the heavyset man's forehead and shoved him back into the apartment.

The man thumbed the off button hard enough to break it. "Where's Alex?" he asked, with a heavy Russian accent.

"Dead." Jonathan closed the door and put his back against it. "You're Shvets?"

"Call me Papi. Lara does. Or would you prefer it if I called her Emma?"

"Call her whatever you want. I saw the file. Now turn around and walk into the living room. Sit down on the couch. Hands on your legs where I can see them."

Shvets turned and walked into a sparsely furnished corner room with large picture windows. "You've become quite the professional," he said, glancing over his shoulder.

"Yeah, well, I learned from the best."

"I'll take that as a compliment. **Spacibo.**"

"Fuck you, too."

Shvets lowered himself onto the couch, placing his hands squarely on his legs. "Happy?"

"Great," said Jonathan distractedly, his attention drawn to the hive of police vehicles jamming the street four stories below and the swarm of uniforms buzzing among them. He'd jumped from one hornet's nest to another. "Why are the police down there?" he asked.

"They think that your wife and I are in the building on the corner," said Shvets.

"Where is she?"

"Not there. You needn't worry."

Jonathan looked back at Shvets, wincing as pain radiated across his upper back and neck. Once the police had started banging down the door in Èze, he'd quickly come to the conclusion that there was no other way out than to fake his own death. It had worked for Emma, he'd reasoned. Why not him?

Jury-rigging the Peugeot to drive without him wasn't a problem. He'd set cruise control at a hundred, hauled the dead Russian's body into his seat, then opened the door and bailed out. Landing on the macadam road was another matter. He'd done his best to drop and roll, but somewhere between the drop and the roll, he'd impacted squarely on his left shoulder, resulting in a partial dislocation and, he suspected, a hairline fracture of the collarbone. It was raw, undistilled anger that had driven him to his feet and propelled his first uncertain, excruciating steps down the hillside. It was over, he'd told himself again and again as his shoulder cried out and his elbows bled. He was done being screwed with.

Half an hour later he'd limped into the station in Monaco, where he'd cleaned himself up in the lavatory before boarding the local to Nice. From there, he'd connected to the 22:58 to Paris, a TGV or **train à grande vitesse,** and had arrived at the Gare de Lyon at 5:24.

"What's La Reine?" he asked. The words had figured prominently in a series of dispatches he'd found on the laptop written by Shvets to an agent referred to only as "L." The dispatches were written in a furious shorthand, full of euphemisms and monikers, few of which he could suss out. He was able to decipher enough, however, to learn the address of Shvets's apartment in Paris and that Emma was involved in an operation that called for blowing up a well-guarded facility, which was set to take place today.

"La Reine," Jonathan repeated. "What is it?"

Shvets didn't respond. He sat massaging his bruised jaw, a confident, almost cheerful expression lifting his great jowls.

"If you don't tell me, I'll ask them." Jonathan nodded his head toward the police below.

"Go ahead. They'll arrest you and throw you in jail before you can get two words out. From what I understand you're looking at a lengthy stretch in a British prison." Shvets spoke in a languorous monotone, as if he'd seen the worst the world could throw at him and he wasn't impressed.

"Right now I'm not thinking about myself. I want to know about Emma."

"If you like, I can arrange for you to see her. Tomorrow you can be together. Far from here."

"Not tomorrow. Today. Where is she this minute?"

"You would do right to consider my offer. I can make sure that you're safely away from here. Free. Without the risk of lifelong incarceration. What do you say?"

"No," said Jonathan. "I'll take a pass."

From the street below came the whoop of a siren. Jonathan glanced out the window to see two ambulances parting the sea of police officers and first responders. He looked back at Shvets, trying to imagine that this tired gray man in a rumpled suit was the director of the FSB.

"Where did you find her?" asked Jonathan.

"Lara? She comes from a town in Siberia on the Kolymsky Peninsula. A bleak place. Her father was a deckhand on a fishing vessel and was absent eleven months of the year. Her mother worked in a fish-processing factory and drank. She beat Lara. It was after she'd broken her arm and leg that an agency intervened. Lara was seven. We have a unit that searches for people like her. Bright, rootless, in need of the state's assistance. Diamonds in the rough, you might say. Lara was brought to our attention by the director of her school. At thirteen she was doing differential calculus and had taught herself Italian, French, and German. Her IQ was off the charts." Shvets looked away, his eyes suddenly alive, illuminated by the past. "I brought her to Moscow myself. You should have seen her. Such desire. Such ambition. Such emotion. And, of course, such beauty. Without a trace of Western corruption. She was a little thin, perhaps, with terrible eczema, but a man could see that with the proper nutrition and medical care she would ripen into something special."

"Did you bother to ask her if she wanted to join the KGB?"

"We didn't have to. It was her idea from the start. She was born to it. One of the rare few. She's like a shark that will die if it stops swimming. Except in place of oxygen, she requires adrenaline. Don't fool yourself, Dr. Ransom. She was never a nice girl."

Jonathan stepped closer to the Russian. He felt the weight of the pistol in his hand. Closing his fingers more tightly around the grip, he thumbed the hammer into the cocked position. He'd killed before. He'd put the barrel of a gun to a man's head and pulled the trigger. He had felt nothing. No remorse, no recrimination. Only a dull rumble somewhere deep inside that he'd done what was necessary. He decided that he despised Shvets. It would be easy to kill him. "Where is she?"

Shvets shook his head, staring at Jonathan as if he were an object worthy of pity. "I know why you're here. You think you've come to stop her, but that isn't really the truth. The truth is that you still love her. You think that somehow she will listen to you and abandon her mission. You're wrong."

"Be quiet."

"Let me ask you something."

"What is it?"

Shvets looked into Jonathan's eyes. "Do you really think she betrayed Division just because she wanted to stop a jet full of civilians from being shot down?"

Jonathan didn't answer.

Shvets continued. "The same woman who without the slightest qualm detonated a bomb on a busy street at midday in central London? Did they tell you how she killed Robert Russell? She broke his neck with her own hands, then pushed his body off the fifth floor."

"The plane was different," said Jonathan. "There were too many passengers. Too many innocent lives. She differentiated between people in her business and people out of it."

"And what about all the others in her past? Do you even know how many operations she undertook on behalf of Division? How many innocents did she kill then?"

Jonathan fought to find an answer, but his mouth was suddenly dry. "What are you trying to say?"

Shvets rubbed his cheek, his steadfast gaze conveying a comradely understanding, some fraternal bond, as if he didn't want Jonathan to suffer any more than he already had.

"No," said Jonathan, without prompting. "I don't believe you."

"Surely you've suspected as much," said Shvets. "You're a smart man. You must have asked yourself why the sudden change of heart."

"The plane was full of innocent civilians. Division had gone too far. She refused to allow it."

"No, Jonathan, that isn't the reason, and you know it."

Jonathan shook his head, not wanting to hear what he knew in his heart to be true. What he'd suspected ever since he'd seen Emma in London.

"Emma has been working for me longer than you know," said Shvets. "It was I who ordered her to stop Division from bringing down that jet."

"You're lying." The words were weak, a rote response to an unimaginable treason. "I don't believe you."

"But you do. I can see it. I ordered her to thwart the attack on the El Al jet, not because I cared about the passengers, but because I intended to destroy Division." Shvets scooted to the edge of the couch. "And you, Jonathan, helped me. It was you who killed General Austen. It was you who stopped the drone even when your precious Emma was too injured to complete her mission. The way I see it, she isn't the only one working for me. You are, too."

Jonathan sat down. Suddenly he was exhausted, the weight of too many hours awake and too few hours of sleep overcoming him. He knew that Shvets was telling the truth. Not because he felt it, or because he could see it in his eyes. But because nothing else made sense. In the end, there was no other logical explanation for Emma's actions.

Jonathan turned and stared out the window. The police had come back down out of the building and he watched as someone was stretchered through the front door. He recognized a familiar face and looked closer. It was Graves, and behind him, DCI Ford. Jonathan had come so far. And now to learn this . . .

Jonathan caught a movement out of the corner of his eye. He spun in time to see Shvets leveling a pistol at him. He threw himself to the floor, raising his own pistol and firing. He saw a spit of flame and felt something cut the air close to his ear. Landing on his side, he cried out as his injured shoulder gave way, but somehow he kept pulling the trigger, the pistol bucking in his hand, the shots wild, undisciplined. Rolling to his feet, he brought the gun to bear, the sight centered squarely on Shvets's chest. He pulled the trigger, but the clip was empty. He fired dry.

Sergei Shvets sat on the couch, one hand clutching his stomach. The other hand still held the gun, but it lay limp in his lap. "Bravo," he said, in the same dull, unflappable tone. "I didn't know marksmanship was one of your skills."

Jonathan eyed the Russian warily. Approaching with caution, he knelt and pried his fingers off the pistol, then tossed it onto the floor out of reach. "Let me take a look."

Reluctantly, Shvets lifted his hand. "And so? Will I live?"

Jonathan unbuttoned the shirt. The bullet had struck below the liver. Very little blood came from the wound. "How's this? Tell me about La Reine and Emma, and I'll save your life."

"You're not so mercenary."

"No," admitted Jonathan. "I'm not." He retrieved some towels from the bathroom and wiped away the blood. "Lean forward," he said.

Shvets grunted and did as instructed.

"Hold these firmly against your stomach and

don't move. I'm going to call an ambulance. I'll let them save you."

"Not necessary," came a dry British voice. "We'll take it from here."

Charles Graves stood in the doorway, flanked by a squad of men in black assault gear.

"Ransom? What in the . . . How can you . . . ?" Kate Ford slipped from behind Graves and walked into the apartment, bewilderment and anger playing across her sharp features.

"Stay where you are," commanded Graves, a pistol leveled at Jonathan. "Your run's over." He motioned to one of the men at his side. "Arrest him," he said. "And make sure the cuffs are tight."

72

Exiting from the central processing facility, Emma walked down a protected passageway across a broad courtyard and into the main administration building. Again there was a guard desk. She showed her site badge and passed through a man-trap, a floor-to-ceiling turnstile that regulated entry into the main reactor complex. On the other side of the man-trap, she cleared a metal detector for the second time. Her purse was checked again, and she was led into an explosives detection booth. A puff of air dusted her body. A green light flashed, and she was waved through. Another man-trap waited. Emma passed through it, then crossed a small lobby toward a set of glass doors leading outside. She swiped her key card, waited for the lock to disengage, then walked through the doors into the morning sunshine.

She stood for a moment, looking at the administration building behind her and the fence topped with razor wire that ran the perimeter of the reactor complex.

Getting in was the easy part.

The reactor building stood in front of her, a gargantuan, windowless four-story block of concrete.

Inside it were the reactor control room and the reactor vessel itself. But Emma did not go inside. She had no interest in getting anywhere near the control room. Instead she drew up a map of the complex on her phone. Skirting the reactor building, she crossed a wide storage area and headed toward an immense warehouse the length of a football field. The walk took five minutes, and in all that time she saw only three or four men. No one paid her the slightest attention.

Swiping her key card, she gained entry to the warehouse. Massive lights hung from the ceiling. Shipping containers stacked three high were divided into neat rows. A forklift drove past her, searching for cargo. Halfway down the warehouse to her left, giant doors stood open, and she could see the blunt snout of a locomotive advancing slowly inside.

Every twelve months it was necessary for the reactor to power down and temporarily cease operation. During this time, spent fuel rods were replaced with "hot" new rods, aging equipment was changed out, and a general maintenance of the facility lasting four to six weeks was carried out. The upkeep required that nearly one hundred containers of new equipment be ferried into the plant.

The last power-down had been completed two weeks earlier.

Emma made her way through the maze of containers to an isolated area far to the north side of the warehouse. Instead of containers, there were pipes.

Hundreds and hundreds of sixteen-inch-diameter lead pipes stacked upon one another. She continued to the wall. She checked her phone and registered her current GPS position. A red dot appeared on the map. She scanned the wall of pipes. Then she saw it. A length of green tape tied around the end of one pipe. She counted down four pipes below and looked inside. She saw nothing, and her breath left her.

Pulling back the sleeve of her jacket, she pushed her arm into the pipe, feeling for a package wrapped in wax paper. Her fingers touched only air. A frisson of panic welled up inside her.

Start over.

Emma counted down four pipes from the length of tape. This time she checked the pipes to her left and right. Again there was nothing.

She lowered herself to one knee and began looking into all the pipes in the vicinity, pushing her hand into each, searching, to no avail. She wondered if somehow the pipe had been taken already, but didn't see how it was possible, given that the green tape was still in place. Then she stopped. If it wasn't below, it might be above. Standing on her tiptoes, she counted the fourth pipe above the green tape and felt inside it.

Her fingers scraped cold lead. Another false lead. Yet she knew the package had to be here somewhere. Papi had confirmed it, and his word was enough for her. Perching a foot on one of the lower pipes, she stood and thrust her arm deeper inside. Her fingers touched something firm and slick. Clawing with her nails, she inched the package out of the pipe until it fell into her arms.

She looked around. The aisle was deserted. She noted that she was breathing harder than her exertion demanded. She took a moment, then carefully unwrapped the box. Inside were two explosive devices, each measuring 6 inches by 6 inches and 3 inches thick, packaged in glossy black electrical tape. On top was a paper-thin LED readout and keys to program the time and initiate the detonation sequence. She set the first device to thirty minutes and the second to six, then put them inside a pipe at eye level. Once more she consulted her phone to study the layout of the complex, running over her route again and again.

"What do you have there?"

Emma spun. Three meters away stood Alain Royale, the plant's deputy director of security. She studied his expression but could not tell if he had seen her program the explosives. She selected one of the bombs and said, "M. Royale, I'm happy to see you. Do you have any idea who put these here?"

Royale took a step closer, then stopped. "There's nothing for you to inspect in the warehouse."

"Not usually, but today's an exception. Did you place this green tag on the pipe?"

"Of course not."

"I didn't think so. You have a smuggling problem. Drugs, I'd say." Emma held out the bomb. "Take a look. Maybe you can tell me what it is."

Royale took the bomb in his hands.

"Well," she continued, "what is it? I've never seen anything like it."

Royale shook the square package, then ran a fingernail over the LED. "It appears to be a timer of some kind."

"Look underneath it," Emma said—a command, not a request. "There are some curious markings."

Intrigued, Royale lifted the package high and examined it. "I don't see anything."

"Look closer. You can't miss it."

"No . . . there's nothing—"

Emma struck his jaw with her flattened palm, stepping up and into the blow, so that it crushed his molars and rendered him immediately unconscious. She caught him as he fell and lowered him to the ground.

Just then the two-way pager on his belt cackled. "M. Royale, we have an urgent call from the National Police. Please contact me immediately. A Code Nine emergency."

A moment later a siren sounded inside the warehouse. Red strobe lights positioned at every exit flashed at two-second intervals.

Emma paid no attention to the commotion. Kneeling, she removed Royale's key card from a retractable lanyard. Then she scooped up the explosives, placed them in her purse, and ran for the closest exit.

73

Graves shook Sergei Shvets by the collar. "What the devil do you have planned? You'll tell us now, or by God, I'll kill you with my own hands."

"He's wounded," said Ford. "Go easy."

"I'll go easy after he talks." Graves yanked Shvets's shirt so hard that the Russian bounded off the couch. "Where is she? Where's Emma Ransom?"

Shvets grimaced. "You're too late," he whispered. "It's done."

"Too late for what?" demanded Graves.

"Go to hell," said the Russian.

"Oh, I will. I'm sure of that. But I'm going to do my best to make sure you get there before me." Graves balled his fist and ground it hard against the wound in Shvets's gut. "Where—is—Emma—Ransom?"

Shvets's eyes bulged, and a moan escaped his clenched teeth.

"Enough!" Kate Ford grabbed Graves from behind and forcibly separated him from Shvets. "Leave him."

Graves shook her off, and took a step back toward Shvets before thinking better of it. "They'll have your head on a pike looking over Red Square, **to-varich,** before I'm done with you."

Shvets didn't answer. He sat hunched over his stomach, sucking down great drafts of air.

"Get him out of here," said Graves, delivering a last glancing blow to the top of the Russian's head. "And make sure you don't leave his side. I want guards at his door, even when he's in the operating theater. Do you understand me?"

A team of medical technicians lifted Shvets onto a gurney and wheeled him out. No fewer than six Black Panthers accompanied the director of the Russian FSB to the ground floor and all the way to the hospital.

"La Reine," said Jonathan.

Graves looked over to where Ransom stood in the corner, held in an armlock by a policeman.

"What did you say?" asked Graves, who was wiping his brow with a handkerchief, barely listening.

"La Reine. That's what Emma's going to try to blow up."

Graves shot an impatient glance at Ford. "Do you have any idea what he's talking about?"

"Yes, I do," she said. "La Reine is France's newest nuclear power facility. It's on the Normandy coast, near a town called Flamanville."

"Let him go," said Graves with a casual wave.

The police officer released Ransom.

"There's going to be some kind of bomb," said Jonathan. "I read about it on a laptop I found at

Shvets's house in Èze. It's supposed to happen today."

Graves gave Ford a look. "You see that laptop?"

"No."

"It was in the car," said Jonathan.

"Sure it was." Graves eyed him with skepticism. "And why should we believe you?" he asked, crossing the room toward the American.

"Give it a rest," said Jonathan. "Can't you see we're on the same side? I want to stop Emma as badly as you do."

Graves halted a foot away from Jonathan. "All I see is a fugitive from British justice wanted for the car bombing of Igor Ivanov's motorcade, as well as for the murders of a doctor in Notting Hill and a yet-to-be-identified corpse burned beyond recognition currently resting in a Monaco morgue. That's what I see."

Jonathan appealed to Ford. "She's going to plant a bomb inside the reactor somewhere."

"And just how is she getting in?" broke in Graves.

"She's pretending to be someone named Anna School," said Jonathan, fighting to extract a kernel of grain from the pages of chaff he'd pored over. "I mean, **Scholl.** Yes, that's it. She's some kind of an investigator."

"Go on," said Ford, in a less hostile manner, which was a signal to Graves to take it easy.

"All the material was written in Russian," explained Ransom. "Most of it went over my head. But

I remember a few things. Emma's supposed to pick up something in the northeast corner of something called W-4. Maybe if I could talk to the engineers or the plant manager, I could figure out more of it."

"Not a chance," said Graves. "Your merry flight from justice is officially terminated. From here, you'll be transported directly to one of France's darkest and most secure jailhouses. And there you'll remain until we file all proper diplomatic papers in triplicate and see to it that your extradition to England goes off without a hitch."

"Don't be a fool," said Jonathan. "I can help."

"And you, sir, are a liar, and as far as I can tell, an agent with extensive training and experience in the employ of a foreign government to be determined at a later date. This nonsense about being a simple doctor stops now."

"No," said Kate Ford. "He has to come."

Graves shot her a whiplash glance. "You're not serious?"

But Ford kept her eyes locked on Ransom. "Call the plant," she said. "See if anyone named Anna Scholl is visiting or if there's been an inspection from the IAEA."

Graves hesitated.

"Do it, Charles."

Graves first consulted with the captain of the Paris gendarmerie, who gave his blessing and provided the plant's emergency phone number. It took another five minutes to be put in touch with the plant manager and five minutes more to explain in his perfect schoolboy's French who he was and why he was calling.

"She's there," said Graves, lowering the phone to his side. "She arrived at shift change. Security checked her out. She passed with flying colors. Even the palm print."

"God," said Kate Ford. "This is it."

Graves put the phone back to his ear. "Do you know where she is right now?" he inquired in French. And then his face fell. "She's inside the main complex somewhere. There are fifteen buildings. She has an all-access pass card."

Kate turned to the French police captain. "How far to Flamanville?"

"Three hundred kilometers. One of my choppers can have you there in fifty minutes."

"Please get it here as quickly as possible," she said, before turning toward Jonathan. "Dr. Ransom, you're coming with us."

"Lock down the plant," said Graves. "We'll get them a photo and description of Emma Ransom within the next five minutes. And tell your people that she's armed and dangerous, and that she's most likely carrying high explosives. Don't take any chances. Shoot to kill."

Jonathan clutched the safety webbing as the Aérospatiale helicopter dipped its nose and plummeted toward the Normandy coast. Staring out the window, he had a clear view of the La Reine nuclear complex. To the casual eye, the area appeared calm, as if nothing were out of the ordinary, and purposely so. It was paramount that no word of the threat leaked to the general public. The mildest panic would have long-lasting consequences. Only after looking closely did he spot the unmarked cars blocking the entry road, and the armored personnel carriers stationed near the guardhouses, and the large black vans belonging to the GIGN—the Groupe d'Intervention de la Gendarmerie Nationale, the elite force trained to deal with threats to the country's nuclear infrastructure—parked adjacent to the main administration building. In the sky above, he caught a glimmer of metal in the morning sun. It was the Mirage jets from the French Air Force, executing a box holding pattern to freeze air traffic above the target area.

Throughout the fifty-minute flight they had maintained an open channel of communication with La Reine. A running update of events delivered in urgent telegraphese.

"She tampered with the closed-circuit video feeds so we wouldn't be able to see her," the plant manager had reported soon after takeoff. "M. Royale discovered what she'd done and is going to try to find her. He spotted her in the warehouse, but she could be anywhere."

"Is that warehouse also called W-4?" asked Kate, referencing Jonathan's information.

"Yes, it is."

"What do you keep there?"

"Pipes, equipment, maintenance supplies."

"A lead pipe might conceal a high explosive from any detection system," said Graves. "She may have gone to the warehouse to pick up the bomb."

Kate nodded, then asked, "Who is Royale?"

"He's the deputy security director. He met with Mrs. Scholl because M. Grégoire, our chief of security, didn't come in today."

"Have you spoken with Grégoire?" asked Graves.

"He isn't answering his phone."

At which point Graves asked the pilot to radio the police and instruct them to send a car to Grégoire's home as quickly as possible. Then, to the plant manager: "Contact M. Royale and ask him if he's found Mrs. Scholl yet."

The minutes ticked past and the news grew more frantic.

"Royale isn't answering," said the plant manager. "He always has his phone with him. Something's wrong."

"Go find him," ordered Kate in a drill sergeant's tone, which made everyone look at her with trepidation.

Ten minutes passed. The first to report back was not the plant manager but a local policeman sent to rouse Grégoire. "I found him and his family in their house, tied up in their beds. The wife had a broken nose, and Grégoire, he is in shock. He said it was a woman who did it. She Tasered them."

"And the children?" asked Kate.

"Fine."

Another two minutes passed before the plant manager finally reported back. "We located Royale. He was in the warehouse. He is unconscious and his jaw is broken. What shall we do?"

Seated behind the pilot, sunglasses hiding his tired eyes, headphones clamped firmly over his ears, Jonathan was privy to it all.

The helicopter flared, nose up, and landed with a jolt. Graves slid back the door and leaped to the ground. Jonathan followed, with Kate Ford and several representatives of the French DST behind him.

Waiting nearby was the plant manager, his face damp with sweat. "She's inside the reactor building," he said, leading them into the administration building. "I saw her on the monitor myself."

"Is she alone?" asked Graves.

"Yes, she's carrying a large purse, that's all."

"Can she get into the control room?"

"Never. The room is locked from the inside. My men have orders to stay where they are."

A few feet away, the rear doors of the vans stood open. GIGN troops clad in black assault gear sat with their backs to the walls, machine guns resting on their laps, looking very much like sticks of paratroopers readying for a jump.

Graves introduced himself to the chief of the counterterrorism squad, who joined them as they filed into the manager's office. A map of the plant hung on the wall. Every building was marked with initials, with a legend in the lower left-hand corner.

"Any of this look familiar?" asked Graves. "Time to sing for your supper."

Jonathan pointed to the main reactor complex, a grouping of four buildings inside a fenced perimeter. "Where is the containment building?"

"Right here," said the manager, pointing to the largest building of the four.

"Do you store fuel there?"

"Of course, prior to inserting it into the reactor."

"That's it," said Jonathan. "That's what I read about."

Graves spoke to the chief of the commandos. "Get your men to the containment building. She's either carrying explosives in that bag or carrying the means to detonate devices that have been previously planted. Don't take any chances."

Jonathan stepped in between the two men. "Let me talk to her," he said. "Give me a minute to reason with her."

"Did you a lot of good in London," said Graves. "Get out of my way."

Jonathan placed a hand on his chest. "This is different," he said. "Emma wouldn't do this." He looked at Kate Ford. "I know her. Let me try."

"Absolutely not," she said.

Graves knocked away Jonathan's arm. "See that Dr. Ransom stays here until we resolve the situation. Oh, and put the cuffs back on. We don't want any more trouble."

74

Emma Ransom was nowhere near the containment building. Two hundred meters away, she crouched beside the outer wall of the spent-fuel cooling pond. The wall was made of standard poured concrete and measured 45 centimeters thick. Unlike the containment building, which was designed not only to keep projectiles from penetrating, be they laser-guided munitions, air-to-ground missiles, or supersonic aircraft, but also to prevent radioactive gases from escaping in the event of an accident, the spent-fuel building was deemed neither a "risky environment" nor a priority target. Positioned at the southwestern corner of the building, she dug in her bag for one of the explosive devices she had retrieved from the warehouse. Ripping off a strip of adhesive backing, she affixed the bomb to the wall approximately 20 centimeters above the ground. As determined by the handheld theodolite two nights before, the spot corresponded to a point 5 meters below the surface of the giant cooling pond that lay on the other side of the wall.

Flipping open the control panel, she set the timer to ten minutes. Papi had instructed her to set it to thirty minutes, thus ensuring her enough time to escape. But plans had changed. She had no doubt that within thirty minutes the bomb would be discovered. Ten minutes left her enough time to set the second device and reach her extraction point before detonation. If, that is, she was not captured. It was the sole eventuality for which she had not planned.

Without delay, she switched the device to "run."

The red numbers displayed on the LED clock began to run backward.

9:59

9:58

9:57

Emma checked in her bag for the second explosive, looked to her right and left, then set off for her final target.

75

They put Jonathan in the manager's office with one policeman to guard him and another to stand watch outside the door. The cuffs were too tight, but he was allowed to sit where he pleased or wander around the desk and, as was the case, study the bank of color monitors arrayed across an entire wall of the office.

With mounting unease he followed the assault team's progress through the complex, their images moving from one monitor to the next. He watched from above their shoulders as they gathered outside the main administration building and checked their weapons, and then as they hit the reactor building at a run, hugging the wall as if Emma were about to open fire on them. The assault team turned a corner and disappeared from view, and for a few frantic seconds Jonathan thought he'd lost them. But then he spotted the black-clad troops, followed by Graves and Ford, on a monitor a few rows lower. The leader gave a signal and they entered the main reactor building, taking turns covering one another as they advanced down a corridor. And all the while Jonathan had a running commentary, courtesy of the policeman's walkie-talkie, which blared at full volume so that he might follow his comrades' movements step by step.

But even as Jonathan kept one eye on the assault team, he searched among the myriad other monitors for a sign of his wife. He had lied about the containment building. He had never seen a single mention of it. A sole term was imprinted on his mind: SFCB, and according to the block letters printed on the map, it corresponded to a structure abutting the cliff at ocean's edge named the Spent-Fuel Cooling Building.

The clock on the wall showed that three minutes had passed.

On the screen, the troops stormed into a conference room and a dozen plant workers threw their hands into the air.

Jonathan couldn't wait any longer.

Suddenly he bent over double, gave a horrifying groan, and fell to the floor.

The policeman immediately came to his aid, kneeling by his side. **"Ça va?"** he asked. "What is wrong?"

"Can't . . . breathe," said Jonathan.

The policeman came closer so that he could check Jonathan's respiration. As Jonathan expected, he had been trained in first aid. His first action was to lift Jonathan's head and attempt to clear his air passage. As the policeman bent lower to listen for breathing, Jonathan brought his cuffed hands around and clubbed him on the side of the head. The policeman toppled onto his side. Before he could cry out, Jonathan slugged him again, and nearly passed out himself because of the pain in his shoulder. The policeman lay still.

Jonathan found the keys to his handcuffs and, after a minute's struggle, managed to free himself. He drew the policeman's gun, checked that the safety was on, then grasped it by the snout and banged on the door. **"Viens vite,"** he said. **"J'ai besoin de ton aide."** Come quickly. I need your help.

The door opened at once, and the guard stormed into the room. Jonathan struck him from behind at the base of the skull. The policeman collapsed to the ground. Jonathan looked between the men, searching for the key card necessary to get from building to building, like the ones he'd seen the plant manager hand to several of the assault troops. Digging through their pockets, he found it, marked with the initials of Électricité de France, and grasped it tightly.

Standing, Jonathan looked once more at the map, scouting out a path to the spent-fuel cooling building. Then he opened the door to the hallway and ran.

"Stop," he said.

Emma knelt at the far end of the pool. At her side, contrasting with the white ceramic tiles, was a black metallic box. Even from where he stood, Jonathan could see that the top of the black box was flipped open, and he knew instinctively that it was a bomb.

"Leave," said Emma, looking at him for a brief

moment before returning her attention to the box. "Get out of here. You don't need to be here."

"The French authorities have Shvets in custody," said Jonathan, his voice echoing across the water and off the immense walls. "It's finished, Emma. Give yourself up. It's your only chance. There are police everywhere. I told them you were in the reactor building, but any minute they're going to figure out I was lying. They have orders to shoot on sight."

Jonathan advanced along the narrow walk bordering the pool. The spent-fuel pond was 50 meters long and half again as wide. The tank was built from stainless steel, the water as clear as glass, clearer than any water he'd ever seen. Beneath the surface lay row upon row of spent fuel rods, grouped into squares seventeen wide and seventeen across and held in place by titanium racks. The rods pulsed with a deep blue glow that danced off the walls and the ceiling and dressed the high cavernous ceiling in an eerie and menacing light.

"Is that why you came?" Emma asked. "To save me?"

"No," said Jonathan. "It isn't." The words came without forethought, and he knew that his relationship with Emma was over. "I came because I'm not going to allow you to kill thousands of people."

For the first time Emma looked up from the black box. "You have no idea what you're doing," she said.

"Shvets told me everything."

"You still don't understand."

"Why, Emma? Why did you go back to him? I saw your file. I know what he made you do."

"Because more than Shvets, I hate Division. I hate how they manipulate the world. How anything went as long as it was stated to be in the country's interest. You think I'm the bad guy. You're wrong. I just pulled the trigger. Someone much higher up chose the target, loaded the gun, and handed it to me."

"And how is that different from what you're doing now?"

"Now I'm helping my country. My real country." She glanced up. "My God, is that a gun you're carrying?"

Jonathan looked down at the pistol, then tossed it into the pond. Threats were worthless. He could not shoot his wife. "And me?"

"What about you?"

"Was it ever real?"

"No," she answered indignantly. "It wasn't real. You were a tool. Nothing more. You got me into places I couldn't go to by myself. Cover, Jonathan. That's all you've ever been."

"Then why did you come to see me in London?"

"Because I like you. Because I needed a good screw. OK?"

"Tell me the truth, dammit! That's all I ever wanted."

Emma stared at him, her eyes narrowed. "The truth?" she said, shaking her head. "What's that?"

She flipped a switch, shut the top of the box, and stood. "Four minutes. You still have time."

Jonathan didn't budge. "You didn't have to come to London just to tell me that we couldn't see each other again. You could have done it a hundred different ways. A phone call, for one. It doesn't fit, Emma. You broke every one of your own rules."

"So now you're an expert? You were a decoy. That's what you were. I was the one who convinced that bunch of doctors in London to book you as their speaker. I allowed you to follow me. I knew I couldn't blow that car bomb without being spotted. I needed something to take the English police off my trail. It made things easier for me if they were wasting their resources following you." She checked her wristwatch. "Now get out of here—"

Just then there was a terrific explosion. The entire building shuddered for several seconds, and one of the massive overhead lamps snapped and dropped into the cooling pond. Jonathan fell to a knee, almost toppling into the water. The lights flickered. Giant bubbles rose to the surface of the water. A Klaxon began to wail. Jonathan stood shakily, observing the bubbles that continued to break the surface. He noted with alarm that the water level in the pool was sinking rapidly. Deep below the surface, he could see a gaping hole in the wall where the water was escaping.

Finding his balance, he ran to the far end of the building, where Emma was rising to her feet. "Get up," he said, grabbing her arms and lifting her. "Turn off the bomb."

Emma struggled to free herself from his grip. "I can't do that," she said, knocking him away.

"You can't or you won't?"

"Take your pick."

Jonathan stared at her, seeing her for the first time as she really was. "What kind of monster are you?"

The words ricocheted off Emma, and despite a sudden tic pulling at the corners of her mouth, she might not have heard them. "Get out of here. You still have time. Do you know what will happen when the water dips below the rods? The second the uranium is exposed, it will cook off and bombard this place with gamma radiation. You'll be roasted like a Christmas goose inside a minute."

"And what about that one?" said Jonathan, pointing at the box at Emma's feet.

"That one takes everything up with it. The exposed rods, the building. Everything. Now go."

But Jonathan stayed put. He looked at his wife and realized that she was a stranger. "Help me, Emma. You can turn off that device. I know you. I know you don't mean to do this."

"No, Jonathan, you don't."

And then Emma turned and ran away from him, pushing open the nearest door. For a moment he caught her silhouette in the sunlight, and then, without looking back, she was gone.

Jonathan got down on his knees beside the black

box. An LED timer on its cover read **1:26. 1:25**. He ran his fingers around its sides, but he was unable to feel any hinges or see any screws. No one had bothered searching him since he'd left Paris, and he still had the Swiss Army knife he'd carried for twenty years in his left pocket. Freeing the main blade, he tried to slip it beneath the LED panel. At first it resisted, but he gave the knife an angry shove and the blade slid in. He hammered the knife with his fist, but instead of the LED panel flipping open to reveal its controls, the entire panel popped free of the box, revealing three wires—one red, one blue, one green—running into the interior of the device.

Years ago he'd accompanied a UN team on a mine-clearing operation in Angola. He'd paid close attention as the engineers had located the mines, cleared the dirt, then carefully unscrewed the base plates. They were Russian antipersonnel mines, and each time the engineers had disarmed them simply by snipping the yellow wire connecting the pressure pad to the detonator. But Emma's bomb had none of those things. No yellow wire, no pressure pad, and no detonator.

His eyes rose to the pool. The water had descended a full 2 meters from the lip of the tile. At most, another 2 meters of water covered the tips of the fuel rods. The blue glow radiated stronger, more malignant than ever.

He looked back at the bomb.

:45.

Jonathan removed the scissors from the body of the knife. He probed each wire, unsure what would happen if he cut any of them. Detonators functioned by delivering a charge to a blasting cap, which in turn ignited the explosive, resulting in a blast. The idea was to cut the wire that delivered that initial charge, thus rendering the blasting cap inert. He didn't know if cutting any of them would result in an instantaneous detonation.

:20

He placed the scissors around the blue wire, then changed his mind and positioned them around the red wire.

:10

He snipped, but the wire did not cut. He pressed harder, but still the blades did not penetrate the plastic sheathing.

:05

Using both hands, he tried again, harnessing all his strength in his fingers. The wire began to give. He watched as the numbers ticked down, pressing the scissors harder still until the hard metal cut into his fingers. He glimpsed a filament of copper and mustered a final effort.

:00

The scissors sliced through the wire.

Jonathan collapsed on his haunches, staring at the LED's glaring red digits, at the black metallic box that had not exploded. Or had he in fact beaten the clock? He was too lightheaded to know either way.

He looked at the pool. The crystal-clear water had descended below the level of the titanium holding racks to the very tips of the fuel rods. As if sensing the presence of oxygen, the rods appeared to pulsate.

And there the water stopped.

The water level fell below the jagged hole made by the first bomb. Thirty centimeters, no more, remained above the uranium rods, but 30 centimeters was enough. No more water could escape the cooling pond.

The door through which Emma had fled opened. Colonel Graves and DCI Ford entered the building, followed by a dozen commandos and the plant manager. Jonathan counted at least ten machine guns pointed directly at him and decided it might be wise to stay where he was.

Graves took in Jonathan and his bloody hands and the partially dismantled bomb situated between his knees. Then he extended a hand and helped Jonathan to his feet. "We saw everything from the monitors in the reactor control room."

"I thought I could talk her out of it," said Jonathan.

Graves considered this, but offered no comment.

Kate Ford stepped forward, put an arm across Jonathan's back, and guided him toward the exit. "Let's get you cleaned up," she said.

Jonathan halted. "Where is she?" he asked.

Graves looked at Ford, then back at him, and Jonathan braced himself for the news. But Graves just shook his head. "We haven't found her yet. But don't worry. We're searching the complex. She can't have gotten far."

Jonathan nodded. She was gone, and they all knew it. He looked over his shoulder at the gaping hole torn out of the wall of the stainless steel pool. "It wasn't low enough," he said, almost to himself. "The water never exposed the rods."

"What's that?" asked Graves. "Didn't catch what you said."

But Jonathan didn't answer. Suddenly he felt too tired to explain.

"Let's go," said Kate. "We have a plane to catch back to London."

"Do I have a choice?" asked Jonathan.

"Hell, no," said Graves. "If you think this clears you of anything, you're sorely mistaken."

76

One hour later, Sir Anthony Allam, director general of MI5, picked up the phone and called Frank Connor. "Your girl just turned up."

"Where?"

"The La Reine nuclear power plant in Normandy. She tried to bring off some kind of incident to paralyze the country's nuclear grid. Wanted to blow the place to the high heavens. Damn near succeeded, too."

"Do you have her in custody?"

"No," said Allam. "She escaped."

"Dammit," said Connor.

"The French police have issued a nationwide alert for her arrest. Interpol is cooperating as well."

"Little good it'll do them. She's a ghost, that one. They'll never find her."

"Perhaps," said Allam. "But we do know that she was working for Sergei Shvets of the FSB. Turns out she was Russian, but then, you must have known that all along."

"Of course I knew. I brought her into the fold eight years ago. Hard to believe she went back to them." Connor sighed. "The whole thing is my fault. If only my men hadn't botched the job in Rome. I don't like leaving a mess."

"French intelligence has Shvets in custody. Apparently he was supervising the operation himself. We managed to track him to a safe house in Paris and nabbed him there. We're keeping the news quiet until the prime minister speaks to the Kremlin."

"I wouldn't give two nickels for his chances back home."

"Be that as it may," continued Allam, "your actions these past days in London have been nothing short of disgraceful."

"Emma Ransom betrayed Division," said Connor. "I did what needed to be done. My apologies if I stepped on any toes. You don't have to worry any longer. I'm flying out tonight."

"Safe travels. I'll let you know how things turn out in France." Allam paused, staring at the clock on his wall. He'd been on an unscrambled line for over two minutes now. He hoped it would suffice. "Oh, Frank, any idea where she might have gone?"

"Who knows? Like I said, she's a ghost."

Frank Connor hung up the phone. The connection wasn't bad, considering he was kilometers from the nearest tower. A wave lifted the schooner and he grabbed at the wheel to steady himself. **One hand for the boat,** his father had taught him. The cardinal rule of sailing. Off the port bow, the coast of France was still visible, and, far off in the haze, La Reine's massive white dome.

"So," he said, handing Emma Ransom a towel. "Where **are** you going?"

"I don't know yet," she answered, drying her hair. "It all depends on what happens now, doesn't it?"

Connor patted her on the back. "Yes, Lara, I suppose it does."

"My name is Emma," she said. "Emma Ransom."

Connor nodded. He knew better than to argue. It was natural for agents to grow emotional at the end of an assignment, and this one had been tougher than most. "You won't try to reach him."

Emma looked at Connor, then quickly away. "No, I won't."

"He can never know."

"I understand."

Connor smiled, and said some words about duty and country and the price that they in their profession had to pay. They were trite, and he'd said the same things a hundred times before, but still he believed them. Every word.

Emma Ransom shook her head and gazed at the distant shoreline. "Hey, Frank, shut up and drive the boat."

77

It was late September and a chill wind swept down from the Arctic Circle, blanketing Moscow and sending temperatures plummeting into the thirties. Everywhere people donned heavy coats and wrapped their necks in woolen scarves. In Gorky Park, the ice rink froze and was opened two weeks ahead of schedule. Weather forecasters were quick to predict another long and bitter winter. But nowhere was it colder than in the basement of the Lubyanka, the century-old granite fortress that was home to the country's most notorious political prisoners.

"You have left us in an embarrassing position, Sergei," said the Russian president. "The evidence is compelling, and that is without taking into account your capture in Paris."

Shvets sat at the bare wooden table, his head held high. "I expect it is," he said. "After all, they planted it."

"Ridiculous," said Igor Ivanov. "Next you'll be claiming that the Americans planned the operation. Tell me, was it Frank Connor who suggested you kill me?"

"That was my own idea," said Shvets defiantly.

The three men sat in a small, dank room two floors belowground. There were no windows. Walls, ceiling, and floor were of the most rudimentary concrete and without adornment. A stuttering fluorescent bulb provided the sole light.

An immaculate leather dossier bearing MI5's seal sat in the center of the table. With ceremony, the president untied it and examined the documents one by one. "A hospital bill for twenty-five thousand euros paid on behalf of one of your agents and traced back to an FSB shell company. Five kilos of Semtex identical to that used in the London car bombing found in a Paris apartment loaned to the FSB by our Iranian allies. And the pièce de résistance, a laptop containing confidential files indicating ties to the same agent, as well as a step-by-step breakdown of the operation. It goes on and on." The president replaced the documents and meticulously retied the dossier. Clasping his hands, he said, "You leave our government no choice but to admit to it all."

Ivanov leveled his darkest glare at Shvets. "We'll be kissing the Brits' asses for a decade because of this."

"You're their man," said Shvets, holding Ivanov's eyes. "The whole thing was a plan to eliminate me. A setup. Ask her. She'll tell you."

"We have. Many times," said the president. "I for one am convinced that Larissa Alexandrovna

Antonova is telling the truth, and that she is a selfless, brave citizen. Viewing the circumstances of her recruitment, she had no choice but to show her loyalty to you. We have forgiven her and hope to make use of her many talents in the future."

Shvets lowered his head. "My God," he said. "They've done it."

"That will be enough," said the president. "Rise. We will accompany you back to your cell."

Shvets stood, his knees strong, his posture that of the soldier he had once been. He left the table and opened the door to the corridor. As he walked, he kept his head held high.

He did not feel the barrel of the pistol touch the nape of his neck or the bullet crash into his skull. He saw a brief flash of light, and then there was nothing.

The president lowered the gun. "I told him that if I discovered that a Russian had tried to have you killed, I would personally execute him."

Ivanov looked at the corpse. "Good riddance."

The president suddenly cocked his head, eyeing Ivanov with suspicion. "You aren't, are you?"

"What?" asked Ivanov.

"An American agent."

Ivanov looked at the president. A smile broke on his lips and he began to laugh. A moment later the president joined him, and for a long time the laughter echoed off the cold stone walls.

"You know," said the president, catching his breath, "it occurs to me that there is a sudden opening that requires filling. Would you have an interest in assuming the directorship of the FSB?"

Igor Ivanov swallowed. "It would be an honor."

78

The call came at 6 a.m. Eastern Standard Time. Alone in his bed, Frank Connor took the cell phone from beneath his pillow and studied the incoming number. At once he sat up, wide awake. "Yeah," he said. "What is it?"

"It's me," responded Igor Ivanov. "I'm in."

Epilogue

Lashkar Gah, Helmand Province Afghanistan

It was close to sunset when the battered pickup arrived. Before the dust could settle, a half-dozen children ran from mud huts and sturdy stone dwellings and surrounded the truck. Massoud, the village's three-legged mongrel, led the charge, barking madly and baring his teeth. Once Massoud had belonged to the United States Army, but the soldiers left him behind after a grenade claimed his leg and the valley was no longer friendly.

None of the twenty or so men seated around the communal fire made a move toward the truck. They continued to chew on naswar, the sticky brown powder blended from tobacco and opium, while keeping their eyes glued to the goat slow-roasting over the flames. It was their first meat in a week, and a good meal took precedence over a visit. No one of importance arrived at dusk and without prior warning.

Only Khan, the village elder, rose to greet the tall stranger who jumped from the rear of the truck. The visitor was dressed in native clothing, with the region's white scarf bound around his head. A coarse black beard flecked with gray covered much of his face, yet even in the failing light one could not help but notice his dark, searching eyes. Over his shoulder, he carried a leather bag, and he approached with respect.

"Who are you?" asked Khan in Pashto, one Afghan to another.

"A doctor."

Khan recognized the accent at once, but hid his surprise. It had been more than a year since the crusaders dared venture so far south. It would take only a word to have the man executed. Yet, there was something in his regard that begged attention. "What is your name, my friend?"

"Jonathan."

Khan shook the visitor's hand and held it in his grasp long enough to know that the man was good and to be trusted.

"My granddaughter is ill, Dr. Jonathan," said Khan. "Can you help?"

Jonathan Ransom looked at the mud huts and the open fire and the faces of the children raised to him in expectation. High on the mountain, the sun's dying rays cast a calming purple light over the rugged landscape. He was home.

"I will try."

Acknowledgments

As always, I am indebted to a great many people for their efforts and assistance in bringing this book to life.

First, I would like to thank Detective Superintendent Charlie McMurdie of the London Metropolitan Police.

Also, at New Scotland Yard, I would like to thank Detective Chief Inspector Chris Nolan.

Other assistance in London was given by David Cleak and Ken Laxton, as well as by a former member of MI5, who wishes to remain nameless. Or else!

Thanks to my friend Thomas Sloan for making the introductions.

Back Stateside, my thanks to Dr. Doug Fischer, Special Agent with the California Department of Justice; to Dr. Andrew Kuchin at the Center for Strategic and International Studies, for his expertise in all matters Russian; and to Dr. Jon Shafqat, for his medical expertise and subsequent close reading of the manuscript. And to Tom Rouse at Qualcomm, who helped me take apart a cell phone and explain what was inside.

A certain individual gave tremendously of his

time to offer a primer on the nuclear energy industry. I came away convinced that nuclear energy offers us a safe, sustainable, and clean path to energy independence. For the many hours we spent together, and the umpteen cups of Starbucks hot chocolate, I'm grateful.

At Doubleday, I offer my heartfelt thanks to every member of the **Rules** team: Bill Thomas, John Pitts, Todd Doughty, John Fontana, Alison Rich, Bette Alexander, and especially to my brilliant editor, Stacy Creamer. And now is a good time to welcome my new editor, Jason Kaufman. Last but not least, a special nod to the one and only Steve Rubin. It's a privilege to work with such a tremendous group of professionals.

I reserve a special thanks for my agent, Richard Pine, and his talented and hardworking colleagues at Inkwell Management, notably Michael Carlisle, Elisa Petrini, Masie Cochran, and Charlie Olsen. Over the years, our relationship has grown from professional to personal. Inkwell is family. Richard, you're my brother.

On a personal note, I'd like to thank the team at the Body Refinery in Encinitas, California, especially my trainer, Michael Barbanti, who goes the extra mile to find new and imaginative ways for me to work off my creative anxieties. **Res firma, mitescere nescit.**

Finally, I would like to give a "shout-out" to my family, who inspire me to give it my best day in, day out: to Noelle and Katja, who I love more every day, and to my wife, Sue, who is always my first and best critic.

This book is dedicated to James F. Sloan. I got to know Jim while researching **The Devil's Banker.** Back then, Jim headed up the Financial Crimes Enforcement Network (FinCEN). He and his team pulled out the stops to illustrate the varied ways and methods used to track terrorist finances. When I met with Jim in his office, I sensed right away that I was in the presence of an extraordinary individual. Jim possesses the quiet confidence and steely competence of the born leader. Prior to working at FinCEN, he put in over twenty years with the Secret Service, retiring as Special Agent-in-Charge of the Baltimore office. I'll never forget the smile on his face when he showed me the photograph of him driving the Popemobile during John Paul II's visit to the United States in 1979. The Irish Catholic boy from Springfield, Massachusetts, had made good!

Over the years, I never stopped in D.C. without paying Jim a visit. I followed his career ever upward as he left FinCEN and joined the Coast Guard as their first civilian Deputy Commandant for Intelligence. In that time he had several opportunities to leave government service for the far richer fields of private security. He turned them down, feeling (rightly) that he could make a greater contribution to the country and to our society by continuing to serve in the government.

Two years ago, Jim contracted ALS, better known as "Lou Gehrig's Disease." It was a bitter and incomprehensible blow. This was not supposed to happen to a healthy, vital man who had so much left to accomplish, so very much to live for. My initial reaction was disbelief and sadness. Then, I got mad. How dare this disease strike a man who exemplifies the best in the human spirit?

At this printing, Jim continues his valiant battle against this terrible illness. He is weakened in body, but not in mind. That same confidence, charisma, and steadfastness that I observed when we first met hasn't deserted him.

It never will.

About the Author

Christopher Reich is the **New York Times** bestselling author of **Rules of Deception, Numbered Account,** and **The Patriots Club,** which won the International Thriller Writers award for best novel in 2006. He lives in California with his family.